IN THE WOODS

A Selection of Recent Titles by Merry Jones

The Harper Jennings Series

SUMMER SESSION *
BEHIND THE WALLS *
WINTER BREAK *
OUTSIDE EDEN *
IN THE WOODS *

THE NANNY MURDERS
THE RIVER KILLINGS
THE DEADLY NEIGHBORS
THE BORROWED AND BLUE MURDERS

* *available from Severn House*

IN THE WOODS

A Harper Jennings Mystery

Merry Jones

Severn House

This first world edition published 2014
in Great Britain and 2015 in the USA by
SEVERN HOUSE PUBLISHERS LTD of
19 Cedar Road, Sutton, Surrey, England, SM2 5DA.
Trade paperback edition first published
in Great Britain and the USA 2015 by
SEVERN HOUSE PUBLISHERS LTD.

British Library Cataloguing in Publication Data

Jones, Merry Bloch author.
In the woods. – (A Harper Jennings mystery)
1. Jennings, Harper (Fictitious character)–Fiction.
2. Murder–Investigation–Fiction. 3. Women veterans–
Fiction. 4. Iraq War, 2003-2011–Veterans–Fiction.
5. Suspense fiction.
I. Title II. Series
813.6-dc23

ISBN-13: 978-0-7278-8444-2 (cased)
ISBN-13: 978-1-84751-551-3 (trade paper)
ISBN-13: 978-1-78010-597-0 (e-book)

Typeset by Palimpsest Book Production Ltd.,
Falkirk, Stirlingshire, Scotland.
Printed and bound in Great Britain by
TJ International, Padstow, Cornwall.

To Robin, Baille and Neely

ACKNOWLEDGEMENTS

Heartfelt thanks to:

the team at Severn House, especially my editor, Rachel Simpson Hutchens;

Rebecca Strauss, my agent;

supportive colleagues and pals at the Philadelphia Liars Club;

encouraging family and friends, most of all my first reader and much loved husband, Robin.

Al Rogers unzipped his tent just before sunrise. The air was chilly and smelled like dead leaves. Nothing moved; it was too early or too late, that time when night creatures had found their dens and day creatures hadn't begun to stir. That time when nothing ever happened. Even the trees looked drowsy. Still, Al hesitated before going out. He hadn't slept much. Kinsella had kept him up, calling him on the radio, whispering that some beast was outside his tent. Al had checked and seen nothing. But every time he'd fallen asleep – boom, Kinsella had radioed again.

'Do you hear it?' he'd asked.

'All I hear is you, Kinsella. Go the hell to sleep.'

'Listen – wait. Did you hear that?'

Al had listened. Had heard something that sounded like an owl. 'It's a hoot owl.'

'No. Not that. I mean the creeping and thumping.'

The what?

'Something heavy. And big. I swear. It's that Bog Man.'

Christ. 'Grow up, Kinsella. There is no such thing as a Bog Man. He's like the Bogey Man. He doesn't exist. If you're hearing anything, it's an animal looking for food. Shit, did you hang the bear bag high enough? He'll eat all our—'

'I'm not goofing around, Al.' When he was nervous, Jim's voice rose in pitch. It had become high falsetto. 'Don't tell me it's a bear or a fox. It's not. It's something heavy and huge. Jesus – I hear it. It's right outside my tent.' His voice was tight. Soprano.

Once again, cursing, Al had opened his tent and peered out. Once again, he'd seen no one. Nothing but the woods, the sky, and the curving hulk of Kinsella's tent. 'You ought to know better,' he'd scolded Kinsella. 'You've been walking the pipeline, what? Two years? By now you should be used to it. If you spend too much time out here, you start to imagine things. You got to learn to ignore it. Take charge of your mind.'

'I am not imagining—'

'Look, Kinsella. I don't know what the fuck you been smoking.

But you're fine. Relax. I'm going to sleep.' He'd promised that if Jim called again, he'd suffer a fate worse than any Bog Man could bring on. So Kinsella had stopped calling. And apparently he'd fallen asleep; his tent was closed up tight. Silent.

Good. Al would have some time to himself before Jim got up. Not that Jim was a bad guy; just that Al was better alone. Companionship that lasted more than an hour or two intruded on him, wore him out, and he and Jim had been together non-stop for weeks. Well, only eight more days. Then he'd have seven days off. No miles to walk, no pipeline to inspect. Nobody around him twenty-four-seven. He'd hole up in his condo outside Pittsburgh, take long, hot showers, sleep on an actual bed, order pizzas, stare at the tube, and stay there, avoiding traffic jams and jabbering humans until it was time to come back to work. Maybe he'd call Miranda.

Maybe not.

The morning was brisk, dewy. Al pulled on a plaid flannel shirt, jeans and boots, crawled out of his tent and looked around. Despite himself, Jim's bullshit had crept into his head. Not that he believed for one second that some abominable bog creature was lurking in the mist. Or that the indentations in the dirt were monstrous footprints. No, it was crap, all of it. The woods were simply a bunch of trees full of wildlife. A place that belonged to animals. Where humans were just visitors.

Above him, birds began to wake up, began twittering. Al took a deep breath and stepped away from camp, following a narrow path, savoring his solitude. He wasn't going to go far. He just needed a few minutes with no soil or water samples to take, no destination to reach, no responsibilities, no conversation. Nobody.

He stayed on the path, careful in the shaded light, dodging occasional puddles of old rainwater, fallen branches, rocks, logs. He loved the stillness, the crunch of his footsteps on fallen leaves, the sense of being where nobody could find or bother him. And these woods fit him like a coat. Snug. Close. But up ahead he saw a burst of light, as if the woods were coming to an end. How was that possible? According to the pipeline charts, the forest continued for miles. Probably it was just a small clearing. Al kept going, and sure enough, he came to a small open field, maybe an acre. He stopped at the tree line, gazing across. The grass stirred. A startled rabbit darted away.

The sky was brightening. Al's stomach rumbled. Time to head back, make coffee. Wake up Jim and start the day. Al stopped beside a tree to take a leak. At first, he thought the sound was his piss hitting the ground, but then he noticed it was getting louder and coming from behind, as if someone was rustling the foliage, coming up the path. Shit. Had to be Jim. Couldn't the guy leave him alone for a half hour? He looked over his shoulder to tell Jim to back the hell off. But the figure moving through the trees wasn't Jim. It wasn't even human. Al stiffened. Was it a bear? No, not a bear. Bigger. And it was stomping. Lifting its knees like a damned drum major. Shit – what the hell was it? Al peered through branches and watched in disbelief. It was coming toward him, covered head to toe with fur. And – oh fuck – it had fangs.

Al didn't stick around to see more. He whirled, his wrist scraping a broken branch as he tore ahead. Twigs scratched his face, snagged his shirt, but he didn't dare slow down or look around. He just ran, zigzagging, not sure in which direction he was heading, hopping over rocks, skipping over puddles, his heart flipping, breath raging.

Finally, panting, he stopped behind a fat oak and peered around. Saw nothing. No hairy fanged creature. Even so, he couldn't stop shaking, couldn't catch his breath. What the fuck had just happened? Had he actually seen the Bog Man? Had Jim been right about it stomping around their campsite? No. Couldn't be. The Bog Man wasn't real – it was just another Big Foot or Yeti myth.

But what he'd seen *had* been real. Big and hairy and marching down the path.

Al's teeth were chattering. Christ, he'd somehow gouged his wrist; blood streamed all over his sleeve and hand. Damn. He pressed on the wound. Would have to clean it when he got back to camp. But where was camp? He looked around, trying to orient himself. Nothing looked familiar. Shit. Okay. He'd just go back to the clearing and find the path again. As soon as his legs would support him.

Still shaky, Al doubled back toward the clearing, his mind on the creature. He moved slowly, quietly, cautiously. When a twig crackled somewhere, he jumped. When a squirrel darted in front of him, he froze. When he finally got to the clearing, the sun was peering over the treetops. Full out morning. He scanned the perimeter for his path. Maybe the thing had left footprints. If so, he'd call the forest ranger and have him come out. They'd track it, catch it. Figure out what the hell it was. He walked along the edge of the field, looking for the path, picturing fangs. Not noticing a person in the trees behind him, aiming a rifle at his back.

Before the bullet shattered his ribs and ripped through his right ventricle, Al had three final thoughts. The first was that if they captured the creature, he'd be famous and the press would hound him. The second was that he wished he'd brought his rifle, so he could have caught it right then. And the third was, oh damn, with all his running around, he'd forgotten to zip up his fly.

Harper Jennings couldn't sleep. Not because of the hard ground or the close fabric of the tent. She'd slept in much less comfortable conditions. No, the reason she was awake was that, for the first time since her daughter had been born two and a half years ago, she was spending the night away from Chloe. She hadn't even been able to talk to her by phone. They'd tried, but out here there was no signal. She wasn't worried; Chloe would be fine with Vicki and Trent, hadn't even cried when they'd said goodbye. She was growing up – she went to preschool three mornings a week, had play dates with little friends. Swim lessons, music classes. Chloe had her own life, apart from Harper. The problem was that Harper had no life apart from Chloe.

Ever since her birth, Chloe had been Harper's companion, the focus of her attention and her passion. Her full-time job. Now the baby wasn't a baby any more; she was a little girl, and Harper needed to back off and find something else to do.

Hank let out a ragged snort, began snoring. They lay side by side, their sleeping bags zipped together. She nudged his back; the snoring stopped for a breath, then resumed, louder. Never mind. It didn't matter what symphony Hank performed; she wasn't going to sleep anyhow. She felt disconnected, as if she'd left a limb at home. Couldn't stop thinking about Chloe. What book had Vicki read to her last night? Had she brushed her teeth? Had she sung the good-night song? Had Chloe asked for her mommy?

Stop it, she told herself. Cut it out. Nothing was wrong. Chloe was fine. Hank was fine. She was fine. It was okay – in fact, it was healthy to spend some time apart. She turned onto her side, brushing her leg against Hank's. In his sleep, he responded, reaching an arm out, covering her hip. His body was always warm when he slept. In a minute, his arm would weigh heavy, roasting her. But for now, it felt snug. Solid, reassuring. Harper stroked it, amazed. How was it possible that they were in their brand-new tent, camping the way they used to before Hank's accident? She'd never imagined that they'd do this again. But there they were.

When he'd suggested it, she'd gawked. 'Camping?'

Hank had grinned. 'Why not?'

She hadn't known where to begin; the list of 'why nots' was long. 'We don't even have equipment any more.'

His grinned had widened. 'Yes, we do.'

He'd bought new stuff. He'd rattled off the list. Harper had panicked. 'I don't know – neither of us is in shape to climb.'

'We won't do anything strenuous. Let's get away. Just us. Look, we haven't been alone together since Chloe was born.'

He'd been right. They hadn't been. Even before Chloe had joined them, they'd needed time alone, just the two of them. They'd had a lot to recover from: Harper's service in Iraq had left her with Post Traumatic Stress Disorder and a permanently injured left leg. Hank's fall from their roof had almost killed him and left him with a limp and aphasia that had limited his ability to speak. And then, they'd been shaken by a series of freakish incidents – fraternity boys committing murders in the house next door, smugglers trying to steal the artifact collection Harper had been cataloging, terrorists kidnapping scientists at a symposium Hank had been attending. Now, Hank's aphasia had passed. He was speaking again, working as a geology professor at Cornell. But with the whirlwind of the last few years, they needed to reconnect. To be together, just Harper and Hank.

And so they'd gone camping. Chloe was gleefully spending the weekend at Aunt Vicki and Uncle Trent's, where she was completely in charge and over-indulged. And Harper was lying awake, listening to Hank snore and owls hoot, thinking about what to do with her life now that her baby didn't need her as much. Cornell's Archeology Department wasn't hiring. But even if they were, she couldn't imagine taking a regular job, working regular hours. Being away from Chloe all day every day.

Damn. She needed to let go, let Chloe grow up.

Maybe she and Hank should have another baby.

But wasn't that just postponing the question? Who was Harper? What did she want to do now that she finally had her degree? What did a PhD in archeology qualify her to do? She turned onto her other side, removing Hank's arm. Hearing a loud, sharp crack just outside the tent.

Reflexively, Harper rolled over and grabbed the Winchester. It was a conditioned response, left over from Iraq. She had her hands on the rifle and was ready to pull the bolt back when Hank grabbed her arm.

'Harper?'

In the dark of their tent, she could see only his outline, a long lump of sleeping bag. She held still, listening. Hearing only the night.

'What are you doing?' He sounded clueless.

'Shh.'

Neither of them moved. They heard nothing.

'What was that?' Hank asked. 'A flashback?'

No, it hadn't been a flashback. Why did everyone assume everything she did was because of a flashback? 'I heard something.' Actually, she wasn't sure that was true. She assumed that she'd heard something because she'd reacted as if they'd been under fire.

'What kind of something?' Hank reached out, took the rifle. 'An animal?'

Harper thought back, tried to recapture it. 'Maybe a gunshot.'

'A gunshot?'

'I think so.'

'Harper. We're in the woods. People are hunting here. Hunters shoot. Gunshots are normal.' He pulled her close.

Wrapped in the sleeping bag with Hank, Harper didn't think about the sound that had startled her. When she heard it again, she didn't even react. They were in the woods, like Hank had said. Hunters were hunting. She dismissed the sound as soon as she heard it and concentrated instead on Hank's lips. By the time she crawled out of their tent an hour later, Harper had forgotten all about it.

If Josh lifted his knees, the new legs worked smoothly, much better than the old ones. He was pleased with himself. Hell, he should forget about being a damned mechanic, should work in prosthetics, making limbs for amputees – or maybe some of those arms for astronauts, the ones they used in space walks. Because, damn, he was good. He'd designed and built these all on his own. And the wide supports at the bottom fit perfectly into the molded plastic feet, balancing him securely. And the bear pelts were smooth, covered him like his own skin. In fact, as he stomped through the woods, looking down from seven feet and four inches, Josh almost forgot that he was wearing a costume. He felt comfortable, bending his knees, practicing his stride, moving swiftly, even running along paths, into campsites. Leaving footprints. But he didn't have time to accomplish much now. The eastern sky was already glowing. In minutes the sun would peek over the trees, and he didn't want some half-assed weekend hunter to see him and take shots, thinking he was a bear.

Josh turned around, heading back to the compound, satisfied with his new improved legs. Loping along through the woods, he figured the shortest way would be through the clearing and that, at this hour, probably nobody would be around. At the edge of the clearing, though, he saw somebody. A guy standing by a tree, taking a leak. The guy must have heard him because he turned to look at him. His mouth opened, his eyes popped, and he stood there, just staring as if he was seeing the Devil himself.

Josh couldn't help it. He let out a howl and lunged toward the guy, watched him take off like he'd gotten shot out of a cannon, smashing into low branches and weaving his way around trees. Josh followed for a few yards, lured by the smell of him. It was strong, more potent than the dead bearskin. And intoxicating. Josh had to force himself to stop chasing the guy and go back. But it was tough; the smell of fear was even more appealing than the smell of blood.

The Impala made a grumble and groaned.

'I told you a hundred times to fix the muffler.' Pete was jittery.

'Just be cool. Act normal.' Bob pulled into the campground just before sunrise, parked near the RV area.

'What if somebody stops us?'

'Jesus Holy Christ. Nobody's going to stop us.'

'What if they do?'

Bob's nostrils flared. 'We've talked about it. What don't you get yet? We're a couple of dudes backpacking for a day, that's all. We don't need no hunting permits. No reservations. Nothing.'

'Right. Nothing.'

'You okay?' Bob turned, looked at him.

Pete nodded. He chewed his thumbnail.

'Because you're doing that thing you do with your eyes.'

'What thing?'

'Where you blink real fast.'

Pete shrugged and tried not to blink.

'You got to tell me you're okay. Because once we get out of this car, there's no going back.'

Pete blinked a bunch of times. 'I know.' He reached for the car door.

'Not yet. Hold on. Let's double-check the packs.'

Pete twisted around and climbed onto his knees, facing the back seat.

Bob reached into the pocket of his down vest, took out a list. 'Okay. Dynamite.'

'Check.'

'Rope.'

'Check.'

Bob read the list: cable, wiring, tool kit, blasting caps, detonators. Maps. Flashlights. Spare clothes. Tarp. Beer, beef jerky. Baggie of grass. Matches. Pipe bombs. Pete's phone with the GPS.

'Check.'

Bob's eyes were glowing. 'This is it, man.'

Pete's hands were shaking.

'Scared?'

'Shittin' my pants.'

Bob laughed. 'That's okay, man. Think of it this way. Before a tough football game – before anything tough, your body revs itself up. You feel scared sick, but it's not fear – it's just hormones or chemicals. It's your body preparing itself for something big. So it's a good sign if you feel sick.'

Pete remembered Homecoming, senior year. He'd been scared sick then, too, and they'd won 28-11. Bob was right. His body was revving up to do something great.

'How about you? Do you feel sick?'

Bob grinned. 'Me? I'm so revved my eyes might pop out of my head.'

Pete nodded, stared out the windshield. In a few minutes, the sun would come up. But, for now, darkness would cover them.

'Ready?' Bob punched his shoulder.

Pete didn't answer, he just returned the punch. This was it, the day they'd been planning for months. This day, today, they were going to do something mind-boggling. They were going to become famous and change history.

This day was going to be great.

* * *

Just as the sun peeked over the horizon, Angela Russo led her husband Phil to the edge of the field.

'This is probably the best place to spot small game. You want to stay still, watch for movement. Don't move because, if they spot you, they'll freeze and you won't see the grass moving.'

Phil nodded. 'I'll be fine.' She looked so beautiful out here, without make-up. Her hair up under her cap. Freckled like a tomboy. Or a modern Annie Oakley.

'You remember how it goes? Aim, deep breath, hold it, aim, squeeze off the shot, breathe.'

'Got it. I'll be fine.'

'Be careful. Don't take any chances on your first time out.' She patted his arm.

'I'm fine. It's you I'm worried about.'

'I've been hunting half my life, Phil. I know what I'm doing.'

'But you've never gone after bear before. At least not by yourself.'

'That's the point, though, isn't it? I want to bag one. Just me. All by myself. Without goddam Stan. Without anyone.'

Phil put a hand under her chin. 'I know it's important to you, darling. I just wish you knew you don't have to prove yourself. Certainly not to me. To me, you're already perfect.'

Angela pursed her lips.

'Okay, sorry. I know. This isn't about me. It's about you.'

She smiled stiffly. 'Bring home a rabbit, Phil. I'll be back for you in a couple of hours.'

He watched her go, the sway of her round bottom inside her coveralls. He waited until she disappeared into the trees beyond the field. Then, alone, he found a spot near the edge of the woods and waited, motionless, the way Angela told him. As the sun came up, he saw a bird or two, but no squirrels or rabbits. Damn, he wanted to bag something just to show her that he could. To gain her respect. Not that he'd ever compare to Stan, hunting-wise. Stan and Angela had hunted together their whole marriage. They'd come here every year and bagged venison every season. Stan was supposedly a crackerjack shot, whereas Phil had just this year managed to hit a tin can. But if he could hit a rabbit, maybe he could show Angela that he was competent.

Phil gazed across the field, watching for movement. A chilly breeze rattled the leaves of the trees, swayed the grass and weeds.

Occasionally, a bird called out. Other than that, the woods were silent. He looked across the clearing at the trees with their vibrant colored leaves, wondered if Angela had found tracks yet. If she'd actually shoot a bear. Jesus. What if she did? What would they do with it? Mount its head on a board and put it in the den? The thought made Phil queasy. Up ahead, something moved through the grass, making a line. He lifted the rifle to his shoulder, reminded himself: aim, breathe, hold, squeeze. Saw the rabbit through his scope. Took a breath. Held it. Aimed.

What in God's name was he doing? Was he really going to shoot at that defenseless little creature? Was he going to kill it? He watched it hold still, trying to become invisible as if it sensed a predator. All he had to do was fire, and he'd have a prize for Angela. He pictured the rabbit, skinned and gutted. Its feet would be good-luck charms on key chains. It was up to him. He had the power over the rabbit's life or death. Gracious – what was he doing? Phil lowered the rifle. He stared at the weapon, at his hands. Felt sick.

But what about Angela? He wanted to impress her, ached to have her look up to him the way she looked up to Stan. But Phil could never be like Stan. He was a pharmacist, not an outdoors man. He preferred to garden, watch films, play bridge, drink fine wines. He hoped that Angela loved him for the man he was. Of course she did. She was married to him now, not to Stan. Hunting was simply a passion that she hoped they could share, the way he hoped she'd learn to play bridge.

The gun was heavy. His new boots felt stiff. The ground was rocky and, even with his flannel shirt, he felt the nip of the air. Phil looked back at the bunny. It was gone.

He sighed, annoyed with himself. It was just a dumb rabbit – it wasn't like he was murdering a person. He had to do this for Angela. Just this once. He had do it to prove that he could, and then never again. He held very still, watching the stillness of the field. Recognizing some of the plants – bull thistle over there, day lilies all over. Purple loosestrife. And weren't those Spanish bluebells? He held still, staring at the plants as the sun peaked higher. There was something Zen-like about standing so still and silent, waiting. He was staring at a privet blossom, letting his eyes drift out of focus when, close behind him, he heard a shot.

He didn't move, didn't even breathe. He could swear he'd felt a whoosh of air along with the crack of the shot. But certainly that had been his imagination. In fact, the shot probably hadn't been all that close. He wasn't familiar with the sound of shots fired in the woods; quite possibly, the sound had rebounded off trees, bouncing and ricocheting in all directions, so he couldn't really be sure where it was coming from, let alone how far away.

Even so, that crack had alarmed him. Had sounded as if it had come from a copse of trees not far away, toward the south end of the clearing. He looked that way, hoping he wouldn't see a bloodied deer or, worse, a hunter gutting it. Would the guy gut it right there, in the woods? Phil didn't know about the gutting process. Didn't want to. Hunting, he decided, was not for him. It was barbaric, the whole sport – even calling it a 'sport' was barbaric. It was not a game; it was killing, pure and simple. And calling the victims 'game' – as if killing them were somehow playing – that was twisted, too. Phil scanned the area where he thought he'd heard the shot. Didn't see any animals, dead or alive, but under a tree on the ground, he saw a patch of blue.

Blue. Not flowers. A solid patch like fabric, the color of his shirt.

He stared at it for a few seconds, curious. Nothing in nature would be that color and size. Wary, clutching his rifle, he moved closer, watching the blue patch. As he got closer, it became more defined. It wasn't entirely blue; it was plaid, much like the blue and gray plaid of his own shirt. Something cold rippled up his spine, but he kept going, keeping his eyes focused on the plaid fabric until he got close enough to see, among clumps of Devil's tails and Japanese stiltgrass, the arms and hands of the man who was wearing it.

Oh Christ. Half the shirt was drenched with blood.

Phil stared, trying to make sense of what he was seeing. The man must have been shot. Oh God, there'd been a terrible accident. Phil ran to the guy; maybe he was still alive. He could do CPR, stop the bleeding. He looked around – maybe someone was close enough to go for help. Sure enough, up ahead in the early-morning light, half-hidden by the trees, he saw a figure, holding a rifle.

'Help!' Phil shouted. 'There's been an accident. A man's been shot – help!'

The person stepped out, faced him, raised the rifle and took aim.

For a moment, Phil didn't understand. By the time he did, it was too late to run, let alone to use his rifle.

*   *   *

The stream was icy cold. Harper didn't mind. She spread a towel over a flat rock, sat down and sponged off. The chill of the water stirred her. She watched it rush over pebbles, run over her feet as if in a hurry. The surface rippled in the early light, reflecting silver, blue and gold. Harper dipped her sponge into the water, washed her face, her neck. She thought of Chloe, wondered if she were awake yet. As she washed her feet, she hesitated. Something moved in the trees, and she sensed that she was being watched. But that was unlikely. She and Hank had camped off by themselves, away from the campgrounds. No one was around. Maybe it was a hunter.

Harper squinted into the woods, saw only trees, tangles of vines and weeds, speckles of colored leaves. A bird flittered off a limb. A squirrel leapt off a trunk. But no hunter. Nobody was lurking in the woods, watching her. Harper dipped her sponge in the stream again, soaked it.

The water was clear, but Hank had warned that it wasn't clean. He'd brought bottled water because he thought the streams were probably polluted. Something to do with fracking, not that Harper completely understood what that was. All she knew was that it involved cracking rocks deep under the earth's surface to get fossil fuels. And that it was controversial. Those opposed to it blamed fracking for everything from pollution to fires to explosions to earthquakes. Apparently, fracking had been done upstream and a pipeline had been built through the forest. While they were here, Hank was going to take samples of soil and water for testing. Doing his geology thing. He couldn't help it.

Rinsing off, Harper looked up the slope to their campsite. Hank was mixing up batter from powdered milk, flour, eggs and bottled water. Engrossed. Completely at home. No, at home he had less energy. It was barely seven, and already he'd taken samples of their campsite soil, the stream and the mud under and around it. He'd washed yesterday's clothes, cleaned up in the stream, planned their morning hike along the bog. Now he was cooking. Hank was a dynamo, healthy again, tireless, the way he'd been before his accident. He'd started up the propane stove. Who would have imagined that he'd recover so completely? She saw him again, falling off the roof, sliding. Landing on his head. She saw him unconscious in the hospital, tubes emanating from every part of his body. Monitors beeping, screens showing his heart rate, his oxygen levels . . . No. That was over. She didn't need to revisit it.

Harper closed her eyes, erasing the memory. Hank was fine. She dribbled cold water down her back, watching him lean over their little propane stove. The cloth of his sweatshirt stretched across his shoulders.

Hank looked up. Had he felt her watching him? 'Come and get it!'

Harper dried her feet, put on her socks and boots, and joined him. They ate pancakes in the crisp air to the music of birds. Hank talked about where they'd hike, the samples he wanted to take. What he expected to find. He went on talking. Harper still couldn't get used to his conversation. For more than two years, he hadn't been able to articulate complete sentences or clearly express his thoughts. Now, he wouldn't quiet down. Harper tried but couldn't feign interest in chemistry and mineral deposits and so on. Her mind wandered to Chloe. Was she eating breakfast now? Asking where mommy was? Had she used the potty? Lord, she missed her. But Chloe was fine. She needed to experience a few days without her mom. And her mom needed to experience a few without Chloe.

Hank was still talking, saying something about people complaining about foul-tasting water. She needed to pay closer attention.

Except whatever Hank was talking about wasn't all that appealing. She understood the importance of leakage and wastewater and natural gas, but honestly, pipeline safeguards didn't stir her blood. She drifted, watching Hank's mouth move, not listening to what he was saying. Realizing how much he loved his work. How Hank had it all – a loving family, a challenging career. Health. His life was full.

Harper chewed a mouthful of pancake, swallowed. Nodded at Hank as if she understood. And realized that Chloe's life was also full. Chloe had preschool, swim class, gymnastics, library, music group, play dates. Harper swallowed coffee, burned her tongue. Damn.

'You all right?'

'Fine.'

'You looked like you were choking.'

'No. I'm fine.'

He looked doubtful, eyed her as he swirled syrup onto the last bite of his pancakes. Harper's tongue felt on fire, but she smiled to reassure Hank. She even took another sip of coffee, careful this time to cool it first. She went through the motions of being happy and relaxed, for Hank's sake. What would be the point of letting him know how lost she felt? He couldn't fix her situation, couldn't make a life for her. Couldn't stop her from becoming clingy or needy or from sinking into self-pity. No, finding a way to fill her life was her responsibility, hers alone.

Hank had stopped talking a while ago. They sat in silence.

'Delicious.' Harper got up, kissed him. She picked up the pan, took the plates and a dish towel, headed for the stream.

'Hold on, Harper. I'll do it.' Hank came up behind her. He had their mugs.

'But you cooked.'

Hank stood close, nuzzled her. 'I want to. I feel great, being out here again. It's like coming back to life. I'll clean up and hang the supplies. Why don't you just relax?'

'Relax?'

'I'll be fast.'

Harper watched him scamper down the slope to the stream. Why didn't he want her to help? Was he so self-sufficient that she seemed in the way? Did he think she'd slow him down or do things wrong? Not long ago, Hank had depended on her for everything – even for speaking. But now, she stood alone, feeling useless. Not needed.

Stop it, she told herself. Cool down. She was being oversensitive. She should let Hank do his manly Hank-in-the-wilderness things. She went back to their tent, then wandered onto a path just beyond it. She wouldn't go far. Just take a couple of minutes to be alone. Maybe she'd figure out her future. Harper stepped over fallen red and yellow leaves, thistles, creeping vines. Her boots crunched, birds and crickets chattered, and Harper strained to imagine a career, a daily routine involving meetings, a wardrobe, an office, a purpose. No use. She couldn't see herself there. So what did that mean? Would she be a stay-at-home mom, volunteering at bake sales for the PTA, playing tennis? No, not tennis. Not with her leg. Maybe she'd be like her mother and stay home and drink. Harper saw her childhood self, coming home from school, finding her mother passed out on a sofa. Never mind. Don't go there. *You are not your mother.*

The light ahead was brighter. The trees seemed to stop. What was up there? A clearing? Maybe a park facility? She kept walking, curious, looking ahead. The field was maybe an acre. Golden, swaying to a breeze, dotted with blues and purples, whites and yellows. Harper's foot snapped a stick, startling her. It was time to head back.

She turned, looked over her shoulder at the field again. And noticed a patch of blue about ten feet away, to her left.

The boy lay sprawled flat in the middle of the square. He had no face.

Harper told herself to leave him. To keep moving. The boy was beyond help. Smoke clouded around her, gunfire burst rapidly somewhere nearby. Dusty heat seared her lungs, smelled of burning rubber, burning flesh. Men were screaming. She crouched and dashed for cover, clutching her weapon. Where was her patrol? She couldn't see through the smoky haze. Where were they?

'Sergeant?' she called. 'Phyllis? Cooper?'

No one answered.

'Marvin?'

Shit. Where was her damned patrol? She held her rifle up and ready, aimed it toward the square. Her head felt jangled. Christ, what had happened? The boy. He'd been crossing the square, walking toward the checkpoint. And now he was dead. Something had happened. An explosion? An ambush? She'd missed it. How had she missed it?

Footsteps. Coming closer. Harper hunkered down, ready to fire. 'Stop,' she warned. 'Don't come closer.'

But the figure came closer, repeating foreign sounds. Or wait – maybe not foreign. 'Harper. It's okay. It's okay.'

What? He knew her name. He kept talking, repeating himself. And his voice – wait. Hank? Hank was here? At the checkpoint?

Harper bit her lip, hard. In moments, the smoke vanished, replaced by trees. The gunfire and screams quieted, stifled by Hank's voice. Her rifle became a broken branch. The flashback of flames and destruction faded into autumn leaves and her husband's embrace.

And the boy with no face had a face again. It was older, though. And he was still dead.

Their cell phones didn't work. They'd known that, but they tried anyway, got no signal. Hank shoved his back into his vest pocket.

'You all right?'

All the way back to their campsite, he'd kept asking her that. She'd kept answering that she was fine. 'It was just a mental lapse, Hank. It passed fast.'

He didn't say anything, just watched her. His gaze had a wary edge as if he didn't believe her.

'I haven't had a flashback in over a year. It was just the shock.'

The shock of finding a dead man in the woods where they'd come for serenity and togetherness.

'Harper. You were shouting. Holding a stick like a—'

'I thought it was a rifle—'

'You thought it was a rifle.' It sounded crazy when he said it.

Damn. Hank thought she was crazy. He'd never seen her in the full throes of a flashback before. So now what? Was he shocked? Repulsed? 'Yes, that's what I thought. But only for a moment. The flashback is over, Hank. Can we move on? We have to get somebody out here.'

Hank eyed her as he walked closer, put his hands on her waist, sat her down on a log. Sat beside her. 'Two things before we do anything, Harper.'

'Shoot.' She still felt wobbly, talked tough to cover it.

'First, you are never going to wander off alone like that again. You always tell me where you are out here; we never lose sight of each other. If for some reason you absolutely have to separate from me, you take a real, actual weapon with you. Sticks won't help you fight off a bear. Agreed?'

She nodded. 'And second?'

'Second is harder. Because if you have a real actual weapon, how do I know you won't have a flashback and start shooting randomly? How do I know when some sound or sight – like that hunter's shot you heard this morning – how do I know that won't set you spinning off into some alternative reality?'

Harper blinked as if he'd slapped her. Hank had known about her Post Traumatic Stress Disorder. But until now, she'd never known that it bothered him. Did her condition mean he couldn't trust her? Apparently, he thought she might flip and start full-out combat at any moment. How could he think that, after all they'd been through – those terrorists, the sociopath fraternity brothers, and before that, the gang of artifact smugglers. After his accident, she'd saved Hank from a crazed medical researcher. She'd sat by his bed for weeks, holding his unconscious hand, talking to him. Every time they'd faced a crisis, she'd come through. But now, Hank had seen her have one lousy flashback and . . . what? He'd lost all faith in her?

Harper wanted to scream. She wanted to sob. Instead, she stood tall and met his eyes, Army strong. 'You're asking how you'll know what I'll do under stress. The answer is simple. You won't.'

He turned away, let out a breath. 'So.' He faced her again. 'When you have a flashback, what happens to you? What did you think was going on back there?'

'It doesn't matter what I thought. Each time is different. I relive various moments. Or combinations of moments, but that's—'

'You've never talked to me about this.'

'I don't want to honor it by discussing it. I won't let PTSD rule my life. Besides, this isn't the time.' She started to get up; he put a hand on her arm, stopped her.

'Hank, we have to go get the police. That guy is dead.' She began again to stand. Hank tightened his grip on her arm. 'He'll stay dead until we finish here.'

Harper's eyebrows raised. She wasn't yet accustomed to Hank physically taking charge. Or telling her what to do. It was a role reversal, and she wasn't real happy about it. 'Okay. Leslie has shown me ways to fend flashbacks off or at least minimize them. And the techniques have helped. Like I said, it's been over a year since the last—'

'What ways?'

Harper sighed, rolling her eyes. 'Hank, do we really have to go through all this? Now? Why are you being so – so controlling?'

'Tell me.' His voice was firm. 'What ways?'

'You already know about the lemon. The taste shocks me back into the present.'

'So you didn't you have your lemon with you this morning?'

'I did. In my vest pocket. But I didn't have time, Hank. I saw him and reacted.'

'But you had a lemon ready to use?'

'Of course.' She always did. She carried lemons the way other women carried lip gloss. Standard operating equipment.

'What else works? Besides a lemon?' His eyes were steely, probing.

'Why are you questioning me? Are you angry? You sound angry.'

Hank crossed his arms. 'I'm not angry, Harper. I just need information. Tell me what else works?'

Harper sat rigid. She didn't want to argue with Hank, but he was pushing her on a topic she tried to avoid. Besides, they had to get going and alert authorities that a man had been killed. Why was Hank choosing this particular moment to discuss her PTSD? Damn. She saw the determination in his eyes. Resisting would be futile.

She took a breath, rattled off her response. 'I can inhale a sharp scent, like smelling salts. Or cause pain by biting my lip or jabbing myself with a sharp object – any intense sensory stimulation will help ground me in the present moment by shocking me out of the flashback. If I don't have any shockers to work with, I can use my own mind and concentrate on some physical aspect of the present moment. Like counting the tiles on a wall or—'

'Okay, I get it. Why didn't anything work today?'

'Because today, I came upon a dead body unexpectedly. It triggered a flashback so quickly that I was in it before I could try to prevent it.'

Hank looked away. Looked back at Harper. Met her eyes. Took her hand. 'Okay. I need to understand this, Harper. The PTSD. You need to talk to me and be more open about it—'

'I don't like to—'

'Hold on. Don't interrupt. For much of the time we've been together, you've been the caretaker. You've been the tough one. And you've put your problems aside. But, Harper, you don't have to deal with them alone. I'm healthy again. And I'm your husband. It's okay to let me inside those walls.'

Harper didn't say anything, but she felt a heaviness lift, rising out of her belly, passing through her shoulders. She looked at Hank, but he'd become blurry. Damn. She puffed her nostrils, took in air. Blinked tears away. She was not going to get all wimpy and cry.

'For now, though, for this trip, I think the best way to make sure another flashback doesn't occur is for you to stick close to me.'

Harper sniffed, nodded. 'Fine.'

'And keep your lemon handy.'

She nodded again, ready to go.

'Somebody shot that guy, Harper. It might have been an accident, but just in case . . . I don't want you flashing back to Iraq if real bullets are flying.' Hank leaned over, kissed her, and stood, still holding her hand. 'Ready?'

She felt like a bobble-head, nodding again. But finally, they were on their way.

The forest ranger called the Philipsburg police captain on a landline. Harper and Hank sat on a bench outside the ranger's station at the campground, waiting for him to arrive. A few people walked by, on the way to their RVs, the convenience store, the snack shop next to the ranger's office. A woman sat at a picnic bench, eating a pepper and egg sandwich, staring at them.

'Why is she staring at us?' Harper nudged Hank.

Hank didn't turn his head to look. 'Don't know. But who can blame her? We're pretty dammed hot.'

The woman chewed, watching them.

'Seriously, Hank. She's bugging me out.'

'Ignore her.'

Harper tried to ignore her. She looked at Hank's hands. She loved those hands. They were muscular, large, confident. Manly, with just the right amount of dark hair on the back, and sturdy steady fingers. She reached for one. It made her own hand look tiny.

'Captain Slader should be here any time now.' Ranger Daniels stepped out of his office, checking his watch. 'You want some water or soda pop?'

Hank stood. 'I'm good. You want anything, Harper?'

'No thanks.' She felt awkward, being the only one sitting. She got to her feet even though her left leg hurt from racing there from their campsite.

The three of them stood, arms crossed, staring at air. Almost two hours had passed since Harper had found the body. In Iraq, flies would have claimed the corpse by now. Here, she pictured crows tearing at its eyes, coyotes at its flesh.

'You remember, I told you two that you should camp here at the campgrounds. I warned you about hikers getting lost, accidents happening out in the woods.'

'We didn't get lost, Ranger Daniels,' Harper answered. 'And this man would have been killed regardless of where we'd stayed.'

Daniels looked into the distance, widened his stance. 'You know, I probably shouldn't say this. I don't want to stir things up. But the thing is I feel responsible for you two. You're strangers here. You're not familiar with the area.'

'That's right.' Hank cocked his head.

'Well, some people live here, year round.' He said that as if it made sense.

'Okay.'

Daniels looked around. 'Most of those people are fine folks. But some of them have issues – and I won't say they're wrong. Their people have been here for a couple of centuries. And they don't like outsiders.'

Harper digested that for a moment. 'Are you saying you think the dead guy was killed by someone local?'

The ranger looked down at her. He was Hank's height but he seemed immense. 'All I'm saying is that some of these people are very protective of the land. They don't want others messing with it. Not the government with their hunting and mining licenses, or the energy companies with their fracking and pipelines. Not seasonal hunters. Not weekenders like yourselves. It's best to leave their part of the woods to them—'

'Wait a second,' Hank interrupted. 'You work for the government, don't you? And this is a state forest. Owned by the government. So you're aware that, no matter how long their families have lived around here, they don't own the land. So they have no right—'

'I don't believe I said anything about legal rights, Mr Jennings. I'm just being real. These people are a tight community. Some believe that outsiders are taking away their rights and their heritage, and they're protecting what they see as their birthright.' He leaned close to Hank, lowered his voice. 'They're good people, mind you. But they're well prepared for catastrophes. Anything from a tornado to an invasion. They have provisions and weapons. And not all of them, but a good number, have lately become convinced that outsiders are conspiring to move in and throw them off the properties they have left.'

Harper watched Hank's reaction. He was meeting Ranger Daniels' eyes, kind of wincing. 'Are you talking about some kind of militia?'

'Sounds like survivalists,' Harper said.

'And you're saying they think we're part of some invasion?'

'I'm just pretty protective of the area where you say you found the body.'

'So you think they shot this man.'

The ranger didn't answer; just then, a police car pulled into the parking area, splattering through old rain puddles. The captain had arrived.

Captain Slader was a lithe, thin-lipped man with dark, bushy eyebrows, graying hair and a salt-and-pepper mustache. He said they could talk on the way to the body and asked Hank and Harper to lead the way. His arrival had drawn the attention of some campers, though. About a half dozen clustered across the road, eyeing them.

'What happened, Joe?' A leathery woman holding a coffee mug ambled over, joining them.

'Nothing you need to worry about, Sylvie,' the captain said.

'Don't condescend to me. You wouldn't be here if it wasn't something to worry about.' Her voice was raspy. She walked beside the captain, craning her neck to look up at him. 'Somebody die?'

'Sylvie, this is none of your concern.'

'Hell if it isn't. If it's out there hunting people, we have a right to know. We don't want to be next.'

The captain stopped; so did Ranger Daniels, Harper and Hank.

'I've told them it's just made-up rumors,' Daniels said.

'We know better,' Sylvie insisted. 'It's back. That hiker saw it. And the footprints – you saw them yourself . . .'

'Sylvie, stop.' The captain spoke gently. 'You're getting yourself all riled up. If something's out there – and I'm not saying there is or there isn't – it's best you tell people to stay away from the area near the bog. Stay where you know it's safe—'

'Oh, come on, Joe,' Ranger Daniels broke in. 'You'll start a panic. Sylvie, I told you there's nothing to worry about, and there isn't.'

'And I showed you the articles. Did you read The Sasquatch Genome Project? They've found evidence, scientists have. From fourteen states and Canada. Not just footprints, either.'

'Sylvie. This isn't the time.' The ranger tried to brush her off.

'Then when is the time, Ranger? When the creature kills again? The articles prove it's real. They found samples of hair, skin, blood and bones—'

'Not now.' Daniels tried to move away, but Sylvie moved along with him.

'—one hundred and eleven different specimens with DNA that's almost human but doesn't match any known animals. It's proof, whether you want to believe it or not.'

'If you're worried, Sylvie, do like I said. Stay away from the bog area. I think that's easy enough to do.' The captain turned away, motioned for Daniels to accompany him into the woods.

Sylvie trailed after them. 'They found DNA in Denmark, too. It's all in those articles. Just read them.'

Daniels stopped and put his hand up, spoke in a gentle tone. 'Slader and I've got business to take care of, Sylvie. Tell your friends to calm down. This isn't about your Bog Man.' He nodded to the group across the street and took off after the captain.

Hank took Harper's hand, gave it a squeeze. She squeezed back, a silent confirmation that she'd been listening to this strange exchange, and they walked along, following the ranger and the captain. As they entered the woods, Harper looked back over her shoulder. Sylvie was standing alone in the road, holding her coffee, watching them leave.

'What was that?' Hank asked.

'Nothing,' Daniels said. 'Just people getting spooked.'

'It's not nothing.' Captain Slader scowled. 'I saw the tracks.'

'Tracks?' Hank asked.

'Some folks have it in their heads that there's a big scary ape creature prowling out near the bogs.'

'And there might be something to it.'

The captain's stride was long. Harper struggled to keep up. Her left leg ached, and they'd just started the hike.

'A couple of local hunters say they saw it,' Slader went on. 'And last week, a hiker got lost out near the bog and said it came after him.'

'The guy was half-drunk, half-delusional from being alone in the woods all night.' Daniels pushed a branch out of the way, held it back for Harper.

'Daniels here is skeptical. But I keep an open mind,' Slader said. 'The hunters who reported it were locals. They live around here and know the woods. I trust them. They said it might be violent or rabid, and people should steer clear of the bog area.'

Rabid? Harper glanced at Hank. What were these people talking about? A rabid ape-creature from the bogs?

Daniels shook his head. 'I know the fauna here, Joe. There's no such animal—'

'How about we leave the locals to deal with it?' Slader suggested.

'I just said there's nothing to deal with.' Daniels bristled. 'If there were, the forest service would take care of it.'

Slader stepped over a rock. 'You're right. Let's just forget the whole idea.'

Slader changed the subject to the body. Where had Harper found him? Did she know who he was? Was he armed? What did he look like? Had she seen anyone else around? Was she sure he was dead?

'Captain,' Hank cut in. 'My wife is Army. She saw some heavy combat in Iraq. If she says a guy is dead, he's dead.'

Harper felt her face heat up. Slader and Daniels slowed and

looked her over, reassessing her. She was short for a soldier. Only five feet, three-and-a-tiny-bit inches. A pint-sized blonde. Not typical military.

'Iraq?' Slader an eyebrow rose. 'Grunt?'

'She was a lieutenant.'

Slader's eyebrows rose.

Daniels let out a low whistle. 'She outranks you, Joe.' He grinned. 'Captain was just a lowly sergeant.'

'Sergeants run the Army,' Harper replied.

Slader's face had reddened; his smile seemed forced.

'Anyway, I'm sure he was dead,' Harper went on, didn't want to get into combat conversation. 'The bullet hit his heart, went in through his back.'

They walked a few steps before Slader resumed his questioning. Had she been alone when she'd found the dead man? What had she been doing? Had she heard anything unusual?

Harper answered concisely, trying to recall the facts without revisiting – or reviving her flashback. Talking about one brought up memories of the other, though. She slid her hand into her vest pocket, clutching her lemon, just in case. She answered the captain as well as she could, omitting the parts about the insurgent attack and stepping over the body of the boy with no face.

By the time they got back to their campsite, Harper's leg was throbbing. She asked if they could stop for a moment so she could take ibuprofen.

'Leg hurt?' Hank asked.

'Are you okay, ma'am?' Daniels asked.

'War injury.' Hank took a bottle of pills from his pocket and set up the folding steps under the bear bag.

Slader watched. 'Did you serve, too?'

'Me? No. I'm a civilian.'

'He was a contractor. Consulted the military.' Harper sat on a rock, stretched her leg muscles.

'Is that how you got injured? Consulting the military?'

Hank looked down the steps at him; Harper looked up from the rock.

'You seemed to have trouble walking.'

'I had an accident. At home. Nothing to do with the war.' He lowered the bear bag, opened it. Took out some snack bars. Unlocked the cooler and got some drinks, handed a bottle of iced tea to Harper, offered some to the men. He'd relocked the cooler and was repositioning the bear bag, tying the rope to the trunk of the tree when a woman burst out of the woods.

'Oh, thank God!' Her hair was loose and tangled, her clothes muddy. 'Help me!' Her voice was raw. 'Please, help me! I can't find Phil—'

Captain Slader stepped over to her. 'Ma'am? Are you all right?'

'No, I'm not all right.' Her eyes darted from Slader to Harper to Hank to Daniels. She panted, pushed hair off her face. 'Phil – my husband – he's missing . . .'

'Missing?' Slader glanced at Daniels.

'He was supposed to meet me at our tent and he hasn't shown up – you haven't seen him, have you?' She gulped air. 'He's about five foot ten, sandy hair—'

'Hold on a minute, ma'am.' Again, Slader exchanged glances with Daniels. They now had a dead man and a missing husband. One and the same? 'Why don't you sit down a second? Got any of that iced tea?' He held his hand out; Hank handed him a bottle. 'Now, take a drink. Settle down a minute.'

The woman perched on a tree stump near Harper's rock. She drank Hank's iced tea but she wouldn't relax. Her body was taut, ready to take off.

'What's your name?' Harper asked.

'Angela. Angela Russo.'

'I'm Harper Jennings.' Harper reached out, shook her hand. 'This is my husband, Hank. Ranger Daniels and Captain Slader from the Philipsburg police.'

Angela looked at each of them in turn.

'So tell us what happened?' Harper made her voice soft.

'If you're ready.' Slader glared at Harper, hands on hips. This was his territory. He alone had the authority to ask the questions.

'See, Phil never hunted before.' Angela gripped her iced-tea bottle, addressed Harper. 'I shouldn't have left him on his own. I thought he'd be okay, though. He'd practiced his aim, and he was only going for small game. He was hoping to bag a rabbit.' She smiled sadly. Mud was smeared across the freckles on her cheek.

Slader had a notepad out. 'What's your husband's name, ma'am?'

'Philip Russo.' Her hand went to her mouth. 'Oh God. Something's wrong. I just have a feeling.'

Harper reached over, put her hand on the woman's arm. She had a feeling, too. 'What was he wearing?'

Slater scowled, took an official stance. 'Do you remember what he had on?'

Angela nodded. 'Khaki coveralls. And his blue plaid flannel shirt.'

Slader and Daniels looked at Harper for confirmation. Harper gave a slight nod. She closed her eyes, saw the body at the edge of the field. Its blue plaid flannel shirt. Damn. Hank stepped over and put a hand on her shoulder. She leaned her head against his arm. No question. The body had to be Phil's. And his poor wife was the only one there who had no idea.

Angela kept talking. 'I don't know where he can be. I went back to the clearing where I left him. I looked all over. Called his name. Whistled – we have a certain whistle, just for us to signal each other.' She demonstrated a piercing three-tone sound. Shook her head. Folded her hands. 'Maybe he's just lost. But I shouldn't have left him. It's my fault because I thought he'd be okay by himself, just hunting small game, and I wanted to go off by myself because this year, I want to bag a bear.' She looked at Daniels. 'I come out here every year. I've bagged deer and elk. Pheasants. Almost everything but bear.'

'Season just opened.' Daniels crossed his arms. 'You have time.'

'Daniels.' Slader rolled his eyes.

Daniels' ears turned red. He looked at his shoes.

'Here's what we're going to do.' Slader tucked his notepad into his pocket. 'Mrs Russo, you'll stay here with Ranger Daniels. The rest of us will go look for your husband.'

'No, I need to go with you.' Angela stood.

'No. For now, you need to catch your breath. I promise we won't leave you for long.' He nodded at Harper and Hank, indicating that it was time for them to lead him to the body.

Harper gave Angela's arm a squeeze. Then she stood, trying to feign hopefulness, even smiling and giving a thumbs-up as she led the way to the body of the man wearing a blue plaid shirt.

The path led right to him. The body was right where she'd remembered it, and this time, Harper saw no sniper fire or explosions. This time, she simply saw a man sprawled out face-down under a tree, the back of his shirt stained with blood. No flashback. Also no onslaught of bugs or coyotes, no voracious vultures circling above. In fact, the scene was extremely still. Disturbingly still.

Harper shivered, put her hands in her vest pockets, held onto her lemon.

Captain Slader smoothed his mustache as he walked around the body to get a look at the guy's face.

'Aw, shit.' He stooped near the guy's head. 'This guy's her husband?'

'Looks like it.' Hank stepped around the dead guy's feet, gazed at his face. 'He's wearing a blue plaid shirt.'

Harper watched them but didn't go close. She had no desire to see another face frozen by death. She stared at a mottled tree trunk, dreading giving the news to Angela. The poor woman was back at their tent, waiting. Hoping for good news. For her, Phil was still alive. She pictured the captain, telling her. Angela collapsing in grief, wailing.

Stop it, she told herself. Think about Chloe instead. Maybe she's at the playground. On the swings . . .

'Thing is, I know this guy.' Slader frowned, interrupting her thoughts. 'I've seen him before.'

'Didn't his wife say she came up here a lot?' Hank squatted, looking at the guy more closely. 'So probably he's been with her.'

Slader pursed his lips. One of the guy's vest pockets was exposed. He reached in, retrieved a pack of tissues, an Almond Joy. No information.

'I should wait for the medical examiner,' he sighed. 'But that poor woman's waiting. Let's roll him so I can get to his pockets.'

Hank took his legs, Slader his shoulders. They turned him over.

'My my,' Hank said.

Harper followed his gaze. The guy's fly was open, his privates partially exposed.

'What the Sam Hill?' Slader looked up at them, shaking his head. 'Guy got shot with his junk out?'

Harper opened her mouth, closed it. She looked at Hank. No way was she going to answer that question.

'Maybe he was taking a leak?' Hank suggested.

'And they shot him in the middle? Hell of a thing.' Slader gazed up at the trees. 'So, in that case, he'd be standing still. Hard to mistake him for a deer.'

'Wait. So you think it wasn't an accident?'

Slader didn't answer. He scowled, stood beside a tree, took his pocket knife out, and dug a bullet out of the trunk. 'Thirty caliber.' He stuck it into his pocket. 'I'll have to confirm back at the office.'

Harper glanced at Hank. Slader hadn't bagged the evidence, had just popped it into his vest. Was that police procedure around here?

Slader returned to the body and rooted around in the guy's vest pockets. Finally pulled out an ID.

'Damn. This says "Albert Rogers".'

Harper stiffened. 'But Angela's husband's name is Phil—'

'Well, like I said, this isn't him.' Slader looked at the guy's face again. 'But now I know why he looks familiar.'

'Why?'

Slader held up the ID card. 'Albert Rogers worked for an energy company. He was a pipeline walker.'

Harper looked at Hank.

'They walk along pipelines, checking for leaks,' he explained. 'They look for stains or dead vegetation, and they sniff around for odd odors.'

'I never heard of that,' Harper said.

'A lot of the pipeline controls are centralized now, done by computers.' Slader stood, let out a sigh. 'But there are over two hundred thousand miles of pipelines in this country. So they send guys like him out to eyeball them.'

'The pipeline here – it's natural gas?'

'Oh, yes, ma'am. It goes right through the forest preserves. And they've been doing the fracking right near here, too. You heard of the Marcellus Shale?'

Harper nodded. She waited for Hank to explain that he was a geologist and that he was taking soil and water samples to test for fracking pollution. But Hank said nothing. She wondered why.

'So what now?' Harper turned to Slader. 'What do we do now?'

'Now?' Slader gave her a blank look. 'You go on back to Ranger Daniels, and I get on the radio and do my job.'

'What about Angela Russo?' Hank asked.

'I'll talk to her when I can. I got to deal with this first.'

Hank took Harper's hand and they walked in step back down the path. She didn't want to face Angela Russo. Didn't want to tell her that they'd found a man, just not the man they'd been looking for.

On the bright side though, they wouldn't have to tell her that her husband Phil was dead.

* * *

By mid-afternoon, they were back at Ranger Daniels' office. Angela Russo sat slumped in the corner, holding a Styrofoam cup with a tea-bag string hanging out.

Daniels said Harper could use the office landline to check on Chloe. Harper made the call, but Trent's voicemail answered. At the beep, she left a message, her voice overly cheery, saying that she missed them and hoped they were having fun. She hung up with a knot in her chest. What was she doing out in some dark state forest, finding a dead man? She should be home with her little girl, taking trips to the playground and the library. She closed her eyes, picturing Chloe, trying to recreate the sound of her laughter.

'No luck?' Hank asked.

She opened her eyes, took a breath. 'Nope. I left a message.' She forced a smile.

'It's okay, Harper. She's fine. And you'll be back in two days.'

Two days. It sounded like a prison sentence, not a vacation.

Daniels ordered sandwiches from the snack bar. Harper was halfway through her Italian hoagie when a short, brawny guy stomped in, unshaven, his reddish hair disheveled, demanding to talk to the police.

'Jim. So sorry about Al.' Daniels went over to the man, tried to embrace him, but the man pushed him away.

'What the fuck happened? Can somebody give me a straight answer?'

'Jim, come sit down—'

'Fuck no. I won't sit down.' Spit flew from Jim's mouth. He turned in a circle, running a hand over his head, his gaze passing over Angela, Hank and Harper. He pointed at Daniels' chest. 'Where's the cops?'

'Captain Slader's on his way over—'

'Fine. Where? Because he better tell me what happened. How is it possible? Al's dead?'

'When did you last see him?'

'Last night. This morning, I wake up and he isn't there. I wait a while and try him on the radio, but I can't reach him. So I go looking for him and I'm freaking out. And then I get a radio call from our supervisor. He's saying that Al's dead and the police need me to identify the body. So tell me, Daniels, what the fuck happened to him? It was that damned survivalist militia, wasn't it? Those people who hate the pipeline? I bet they shot him.'

Daniels was taller, broader than the man, but he didn't use his size to intimidate him. He let the guy shout and gesticulate and stamp his feet. When he finally quieted down, Daniels went to his desk and took out a bottle of Jack Daniels. He poured some into a coffee mug.

'You buying, Ranger Daniels?' Angela perked up. 'I could use some of that.'

Daniels smirked, held the mug out. Jim was wild-eyed, breathing fast. He eyed Daniels, then the mug, then Daniels. He took the mug, downed the Jack.

Daniels put an arm around him, led him to the table where Harper sat with Hank. 'Have a seat, Jim.'

'Don't want to sit.'

'Sit anyway.'

Jim sat on a folding chair near Harper.

'This here's the woman who found Al.' Daniels nodded at Harper. 'That's her husband.'

Harper gave the kind of smile that indicates sorrow. 'I'm Harper Jennings. This is Hank.'

Hank reached over, shook hands.

'Jim Kinsella,' the man said. 'I'm . . . I was Al's partner.'

Harper nodded.

'So what happened, ma'am? How'd he die?'

'He was shot, Jim,' Daniels answered. 'Might have been a hunting accident.'

Jim glanced at Daniels, then back at Harper. 'He was shot?'

Harper nodded.

'They were searching for my husband, Phil, because he's gone missing,' Angela called from the corner. 'But they didn't find Phil. They found your friend instead.'

It wasn't exactly what had happened, but Harper didn't correct her. Dead was dead.

'Where was he shot? In the head?' Jim looked at Harper, pointed to his head.

Harper hesitated, not sure what she should tell him.

Ranger Daniels intervened. 'Jim, it's been a rough day for Mrs Jennings. When Captain Slader gets here, you can ask him everything—'

'Was he shot in the head?' Jim kept his eyes on Harper. 'Was it execution style?'

'Now Jim, let her be—'

'Because you and I both know it wasn't a hunting accident, Daniels.' Jim was on his feet again. 'These locals have to be stopped. Al and I complained to Slader and we talked to you. We told you that sooner or later something would happen—'

'Jim, calm down.'

'Uh-uh, no. Not this time. It was them – what do they call themselves? The Hunt Club? I know it was them. It wasn't enough for them to leave us threatening notes or mess with our gear. Not enough to vandalize our truck. No, they had to go and take Al's life. They fucking killed him, and you know it as well as I do.'

Ranger Daniels took a wide stance, crossed his arms and gazed down at Jim. 'Until we know that anybody deliberately killed him, it was an accident.'

'Not if he was shot in the head, execution style. Was he?'

'No, as a matter of fact, he wasn't.'

'Where then?'

Daniels flashed a look at Hank.

Jim walked up to Harper, bent over and put his face in front of hers. 'You found him. Tell me. Where was he shot?'

Harper hesitated. Hank got to his feet, put a hand on his shoulder.

'With all due respect and sympathy for your loss, sir, I think it's best you step away from my wife and wait to get your information from the police captain.'

'Really. And if I don't?' Jim wheeled around, facing Hank.

'In the back,' Angela's voice was flat. 'They said he was shot in the back.'

For a moment, everyone froze. Then, like air from a deflating balloon, the tension eased.

'So. They did it.' Jim's shoulders sagged. 'They chased him down and shot him like a fucking rabbit.' He sank onto a folding chair and stared at the floor.

Harper sat, too. Hank handed her a can of Dr Pepper.

They all sat quietly until, some minutes later, Captain Slader stepped back into the office.

Before Slader could say anything, Angela began talking to him. 'Captain, what about my husband? We still need to find him.'

Jim started at the same time, talking right over Angela's words. 'What are you going to do about these locals, Slader? That Hunt

Club – or whatever they call themselves – they've gone too far this time—'

'Do you think the people who killed that pipeline worker shot my Phil, too? Oh, God. Please, you need to go back out and find him.'

'—because, trust me, the pipeline company's not going to put up with their employees being murdered. They'll send out investigators and security – there are going to be repercussions. You better make it clear to these people—'

'Hold on, both of you.' Daniels had his hands up again, trying to quiet everybody down. 'One at a time.'

But Captain Slader ignored all of them. He went to the coffee pot, poured himself a mug. Added some creamer. Took a long swallow.

Angela and Jim kept jabbering, competing for attention. 'Back off, asshole. My husband's missing—'

'"Back off"? A man's been murdered—'

'My Phil might be hurt—'

'My partner's dead. Dead takes priority—'

Harper stood beside Hank, holding his arm. Angela's ragged voice jangled her. As Jim and Angela squabbled, she looked up at Hank. 'You okay?'

He sighed, met her eyes. 'You?'

'Keeping my lemon ready.'

He leaned over, kissed the top of her head. 'We should be out of here soon. We can—'

'Okay,' the captain bellowed. 'Listen up, everybody.'

Angela and Jim quieted, their eyes fixed on Slader, his blue eyes glaring under thick wild eyebrows.

'Nobody talks till I'm finished, okay? Here's the situation. Al Rogers' death is being investigated like any other shooting. Clearfield County coroner's examining the body, and forensic evidence is being gathered. But you're right, Jim, I'm sure the pipeline company will send its own people down here. Thing is, that's going to cause a whole new round of resentment among the locals—'

'You mean the ones who killed him—'

'Did I say I was finished?' Slader's eyes darkened. 'Keep your yap shut until I say you can open it.' He waited a beat, jaw rippling.

Harper gave Hank's arm an uneasy squeeze.

'You ought to know by now, Jim. These people don't like outsiders messing around their land. Doesn't matter who it is or why they're here – the pipeline or the gas company or the government – anybody bringing in more outsiders is only going to rile up more Hunt Club trouble. I'll deal with that and make sure nobody gets hurt—'

'You mean, nobody else.'

Slader raised an eyebrow. 'What I want, Jim, is for you to lie low. Stay the hell out of it. If – and I said *if* – local people or anyone in their organization are involved in Al's death, we'll figure it out and deal with them. But, meantime, there's no sense making assumptions and stirring up trouble. All that'll do is start a confrontation.'

'What are you talking about?' Angela interrupted. 'What people?'

'The Hunt Club,' Jim said. 'It's a militia group.'

'Not necessarily,' Slader said.

'Well, whatever they say they are, they're armed and preparing for a war with the government, the gas company, the pipeline, frackers, tourists, hikers, hunters – anyone and everyone.'

'Come on, Jim.' Daniels spoke up. 'They're not that bad. They just want to live their lives in peace. If you don't bother them, they won't—'

'Bull fucking shit, Daniels. Somebody bothered Al, didn't they? And I promise you, he wasn't bothering them.'

'Wait – you think this group – that Hunt Club – hurt my Phil?' Angela's hand went to her throat. 'You do, don't you? You think they killed him the same way they killed that other man? Oh, dear God.' She swooned.

Harper dashed to her, helped her into a chair. Hank got her a bottle of water. The men continued arguing about the locals.

'Besides, it's not a militia,' Daniels insisted. 'They're just regular citizens, prepared for any disaster. I prefer to think of them as survivalists.'

Jim sputtered. 'Survivalists don't shoot people.'

'Doesn't matter what you call them.' Slader eyed Jim. 'It's best not to mess with them. You hear me, Jim? Let the authorities investigate and work this out. For what it's worth, I personally doubt that Hunt Club members had anything to do with Al's death.'

'Because?'

Slader blinked slowly, bit his lip. 'Because I know these people. And that's what I think.'

Jim pursed his lips, nostrils flaring. 'I'll tell you what, Captain.

I'm not about to let this go and neither's my employer. If I were you, I'd do my job and catch Al's killer quick, before the big guns bring the wrath of God down on you.' He paused, met Slader's eyes. 'Anyone needs me, I'll be back at our – at my campsite.' He turned and marched out of the office, banging the door behind him.

Slader's eyes narrowed and he folded his arms. Before he could speak, Angela started up again.

'Can I just point out that nobody can help this dead guy, but my Phil might still be alive and saved? Can we please get back to looking for Phil?'

Daniels reminded her that he had two teams and a number of volunteers out looking for him. 'We've got a few more hours of daylight. I'm heading back out myself now. Want to join me?' He looked at Hank and Harper, who looked at each other.

'You up for it?' Harper asked.

'If you are.'

'I'm coming, too,' Angela insisted. She stood and joined them.

Daniels gave them each bottles of water, excused himself to exchange a few words privately with the captain, and led the little search party back out into the woods.

Damn damn damn damn! This shooting was bad news. Those idiots. What were they thinking?

The sector chief paced, lit a cigarette. Finally, he used his landline to contact his number-two man who was probably out picking pumpkins for his kids and didn't pick up. He left a message, still steaming.

'Do you know what the hell is going on? Campers found one of those pipeline walkers shot this morning. Nobody said anything about shooting anybody. Now they're going to send in state cops and industry people, maybe Feds. The woods will be crawling with who knows what kinds of badges—'

In the middle of his sentence, Hiram picked up. 'What was that, Chief?

'Oh, you're there. Did you hear what I said?'

'I heard you say a pipeline walker got shot. Which one?'

'The dark-haired one. Named Al Rogers.'

'Shit. He wasn't so bad. It's the other one who's the pain. You ever run into him?'

The chief blew out a cloud of smoke. 'What's wrong with you, Hiram? Don't you see what's going to come down now? Cops. Investigators. The pipeline company'll send an army—'

'Don't get your panties in a knot. People get shot out in the woods every now and then. What's the big deal?'

The chief took a drag on his cigarette. Hiram sounded way too complacent. 'Hiram. What do you know about this?'

'Nothing. This is the first I've heard about it.'

'Seriously? A man gets shot in these woods and you know nothing about it? You expect me to believe it? You have eyes and ears every-damn-where. And when I'm not around, you're supposed to keep a handle on these people.'

Hiram was quiet for a breath. 'I'm not in charge of anybody.'

'Bullshit. We have a shared interest. We've agreed to agree on any action – *any* action – before implementing it. If you know something about this, Hiram—'

'I don't. I'd tell you. All I know about is the thing Josh has been doing.'

'You're shitting me.' The sector chief sat, leaned on the desk. 'He's up to that again? You didn't stop him?'

'I tried to reason with him—'

'But I told him – we all told him – that will backfire. He's more likely to bring more tourists than to drive them away. Damn fool.'

'I know.'

'When did he start up again?'

'As far as I know, last weekend. He got some newfangled hi-tech legs.'

The chief snuffed out his cigarette, turned to look out a window. The leaves glowed golden, red and orange in the afternoon sun. This land was God's bounty, and it was his duty to protect it.

'We need a meeting. Everybody. Tonight.'

'Tonight? I don't know if I can get all—'

'Hiram, we got a dead guy and Josh is going rogue. We better get ourselves together. We're about to be swarmed by cops and investigators and who knows who all, and we've got no plan.'

'Right.' Hiram sounded less than enthusiastic. 'I'm on it.'

The chief hung up and rubbed his eyes. His chest was tight, blood pressure rising, and his stomach felt like soup. Not that he was scared, though. No, he'd been preparing for decades for a confrontation with the government. He'd trained with his neighbors in everything – weaponry, marksmanship, strategy, survival techniques. They had their arsenal, and they were ready, all of them. Even so.

He stood up, walked to the window, and watched a couple of wrens flutter by. The weather was crisp, clear. His sons were out there, hunting pheasant today. Life wasn't bad, over all. He and the ex-wife mostly got along, and Mavis wasn't giving him grief. His pants were a tad snug at the belt from some pounds he'd gained this last year, which was good because he tended to be skinny. Thing was, though, he wasn't young any more. He needed reading glasses, and his sideburns were almost silver. Now that the showdown he'd been preparing for was finally coming, he'd lost a lot of his fire.

He stared out at the colors, the bright light, the shadows, and he considered the jokes of life. One in particular was that by the time life finally let you have what you wished for, you just might not want it any more.

But it was no use philosophizing. Thinking too much never got anybody anywhere.

Bob climbed the rocky slope, pushing through vines and branches. Up ahead, where the ground leveled off, he saw what appeared to be an abandoned skeleton of a building. He let out a whoop. They'd been hiking for three hours, trying to follow the map, getting lost, reorienting themselves. And now, finally, they'd found it: the old campground.

'What?' Pete called. 'You see something?' He was tired, trailing behind Bob.

'I think this is it.'

Pete joined him, peered through the trees at what was left of a burned-out structure. The roof had caved in, but the frame was still recognizable.

Bob pulled out his frayed old map. 'This has got to be the main building. Yeah, look . . .' He walked closer to the ruins, pointing to the left. 'Those stones? See how they're laid out in squares? Those must be what's left of the cabins.'

Pete looked at the stones. The sides of the squares were at most five feet wide. 'Wouldn't cabins be bigger?' He scratched his hands.

'Maybe not.' Bob scanned the area. 'Besides, when they laid the pipeline, the workers probably moved things around. They must have cleared a road for their equipment. Everything would be dug into and moved around.'

'I don't know.' Pete peered at the map. 'Are you sure this is the right spot? Because the map shows that the old campground had a trailer lot. I don't see a trailer lot. And the main building didn't look as big as this place. It looks smaller, same size as the cottages.'

'So? They dug up the lot when they laid the pipeline. And that map is just, like, a sketch. A plan. It shows the locations, not the exact actual structures.' Bob pointed to a row of boxes on the map. 'See? These things are those squares. We're here.'

Pete studied the map again. Saw only one other building in that area of the woods, a hunting lodge located a few miles from the old campground. And this sure didn't look like a hunting lodge. This place was deserted, in ruins. It had to be the old campground, torn up to make way for the pipeline.

'Okay.' He referred to the map. 'So if those are the cottages, then the pipeline must be buried over there, behind them.' Pete took five giant steps and stopped, turned to face Bob, and raised his arms. 'Right underneath me.'

Bob broke into a grin. 'YEE HA!' He ran around, waving his arms, hooting. 'We fuckin' found it!'

Pete scratched his palms, wincing.

'Come on, Pete. Stop carrying on. What's wrong with your hands?'

'I think it's poison ivy.'

'No shit. Well, never mind. Show some jubilation.' Grinning, Bob opened his backpack and pulled out a bag of weed. 'We found the spot. This is celebration time. Where's the paper?'

'You have it.' Pete folded the map, stuffed it into his pocket.

'No, you do.'

Pete looked in his pack, dug deep, taking out their explosives, wiring, beer, blasting caps, beef jerky, matches, walkie-talkies. He was pulling out rope and flashlights when Bob said, 'Oops, you're right. I got the paper.'

They smoked for a while and feasted on beef jerky. Then, feeling mellow, they decided to set up their devices.

'You should have brought more food.' Bob wrapped explosives in wire.

'Me? Why me? Were your legs broken?' Pete messed with a walkie-talkie, took another hit on the joint. Maybe marijuana would stop his itching. He'd heard that it helped cancer patients – so why not poison ivy?

'Dude. Seriously, I'm frickin' starving.'

'You just think you're hungry because you're fuckin' stoned. You just smoked a pile of weed and ate about a ton of beef—'

'I could eat a frickin' antelope.'

Pete closed up his tool kit, chuckling. 'Who knows? When these little darlings go off, they might roast an antelope or two.'

'I'm not kidding. I could go for some curly fries. Or no – wings. Christ, I could do with some wings.'

Bob went on, listing various foods he could eat while he and Pete set up the explosives, connecting them to the blasting caps and the walkie-talkie that would act as a detonating device.

When they were finished, Pete blew cool air on his hands. They were red and blotchy, and the itching was making him crazy.

'We're ready.' Bob beamed.

'Just a second.' Pete went to the toolbox, took out a hammer, started pounding on one of his palms.

Bob watched. 'What the fuck are you doing?'

'Killing this itching motherfucker.' He pounded it again, winced, cursed.

Bob picked up his backpack, rooted around, took out a first-aid kit. Handed Pete a tube of something. 'Use this.'

'What is it? Shit. You had this all the time?' He rubbed cream on his swollen, now bruised palms. Felt the itching fade, could almost see it wither and die.

Bob rolled another joint, lit it, took a hit. Passed it to Pete before taking two beers out of a backpack. Opening them, he handed one to Pete, sat against the trunk of a tree, took a pull at his beer and another hit on the joint. 'We've done it. We've really done it.'

Pete took a seat beside him. 'Now all we have to do is wait for the perfect moment, press a button, and cover our asses.'

Bob chugged beer. Looked into the distance. 'I could do with a nice thick steak.'

Pete smirked. 'Seriously, dude. This is our moment. No, no. I mean this is the moment right before our moment. Once we move onto the next moment, this one will be gone, completely in the past, and we'll already have blown that thing to bits. So, right now, let me ask you this: in this last moment before our moment, if you could have anything in the world you wanted, what would it be?'

Bob swallowed beer and turned to Pete. 'What would I want?'

Pete nodded.

'That's a heavy question.'

'I know.'

'You mean not just like a steak. You mean like eternal life? Or Halle Berry? A billion dollars? That sort of thing?'

Pete closed his eyes. He felt smooth and light. As if he could lift off the ground and float.

'You mean like a sailboat? Or maybe – how about I could be president of the world? Shit. That would be intense.'

Bob went on, naming things he might want while Pete drifted, lulled by the light breeze, the chirping of insects, the rhythm of Bob's wish list, and the smoke from the joint he occasionally lifted to his mouth. This was a moment to savor, full of anticipation. Wow, what a great word, anticipation. He'd never really appreciated it before. But it really did say it all, didn't it? It captured the best of everything – that feeling right before the first bite of a burger. Right before sliding his dick inside a pussy. And now, right before making the phone call that would change the world, taking him to the apex of his life. At least, of his life so far. Anticipation. He was drenched in it. He almost wanted to stop time, to soak in this hot, wet moment forever.

Ranger Daniels took a short cut, leading them along a narrow trail back to the clearing where Angela had last seen Phil.

'What kind of footwear's he got on, ma'am?'

'Footwear?' Angela frowned. 'Hunting boots.'

'What's his size, ma'am?'

She bit her lip, concentrating. 'I never asked him. Ten? Ten and a half?'

'Never mind. With all the leaves falling, there won't be many clear prints around here anyhow.'

As they walked, Harper and Hank lagged behind, occasionally calling Phil's name. Angela didn't call out. Occasionally, she repeated herself. 'I don't get it. Where could he be? I left him right at the edge of the field, hunting rabbits.'

'If he's hurt or wandering around lost, ma'am, we'll find him. I've got two other teams looking.' Daniels sounded confident.

'How can you be sure? There are, what? Like four hundred thousand acres of woods around here?'

'We don't have to cover all of them—'

'We should get dogs. Do you have any of those sniffing dogs?'

Angela picked at the dried mud under her fingernails. It was all over her. On her pants, in her cuticles. 'Dogs could follow his scent.'

'I don't have dogs, ma'am. But I know the woods. We won't have to search the whole state park. Just the areas where he could have gotten to.'

'No, you're right. He couldn't have gone far. He wouldn't. He's not outdoorsy. Phil's a city guy. Honestly, he's not even a city guy. He's more of a homebody guy, doesn't have a lot of flair or natural instinct. Oh God, what was I thinking? I shouldn't have brought him up here. He was a complete newbie. What if they shot him like they shot that pipeline worker?' Angela didn't stop talking. Kept picking at her fingernails.

'We have no evidence of anything like that, ma'am.' Daniels kept moving.

Harper called out, 'Phil? Phil Russo?'

No answer. She and Hank walked side by side, peering into the forest. Harper watched the shadowy spaces between trees, listened for sounds beyond Angela's grating voice. Heard the usual insects chattering, birds calling. Leaves rattling on branches overhead or crunching under their boots. But more than anything, even louder than Angela's voice, she heard the bellowing silence of a lost man.

'He should be right where I left him,' Angela went on. 'He shouldn't have wandered off. I told him, I warned him to stay here until it was time to meet me. Why couldn't he for once listen to me?'

Harper's jaw tightened. Angela didn't seem able to take a breath without talking. She made herself tune out Angela's voice, redirected her focus by calling out for Phil. Watching for him. Taking notice of the pigments of the autumn leaves, the light beaming through the trees. Hank's wide shoulders. The pulsing ache in her leg. Anything that wasn't Angela's cloying continuous chatter.

Finally, they reached the clearing and separated, searching the area independently. Just steps from the path, Harper stopped and backed up, took a closer look at a vine. At first glance, she'd thought it was speckled. But no. It wasn't speckled. Splattered on its leaves were reddish-brown spots. Teardrop shaped, kind of horizontal. The color and texture of dried blood.

'Hank,' she called.

Hank stepped over. As soon as Angela saw them talking, she rushed over, followed Hank's gaze. 'Oh God. Is it blood?' She held her stomach. 'It is, isn't it?' She turned in a circle. 'Phil?' She yelled into the trees. 'Phil? Can you hear me? Phi-il?'

Hank and Ranger Daniels huddled by the vine, examining its leaves. Harper was sure it was blood spatter, but they'd stepped all over the ground below, obliterating whatever footprints or other markings there might have been.

Angela began wailing. 'Oh God. He's not answering me. They've killed him . . .'

'Ma'am,' Daniels began, 'we don't know that.'

'For all we know, that's squirrel blood.' Harper's voice was abrupt. 'Or wait – is this where I found the gas worker?' She looked around, as if unsure.

Hank shook his head, pointing. 'No, he was over there, closer to the main trail.'

Harper rolled her eyes at him. Why had he said that? Now Angela would start again.

'What?' Hank asked her.

Harper lowered her voice and mouthed. 'I'm trying to calm her down.'

'Well, how was I supposed to know that?' Hank answered aloud.

'To know what?' Angela asked.

'That it's probably animal blood.' Harper glared at Hank.

Angela began wringing her hands. 'But what if it's not? What if those crazy local club members shot Phil? That could be Phil's blood—'

'Now, calm down, ma'am.' Ranger Daniels had joined them. He put an arm on Angela's shoulder. 'The lady's right. It's probably deer blood. Think about it. It doesn't make sense that anyone around here would shoot him. Nobody here has a beef with your husband—'

'So? They shot that gas man for no reason—'

'No, see, here's the thing: you got to stop jumping to conclusions.' He withdrew his arm. 'We don't know for sure that the local organization shot him. But if they did – and that's a big if – it's different. The locals have been feuding with the gas company and the pipeline people for years—'

'Ranger Daniels?' Harper interrupted. Her left leg was throbbing, and Hank's limp was pronounced. She wanted to stop talking and get something accomplished. 'Should we take a sample of these leaves? Could they be evidence?'

Angela wheeled around. 'Evidence? So you don't think it's deer blood. You think it's Phil's.'

Harper didn't answer her. She kept her eyes on Daniels, who scratched his ribs, considering the question.

'Oh. Yes, why not. I suppose we should.' He took what looked like an old payroll envelope from his vest pocket, plucked some stained leaves from the vine. Stuffed them inside. Marked the envelope with a pen, stuck it back into his pocket.

Harper looked at Hank; he shook his head, telling her to let it go. Procedures were apparently relaxed out here.

Angela fretted, worried her hands, turned in circles. 'Oh God, oh my God,' she panted.

'You okay, ma'am?' Daniels asked. 'How about we sit a minute. Drink some water.'

'But if that's Phil's blood, where's Phil?' Her skin had turned ashen.

'All we know for sure is that your husband isn't here, ma'am. So we need to take a minute to regroup and figure out how we'll proceed.' He guided them to a fallen tree trunk, took a seat. Gestured for the others to join him.

'How can you sit down and rest? My Phil could be lying hurt somewhere—'

'Give it a break, Angela.' Harper used her most commanding lieutenant's voice. 'Just sit down and be quiet.'

Angela looked startled, but closed her mouth and took a seat. They all drank water. Harper rested her aching leg. For a full minute, nobody spoke. Even the insects seemed to quiet down.

Harper took out a bottle of ibuprofen, handed some capsules to Hank, swallowed a few and rubbed her sore thigh. Hank reached over, helped her massage the muscles. She closed her eyes, almost moaning at the soreness. Enjoying the silence. But it ended sharply.

'What did you mean they'd been "feuding"?' Angela's voice was a hook, latching onto Harper's nerves and yanking them.

Daniels drank water.

Angela pressed him. 'You said the locals and the gas people have been—'

'It goes way back.' Daniels wiped his mouth. 'From the beginning, the locals were against having any kind of pipeline go through here. They didn't like fracking and wanted the land to be left pristine. But the government caved, and the gas company got its way. They destroyed the old campground – ran the pipeline right through it.

In fact, that's how come we got our new grounds – brand-new cottages and shower facilities. New ranger station. Everything state of the art.'

'I remember the old campgrounds,' Angela said. 'They were a mess.'

'These are nicer, for sure.' Daniel smiled. 'So anyway, we moved the campground and everything was fine. Until they started the fracking. After that, people around here started having problems. Wells got contaminated. Folks still can't drink their own water – it's discolored, tastes bad. It burns their mouths, gives them headaches. Some can't even shower at home – the steam burns their lungs. The water's been so bad that fish died in the rivers and creeks.'

'My my.' Angela tsked.

'Oh, but that's not the worst of it. The locals really lost it when a drilling rig exploded.'

Harper was appalled. 'Exploded?'

'Yes, ma'am. It was bad. The explosion blew away the old hunting lodge. Killed a guy who was staying there.'

Harper looked at Hank. Hank's face was completely neutral, didn't register the slightest surprise. Didn't he find this information the least bit disturbing? Unless . . . Of course: Hank was a geologist. He would have already known about all these fracking problems. In fact, he probably knew more about them than the ranger did. Damn. Was that why he'd suggested this spot for their trip? Was that the real reason he'd brought her here? Pretending that he wanted a romantic getaway, but really doing research on fracking, collecting water and soil samples?

Hank felt her looking at him and turned to her. 'You okay?' His face was blank. Feigning innocence.

She squinted, letting him know she was onto him.

'What?' He tilted his head.

Daniels continued. 'Yeah, when that rig blew, it was like hell bursting up through God's green earth. A geyser of gas and fracking wastewater blasted out of the ground, and it kept spewing sky high for sixteen hours straight. The stink was everywhere. You could taste it. It got in your skin. And the hunting lodge – phwoom. Gone. Place was, I don't know, fifty or a hundred years old. Lots of locals belonged to it – they formed a new organization, named it the Hunt Club to remember the lodge and what happened to it. But all that's left of the original place is the foundation, just bare bones of the lodge. Nothing's there but old septic tanks.'

For a moment even Angela was silent. But only for a moment.

'So that's why the locals don't like the gas company,' she announced. She folded her hands. 'But that's not exactly a feud.'

'Oh, it is. The local folks in the Hunt Club are determined to get rid of the frackers, pipeline, gas company, government and every other outsider – including hunters and hikers like you. As a government employee, I watch my backside, but I've made peace with most of them. They're not bad people. Still, there's a number of them who want to take up arms and go guerrilla. They've got an arsenal and a trained militia. A compound where they can survive for months under siege if they have to.'

Harper stiffened. She looked into the trees, half-expecting to see armed men in camouflage.

'Now, I'm not saying they plan to start an all-out war,' Daniels went on. 'They're angry, not stupid. Instead, they mess with the gas company's equipment. They let the air out of their tires. Vandalize the pipeline walkers' campsites. Try to scare them. But so far, it's been mischief. Not murder.'

'Until today,' Angela said. 'Today was murder.'

'We don't know that yet,' Daniels said. 'Could have been anything. An accident.'

'I feel it. I just know it. What have they done to my Phil?'

Daniels didn't answer.

'You knew about this fracking stuff?' Harper whispered to Hank.

He shrugged. 'Which part?'

She scowled.

'What's wrong?'

Did he really not know? Did he think she wouldn't figure out that he'd pretended to want to hike and camp and be alone with her when really he'd devised this trip so that he could study the environmental effects of hydraulic fracturing? What he'd presented as romantic time together, away from work and responsibility, was instead some preliminary geologic field study. And he wanted to know what was wrong? Damn. Harper stretched her aching leg. She thought of Chloe and ached even more. What the hell was she doing here?

Not that she belonged anywhere else.

Hank took her hand. 'Come on, Harper. Don't be like that.'

Really? Had he read her mind? Her nostrils puffed. 'Like what?'

'Can we talk about what's bothering you later?' He leaned over to kiss her cheek.

'Fine.' She sat rigid, even as his whiskers brushed her cheek, raising goose bumps.

Daniels stuffed his water bottle into his backpack. 'So. How about we go back to the exact point where Phil was last seen and start again from there.' He stood. 'We'll break into teams of two.'

Harper got to her feet, ignoring the complaints of her leg.

Hank put an arm around her waist.

'I don't understand.' Angela stayed at the ranger's heels. 'Where could he have gone? I left him right at the edge of the field.'

Phil wasn't in the field. They'd separated into pairs and fanned out, checking the clearing and the two trails heading to Angela's campsite. No Phil. When they reconvened, Angela frowned. 'I don't understand where he could be,' she began again.

Harper chewed her lip, told herself to be tolerant. It wasn't Angela's fault that she was upset. Or that she had a voice like a rabid hamster.

Daniels radioed his other search teams. They'd had no luck either. His face was strained as he faced the group. 'We're getting tired, and we have only a couple hours of daylight left. So let's stay split in two groups. Angela, you're with me. We'll head north.'

'Good idea.' Angela nodded. 'Except I've been thinking. Maybe we should go check out the bog.'

Everyone looked at her.

'I remembered something. While I was over there, looking into those thistles, I remembered that last night, Phil and I were talking about the bog trail. He said he wanted to hike it. So maybe he got tired of hunting . . .'

'And maybe he took it in his head to go check it out?' Daniels finished her sentence for her.

'You want to split up first?' Hank asked.

'No, let's all go,' Daniels said. 'We'll divide up there and search the bog area. If there's no sign of Phil, you two can backtrack on the main trail, and I'll go on with Angela the opposite way.'

It took about twenty minutes to walk there, and the trail got narrower and muddier as they went. The ranger narrated their trek as if they were a tour group, telling them that they were surrounded by 430,000 acres of remote and wild state forest. That Black Moshannon State Park, where they were, was in the heart of that forest, and that it got its name from its black-watered bog. The water wasn't actually black, but was stained a dark tea color by sphagnum moss and plant tannins. The other part of the park's name, 'Moshannon', came from the Indian words 'Moss Hanne', which had nothing to do with moss, but meant Moose Stream.

Harper was grateful for the narration. As long as Ranger Daniels talked, Angela didn't. But she only half-listened, concentrating instead on her annoyance with Hank. She walked apart from him, not holding his hand or even making eye contact. After everything they'd been through, didn't she deserve a weekend of his undistracted time and undivided attention? Why did she have to share him with samples and tests and passion for his career? Hell, she didn't even have a career to have a passion for. She was dangling, disconnected. And there it was again, her sense of being lost and useless. Of having no purpose aside from being Chloe's mom.

Maybe it wasn't Hank she was angry at; it was herself, for losing her direction. She kicked a rock, heard it plop into a puddle. Felt alone.

'Bastard!' Angela bellowed. She took off running up the path, her boots splashing mud. 'I can't believe you're here, you damned bastard!'

'Phil?' Daniels ran after her. 'You found him?'

Harper tried not to slip in the muck as she followed. She didn't look at Hank, heard him sloshing behind her.

'You sonofabitch!' Angela yelled. 'Stan? Where are you? Get some pants on and come out here.' She kept hollering, taunting someone named Stan.

Harper came to a small, circular cove. She stayed back, quickly scanning the area, assessing it. Tarps covered the ground, separating the mud from a high orange tent and adjacent canopy. Underneath the shelter was a small propane stove. Two collapsible chairs. At least two gun cases. A portable cabinet that might hold more. Hank caught up with her, stood close.

A shaved head emerged from the tent. 'Angela? What the hell?' The head disappeared again.

'Come on, Stan. I got a ranger with me. Get your sorry ass out here.'

A moment later, the man came out of the tent, buttoning a flannel shirt. He frowned at Angela, then the rest of them. 'What are you doing here, Angela?'

'I should ask you that question, Dickwad.'

'Any of you guys want to tell me?' The man looked at Harper, then Hank, then Daniels. 'What's going on?'

'I'll tell you what's going on.' Angela darted closer to him. 'What's going on is that Stan's going to tell us what he did to Phil.'

The man's eyebrows went up, his head tilted, and he put his hands on his hips. He stood that way, looking at her. 'I don't know what you're talking about, but you better leave, Angela.' His tone was flat. Ominous.

Harper and Hank exchanged glances, not sure what was happening. Clearly, there was bad history between this guy and Angela. But who was he? Why did Angela think he'd harmed Phil? They stood at the edge of the cove, ready to move quickly. The guy was solid muscle. But with Hank and the ranger there, they could easily take him down. Except that he probably wasn't alone.

'Sir.' Ranger Daniels cleared his throat. 'I'm a park ranger. We're out here looking for a lost hunter—'

'Well, look what scum has crawled out of the bog.' A round face edged with tangled brown curls popped out of the tent, followed by a short woman in an overly large sweatshirt, wool socks, and possibly nothing else.

'Suck it, Cindi. Everybody, meet my lying cheating lowlife shit of an ex-husband Stan, and his lying two-faced housebreaking slut cow whore.'

Cindi cracked her chewing gum and waddled across the tarp to stand beside Stan. 'Pleased to meet you, Officer.' She stuck her hand out to Daniels for a shake.

'I'm actually a park ranger.'

'Well, pleased anyhow. I'm Cindi. Stan's wife.'

'Oh, please. You are not—'

'Oh yes, I am.' Cindi held up her ring finger. It sported a large rock and matching gold band. 'Musta forgot to invite you to the ceremony.'

Stan wrapped an arm around her. 'Pay no attention to her, doll—'

'No, you better pay attention to me, doll. Start by explaining what you're doing up here.'

'Excuse me . . .' Ranger Daniels tried, but everyone kept shouting at once.

'Fuck you, Angela. Why shouldn't we be here?'

'Because you shouldn't be anywhere I am, that's why. I have a restraining order, motherfucker. I'll have you arrested—'

'Not any more. Not for a year. And anyway—'

'Where's Phil? What have you done to him?'

'—how would I even know you were here?'

'Phil?' Cindi looked up at Stan. 'Who's Phil?'

'Everyone, please!' Daniels held his hands up for attention.

Angela's face was bright red. She shouted, 'Phil's my husband, bitch.'

'She got someone to marry her? Poor fuckin' Phil.'

'Don't you even say his name with your filthy mouth—'

A spine-piercing, ear-shattering whistle blew, startling them all into silence. Harper removed her fingers from her mouth, whispered, 'Sorry,' to Hank, who was rubbing his ears. Then she stood tall and issued an order. 'Everybody shut your yaps and listen to the ranger.'

'Okay.' Daniels eyed her warily, took a breath, and turned to Stan and Cindi. 'I've been trying to tell you folks that we're out here looking for a missing hunter. Philip Russo. This woman's husband. He was last seen about a mile from here early this morning. You wouldn't happen to have seen him?'

Cindi shook her head, no. She kept chewing her gum, staring at Angela.

'No, we haven't seen him. Why would we?' Stan crossed his arms, faced Angela. 'But here's a thought: maybe old Phil isn't lost. Maybe he came to his senses and high-tailed it out of here to get his ass away from his batshit old lady.'

Harper expected Angela to make a move and stepped forward, ready to block her.

But Angela didn't attack. She walked slowly forward, her finger aimed at Stan's heart. 'You prick. You just can't stand to see me happy—'

'Honestly, Angela, I couldn't care less if you're happy.'

'Bastard. You did something to Phil.'

'I don't care what you are—'

'Otherwise, why would you be up here now, the same weekend as us?'

'—as long as you're not near me.'

'Okay, you two, settle down.' Daniels raised his hands again, waved them up and down to no avail.

Harper stepped forward, stood beside him, preparing to whistle again, but Angela stopped. She didn't say anything for a moment, just stared at Stan.

When she spoke, her voice was sharp and thin. 'I swear, Stan, on my mother's grave. If you did something to Phil, I'll see you fry in hell – you and your little dolly.'

'Oh, go lay an egg, Angela. You're a whack job.'

Ranger Daniels finally asked Harper to escort Angela away from the campsite so he could speak to Stan and Cindi uninterrupted. Harper led her back to where Hank was standing, but kept a distance from her. Angela seemed altered. Her features had twisted, eyes narrowed, lips curled like a snake. Sweat beaded her forehead. Venom radiated from her pores. How was it that Stan and Angela had ever been married? She couldn't imagine that they'd ever loved each other. Respected and trusted each other. How had their relationship turned so ugly? And how deep did the ugliness go? Deep enough for murder?

Harper eyed Stan and Cindi, their weapon cases under the canopy. With Angela beside her, sputtering bitterness, she gazed out toward the bog. It would be easy enough to dump a body in that dark water. She watched the surface, imagined a body floating just underneath, half-expected it to pop up and reveal itself. When Hank came up behind her and put a hand on her back, she spun around reflexively, her arm back and ready to swing.

Daniels divided them up. Hank was to keep an eye on Angela, and Harper on Cindi while he had a word alone with Stan.

Harper took Cindi to the folding chairs under the canopy. 'Aren't you cold?' Harper nodded at Cindi's bare legs.

'Me? No. I'm always hot.' She curled into a chair. 'Say. Would you like a beer? We have a ton of them—'

'No. No, thanks. But you go ahead.' Actually, Harper wanted several. She was tired, worried about Philip Russo. And the exchange between Stan and Angela had been jarring. Was it possible that Stan had done something to his ex-wife's new husband?

'No, I'll wait for Stan.' She looked at him, talking to Daniels. Then she leaned forward, whispering to Harper. 'How do you know her?' She nodded toward Angela.

'Me? Oh, I don't.'

'Really? So what are you doing – are you with the ranger?'

'No. Angela came to our camp this morning, when she couldn't find her husband. We're just helping out.'

Cindi nodded. 'That's your husband? He's cute.'

Harper had to smile. Hank was 'cute'? She thought of him as rugged or powerful. Maybe even animal. But cute? 'Thank you.' She felt the need to add, 'So's yours.'

'Yeah. Stan's a sweet guy. I don't know how he and her ever got together. She's a witch. With a "b".'

Harper didn't answer. Daniels and Stan had joined them under the canopy. Daniels took the weapons cases, carried them out in front of the tent.

'Thing is, why is she acting so surprised that we were here? We're here most every weekend. She knows that.'

Harper was watching the men, wasn't paying attention.

'It's Stan's spot. The same spot she and him used to camp at. For like nine years. So why was she acting like she didn't expect him to be here?'

'Wait. She used to camp here?'

'You bet. Stan loves the bog. And this little nook is his own personal camping place. Nobody else even knows it's here. He camps here just about every weekend in the fall – with me or by himself.'

'Angela knew that?'

Cindi nodded. 'Yes, that's what I'm telling you. She wants to make trouble for Stan. What she said before about that restraining order? She made stuff up about him and said he'd stalked her and threatened her, that kind of crap. She actually had a court order saying he couldn't come near her, which he was only too happy to obey. He was never bothering her. She did it out of spite, just because she can't stand that we're together.' Cindi paused, blew a bubble with her wad of gum. Popped it.

Daniels opened one of the cases, removed the rifle. Harper watched, thought it looked like a bolt-action Beretta. Daniels checked it. Talked to Stan. Took a few boxes of thirty-caliber bullets out of the case.

Across the campsite, Hank and Angela were drinking water. Angela was talking, gesturing. Hank nodding, tolerating. Harper watched, trying to be objective. Was Hank 'cute'? Maybe, in a rough, grizzly-bear-like way. Even so, she was still annoyed with him. Wait. Why again? She tried to remember.

'Okay.' Cindi sounded resigned. 'To be fair, it's not all her fault. We used to be friends, her and me. So she blames me for them breaking up, but really, I wasn't the reason. They were done; I was just the final blow. And honestly? When Stan told me she got married again, we were ecstatic. We thought she'd finally leave us alone. With a new husband, maybe she'd have better things to do than harassing us.'

'When did she get married?'

'Oh, way before we did. We got married eight months ago last week. Angela? Stan told me about it maybe a couple months before that. I didn't ever meet the guy, though. Never even knew his name until just now. Phil?'

So that would make it a year or so? Maybe less? Angela and Phil were still newly-weds. Harper tried to piece together what she was hearing. To make sense of it. Why had Angela brought Phil hunting in the same area as her ex-husband's campsite? And if she'd known all along that Stan would be camping there, why had she acted so surprised to find him? Another question tickled her mind, but she didn't form it because Daniels interrupted her thoughts, raising his voice. She looked, saw him arguing with Stan.

'I told you I have no idea.' Stan put his hands up.

'How about your wife?'

'My wife didn't either. We've been together all day.'

Cindi sat up straight. 'What's wrong, hon?' she called. 'Ranger, you want to talk to me?'

Daniels turned to face them. 'Ma'am.' He towered over them and his face was grave. 'Have you fired this weapon recently?'

'No, sir. Haven't taken it out of the case since we got here.'

He looked at Harper. 'I have to call this in.'

'Hold on,' Stan shouted. 'Call what in? It's no crime to have a weapon. It's hunting season. I'm here to hunt.'

'But you just told me that you haven't fired this gun.'

'Because I haven't.'

Angela bounced up and rushed to join them, Hank at her heels. 'See? They shot him. They must have shot him – where's his body? What did you do with him?'

'Stop.' Hank grabbed her shoulders. 'Just hold still and hush.'

Angela squirmed, trying to free herself, but she didn't make a sound.

'I don't see what the problem is.' Stan faced Daniels.

'Okay, I'll explain it. The problem is that we have the body of a man who's been shot, ammunition that's the same caliber as the fragment we found with his body, a missing man that you've had some problems with, and a rifle that's been fired even though you say it hasn't.'

The blood drained from Stan's face. 'But . . .' He looked at Cindi. 'It hasn't been fired.'

Cindi shook her head, agreeing. 'We don't know anything about a shooting or her husband. Really. Stan's been with me non-stop since we got here.'

Daniels looked at Stan, then Cindi. 'Really? Non-stop?'

Cindi flushed. 'Yes, really. The only time he's left my sight was to go take a piss in the woods.'

Daniels puckered his lips, then turned to Hank. 'Would you and your wife be kind enough to keep the peace while I radio the police?'

'The police? Why?' Stan persisted. 'We didn't do anything.'

Cindi ran to him and held on. 'What's going on, Stan? Does he think you shot Angela's husband?'

Harper suggested that they all go sit down, and Hank herded them under the canopy.

Angela stayed back, picking mud from her cuticles, watching the captain make his call. Harper looked at her, thought she saw a hint of a smile.

Cindi wouldn't let go of Stan. 'Should we call a lawyer, Stan? What's he telling the police? This is crazy. So what if your gun's been fired? People come here to hunt. Everybody fires their rifles. Maybe you forgot you shot at something. Maybe when you were cleaning it. So what if you did? That's not against the law.'

Stan let her cling to him, but he didn't say anything. His face was grim, his eyes set on Angela. Harper watched him, the quiet sizzle of his gaze. He sat calmly, his body relaxed, but his eyes glowed like hot coals. What would happen if Stan let go and released that hot anger? Would he get violent? Maybe kill?

Harper sat on a folding chair beside Hank, thinking about what might push someone to murder. Jealousy? Betrayal? Deceit? All of that was present among Angela, Stan, Phil and Cindi. But it all emanated from Angela and Stan, the unhealed wounds of their marriage. Harper wondered about healing. If she and Hank got divorced and then remarried – no, her stomach flipped at the very thought. She hated Hank's new wife, hated Hank for being happy without her. She turned to look at Hank. Took his hand and squeezed. Was relieved that he squeezed back.

Cindi was still talking when Ranger Daniels got off his radio.

'Ma'am,' he addressed Cindi, 'I could hear you talking the whole time I was trying to speak to Captain Slader. Let me be clear: no one's accusing you or your husband of anything. The captain just needs to come have a look at that rifle and talk to the two of you. He'll probably want you to come back to my office to answer some questions.'

'Why? We don't know anything,' Cindi insisted.

'She's lying, Ranger,' Angela said. 'She's a manipulative, scheming whore who's not capable of telling the truth—'

'Now, now,' Daniels hands went up. 'Let's not start up again.'

But Cindi bolted up, hissing. 'Why can't you just leave us alone, Angela?'

'Me? Leave *you* alone? I think you've got it backwards. Ask your husband—'

This time, Harper's whistle was so harsh and shrill that it rattled their skulls.

Daniels continued, uninterrupted. He told Stan and Cindi to stay at their campsite until the captain arrived. 'Ordinarily, I'd wait here with you, but a man's missing and daylight's waning, and that takes priority.'

'Fine,' Stan agreed. 'We'll wait here.'

Daniels apologized, explaining that, because of cuts in government funding, he didn't have an assistant to help out. He appreciated their cooperation.

'No problem.' Stan stood. 'But since you're short-handed, maybe you'd want Cindi and me to help search.'

'Yeah.' Angela rushed at him. 'You bet. You could help the search a lot because you probably know exactly where to look. Why don't you save us time and just tell us where Phil is?'

'Ma'am . . .' Daniels began.

'You're sick, Angela.' Stan's voice was low, rumbling. 'Get help.'

'What did you do to him, Stan?'

'Nothing,' Cindi shrieked. 'You're obsessed with Stan, Angela. Why can't you let go?'

'Everyone, please. Calm down.' Daniels raised his voice.

'If anyone here's obsessed, Cindi, it's you. You wanted my house, my friends, my husband. Face it. You wanted to be me.'

'I'd sooner be a cockroach.'

Daniels turned to Harper, gave her a nod. She raised her fingers to her mouth, and inhaled, ready to whistle again.

'EVERYONE SHUT UP!'

The voice was thundering. Dangerous. And it came from Hank.

Even the birds didn't make a sound.

Then, in a slow, gentle voice, Ranger Daniels asked Stan where his vehicle was parked. Stan told him that it was back at the campground.

'I'll need your keys.'

'Sorry?' Stan stuck his hands in his pockets, stood tall.

'You'll get them back after you talk to the captain.'

'I told you we'd wait for him. Are you saying I'm lying?'

Harper rolled her eyes. 'He's saying he needs your keys as insurance.'

Stan unleashed a torrent of protests. 'You have no right. This is a free country. You have no cause to take my keys or anything else. I haven't done anything wrong. You're violating my civil rights.'

Daniels waited for Stan to stop. He checked his watch. 'Sorry. Sun's going to go soon and we got to move. I agree this is unconventional. But look at it from my point of view. I've got no way to guarantee that you'll stay put. And I'll remind you again: I have a missing man, a dead man, a bullet fragment that's the same caliber as your ammunition, and a rifle that's been fired that the owner says wasn't fired, and that owner is someone who has conflicts with the wife of the missing man. I'd be remiss if I didn't assure your presence for questioning. How do I know you won't take off?'

'Because I said I wouldn't.' Stan's gaze was steady, aimed at Daniels' eyes.

For a long moment, the two men stared at each other, neither moving, neither talking. Cindi, Angela, Harper and Hank stood waiting. Finally, Stan sighed, reached into his vest pocket.

'No, Stan.' Cindi breathed. 'Stand your ground.'

Daniels took the keys. 'You'll get them back soon as Slader's done with you.'

'How could you do that?' Cindi scolded. 'He's got no right.'

Daniels gave Hank a radio. As planned earlier, the search team split up. Daniels and Angela headed north, Hank and Harper south. They were to meet up at sunset at the ranger's office. If anyone found Phil, they were to get in touch by radio.

As they left Stan and Cindi, Harper turned to say goodbye, but Cindi had gone into the tent and zipped it closed. Stan stood alone on a tarp, eyes on fire, watching Angela walk away.

Hank's brows were furrowed, his eyes on the trail. He was experienced in tracking, knew what to look for. In their hiking trips, he'd taught Harper what to do in case she got lost. The first rule, Phil had already broken. It was to stay put.

Beyond that, a lost person was supposed to stomp as he walked, digging his feet in the ground, making clear prints. And he was supposed to leave a trail of personal objects, like pencils for example, pointing in the direction he was going.

If Phil had followed these rules, they hadn't seen any sign of it. Which would mean they were on the wrong path.

Harper walked in silence, studying the path, looking for a pattern of dislodged leaves and gravel, or twigs broken from the weight of being stepped on. Footsteps, though, wouldn't tell them anything. Any number of people might have walked there.

'Phil,' she called. 'Philip Russo.'

Nothing.

They walked on. In the distance, someone fired a rifle. Twice. Probably hunting.

Harper took Hank's hand.

'Do you think it's just a coincidence?' he asked.

Harper knew what he meant. 'The exes both being here? I doubt it. You?'

'If Stan comes up here every weekend, and camps exactly where he used to camp with Angela, it seems like Angela would have had a pretty good idea where he'd be.'

Harper nodded. 'Then again, maybe she thought it was "their" spot. And that Stan wouldn't go there now that they're not together.'

Hank didn't answer.

Harper called out Phil's name again.

Nothing.

'Those two sure hate each other.' Hank put his arm around Harper.

'It's hard to believe they were ever married.' Harper looked up at him. 'How did it get so nasty? I mean they used to love each other.'

The arm tightened just a tad. 'Maybe they never really did.'

Harper thought about that, couldn't imagine being married to someone she didn't love. Her earlier doubts about Hank's reasons for wanting to go camping seemed trivial now. She walked in step with him, her breathing in sync with his. Probably their hearts were beating together. Had Angela ever felt this linked to Stan?

Hank pulled away, moved to the left. 'What's this?' He pushed a vine away, revealing a KEEP OUT sign. It was attached to a vine-covered chain-link fence, topped with barbed wire.

Harper looked beyond the fence, saw a field, a mound of rocks and dirt among the trees. She'd seen mounds shaped like that before, in the Middle East. They concealed bomb shelters or bunkers.

'This doesn't look right,' Hank said.

No, it didn't.

'If this area is off limits because of the pipeline, the sign would say so. It would be marked with an official logo. Same with the state. State signs are labeled.'

But the sign looked generic. Had no logo, no official marking.

Harper pulled the vine away, exposing more of the fence. She walked along, yanking vines, exposing it, following around a corner. She peered into the blocked off area, studying the mound, sure that it concealed something.

'Fence is fairly new.' Hank touched barbed wire. 'What do you think this is? It's right in the middle of the state forest.'

Harper wasn't sure. She wanted to climb over it, find out what was on the other side. What was hidden by the mound of rocks. She pictured insurgents, dug in, ready to strike.

'That little hill,' Hank said. 'It looks man-made. Maybe some loner built himself a hut in there and wants people to back off.'

Maybe.

'Someone should check it out.'

Harper looked at him. She was ready to jump the fence.

'No.' Hank shook his head. 'I didn't mean us, Harper. We're here looking for a missing man—'

'But maybe he's in there. Maybe he got curious and climbed the fence. Maybe he's trapped there. Maybe the ground opens up and he fell in—'

A sharp boom shook the trees. Reflexively, Harper ducked, pulled Hank down with her.

'We're fine. Harper? It's okay.'

But Harper knew that it wasn't. She was well acquainted with the sound of explosive devices. 'Stay down,' she ordered.

'It's nothing,' Hank said. 'Probably the gas company doing some work.'

The gas company? What? Harper crouched low, waiting. Watching. Listening for sniper fire, for the screams of wounded men. She blinked, looked around. Where was her patrol? And, oh God – where was her weapon?

'Harper.' The voice was far away. 'You need your lemon?'

Her lemon? She gazed into the trees, vaguely aware that they were too green, too lush for the war zone. Expecting insurgents. Maybe an ambush.

Hank knelt beside her, spoke gently. 'I promise. We're okay.' He kissed her forehead, held up a round yellow thing. 'Need this?'

Wait – Hank? She looked from him to the lemon, back to him. The war flickered, faded away. Oh God. No. She didn't need the lemon. She stood, brushed herself off, and turned away so he wouldn't see her flushed red face. She'd almost slipped into a flashback. Damn. She was not going to let that happen, wouldn't allow it. Wouldn't get swallowed by the past just because some gas company was blowing up rocks nearby. But they should warn people about what they were doing, shouldn't they? After all, the area was packed with hunters and campers. Never mind. It was probably fine. Hank seemed to think it was. But Harper remained on edge, ready to bolt. Nothing here seemed fine.

She called out Phil's name again. Got no response.

A breeze rustled the leaves. The sun was getting low. She estimated another hour of sunlight. Felt unsteady. Needed to focus.

'Do you really think Stan did something to Phil?' she asked. 'Because what about that local militia group – the Hunt Club?'

'What about it?'

'Well, they hate the pipeline, right? And fracking, too. So maybe they assassinated the guy from the pipeline. And maybe Phil was there and saw the shooting so they had to take him prisoner. In fact, maybe that explosion was the militia training for combat—'

'Harper, hold on.' Hank stopped walking. 'You're spiraling. You can speculate all day and just go in circles. If that explosion was anything unusual, the fire department, the park service, and every volunteer this side of Pennsylvania will be racing to deal with it.'

He was right.

'And as to Phil? I'm trying to believe he just wandered off. But right now, I'm concerned about you and your flashbacks. Be honest. Finding that body this morning, and searching for Phil, is it stirring up more than you can handle? Tell me. We can stop—'

'No. No, I want to help. It's just . . . something feels wrong.'

Hank started walking again. 'Yep, it does,' he said. He started to say something else, but before he could, a scream shook the forest, soul-searing and female.

The sector chief finally got home, poured himself a mug of lukewarm coffee and went to his landline. Hiram answered on the first ring.

'Where've you been?' Hiram was breathing fast. 'Do you have any idea what the fuck is going on? I've been trying to reach you—'

'Been busy.' He gulped some coffee.

'Well, so have I. You got to be more accessible. Everything's gone crazy. Do you know who set it off?'

'Set what off?'

'Your mama's knickers. What do you think? That bomb or whatever it was that just exploded.'

The chief swallowed too fast, almost choked. 'What?'

'Where the hell were you, in Kansas? You must have heard it. Somewhere out by the old hunting lodge. Not ten minutes ago.'

Come to think of it, he had heard it. Heavy, like thunder. But he'd been concentrating on other problems, hadn't paid attention. Damn.

'I haven't been out there yet, but I sent a couple guys out right away. Meantime, I've called around. Nobody admits to it, but what with everything else that's going on, I wouldn't be surprised if it's some of our own people raising hell.'

'No, can't be.' The chief lowered himself into a kitchen chair. 'We agreed nobody would go off on their own.'

'I wouldn't be too sure. People are pissed off. What with that shooting, the state cops are going to be here, blaming us. And the press. There'll be fucking TV cameras and lights, and the gas company, the pipeline company – they're all going to be here. Plus the woods are already crawling with weekenders. Josh is hopping mad.'

'Tell Josh to sit on it. He needs to stop parading around—'

'It's not just Josh. Mavis and her people swear they won't put up with more outsiders – she's insisting that this is it, the invasion, and she's telling everyone to gather up arms—'

'Shit,' the chief said again. He rubbed his eyes. 'Not again. Mavis and her pigtail vigilantes—'

'I know. But she's just saying what the others are thinking.'

'I'll talk to her. You think she set off a bomb out there?'

'Mavis? No. She'd have said.' For a moment, Hiram didn't go on. The chief heard him breathing. Hiram had a way of hesitating, as if he had to be a damned politician. Practicing tact.

'What? Tell me,' the chief growled. He leaned on his kitchen table, messed with the salt shaker. Knocked it over. Spilled some salt. Damn. Wasn't that bad luck? Weren't you supposed to toss salt over your shoulder when you spilled it? But which shoulder? The chief had no idea. It was bullshit anyway. What was the deal with Hiram? What was he hiding? 'Did you call a meeting like I told you?'

'I did.' Hiram's voice was edgy. Tentative. 'But what I'm trying to tell you is that some of our people are fed up. They're going off on their own—'

'Setting off explosions.' The chief tossed salt over his left shoulder, then his right. 'What else?'

'Lots of things. They're launching a full-out campaign to clear the area.'

'Who are you talking about, Hiram? What kind of campaign?' The chief simmered, felt his face heat up.

'You already know some of it.'

'Our deal is we all work together—'

'But you haven't been around – no one could reach you. Meantime, people are running out of patience. They don't want to wait for committees and discussions. They want the area cleared—'

'I don't give a flying fuck what they want.' The chief's voice was soft, but his fist slammed onto the table. 'Christ, Hiram. We all want the same thing. But we're powerless unless we coordinate and work together. We have to think before we go off half-cocked . . .' He stopped himself, took a breath. Scolding Hiram wouldn't help. Besides, as a leader, he needed to remain calm and controlled.

'I agree. But you're sector chief. You need to step up and remind them. Because they won't listen to me.'

Right. He needed to do that. But how could he if they were all splintering off, conducting their own little mini-wars?

'Tell me. Besides the explosion, who's done what?' He stood and went to the kitchen window, watching the trees, their red and golden leaves.

'You already know about Josh's campaign—'

'Idiocy—'

'Listen. He was out this morning, doing his thing. And he found a guy.'

'What do you mean "he found a guy"?'

'I mean he took him.'

What? Oh God. The chief sat again. 'He took a guy?' So it was Josh? Josh had shot that guy from the gas company? Damn. The chief closed his eyes, reminded himself that he couldn't get angry. Emotions got in the way of leadership. He had to remain calm and rational. Had to think.

'Okay,' he said. 'So what's done is done. They won't be able to trace it to Josh if we all stick together and insist we know nothing. But for sure, Josh is going to have to answer for bringing the gas company people, the state cops and probably CNN and the fucking *New York Times*—'

'What the fuck are you talking about? Nobody even knows about it.'

'Everybody knows, Hiram. For sure everybody at the pipeline and the gas company – the dead guy worked for them. He was a pipeline walker.'

'But what does he have to do with what I'm saying?'

The chief closed his mouth. Dread snaked up from his belly. 'You're not talking about Al Rogers, the pipeline walker who got shot?'

'Did I say anything about a guy who got shot? I said Josh *took* someone.'

Oh. Took? As in kidnapped? The chief rubbed his eyes again. Fatigue washed over him. 'Why?'

'How should I know? Does Josh need a reason? Maybe the guy saw him prancing in his costume. Anyhow, he's got him at the compound.'

Of course he did. So they would all be considered accomplices. The chief pursed his lips. 'So that's it?'

Hiram let out a breath. 'Not exactly. There's one more thing.'

* * *

When he got off the phone, the chief took out a bottle of Old Grand-dad, poured a quantity into what was left of his coffee, and sat at the kitchen table, drinking, trying to lower his blood pressure. The whiskey burned his chest, reminded him of the war. Iraq. He'd led soldiers there, too, making order out of confusion. Keeping his people alive. He'd do the same here.

Number one. Something had exploded out by the old hunting lodge. One of the locals might have set something off. Then again, there were old septic tanks out there. Maybe methane gas had built up and blown. But even if none of his people had done it, others would come in droves to investigate an explosion so close to the pipeline. The pipeline people, of course. And government and environmental groups looking for weaknesses or damage or pollution. Swarms of them. Damn. It needed to be addressed.

Number two. Mavis. She had her contingent ready for all-out war. He had to settle her down. Would have to invest some private time and personal attention. He'd get on it.

Number three. The dead gas company worker. Hiram had found out nothing about who'd shot him. So the shooter might not be one of the Hunt Club members, might just be an accident. In which case, the investigation would pass quickly. All he needed was to make everyone wait it out.

But Number Four was a problem. Fucking Josh. He was out of control. For months, he'd flitted around the park, scaring people, and that was trouble enough. But now, he'd taken a living person. Kidnapped someone. And that would bring cops, the FBI, who knew who else. And that wasn't all.

Because the final thing Hiram had told him on the phone was that Josh had found another dead body. Not the gas company guy – another one. Josh had claimed he'd stumbled over it while he'd been out testing his new legs and scaring campers, before he'd even taken his prisoner. Hiram hadn't seen the body; all Hiram had seen was a driver's license, belonging to Philip Russo.

The chief poured more Grand-dad and drank. He had the urge to find Josh and smash in his skull. Had the damned moron killed Philip Russo? And the gas guy, too? He'd known for years that Josh was psycho. As a teenager, he'd been caught not just hunting small animals, but torturing them. Peeling their skin off, tearing them apart while they were still alive. Saying that he was studying their anatomy. Christ. Even then, he'd been twisted. Probably he had no clue what havoc he was causing – what outside attention he was drawing. And kidnapping? Did he have any sense at all? He'd ruin all of them.

The chief's blood pressure was soaring. He had to slow it down. He'd be no good to anyone if he had a heart attack or stroke. He had to steady his breath. Stay calm, controlled. Clear-headed. That's how leaders kept people alive in wartime. And this was just another kind of war. Besides, it wasn't definite that Josh had killed anybody. Hiram hadn't said he had; in fact, Hiram had implied that some outsider had probably shot Russo by accident. But wouldn't that be an odd coincidence – a novice hunter who didn't know what the fuck he was doing, shooting both Rogers and Russo by mistake? In the same morning?

Either way, that damn Josh had gone too far. Renegade needed to be brought down.

The chief wanted a cigarette. Hadn't smoked in a year. He got up, began searching cabinets, drawers. He must have left a pack somewhere. Damn. Maybe in the bedroom? He stomped through the cabin, tearing things apart until finally he realized that it wasn't a cigarette that he wanted. It was relief. He just wanted a fucking break. How was he supposed to rein in these people when each one of them thought they alone knew what was best and didn't give a crap in hell what their actions meant to anyone else? Who'd blown up the old hunting lodge – and why? Had Josh shot those two guys? And if so, did he plan to keep on shooting?

The chief went back to the kitchen, poured yet another drink.

Damn, the locals were rising up. Three hours until the meeting. And who knew what might happen before then? It was time to take charge. Finishing his drink, he reached for the phone, punched in a number.

'Mavis? Stay put. I'm coming over.'

Before she could talk, he hung up.

Shit. Literally. Pete had it in his eyes. Mucky stinking cold black soup, all over him. Under him. Around him. He blinked, trying to see. Raised a slimy wet hand to smear the stuff off his face. His hands came away blood-streaked. Where was he? What the hell had happened?

Cautiously, he lifted his head up off the ground and looked around. Everything was splattered with the stinking stuff – bushes, weeds, fallen leaves. And Bob.

Bob was there, lying still as a log. Where the fuck were they?

'Bob?' Pete started to say, but stopped. When he opened his mouth to talk, crud seeped in, starting him gagging.

When he finished puking, he was on his knees. He looked over at Bob. Bob hadn't moved. Christ.

'Bob?' he managed. His voice sounded dim and far away.

Bob didn't answer. The silence was long and thick. Why didn't Bob answer? Oh God. Was he dead? Pete strained to remember what had happened. Where they were. Why couldn't he remember? He crawled to Bob, his hands slipping in slime, and he saw something hanging out of his vest pocket, a drenched paper. He pulled it out, unfolded it, his map of the pipeline. He blinked at it, finding jagged shards of memory. The pipeline. They'd come to blow it up. He remembered finding the place where it passed through the old campground. He remembered putting the device together. And waiting for the moment to set it off. Had they done it? Blown the thing up, destroying the pipeline? Making history? He couldn't remember.

'What?' Bob's voice was dim, like an echo, but it sounded mad. He was flat on his back, covered with muck. Blood trickled out of his ear, his nose. He didn't move. Just lay there, moldering.

Maybe they were both dead. This could be hell, the smell, the crap all over. The ringing howl in his ears. The cracking pain in his head. The bomb – they must have done it. Actually blown up the pipeline. The explosion must have sent them flying, knocked them out. He looked down at the map. A red drop landed on it. Splat. Pete stared at the drop, then up at the sky, trying to see where it had come from.

'Fuck.' Bob still didn't move. 'What happened?'

Pete touched his forehead. His cruddy hand came away with red smears. Blood. He looked at Bob. 'I'm bleeding.'

Bob didn't say anything.

'Bob? You okay?' His voice sounded muffled, as if filtered through a feather pillow.

'I'm fuckin' ducky.'

Pete could hardly hear him. Why? Damn – had the explosion blown his ear drums? Made him deaf?

'Chrissakes, Pete.' Bob pushed himself up on an elbow. 'Would you stop doing that thing with your eyes?'

Really? He was half deaf, covered with crud and bleeding, and Bob was on him about blinking too fast? 'I'm bleeding.' He put his head down for Bob to see. 'Take a look. Is it bad?'

'Can't tell.' Bob let out a groan as he sat up. He held his head in both hands and paused before trying to stand. 'Shit. We gotta get out of here.'

Pete didn't move.

'Come on. Get your ass up.' Bob bent one leg, put weight on it. Steadied himself.

'What happened? Did we get the pipeline?'

'You think this is what they pump through the pipeline?'

'Fuck. Then what did we blow up?'

'You want to discuss it? Now? Here?' He pushed himself up onto his feet. Wiped wet clods off his sleeves, plopping them onto the ground. 'Pete? What's wrong with you? Get the hell up. They'll be coming from all over the park to find out what blew. We gotta go.'

Pete looked around, tried to stand. Slipped in some muck and, falling, reached for Bob, grabbed his arm. Pulled him down with him. They both landed hard, with a splat. Bob sat in a puddle of crud, glaring and silent.

'Sorry,' Pete muttered. He fumbled around, got on all fours, trying to balance enough to stand.

Bob got up and held out a hand, pulled Pete to his feet.

They stood for a second, winded from the effort. 'Let's go.' Bob turned and headed for the woods, grabbing their backpacks on the way. They'd been shielded by a tree, were still pretty clean.

'Where we going?' Pete trudged after him.

'Out of sight,' Bob said. 'Then someplace to get this stinking shit off.'

They moved through the woods, orienting themselves. They were looking at the map, figuring out where they were, deciding which way to go to get to the creek when the woods rang out with a sharp, high-pitched scream.

The Bog Man lumbered along on his new legs, tall as a grizzly. He walked stiff-legged, working his prosthetic extensions, swinging his huge feet. He was a marvel of engineering, coordinated and balanced. And fearsome. The hides around his head altered sounds, muffling those of the woods, enhancing those under the bearskin. His amplified breath sounded primitive and hungry; his heartbeat pounded out danger. He was a beast, towering over the other creatures. The only one of his kind. Alone.

In fact, he was beginning to realize how truly alone he was. The

Hunt Club was just a herd of sheep, cowering together, passive and weak. They didn't understand how dire their situation was. And they sure didn't see the significance of his work. Most of them thought he was just a jokester who liked playing pranks. Hiram snubbed him like he was nobody, just a mechanic from the auto repair shop. And the chief was even worse, acting like he was some kind of a pervert ever since that trouble, even though that was what? Like fifteen years ago? Fact was the chief was threatened by him, trying to hold him back. But guess what? He didn't give a damn what the chief or any of them thought. He was on his way, just getting started. He chuckled, thinking of the guy who'd spotted him that morning, the way he'd stood frozen, gaping. And then, the way he'd taken off like his ass was on fire.

The Bog Man pushed his way into the trees, feeling mellow. Must be how a coyote felt after he'd eaten a doe belly. Lifting his legs, crushing plants, he realized that his senses were keener. Not just his ears, but his eyes and nose were sharper. And without being conscious of it, he'd been following a scent. Something animal. Primal. It tugged at him, leading him through the woods as surely as if it had taken him by the hand. Not that it was the only smell pulling at him. No, there were scents all around him, opening like a hooker's legs. Odd how he'd never paid much attention before. But the bearskins had a strong odor. And the trees, the soil, the drying leaves. And something warm – maybe deer? He inhaled, sniffing. Trying to separate and identify each strain in a symphony of scents. Only one, though, compelled him forward. And gradually, as he walked, he identified it: the smell of the dead guy.

Good. He wanted to go back and take another look at him, afraid he'd been too hurried before and done a half-assed job. A cardboard sign? Well, cardboard had been all he'd come up with on short notice, discarded at some campsite. But it wasn't enough. Maybe now that it was getting dark, he'd be able to do more, make the message clearer. Take out the eyes, or peel off some skin. Or wait – the head. Damn, why hadn't he thought of that? He had his pocketknife with him, but he should have brought an axe. He could have chopped the thing off, stuck it on a stake. That would have scared the crap out of outsiders. And the bonus was, no matter what he did, no one would bother him about it. It wasn't like he could get arrested – the Bog Man wasn't human, wasn't subject to their laws.

As he got close, he heard a woman talking. Damn. He wasn't

alone. The bearskins muted her words, but he knew she wasn't far away. He stopped, peered through the trees. Saw the ranger and a woman make their way up the path. But right in front of him, a squirrel quivered on a branch, distracting him, smelling like fear. He watched it stand motionless, maybe a foot away, pretending not to be there.

If he reached quickly, he could scoop it up, feel its heart race and its body squirm. It had been a long time since he'd taken a small animal, and he'd never been able to do much before their hearts stopped. Maybe he could now? He considered it, but never made a move. Even with his ears covered with bearskin, he heard the scream, long, high-pitched, and full of terror. The squirrel scampered off as he stood still, savoring the sound.

Apparently his message had been clear after all.

Harper and Hank followed the scream. It led to Philip Russo. Or to his body. It was grotesque, propped up and tied to a tree trunk on a main trail, about two miles from the ranger's office at the campground. A cardboard placard was duct-taped to his chest, the word TRESPASSER printed crudely in black marker.

Angela was a whimpering ball, collapsed at her dead husband's feet. Ranger Daniels knelt beside her, trying to comfort her, listening to his radiophone. A voice was blaring, talking about the explosion. Describing a geyser fifty feet high.

Hank ran to help, relieving Daniels, offering Angela the flask of bourbon he kept in his vest pocket. But Harper stayed back, taking in the scene, rereading the placard. Had the locals killed Philip Russo? Why? Out of all the hunters and backpackers visiting that weekend, why Phil?

She walked along the path, examining the ground and the foliage, not sure what she was looking for. Noting two parallel lines, partially clear of leaves, leading to the tree. Probably Phil's legs had dragged there. The ground around Phil's body was disturbed, no doubt from the effort of tying him there. Harper walked around the body, looking at Phil. His eyes were open and vacant. And even though his mouth was distorted in a deadly grimace, his body seemed fairly undamaged. His hands were clean, unblemished. His clothes were unsmudged. She saw no sign that he'd been in a struggle. In fact, no wounds were visible at all, just the border of a bloodstain on his blue plaid flannel shirt, visible above the TRESPASSER sign.

Daniels was on his radio with someone else, raising his voice. 'Because who else would leave a sign like that? It's got to be the Hunt Club.'

A male voice answered him, but Harper couldn't make out what it said. She circled the body again, looking above and around it. Just behind Phil's head, she saw a small clump of brown fur caught on the bark. Harper leaned close, examining it. Odd. Was it from a bear? A raccoon? Why was it here, on this tree? Had Phil's killer worn a fur coat?

'Well, see for yourself, Joe,' Ranger Daniels went on. 'But it looks to me like your neighbors are behind this. And if they are—' He stopped mid-sentence, listening to the response.

Harper was too far away to hear what was being said, but she knew who 'Joe' was: Daniels was talking to Captain Slader.

'I didn't say you could control them. But if it's them, there'll be hell to pay. The whole damned world will descend on this place and I promise you they'll start a confrontation—'

More blurting from Captain Slader.

'Well, hurry it up, can you? I've got to get up to that explosion. Which you wouldn't know anything about, right?'

The captain's answer was brief and gruff. Grumbling, Daniels stowed the radio in his vest. 'You all right there?' He turned to Angela.

Hank had her sitting up, faced away from the body. Her skin was a greenish gray, and she was mumbling, hugging herself.

Harper motioned to Daniels. 'Ranger? Want to look at this?' She pointed to the clump of fur.

His radio was blaring again, a static voice asking him to respond. He answered as he stepped over to Harper, told the voice that, yes, he knew about the explosion, and no, he didn't know what had blown, but yes, he'd be heading up there soon. Then he looked at the wad of fur for a long moment, rubbing his jaw. Finally, he reached out and plucked it off the tree.

'Wait – don't you need to bag it?'

His eyebrows raised. 'Why? It's just fur.'

'But it might be evidence.' Harper reached for the hand he held it in, but he raised it over her head. 'What are you doing?'

'There's fur all through these woods, ma'am.' He wadded it up and stuck it into his pocket. 'It doesn't mean a thing, other than some animal scraped against some bark. Probably trying to scratch its back.'

'Or maybe the killer left it.' Harper stood straight, hands on hips, but Daniels leaned down and lowered his voice.

'Ma'am, you're not from around here. Trust me, whoever did this to Mr Russo was not a raccoon or a bear. A tuft of fur has nothing to do with this investigation.'

'Ranger,' she began, but Daniels leaned closer, whispered into her ear.

'Okay. Between you and me, I can think of another possibility.' He looked around, making sure no one was listening. 'Somebody might have planted that fur on purpose.'

Harper blinked. 'Why?'

'To make it look like it was that Bog Man who killed him. To scare people away from the woods.'

What? Was he joking? Harper looked him in the eye. Daniels seemed completely serious. Still, she wasn't going to back down. 'So,' she whispered, 'that fur would be evidence that they tampered with the crime scene. It needs to be preserved.'

'Ma'am, I'm not going to make things worse than they are. There are folks who believe that the Bog Man is real as the nose on my face, who would panic if they thought he was killing hunters. And there are others – mostly Hunt Club people – who just feed the rumors, hoping to scare outsiders away. Thing is, I'd bet my pickup that some local stuck this fur here out of mischief. For the express purpose of distracting us from the real evidence and making it look like the creature killed him. Either way, that piece of fluff is staying with me.'

'No one would believe that a creature—'

'Really? You never heard of Big Foot? Yeti? Sasquatch? Half man, half something else? People come from all over the world to search for them. If publicity gets started about this fur, nobody'll be scared away. It'll be the opposite, like with Sasquatch and the others. Freaks'll descend here from all over the planet, searching the bog.'

Harper scowled. 'The fur is evidence, Ranger. Whether or not the killer put it there. You can't decide whether or not it's relevant—'

'Harper!' Hank called.

Harper turned just in time to see Angela dart toward the body. Hank was behind her, arms out to catch her. Daniels spun around and grabbed her waist, but Angela was already on Phil, tearing the duct tape off his torso.

'Phil!' She pawed at him, threw the cardboard to the ground, stroked his stiff hands and arms. 'Phil,' she wailed, resisting and hissing when they tried to pull her away.

'Mrs Russo.' Ranger Daniels kept his voice gentle. 'Please back away.'

But she didn't. She kept fighting to get to her husband. 'He's my husband – let me go.'

Harper took hold of her hand. 'Angela, stop. You'll destroy evidence.' She glared at the ranger. 'They need to have everything intact so they can find out who killed your husband.'

Angela stopped struggling and looked at Harper. 'But we already know who killed him. I told you – Stan. Stan killed him.'

'Why would Stan put a sign on him?' Harper asked.

'I don't know. Maybe to make it look like it was the people from around here? I don't know why Stan does anything he does.' She went on, giving examples of Stan's inexplicable behaviors – marrying Cindi, for example.

Hank met Harper's eyes, shook his head.

'Look.' Daniels checked his watch. 'I hate to do this. If I had any staff at all, I wouldn't have to ask. But the sunlight's almost gone. And that explosion before sounded serious – the radio hasn't stopped with calls about it.'

'Did you find out what it was?' Hank asked.

'Not for sure. But people have been reporting a spout shooting up like a cloud and raining crap all over the old hunting lodge. I figure gas might have built up and exploded one of the old septic tanks, but just to be sure, I have to go out and take a look. I hate to impose on you civilians, but Captain Slader should be here any minute. Can you two stay and secure the scene, hold onto her until he gets here?'

Hank assured him that it was no problem.

'When you say "secure the scene", you mean protect all the evidence?' Harper eyed his pocket. She didn't mention the fur.

'Yes, ma'am. Exactly.' He looked at her directly, unashamed.

'We'll be fine,' Hank said.

'He was jealous of Phil,' Angela went on, 'that's why he did it. Stan just can't let go; couldn't stand to see me happy. He had to ruin it. You need to arrest him.'

Daniels walked off. Harper took a seat on a log between Angela and Hank, reached her hand into Hank's vest pocket, and, as Angela mumbled on, pulled out his flask.

* * *

By the time they found the stream, it was almost dark. Bob waded in, stripping off his clothes as he went. Pete knelt in the muddy bank, splashing water onto his forehead. It hadn't stopped bleeding. Nothing was going right, and he was getting creeped out. First, the explosion covered them with stinking crap; then they heard that scream. It sounded like somebody was having her guts pulled out. Bob had said it wasn't their business, and to ignore it. Pete wasn't sure he was right, but figured they'd be no help to anyone anyhow in their condition. Still, the scream repeated in his head. What could have happened that would cause that noise?

'Get in the water.' Bob lay back between rounded rocks in the chilly knee-deep stream, letting it wash over him.

Slowly, Pete peeled off his clothes. They were trash now. Nothing would take the stench out of them, and even it if did, he didn't want those things on his body again. Hell, he didn't want them to be in the same town as him. Damn. Vest was new. He'd paid $59 for it at the Target store. All he had in his backpack was an old Flyers jersey and jeans. Not even any socks. He'd freeze his ass off.

Bob surfaced, shook water off his head. Shivered. 'Come on. Get in here.'

'It's fuckin' ice water.'

'Standing there won't make it warmer. You got to get that crap off you.' He slid back, submerged up to his neck. 'Don't be a damn pussy.' He grinned and, letting out a hoot, sprung up, grabbed Pete around the neck, and pulled him into the water.

Pete landed hard, hitting his knee on a boulder, and when Bob released him, he fell face first into the stream. Cold surprised him, enveloped him. It reached into his nose, down his throat, stretched through him like tentacles. He didn't mind it. In fact, spread out flat on stones and mud, he thought about staying right where he was. Going to sleep in the water. But something hooked into his armpit, dragging him up.

'Pete?' Bob pulled his head up by his hair.

'Get off me.' He pushed Bob away, coughing. His voice cracked like ice.

'You okay? I was just messing—'

'Yeah.' He coughed some more, sat up on the pebbles, letting water swirl past him. 'So was I.'

'Shit. You had me.' Bob slapped the back of Pete's head, crouched beside him in the stream. 'I say we burn our clothes.'

'Yeah.' It made sense.

Bob splashed water on his arms, rubbed the backs of his hands. 'I think it's off me, but I keep scrubbing anyhow. I'll probably never feel clean.'

Pete coughed some more, rinsed his face, raised an arm to his nose and sniffed. Didn't smell anything, just autumn air, water and trees.

They stayed where they were, shivering, listening to the water and the woods.

'So what's the deal? Did we mess up? Or do they actually pump shit through the pipeline?' Bob finally said.

'Christ, I don't know.'

'Because that sure wasn't natural gas.'

No, it wasn't. Not that Pete had ever actually seen natural gas. But he knew it wasn't what had burst from the ground.

'Map must be wrong,' Bob said.

'It's not wrong. It's from the plans for when they built it. You must have taken us to the wrong spot. To that old hunting lodge.'

'Fuck if I did—'

'Well, if you didn't, then explain what the fuck happened.'

'Why are you asking me? How should I know? And stop fucking doing that blinking thing.'

An ache rose from Pete's belly, a surge of rage and disappointment. And hunger. They'd eaten all their supplies, and now Bob was getting into one of his nasty, scrappy moods. Well, it wasn't Pete's fault that the day hadn't gone as planned. All he wanted was to eat and get warm.

'Okay, we better get going. But we got to lie low.' Bob stood. 'We got to get dry, get dressed, get these clothes burned and get going. People around here aren't going to be happy with us. And if they dig through the mess and find any parts of our device, they'll have Homeland Security, the ATF, the FBI, and half of every other government agency looking for our asses.' He spit, a contemptuous punctuation mark, and waded out of the water.

The sunset glowed amber and rose, but it was fading. The sky was almost dark. A sliver of moon peeked through the trees. Teeth chattering, Pete got out of the water, the pebbles harsh on his feet. Bob had already gathered sticks and twigs for a fire. Pete stood dripping, feeling useless.

'Matches?' Bob didn't even look up.

Pete opened his backpack, pulled out a bunch of stuff, including his spare jersey and pants, before he found not only matches, but rolling paper and the baggie with the rest of their pot. For the first time in hours, he smiled. His momma had been right: even in the worst of times, pleasure could be found in small things.

Mavis lived all the way out near Philipsburg, a ten-minute drive at sixty. The chief went at eighty. When he got there, she was just putting the 'closed' sign in the window of her beauty shop. She saw him pull up, opened the door. Stepped onto the porch. Said his name.

He took his hat off as he walked up to her, planted a kiss on her cheek. She accepted it as routine. Waited for him to talk.

'I hear you've been talking to people.'

'Damn right.' She was exactly his height. When she looked at him, their gazes just about collided. 'They're killing folks. And I heard a bomb went off—'

'Who told you that?'

'Lots of people. Everyone knows.'

The women had their own network. Mavis's shop processed information faster than the Internet.

'So why are you here? I haven't heard from you in, what? Three weeks? So I doubt you dropped by for a social call. I guess you've come here to get me to tell my people to wait this out.'

The chief sighed, looked at his shoes. 'How've you been, Mavis? I've been meaning to call—'

'Stuff it.' She checked her fingernails. Dark blue with rhinestones.

The chief stepped close enough to feel her body heat. 'Can we step inside?'

She gazed at him, blinked. Let out a breath. 'Oh, what the hell?' She turned, led the way in.

The walls were lined with mirrors, two stations with scissors and supplies. Beyond that a sink for washing hair, a table for manicures, some chairs and sinks he couldn't figure out. Mavis led him through to the back stairs, up to her living room, which adjoined her bedroom and kitchen.

'Drink?'

He ached for one, but said no. He was here on official business.

She got him a beer anyhow, poured herself a glass of white wine, and took a seat on the faded pink sofa. Crossed her legs.

'Really, I'm not lying. It's been on my mind to call you.' He set the beer on the coffee table.

Mavis scowled, leaned over and moved it onto the doily. 'Not on the wood. It'll make a ring.' She sipped her wine.

'I like your hair that color – it's pretty.'

'Screw you. It's the same color it's been for months. I know why you've come down here, but you're wasting your time. We've already decided we're going on patrol.'

'You're what?' Really? He wanted to slap her pretty, overly made-up face. By what right, under whose authority had her little circle of misfits, dykes and spinsters decided anything? But the chief didn't react, didn't slap or even shout. Good leaders remained composed, and he was the club's elected leader. He forced himself to speak calmly. 'There's a meeting tonight. Your people should be there. Because the whole reason we made this organization was so we'd coordinate and cooperate. We're far more powerful if we all work together, not each go off on our own—'

'You weren't really thinking of calling.' She turned, facing him. Was she pouting?

'I was. It's just – I've been crazy busy.'

'A call takes two minutes. Nobody's so busy they can't find two minutes if they want to.'

He reached a hand onto the back of her neck, under her hair. Fondled the downy skin there, the way she liked it.

Mavis frowned, slapped his hand away. 'You think you can have me any time you want, don't you?' She swallowed wine, eyeing him. Her eyes didn't flash, didn't smile. Was she mad? Just playing with him? He couldn't tell.

He shrugged.

'See? That's what I mean. You're so damned sure of yourself, you cocky asshole. You think I just sit here, day after day, waiting for you? That I got nobody else to spend time with? That I'm that much of a loser—'

He leaned over, quieted her by pressing his mouth on hers. He really didn't have time for this, but Mavis smelled tired and flowery. And it had been almost three weeks. The chief knew how to make her moan, and Mavis knew her way around a man. Her bra was off and his pants unzipped when, as if on cue, he got a call he wished he never answered.

A second body had been found, tied to a tree. Damned Josh. Whether he'd killed the guy or not, he'd put him on display, created a spectacle. State cops were already rolling into the campgrounds. And if that wasn't bad enough, that explosion had blown away what was left of the old hunting lodge. The locals were steaming.

He left in a hurry, promising Mavis that he really would call, leaving her sputtering mad. He was halfway to the campground before he realized that, damn, Mavis had never actually agreed to bring her people to the meeting that night, much less to hold them back from going out patrolling with their armaments and making things even worse.

Daniels smelled the site a good ten minutes before he got there. And when he got there, he was glad he'd worn his old boots. The sun was almost setting; he used his flashlight to enhance the light. But there was no question as to what had happened.

A gaping hole marked the spot where the old latrines had been. And the contents of the tanks underneath covered everything – trees, the caved-in, splintered lumber of the old lodge. Damn. Probably a methane build-up. Had to be. Old gases, expanding and confined, nobody flushing them out. Sooner or later, something had to give.

He trudged ahead, shining his light here and there, careful not to slip or trip. Hell, that would be something, falling here. The stench was enough to choke a man, made his stomach queasy. He told himself that he could leave, that there was nothing more to see, especially not in the dimming light. No foul play had occurred. He'd have to make a report, call the environmental people to check it out and arrange a clean up, since it was a public health hazard. What a mess.

He trudged ahead, pondering how strange life was. How nothing had happened for months, and then, in a span of hours, two men had been killed and the old latrines had blown to hell. He doubted he'd ever get over the shock of finding that poor guy, Russo. The sight of him, eyes wide open, mouth contorted in a grim grin. His body propped up, labeled with a TRESPASSER sign. What had set the locals off? Had something happened that he didn't know about? But even if they'd been riled up, why had they gone and killed people? The bloodshed was hard to grasp. Even though the locals had their Hunt Club compound and trained for battle like a militia, they were mostly good folks. It made no sense that they would wake up one day and, unprovoked, go out and kill a pipeline walker. Even though he worked for their sworn enemy, he'd personally done nothing to hurt anybody. And that poor rabbit hunter? That made even less sense. Why would they mess with him?

Daniels sloshed ahead, hoping that Captain Slader and the cops would find out who was behind the killings and stop them before anyone else got hurt. Otherwise, with the Hunt Club armed and ready, the woods could become a war zone. Distracted by his thoughts, he almost slipped off the edge of the blasted-out ditch.

Steadying himself, he aimed his light down into it. Saw muck and stones, stuff he didn't want to look at. The ground under his boots squished. Okay, enough. He'd done his job. He'd checked and found nothing dangerous or suspicious. He could go.

Turning, he waved his light around, noticed a couple of trees not far from the hole. The lower branches were stark and bare, stripped of colored leaves. He stepped closer, saw the scorching. Damn. The branches had been burned. Which didn't make sense if the explosion had been from the pressure of built-up gases.

Daniels looked around, scanning the area. Because of the muck, he hadn't noticed right away, but the ground cover had also been charred. He squatted, looking closer. Sensing trouble.

Okay. He wasn't an expert on explosions. Obviously, there had been lots of heat. If the pressure of the built-up gases had been enough to cause an explosion, wouldn't it have generated enough heat to sear nearby plants? He wasn't sure. Had no experience with an event like this. Wasn't acquainted with the properties of old septic tanks or methane gas that had been confined too tight. Probably, everything was in order, though; he might as well head home and clean the hell up. He'd have to throw the boots out, as they were soaked from the puddles. Nothing would get crud like that out of old leather.

Flashlight guiding him, Daniels headed back to the trail. A few steps away, it lit up something flat and silvery. He stopped, crouched to see what it was. Didn't want to touch it. Took a ballpoint from his pocket and poked at it. Saw it was just a swatch of silver duct tape.

Duct tape? Why would duct tape be found in the residue of the old latrines?

Maybe it hadn't. Maybe some hunter or camper had littered, dropping it before the blast, so it got mixed in with the detritus. That had to be it. Even so, it crossed his mind to mark the spot in case investigators wanted to see it. But why would they? It was nothing. A piece of tape.

He stood, eager to go. The light was fading. Passing the charred trees, he waved his flashlight around one more time, didn't think about the odd-textured bump in one of the trunks. Walked on.

But the bump bothered him, wasn't right. Didn't have the texture of bark. Damn, he wanted to leave. The stink of the air hung still, chilly. The sun was all but gone. He could just ignore it.

Or he could go back, take a quick look and then take off. Fine. Daniels spun around, plodded back to the tree. Shot his light on the trunk and found the bump. Stepped closer. What the hell? Something was jammed there – actually penetrating the bark. It was smooth plastic with a jagged edge. Damn if it didn't look like the casing of a walkie-talkie.

At twilight, sitting cross-legged near the lake, Bob had an epiphany.

'We got a problem,' he announced.

Pete got it. 'Yeah.' He nodded, impressed by the sheer depth of the observation. He took a long hit, passed the joint back to Bob.

'Water,' Bob said.

'It's okay. There's more in the car.' Pete let the smoke out of his lungs. 'We'll go get some.'

'No.' Bob inhaled. Held in the smoke.

'No?' Pete giggled. It seemed funny that Bob said he wanted water, and then said he didn't want to go get it.

'No, no. The problem.' Bob's voice was slow, his words dragged. 'The problem is water.'

What? Pete had no idea what Bob was talking about. But he sure was hungry. Maybe they'd left some beef jerky back in the car. Or some money to get a burger somewhere. With curly fries.

'See, the thing about water is . . .' Bob took another hit, pausing to let his lungs absorb the dope. 'The clothes are soaked with it. They won't burn. If we start a fire, the clothes will probably douse it. That's a problem.'

Pete wasn't entirely listening, was thinking about ketchup.

'So the fire's not a good idea.'

Wait, what? No fire? Pete looked at the pile of twigs they'd gathered as kindling. He'd been looking forward to watching flames in the dark. Seeing the fire devour their stinking clothes. He leaned back against a tree trunk, disappointed.

They sat silent for a while. Pete wondered if there was a pizza place anywhere around. 'I gotta eat something soon.'

'Yeah.'

'So? Let's go.'

'We can't just leave this stuff.'

'Why can't we just make a little fire and see if the clothes will burn?'

Bob didn't answer. He sat up straight, his body announcing the arrival of another idea. 'How about,' he pointed through the trees, 'the stream?'

The stream? 'You want to dump our clothes there?'

'Oh.' Bob frowned, considering it. 'Maybe. But I was thinking we could wash the clothes really good so they don't smell. Then we can take them with us.'

Wet clothes? Bob wanted to carry sopping wet clothes? Bob got up, started picking up the stinking things and strolling toward the water.

'Hey, wait.' Pete followed. He was cold, and his hands were starting to itch again. 'After this can we get something to eat?'

Bob kept walking. 'After this, we return to "Go" and roll the dice again.'

Say what?

'From start. From square one. From zero. We rethink everything, make a new plan, begin again.'

Begin again? Now? 'I can't begin anything on an empty stomach.' Bob was pissing him off, moving slow, talking slow. Acting like he was the boss. Pete wanted to run into a pantry, tear open a box of Fruit Loops and have his way with it. Or maybe Captain Crunch. He scratched his palm.

'Here's what I think,' Bob went on. 'First, we got to go back to the car and take everything out. Take inventory. See what's left. Pack it up again with a new detonator, whole nine yards. Regroup. Then we got to recheck the location. Get it right this time. Set up camp close to the spot, wait for the right moment in the middle of the night. And do what we came here to do.' Bob plopped the soiled garments into the water. Used a stick to swish them around. And around. And around.

Pete watched, captivated. In the dim light, he could see the water swirling, silver and black, and the clothes bobbing up, pillowed with air. He crouched, entranced, forgetting about cereal.

Sometime later, Bob stood, dragging the sopping clothes out of the lake. Sniffing them. Holding them out for Pete to sniff.

'That's okay, I'm good.' Pete backed away with his hands up, refusing.

'They don't smell too bad.' Bob twisted them, wringing out water. Handed some of them to Pete. They started walking toward the trail, carrying wet laundry, heading back to the Impala.

'So, you think that snack bar's still open?' Pete asked.

'Hope so. I could eat a bear.'

Pete was deciding what animal he was hungry enough to eat when he sensed movement in the trees nearby. He stopped. Listened. Heard a rustle. 'You hear that?'

Bob looked at him. 'What?'

Pete looked into the dark woods. Something – or someone – was out there. 'Give me your flashlight.'

Pete turned it on, aimed into the trees. Saw nothing. He moved the light around, examining shadows and shapes. Finally, he gave up. Used it to light up the dirt path ahead.

'Christ.'

The footprints were gigantic. Wide, with ape-like toe prints. They pointed away from the stream, went from the muddy banks to the trail where they disappeared in the fallen leaves. Bob and Pete stared at them.

'Oh, man,' Bob said.

'Big Foot?' Pete asked.

'Get serious.'

'What else could make footprints like that?'

Bob thought for a minute. 'Maybe a mutation. From all the gas leaks and chemicals and fracking pollution around here.' He started walking again. 'That settles it. We gotta get this done right, tonight, and take out that pipeline before it poisons anything else.'

They moved faster, talking and planning all the way back to the Impala. They had a lot to do, and it would be harder to do it in the dark.

Harper's left leg was beyond aching. She dosed herself with ibuprofen, collapsed into a folding chair, and watched Hank light the propane stove. She missed Chloe. She wanted to go home. No, she wanted to *be* home.

'How's your back?' she asked. Hank had seemed to limp less as they'd walked. Maybe the exercise had been good for him.

'I took about a thousand pain pills. With a little wine and some sleep, I'll be fine.' He unfolded the stepping stool, set it up under the bear bag, reached up to untie it.

'I'm not helping.'

'I know.'

'I'm too wiped out.'

'I know.'

'I'll rally if you want.'

'Just sit.' Hank took their supplies down from the tree branch, opened the sack. Retrieved the wine first.

Harper couldn't move. She leaned back, aching all over, watching Hank open the bottle and pour. When he brought her a plastic cup of Cabernet, she almost cried in gratitude.

'I love you.' She lifted the cup, a toast.

Hank bent over, kissed her. 'Having fun?'

She managed a smile. 'More than I can say.'

'We should do this more often.' He moved his chair close to hers and sat. Took her hand.

The sun was setting; the sky glowed pink behind the trees. The air was chilly, smelled crisp and sweet.

'Think Chloe's okay?'

'She's fine. We'll call in the morning.'

He was right. It was no use thinking about Chloe. No use dwelling on the absence of chubby arms grabbing her thigh as they stood in the kitchen, or encircling her neck as they sat on the couch. Or a soft voice piecing together sentences to share her observations and opinions. 'Codge chiz is best,' she'd exclaimed the other day, eating lunch. Harper's throat felt thick, her body disconnected. Cut it out, she told herself. You're Army. You fought insurgents and survived. Surely, you can get through a weekend away from a two-year-old.

They sat quietly, listening to chirps and twitters. Creatures snuggling in for the night. Or emerging to prowl.

Harper swallowed wine. 'You think the local people killed them?'

'That trespasser sign makes it look that way.' Hank swiveled, facing her. 'But who knows?'

Harper didn't answer. She didn't know the people who lived around here. But she was pretty sure that, if she'd killed a man, she wouldn't put a placard on his chest, incriminating herself.

'What about Stan? You think he killed Phil like Angela says?'

Hank shook his head. 'Hard to say.'

'I don't think it was Stan.'

'Why not?'

'Because if I were Stan and I was going to kill someone, it wouldn't be Phil. It would be Angela.'

Hank chuckled. 'You're right. Then again, we have no idea what their history is. I have no idea who killed those guys. But if we get a chance, I'd like to talk to the other pipeline walker – the dead guy's partner.'

'Jim. His name's Jim. Why? You think he did it?' Harper hadn't considered that possibility. But two men alone in the woods for months might get on each other's nerves. Might even drive one to murder the other. She thought back, saw Jim talking to the ranger. Jim had been bereft about his co-worker; hadn't seemed like a killer. Then again, Harper had learned that some killers could seem harmless – even friendly. An Iraqi woman flashed to mind, smiling, meeting her eyes. Putting a hand inside her robe. Disappearing in a white-hot blast . . . No. Harper shook her head, pushing searing wind away. Refusing to revisit the past.

Hank was talking. She'd missed a bit. 'But I'd like to hear his take on the local folks and that Hunt Club. Their animosity level. From what the ranger said, it seems like until now, their pipeline protests have been pretty non-violent. At worst, they've slashed tires or written graffiti. Done mischief to discourage hunters and hikers. So it doesn't make sense. Why would they escalate to killing people? What changed?'

Harper frowned. 'I'm sure the authorities will look into it.'

'But we can ask around, as long as we're here.'

'Hank—'

'What? Think they'll shoot us for talking to them?'

'Are you crazy?' Harper gaped at him. In the past, Hank had raged at her for seeking out danger, taking unnecessary risks. Diving head-first into peril. When had their roles switched? When had she become the cautious one? Again, Chloe popped to mind. 'It's not our job to solve the murders, Hank. We're just weekend campers. Civilians. Besides, we don't know which people are involved or where to find them—'

'We can just chat with people in the area—'

'Why?' Her nostrils flared. 'Why draw attention to ourselves? Why plunge into this? We aren't here to solve murders.'

No, they weren't. But why were they there again? Something

about spending time together? Reconnecting with each other and with nature? Recapturing romance? Well, that sure wasn't happening. Harper wanted to leave. To go back to Ithaca. To hop on her Ninja and roar past familiar places. To read a story to Chloe, kiss her pudgy cheeks and tuck her into bed. Harper closed her eyes, felt them burn. Damn, her wine cup was empty.

'Steaks?' Hank got up, opened the cooler that held their food.

'I want to go home, Hank.'

He took out two New York strips. 'We will.'

'No, I mean now.'

'Now?' He looked at her. 'Tonight?'

Realistically, they were both too tired to pack up and hike back to the car in the dark. 'Tomorrow. First thing.'

Even in the dim light, he met her eyes, studied them. He didn't say anything. Harper could hear his thoughts. He wasn't ready to go home, was debating the pros and cons of arguing, anticipating what she'd say. Weighing compromises. Trying to consider her feelings. 'Fine. If you want to go, we'll check in with the ranger, give the cops our statements, and take off.'

Really? No resistance? He'd just given in? 'Thank you.' Harper leaned back, felt her shoulders unwind.

While the steaks grilled, Harper made a salad. They ate quietly, too tired to talk. While they cleaned up afterward, she moved stiffly with cramping muscles. Finally, the bear bag had been hung from a branch and their teeth brushed with bottled water. They crawled into their tent, rolled into their double sleeping bag. Harper melted into Hank's arms. They made love gently, floated into slumber. Harper's sleep was heavy and dreamless. And it ended prematurely, deep in the night.

At first, she thought the grating noise was Hank's snoring. She shoved him, but the sound didn't stop. Drifting up to consciousness, Harper heard Hank breathing softly, not snoring at all. She propped herself onto her elbow, listening to a repetitive, harsh scraping.

Coming from just outside their tent.

'Hank.' She nudged him.

Hank didn't stir.

'Hank,' she whispered. 'Somebody's outside.'

No response. No surprise. When he was tired, Hank slept like the dead.

But what was that sound? Who was out there? Harper slid out

of the sleeping bag, crawled to the zipper, peeked out the netting at the top of the tent. Saw darkness.

'Hank,' she tried again, pushing his legs.

Hank rolled over, oblivious.

Harper reached for her flashlight, peered out through the mesh again. Heard more scraping. Slowly, silently, she unzipped the front of the tent, just enough to open a slit. The moonlight cast shadows, altering appearances. Changing familiar shapes into hulking night creatures. She gazed out, identified the lump of tarp covering their folded chairs and stove. It was undisturbed. She lowered the zipper to open the tent more and widen her view.

The grating sound stopped. She held still and waited, heard nothing. Opened the zipper enough to poke her head out of the tent. Looked around. Felt the chill of night.

Saw no movement, no intruder.

'Hank,' she repeated. Early in their relationship, he'd responded to her every movement, waking up to see if she wanted anything, to make sure she was okay. Now, she couldn't rouse him with a fire alarm.

Never mind. Whatever was out there seemed to have wandered off. Harper sidled back to the warmth of the sleeping bag. She wasn't even halfway in, though, when she heard a deafening crash. What the hell? She froze, alert, listening. Replaying it in her mind: a crack, a whoosh and a thud.

Hank hadn't even stirred. Harper didn't even try to wake him up. She grabbed their rifle, unzipped the tent and dashed out into night. Hunkering low, she scanned the area, crept toward the source of the sound. Trees hovered darkly around her, their limbs outstretched, blocking the moonlight. Branches reached out, sharp and menacing, and the ground under her bare feet scraped harsh and uneven. She clutched Hank's Winchester and shivered, sensing danger. Crouching, inching forward, Harper prepared to face an intruder, maybe a band of militia members. Maybe a bear.

Wait. Speaking of a bear, where was the bear bag? She looked around, didn't see it. She turned, and – damn. The branch that had held their sack of rations too high for bears to reach was no longer attached to the tree. It lay flat on the ground, torn from the trunk.

Harper didn't move. She looked from the stump on the trunk to the fallen branch. It was sturdy, thick. How could it have broken off the tree? Healthy branches didn't just drop off tree trunks, not without hurricane-force winds or the help of a saw. And yet, there it was, lying in the dirt. What the hell had happened?

She replayed the sounds that had awakened her. The cracking must have been the final break from the tree. But before that – the scraping? Had it been a saw? Had someone sawed the branch? She looked closer at the stump. The break was jagged. So no saw. Then what? A memory floated to mind. She was maybe ten, climbing a tree to retrieve a kite. Crawling out on a limb that gave way under her weight.

Maybe that's what had happened here. Maybe what she'd heard had been the branch shaking, the leaves rattling, under the weight of some creature – probably a bear. Had it been going after their supplies? If so, it hadn't succeeded; their bear bag lay flattened under the branch. Harper contemplated tugging it out, rescuing the contents of their cooler – what was in there? Eggs? Salami? Cheese? Yogurt? She put a hand on the branch, testing its weight. It was solid, too heavy to lift, but if she put down the rifle, she'd probably be able to drag it and rescue their supplies.

The air moved behind her, and Harper held still, aware that she wasn't alone. The perpetrator might be watching, maybe still intending to steal the food. Slowly, she looked into the darkness. Saw no one. Maybe it wasn't the bear watching her. Maybe it was just night creatures – foxes and owls. She looked back at the branch, their crushed bag. Damn, why couldn't Hank get up and help her? She should go shake him awake.

Or she could leave the damned stuff alone and go back into the cozy tent and sleep. They were leaving in the morning anyhow, wouldn't need the food. And the cooler was probably smashed, the eggs broken. It would be a mess to deal with.

Fine. Harper backed away from the branch. She looked up at the trunk again. Had it been a bear? Would a bear be smart enough to figure out how to snap a tree branch? Well, it must be. Because what else could have been heavy enough, powerful enough to do it? The back of her neck tickled. She turned, looked behind her.

At first, she didn't see it standing among the trees, watching her. But then it moved slightly, shifting its weight.

The thing had to be over seven feet tall. It stood erect on two legs, like a man. Its body resembled a bear or an ape, covered, head to toe, with fur. And, with a high-pitched, piercing trill, it started walking in Harper's direction.

* * *

Harper watched in disbelief. What was this animal? Not an ape, not a bear. Not a human.

That woman from the campground – Sylvie – popped into her head, scolding, 'I warned you. It's the Bog Man.'

The Bog Man? Ridiculous. There was no such thing. Even so, Harper had no idea what else it could be. And it was coming closer.

She had to stop gawking and do something. She squared her shoulders, inhaled deeply, and commanded, 'Stop.'

It didn't stop. It moved steadily out of the shadows, coming closer.

Finally, her training kicked in. Even as she doubted what she was seeing, she reacted reflexively, automatically, as she would with an insurgent. She reached for the Winchester, positioned herself, and aimed, prepared to shoot if she had to. Except – wait – what was she doing? This creature hadn't attacked her. And if it was the Bog Man, which it couldn't be, but if it were, then it was a rare, unknown life form, like those elusive Yeti, Big Foot, Sasquatch things – it needed to be protected and studied, not shot.

The creature halted, looked up at the moon, and let out a long, ghostlike wail. Its fur gleamed, fangs glistened in the moonlight.

'Hank!' Harper called, knowing that he wouldn't wake up.

The creature faced her, raised its arms to its chest, gorilla-like, and roared. Harper forgot to breathe. Her limbs felt limp and slow, the rifle flimsy. The creature approached, eyeing her, panting. Oh God. It wasn't real, couldn't be. Had to be a huge, deformed bear. That's right, just a bear. In fact, maybe none of this was happening – maybe it was a dream, brought on by stress and exhaustion.

On the other hand, if it was only a dream, shooting it couldn't do any harm. Maybe she should flip the bolt on the Winchester and shoot.

The creature stepped closer, and she smelled animal fur, unwashed and stale. Its head wasn't like a bear's. But also not like a human's. It watched her, hesitating, releasing so shrill a cry that Harper's ears rang. Then it came running.

Harper took off into the woods.

It was right behind her. She could smell it, feel its heat. Harper's jaw tightened. She dashed behind a wide tree trunk, whirled around and, in a single motion, lifted the rifle, flipped the bolt, and aimed at the spot where the creature had to be, ready to fire.

And waited.

No creature appeared. But it had to be there, couldn't have just vanished. She listened for movement, heard none. Was it hiding, waiting for her? Cautious, clutching the rifle, she stepped back toward the tent, searching for the thing, sensing its presence. Maybe it had run away. Maybe she'd scared it off.

Maybe she could get back in the tent, crawl into the sleeping bag with Hank.

She was only yards from the tent when a twig cracked to her left. Harper pivoted toward the sound and aimed the rifle, unprepared for the dark form that bolted at her from the opposite direction, knocking her to the ground. Harper fired just before the Winchester flew out of her arms. The shot didn't seem to startle the creature. It loomed over her, staring down.

Harper rolled into a crouch. And stopped, eye-level with the creature's fur-covered knees. It stared down at her, not moving, not attacking. What was it waiting for? Was it planning what to do? Was this her last chance to escape? Harper didn't wait to find out, took off scampering toward the tent.

'Hank!' Her voice was raw, came from her belly. 'Hank!'

'Harper?'

Thank God. Hank was awake, had come outside.

'Where were you? Did you hear that shot?'

She glanced at him, kept running. Why was he asking questions? Couldn't he see the Bog Man chasing her? 'Hank,' she yelled again, hoping he'd come after her. Her bare feet winced at every pebble and stick, slipped on damp leaves.

'Harper? Wait.'

Wait? Was he crazy? She kept going, recalling the creature's massive frame. She didn't dare slow down even as low branches scraped her arms and face. Harper ran, weaving between trees, tearing through vines. What if she hadn't fled? Would that beast have torn her apart? How had she been so careless, dropping her weapon? Damn – something thorny pierced her foot. She kept running, her left leg throbbing, slowing her down. Winded, she paused behind a clump of dogwood, listening. Hearing its feet crushing leaves and twigs, its body thrashing through branches and undergrowth.

'Harper? Hold up – where are you?' Hank was following her.

Oh God – had the creature seen him? She didn't dare answer

Hank; the creature would hear. And it was close, hunting her. Speckles of moonlight danced on the ground. Twigs grabbed at her skin, and the night breeze brushed her neck, teasing, urging her deeper into the woods. Where was it?

A white light flashed from behind. 'Harper. Stop.' Hank sounded breathless.

Harper didn't answer. Couldn't risk it. She needed to keep moving, to confuse the creature, so she ran deeper into the darkness, away from the sounds of cracking sticks and rustling leaves.

'Harper? For God's sake, what are you doing?' Hank's voice shot through the woods. He sounded annoyed, and the beams of his flashlight hit branches over her head. Damn, he'd draw the creature to him with all that commotion. Harper had to warn him. She turned back toward Hank, aware of movement to her left. For a moment, she had the sense that she was flying. Maybe she felt a brief thud of impact. But before she could feel any pain, the world went black.

The sector chief waited while Hiram called the meeting to order. Thirty-four people had shown up, including Mavis and most of her ladies' group. It wasn't as many as he'd hoped for, but given the short notice, it was a decent turn out. He stood beside the gong and the big-screen television in the compound's lounge, addressing his neighbors, some on folding chairs, others on the donated sofas, and all talking at once.

'Thanks for coming out tonight,' he began.

People kept talking, so he hit the gong. The room shook, and everybody shut up.

When the reverberation stopped, Hiram began again. 'We don't have time to chit-chat. As you know, our sector's got some serious trouble, and we have to figure out how to deal with it.'

'I say we shoot all the outsiders,' someone called.

'Somebody's already doing that,' someone else answered.

'God bless 'em,' a third voice chimed in.

Hiram hit the gong again. 'Order!' he shouted, but the group was unsettled and yammering.

'Everybody shut up,' someone yelled.

The chief stepped up, scowling, and the chatter quieted. 'This occasion is damned serious. Some of you don't seem to get that. Stop clowning around. Hiram's trying to help us out here. Show some cooperation and respect.'

'Yeah, Hiram!' someone called.

'You rock, Hiram.' A few people clapped.

'Anyhow, I might as well take over for now, Hiram.' He squeezed Hiram's shoulder, and Hiram took a seat. 'I'll get right to it. Remember, we're not here to report anyone or turn them in to the law. As always, what we say here stays here within these walls. Anyone got a problem with that, say so now.'

A slight murmur rose and fell. Nobody had a problem.

'Fine. So, first order of business: who here killed Philip Russo?'

'Who killed who?' a man on the sofa asked. Someone leaned over, explaining.

'Josh told me he found Russo's body. He'd already been shot dead,' Hiram said.

'That's right.' Josh was sitting on the floor, leaning against a sofa. 'I didn't kill him. And I don't know who did.'

The chief asked what happened.

'He was just lying there, on the edge of the clearing. I figured some asshole hunter shot him – you know how they think everything that moves is game. So I dragged him to the main trail, tied him to a tree, and put a sign on his chest as a warning to outsiders. Poor fuck was dead. Why not let him serve a purpose?'

People started responding, all talking at once.

Hiram hit the gong.

While the reverberation quieted, the chief took a breath. 'Josh, what in God's name were you thinking?'

Josh opened his mouth to answer, but the chief didn't let him speak.

'The authorities found a body, and on it was a message that clearly suggested our organization. What impression do you think that made on them?'

Josh's face was blank, unrepentant. How stupid could he be?

The captain stepped toward him, glowering. 'You made it seem like one of us killed him, Josh. Do you not see that?'

Josh's face reddened. He pressed his back against the sofa. 'They can't prove anything. Because that's not what happened—'

'But it's what they'll think. The last thing we need is a murder investigation, a search warrant for the compound. And, in your consummate genius, you probably left your DNA all over the body, so they might well arrest you . . .'

'No.' Josh was mad now, getting to his feet. 'There's no DNA. I was covered, head to toe.' Josh met the chief's gaze with defiant eyes.

The chief faced him, reminded himself to maintain control. Not to look away. Not to back down.

'I believe,' he continued in a quiet voice, 'that we have all accepted the organization pact. If you recall, the essence of that pact says that we are sworn to combine our forces and act as a unit. You should have gotten approval before you started parading around in your monster costume. But aside from that, by moving that body and hanging the sign on it, you acted alone, impulsively, without thinking of the possible consequences to yourself and others, and certainly without the approval of anyone—'

'Bullshit. This is still friggin' America, isn't it? I've got freedom of speech. I saw an opportunity, and I took it. I don't need anybody's freaking permission to hang a sign.'

'Well, some here might say that, since that sign appeared to represent them, you do need their permission to hang it.'

Voices tittered, and tension mounted. But the chief didn't want a showdown with Josh. Not now, anyway. Right now, he needed unity and support, so he stepped back to the speaker's spot and waited for the group to settle.

'Clearly, Josh intended no harm. But let's hope he'll think things through and bring them up for discussion next time he feels inspired.'

'You think you're so smart, Chief?' Josh was still standing. 'What have you done to get rid of the outsiders? Huh? At least I'm doing something—'

The gong drowned out Josh's voice. As it faded, people turned to the chief.

'Those are important questions, Josh. We'll address all of them at the end of the meeting. For now, let's get back to our agenda and the matter of Philip Russo. No one knows who killed him, correct?' He waited for a response. No one answered. 'Fine. Then how about the gas pipeline employee, name of Al Rogers? Anyone here kill him?'

Heads shook, no. Voices buzzed.

'You guys can sit around,' Josh shouted. 'I'm out of here.' He gathered up his bearskins and headed for the stairway leading out. A bunch of people – Mavis, Annie and Wade – called after him, but he stormed out.

The chief watched him go, relieved. The meeting would go better without Josh there. He was volatile and hot-headed, needed to be watched closely. The chief had seen men like him in the war, finding pleasure in violence, taking foolish risks, self-destructing. He'd have to keep an eye on Josh. An impulsive firecracker like that could start a blaze, burning the whole community down.

First thing Bob and Pete did at the campground was make use of the new shower facility. Pete scrubbed himself, lathered up and scrubbed again, would have been tempted to stay there all night if not for his empty stomach.

They got a couple of sweatshirts, a tarp and a fleece jacket out of the Impala's trunk, found a ten and a twenty in the glove box. Used most of it at the snack bar to buy cheesesteaks, curly fries and ham sandwiches to go. The place was mostly empty. A woman drank coffee alone at a table near the window. A couple of senior citizens were sharing a cherry pie à la mode. A young thing, maybe eighteen or nineteen, waited on them. Pete watched her hips sway, the freckles on her arms. The mischief in her eyes.

'Keep your fly zipped.' Bob's mouth was full of fries. 'We got more important things to do.'

Pete didn't answer, didn't want to get into an argument over a girl. Fact was he had to save his argument for the big stuff. After his shower, he was tired. All he wanted to do was eat and sleep – and, if the opportunity presented itself, get laid. He couldn't imagine going back out onto the trail and starting all over again, especially not now, in the dark. Bob's mind was made up, though. He was psyched, raring to go. Eating fast, breathing fast. Revving like a race car at a pit stop.

'I've been thinking,' Pete started. 'About tonight.'

'Yeah, me, too. We got to go through the stuff in our packs, take inventory. Study the map here, where there's light.'

Pete looked around, trying to figure out what to say. He wanted to suggest that they wait until morning, but didn't want Bob to get pissed at him. He had to make it be Bob's idea to wait. Maybe he should talk about the effects of sleeplessness. Like pilots – how they made more errors, crashed more when they were tired. The same kind of mistakes could happen to them.

'Bob,' he started. 'I've been thinking—'

A young couple entered the shop, laughing, talking too loud, interrupting. Pete turned to look at them. Thought they didn't go together. The guy was scruffy, unshaven, wearing grubby jeans. The girl, though, she was shimmering. Clothes fresh from a catalogue. Lip gloss, eyeliner, the whole nine yards.

'Shit.' Bob turned away from them.

'What?'

'Don't you recognize her? That's what's her name. The eleven o'clock news. Shit. I didn't think the press would get here till tomorrow.'

The news team ordered black coffee, sat at a table, huddled over notes.

'You think they're here about us? The bomb?'

'Why else would they be here?' Bob covered his mouth with his hand. 'It's got to be us. Nothing newsworthy ever happens out here.'

The woman sitting near the window stood and walked over to the news reporter. 'Finally,' she said. 'I've been waiting for months.'

The news reporter glanced up. 'Excuse me?'

'I've called every news station in Pennsylvania at least twenty times. Finally, someone listened.' Her voice was raspy, her hands pressed together. 'Thank you. Thank you so much for coming out . . .'

The reporter stiffened, shifted in her chair. 'Yes. No problem.'

'I'm Sylvie Donavon – but you must know that. From my emails.'

The reporter stared at her. The guy with her said, 'Maybe she wants an autograph.'

'No, no,' Sylvie said. 'I mean, of course I would. But see, I'm the one who contacted you. I have first-hand information.'

Pete nudged Bob, nodded toward Sylvie. 'Uh-oh.'

'First hand? You were there?' The reporter lit up, nudged her companion.

'Yes, you bet.'

Bob swallowed, whispered, 'Shit.'

'You've seen the actual bodies?'

Bodies? There had been bodies? Oh God. Pete's eyelids went crazy, began blinking fast.

'Bodies? Well, not an actual body. But I've seen its footprints. They're half as long as I am tall.'

'Sorry, what?'

What? Pete and Bob stared at each other, ready to bolt.

'The Bog Man – I emailed you about it.'

'The Bog Man?' The newswoman's left eyebrow rose.

'He's like Big Foot, only he lives right here in Black Moshannon. A while back, he took a hiker, and now they're saying he's taken someone else. You can interview me if you want. I'll give you all the background you need. He's our very own Sasquatch—'

The scruffy man leaned back in his chair. 'How about this,

Ma'am? We're on deadline now, but maybe we'll talk about a feature later. Why don't you write down your name and contact information, and let us get back to you.'

Pete chuckled. 'Bog Man?'

Bob shook his head, went back to his fries.

'No, see. You already have my contact info. I'm the one who broke the story—'

'The Bog Man story.' The news lady smirked.

'Yes, that's right. I sent emails to all the—'

'How about you write it all down for us.' The man spoke clearly, as if to a child. 'Any facts and events that might help us with the story. Just to be sure we have everything.' He sent Sylvie off to get paper and a pencil.

Bob swallowed his last bite, wiped his mouth. Motioned to Pete that he wanted to get going. But Pete shook his head, nodded toward the news team. He was trying to listen in on their conversation, to find out what they knew about the bombing. Their voices were low, though, and he could only hear snippets:

'So what's the connection . . . Philip Russo and Al Rogers?'

'. . . coincidence?'

'No way. Two men killed on the same day? . . . plus that explosion . . .'

'. . . no story, just an old septic tank . . . Gases . . .'

'. . . where's that ranger? . . . need to scoop . . . two shot, plus explosion . . .'

'I just told you . . . that explosion was nothing.'

'. . . good visuals . . . sensational copy . . .'

Bob's eyes narrowed. 'Let's get out of here.' He got up and went to the door.

Pete rooted in his pocket, took out some money for a tip. The senior citizens had stopped eating pie and were leaning their heads together, whispering, eyeing the news lady. Sylvie sat at her table by the window, writing madly on a yellow pad. As Pete passed, the waitress lifted a hand. Her fingers fluttered in a wave, and she whispered good night. Her voice was like velvet.

Damn.

Someone was jostling her. Pushing on her head? Oh God – that creature? Harper tried to resist, shoving and twisting.

'Harper?'

She opened her eyes.

'Thank God.' Hank's face was a dark oval hovering over her. 'You're conscious.'

She looked up, saw tree branches silhouetted by the night sky. What had happened? She started to get up.

'No, don't move. Stay still.' Hank touched her forehead.

'Ouch.' She pushed his hand away.

'Hurts?'

Yes. It was tender. She opened her mouth to ask a question, but wasn't sure what it was. Maybe why Hank was frowning? Or where the creature was? Or why her head hurt?

'Hank,' she began. 'What happened . . .?'

'You fell. You went down hard and hit your head. What the hell were you doing, Harper? Running off barefoot like the hounds of hell were after you – where were you going?'

She remembered running, being chased.

'A gunshot woke me up.' Hank's voice was harsh. 'Was that you? The rifle was gone – I found it back there on the ground. Did you shoot something?'

Had she? Harper remembered being shoved to the ground, the Winchester firing, flying from her grasp. The memories came in a hodgepodge, flooded her mind. She looked around. Was the creature still there? Watching them?

'Hank, we have to get out of here.' She tried to get up, but he wouldn't let her.

'Hold on.' He checked her forehead. 'You need to take your time.'

'I'm fine.'

'If you say so.' Hank reached under her hips and around her shoulders, lifting her.

'Stop – I can walk.'

'No, you just fell. And it's dark and you're barefoot.' He hoisted her into his arms, carried her back to the tent.

Hank's arms were sturdy and steady. Harper felt childlike, cradled against his chest, trying not to tremble. Struggling to process what had happened. Had she really just seen – just barely escaped from the Bog Man?

'Our campsite's all torn apart.' When Hank talked, his chest vibrated. 'Was it a bear? Is that what you were trying to shoot?'

She leaned against him; his body warmed her.

'Why didn't you wake me up? What were you thinking, going after a wild animal by yourself in the middle of the night?' He went on like that, exasperated and worried, until they were back at the tent. Then he set her down and lit their camp light. Examined her scrapes. While he searched for the first-aid kit, Harper huddled beside the tent, staring at Hank's collection of soil and water samples. They'd been knocked over, scattered across the ground. She couldn't stop shivering. Without the heat of Hank's chest against her, she was unbearably cold.

The others had stayed in their suffocating meeting, gabbing at each other. But the Bog Man wasn't able to waste time like that. He was awake, energized. Moonlight brightened his way as he stomped along trails, leaving well-defined footprints. Entering campsites. Tossing around equipment. Working tree branches until they gave way. Scattering supplies and the contents of bear bags.

The longer he prowled, the more alive his senses became. He'd been listening to his heartbeat, the rush of blood through his veins. And he picked up sounds around him, too. Even through layers of skin and fur, he heard the light steps of a fox, the flapping wings of an owl. The skittering feet of prey.

Sometimes he heard whispers and touches. Bodies thumping together.

Sometimes, the breathing he heard wasn't his own.

It was disorienting, all the smells and sounds, all the movement. Creatures skulked and hid, chased and fled. They killed and died, ate and were eaten. The night cloaked a world he'd known about but never been part of. Until now.

The moon was bright, almost full. Heart pounding, blood roaring, the Bog Man moved on among the trees, leaving footprints, noticing some already carved into the ground. Wait. Had he already walked this way? He didn't think so, but there they were, his footprints, huge and deeply defined in the dirt. He must have doubled back at some point. No big deal. He walked on.

When he came to a campsite, he stopped, confused. Damn. Clearly, he'd been walking in a circle; the place had already been torn apart. Camping chairs lay broken, the bear bag torn down, supplies scattered. What was wrong with him? How had he become so disoriented?

Probably it was over-stimulation. He should go back and rest.

The Bog Man walked back toward the compound, unsatisfied. Messing up campsites wasn't enough. Outsiders needed to be petrified to set foot in the woods, and vandalism just wasn't that petrifying.

Death was, though. If the Bog Man wanted to strike terror, more people would have to die.

Before going inside, he turned to face the woods. The night smelled of cold and predators. He looked up at the moon, filled his lungs with air. And howled.

Bob turned on his flashlight and sat in the back seat of the Impala, studying the map. Pete stuffed the wrapped-to-go ham sandwiches into his backpack.

'What the hell were they talking about in there?' Pete asked. 'Did you hear them? They said people got killed.'

'How should I know?'

'And what about that crazy lady? Going on about the Bog Man? Was she for real? Did you see the look on that news lady's face? She was, like, somebody get this loony tune away from me—'

'Here's the deal, though.' Bob looked up from the map. 'The media are like killer bees. If you see one news reporter, you can bet the rest of the hive is right behind them. By morning, they'll be swarming all over the place.'

'But why? You heard them. They aren't here about the bomb, so what is it? Is some serial killer loose in the woods?'

'No. They're here to catch the Bog Man.' Bob growled like a monster.

'I'm serious. If guys are getting killed out there, maybe it's not safe to go back.' Pete had a full stomach, was happily dry and warm. He wasn't so keen on trekking back out into the chilly night to set off another explosion. Couldn't stop thinking about going back to the snack bar and chatting up the waitress.

'Oh, nobody's going to mess with us.' Bob adjusted the map, 'Thing is, we have a great opportunity here. Something's already drawing the media. So we have automatic publicity. When the pipeline blows, the media will be here, on site, with their cameras ready to film it.'

'Cool.' Pete tried to sound enthusiastic. 'But we can't afford another mistake. We need to do everything perfect.'

'So?'

'So right now, we're both wiped. And it's pitch dark, hard to see what we're doing. So maybe we should wait until—'

'No, we got to move now, tonight. While campers are asleep and before the media start prowling around out there.' Bob's jawbone rippled, a sign that it was best not to disagree with him. 'And stop doing that blinking thing – you look like a damned cretin.'

He looked like a cretin? Really? Pete's nostrils flared. He bit his lip. A cretin? Well, fine. Then it was a cretin who'd gotten the map of the pipeline and researched how to detonate explosives on the Internet. And that same cretin who'd actually gotten hold of dynamite and blasting caps. What had Bob done? Mostly, he'd criticized, complained. Bossed Pete around. And now, he was calling him names. Pete turned away, looked out the car window, blinking rapidly.

'So,' Bob pointed to a spot on the map, 'we're here. And the place we hit before is over there.' His finger traced a path from one point to another. 'The pipeline goes right through there. So how come we missed it?'

'I think because that wasn't where we actually were.' Pete's tone was cold, even condescending. He pointed to the map, showed their mistake. 'I think we strayed from the pipeline. We went too far to the east, should have stayed closer to the bog.'

'Then what was that building? If it wasn't the old campground, then what was it?'

'How should I know? All I know is that we got lost.' Pete looked out at the snack bar. He should have gotten the waitress's number.

'Okay, what's done is done. We're starting fresh.' Bob ran a finger along the map, retracing the pipeline's path through the woods. 'It goes along here, parallel to the road. And passes the bog and the lake, keeps going past Philipsburg.'

He should have at least asked her name, found out how late she worked. Damn. Maybe he should go back in. Tell Bob he had to take a leak.

'So I say we blast here.' He pointed to the map. 'It's not far from the bog trail, so it shouldn't be hard to find. What do you say?'

Pete nodded. Fine. Said he needed to hit the men's room. He'd be right back. He got out of the car, leaving Bob sorting through their backpacks, gathering usable items. On the way back to the snack bar, he planned his move, practiced what he'd say. Not a question, no. Something direct. Like 'call me when you get off.' Or 'meet me for a beer later.' He opened the door, looking for her. And stopped, a stupid grin pasted on his face, when he saw her.

She was talking to the forest ranger. They were leaning toward each other on either side of the counter, their heads close together, whispering. She giggled, nodded, her eyes coy, her lips puffy and moist. Before the ranger went to the table with the news lady, he bent his head down and the waitress lifted hers up. When they kissed it was long, clearly involving tongues.

Pete's smile withered, and he literally stumbled over his own feet as he backed away.

Halfway into the meeting, the sector chief hadn't learned a thing. Nobody claimed to know anything about either of the shootings. Most people agreed with Ax when he stood up and said that it had to be outsiders, killing each other.

'But it doesn't matter to the government who's actually doing the shooting,' he declared. 'They're going to use the killings as an excuse to come on in here and take more control. Whereas if they'd kept out all those hunters and hikers and other outsiders from the beginning, no one would be shooting anybody and we'd be left in peace.'

Wade and Moose, Mavis and her ladies were on their feet, cheering, agreeing with him. Shouting that it was time to get rid of all the outsiders, government and gas pipeline and frackers included.

'The land is rightfully ours – let's take it back,' someone yelled.

'Yeah!' someone else shouted. 'I say we get rid of all of them. From litterers to frackers. Look what they did in just one day – bodies are piling up. We can't just sit here—'

'And it's not just bodies,' Hiram's wife Annie put in. 'Some asshole even went and blew up the old hunting lodge.'

The chief was losing control of the meeting. People were jabbering, exchanging rumors. He hit the gong, but they didn't entirely quiet down. It took Hiram and his booming baritone to stand, raise his arms, and shout for order. 'That's enough. Everyone zip it.'

The sector chief took the floor. 'If you'll bear with me, I'll fill you in on what I've found out. First, the two men killed today were likely shot by the same gun. Bullets have been recovered, same caliber.'

The murmurs started, but the chief kept talking in a controlled tone, not even trying to shout over them. Those who wanted to hear him took over, telling the others to hush up.

'Also.' He looked them in the eye as he talked, one at a time, making personal contact. A good leader, he'd learned, related to people, made each one feel individually valued. 'I've learned that the explosion at the old hunting lodge was not caused by gases in the old septic tanks. A detonator was found at the blast site.'

'What?' Mavis stood again. 'It was a bomb?'

'Why would someone blow up an old latrine?'

'I heard shit was flying all over the place.'

The comments flew.

The chief kept talking, ignoring them. 'You can bet, since this is considered a state park and a bomb was set off here, ATF agents and possibly homeland security will be arriving in the morning, searching for terrorists. State cops are already here about the killings.'

The group was indignant. 'God almighty,' someone said.

'The ATF and state cops? This'll be a police state.'

'Fine. Let them come. We'll show them whose land this really is—'

'I know how you feel.' The chief remained calm. 'I feel the same way. But I think we'd best lay low and wait out this crisis. It's not time to rise up against the Feds.'

'Bullshit,' Hiram blurted. His face was bright red.

The chief was startled; Hiram was second in charge, and he never spoke out against him. 'Hiram?' he managed.

'Chief, with all due respect, that was no terrorist who set off that explosion. I'll tell you who did it: the gas company. Or maybe the pipeline company – they're all connected. Sure, they'll deny it, but they've obviously started blasting again. They're probably expanding their pipeline or repairing it – maybe they made a mistake in their logistics. Whatever. Point is, after the hunting lodge blew the first time, we all agreed we wouldn't put up with one more explosion from them, not even a firecracker—'

'Hiram's right.' Ax stood, addressing the sector chief. 'But I'm not sure it's only about the pipeline. I saw some new ones today. Two of them – one's a woman. They were taking samples. Bagging up soil and rocks. Taking water from the lake. It's just like they did before the fracking. I bet they're an advance team for the frackers, who are planning to do more.'

'Now, Ax. We don't know for sure what they were doing,' the chief said. 'Don't jump to conclusions.'

'I know they were taking samples. I saw them—'

'Fine. For all you know, those samples are for some environmentalist group – they might be testing for pollution or whatever.'

The crowd was buzzing again.

'Everybody settle down. Take a seat, Ax. I'm asking you all for patience. All we know for sure is that the next few days, these woods are going to be crawling with outsiders. If we just keep our heads down and lay low, they'll do their business and go on their way—'

'Until the next time,' Wade said.

'That's right,' Annie said. 'How much are we going to take? Our wells are already fouled. We still can't drink our water. Some of us can't even shower at home. How long do we sit around and let them trample all over us?'

'I say we escalate.' Ax stood.

People shouted their agreement.

The chief watched. Saw rebellion in their eyes, smelled their long-simmering rage. If he wanted to lead, he'd have to listen.

'Okay, everybody. I hear you. All in favor of escalation?'

'Ayes' resounded through the lounge.

'All opposed?'

Silence.

'Fine. The ayes win. Escalation it is. But any plans still need to be approved by committee. And be aware: anyone else gets killed or hurt? The state cops and ATF won't just send a few men; they'll take over. They'll be in your living rooms. They'll eat lunch on your tables. I don't want that, and neither do you. So use judgment.'

The meeting broke up. Mavis and her girls lingered, planning what they'd do.

The chief couldn't stick around to talk with Hiram or anyone. Too much was happening too quickly. If he didn't keep on top of it, the whole sector might stage a showdown with the government, and he seemed to be the only one concerned about the outcome.

* * *

Harper didn't even wince as Hank cleaned the raw scrapes on her feet.

'You okay?' He kept asking her questions, urging her to talk.

'Fine.' She didn't want to talk.

'Why are you so quiet?' Hank had wrapped a blanket around her. He sat beside her outside the tent. 'You're acting weird, Harper. Talk to me.'

Harper didn't know what to say. Was she supposed to tell him that she'd hallucinated? Seen some non-existent creature tear their campsite apart? No, she didn't want to tell him that. Instead, maybe she should tell him that she couldn't stop seeing Phil's body, and that it was reminding her of other bodies. Bodies from the war that had been burned or shot or blown up. Bodies with parts missing, or parts with bodies missing. Or maybe she should tell him that the explosion they'd heard earlier kept repeating in her head, like that explosion in Iraq that had killed her patrol, soldiers she'd been responsible for but hadn't protected.

Hank was waiting. Studying her, worrying.

'What would happen,' she asked, 'if we didn't wait? If we just left?'

'You mean now?'

She nodded.

'We said we'd stay until morning . . .'

'I know. But we don't have to. I mean, we aren't suspects . . .'

'It's only a few more hours—'

'I want to leave.' She wasn't going to cry. Refused to. But she felt the tears welling up. 'Please.'

Hank took her hands. Their camp light beamed up at his face, made him look shadowed and ghostly. 'Harper, it wasn't real.'

How did he know that? 'What?'

'Whatever you saw. Whatever made you run barefoot through the woods—'

'You don't know what I saw.'

Hank let out a breath, tightened his grip on her hands. 'No. Of course I don't. But it's not the first time you've gone off, reacting to things you see in your mind.'

Oh God. He thought she'd had a flashback? 'This wasn't a flashback.'

'No? Because it looks to me like a bear came into our camp and tore it apart. It woke you up and triggered a memory of a raid or an ambush—'

'Stop.'

'—or something from the war, and you took off with the rifle—'

'That's not what happened.'

'—caught in a flashback.'

'Hank!' Her anger startled her. Did he really think she was so unstable? That she'd take off with a weapon in the night, chasing memories? What must it be like for him, living with someone he thought might at any moment slip out of reality and into her own terrible memories? She blinked, but one of the tears escaped, rolled down her cheek.

She didn't want to lie, but wanted to reassure him. Her tone softened. 'It wasn't a flashback. I didn't think we were under attack or anything like that. I thought I saw a big animal. And the way it was acting, I thought it was dangerous.'

'So you took off after it? Alone?' He sounded doubtful.

'I tried to wake you.'

'You did?' He reached a hand up, wiped her tear away. 'Well, you shouldn't have chased after it. In the dark. By yourself.'

She nodded.

He sighed, watching her. 'Harper, you think you can stick it out till morning? Because I'm cold and tired. I'd really like to get some sleep before driving all the way back to Ithaca.'

She sniffed, nodded again. Crawled into the tent, climbed inside the sleeping bag beside him. Her head was against his chest. She could feel his heartbeat, the rise and fall of his breath. She focused on that rhythm, trying to ignore the images of Philip Russo and the others.

'So what was it? A bear?'

A bear? She closed her eyes, choosing her words. 'I don't know what it was. It was huge, and ape-like.'

'Ape-like?'

'It was on two legs. And furry.'

'Really.' He shook his head.

'What?'

'Nothing. But a big, furry creature that stands on two feet? Sounds a lot like a bear.' Hank's breath evened out, and thickened into soft snores.

Harper lay awake, ignoring the snores, listening to the woods, straining to hear the thrashing of branches or the howling of the creature. But it must have moved on. She pictured it, silhouetted by the moon. Recalled its size and hairy, almost human shape. It had been neither a dream nor her imagination. No, she'd been awake and alert. Had seen it. Heard it. Smelled it. Looked into its eyes. She had no idea what it was, but she knew that it was real. And it wasn't a bear.

Bob had everything laid out on the back seat, ready to go. 'I was talking to a guy in the parking lot,' he said. 'He said a lot's been going on up here.'

The guy had told Bob that two men had been killed in the woods that day, one of them a pipeline worker. Police and the press were starting to arrive. By morning, the area would be crawling with investigators. He and his buddies were thinking of leaving; it might not be a great time to hunt.

'So I ask him if he's heard about an explosion. And he thinks a second. Then he says, "Oh yeah. At the old hunting lodge—"'

'The old what? Hunting lodge? So we were in the wrong spot. I knew it wasn't the campground.'

'That's not the point, Pete.' Bob raised his voice, realized he was talking too loud. Lowered it to a whisper. 'The point is that he said it was caused by old septic tanks – he said gases built up until they finally blew.'

'So?'

'So? Really? Don't you get it? No one suspected anything. They think the explosion was natural, an accident. Which means no one's looking for us.' He reached into the front seat for a backpack. 'And also, it means it's a good thing we're doing this tonight. Because tomorrow, there'll be cops and gas company people and who knows who else scurrying around watching everybody.' He opened the zipper, started loading the backpack. 'This is our last chance. So we better get it right.'

Pete yawned, couldn't help it. He was cold and tired. Pissed about the waitress kissing the ranger. Pissed about having to trek back out into the woods. Pissed that they'd blown up the wrong site. Pissed that his plans weren't going the way he'd envisioned.

'Ready?' Bob handed him his backpack.

Pete had cleaned it earlier, and it wasn't quite dry. When he put it on, its dampness penetrated his sweatshirt, chilled his bones. He shivered as he followed Bob onto the trail. Everything looked different in the dark. The trees seemed sinister, the trail menacing.

Even the air felt evil. They walked in silence, guided by their flashlights. Bob held the map, stopping occasionally to check it, as if demonstrating that he was smarter than Pete. That Pete had been the one who fucked up the first time. Never mind what Bob thought. Pete almost didn't care any more. He'd all but given up on success, was going through the motions. His anticipation of greatness and fame had fizzled. The only mark he'd made on the world was the mess from the explosion. All that remained of his dream was this endless traipse behind Bob in the cold and dark, the crunch of their footsteps and the calls of whatever creatures prowled the woods at night. Pete shivered, realizing that the moon looked just about round. Didn't animals go crazy under the full moon? Hadn't he heard that they got aggressive and vicious? He looked over his shoulder, flashed his light around, half expecting to see a wolf baring its fangs. Wasn't relieved when he didn't see one.

Bob finally stopped, pulled out the map. Checked it under his flashlight. 'I think we stop here and get organized. We're almost there.' He held his flashlight in his mouth, pointed to a spot on the map. Looked at Pete for confirmation.

'That's where we are?' Pete had lost track of time. It would have taken at least an hour to get that far. Had they been walking that long? 'So where's the pipeline?'

'Should be over there.' Bob pointed, folded the map, took his flashlight out of his mouth. He lay a tarp on the ground, set down his backpack on top of it. Waited for Pete to put his down, too. And walked off, gesturing for Pete to join him. Sure enough, they'd found the pipeline. Bob had found a long stretch of cleared land, probably the path that the pipeline guys walked. A few yards wide, it looked like some huge power razor had shaved a strip through the woods. It looked nothing like the site they'd blown up before.

A glimmer rose in Pete's chest. Maybe they'd get it done after all. He went back to the tarp and set to work with Bob, laying out the explosives, wrapping them in wire, attaching the blasting caps and adjusting the detonator.

They were back in the groove, moving in sync. An efficient, coordinated team. Experienced, this time. Bob and Pete didn't need words, didn't make sounds. They took their bomb to a spot along the pipeline path and hurried back to their tarp, repacked their backpacks and took positions, lying flat on the ground.

Bob held the phone. He looked at Pete. 'Ready?'

Was he? Pete thought for a second. 'What time is it?'

Bob checked his watch. 'Almost twelve. Eight of.'

'How about let's wait? Do it at midnight.'

'Nice. At the stroke of twelve, the pipeline will turn into a pumpkin – a smashed pumpkin.' Bob smirked and sat up. 'Got any weed left?'

Pete did. They shared it, getting more pumped with each drag. Gloating about how famous they'd be. How this explosion would mark the beginning of the end of fossil fuels, the dawn of a new, clean-energy era. How it would make the national news – hell, it would make the history books. They kept checking the time. At eleven fifty-nine, they began the countdown. Bob picked up a walkie-talkie and, just at midnight, pushed the 'talk' button. They put their heads down, waiting.

A few seconds later, they raised their heads. Nothing had exploded. No earth-shaking bang, not even a tiny pop.

'Shit.' Bob started to get up.

'Wait.' Pete grabbed his arm.

'What for? Something went wrong.'

'Maybe it's just delayed.'

'Bullshit. It's not happening. Did you connect the wires right?'

'Of course I did.'

'Well, obviously, you didn't. Because if you did, the thing would have gone off.' Bob was on his feet, about to head back to the bomb.

'Why do you assume it's my fault? Maybe it's a bad blasting cap.'

'How does that make sense? It's the same kind we used before.'

'Why are you asking me? How should I know?'

They argued as they walked until Bob stopped. 'Wait. Maybe you didn't push the button all the way.' He grabbed the walkie-talkie, pushed the button hard and said, 'Shit,' a nanosecond before the bomb burst, hurling both of them into the air and dropping them, unconscious, onto a clump of hostile bushes.

The sector chief sat in his reclining chair, watching the phone ring, reluctant to answer. It was after midnight, and that landline was designated for Hunt Club business. Hardly anyone ever used it. In fact, no one called that line unless there was serious trouble. So it didn't bode well that the phone was ringing, especially at this hour, especially after the events of yesterday. The locals had insisted on escalating despite the fact that they had no plan. They were disorganized, undisciplined. Unprepared. Emotional. Determined to act on their own. The chief had lost all semblance of control. He'd decided that, under the circumstances, he'd have to resign. He would call another meeting, try one more time to form a cohesive group. And if they refused, he'd quit, absolving himself of any responsibility for what might ensue.

But meantime, the phone was ringing. And he had no doubt that he'd be sorry to hear whatever the caller had to say.

He'd been drinking whiskey by the fireplace, hoping to smooth his jangled nerves. But the phone jangled them again, clanged out a warning: Take cover. Run. Hide. He stared at it, willing it to stop.

It didn't.

Damn. He took a breath. Let it out. Stood up and ambled to the phone, bracing himself.

'Did you hear it?' Hiram's wife, Annie, was on the line.

'Hear what?'

'Another explosion. It's obvious now that we're under attack. We have to do—'

'Annie, dammit, give me the phone,' Hiram barked in the background.

'No, Hiram. I have things to tell him—'

'When did it happen?' The chief's question went unanswered while Annie and Hiram bickered.

'Annie, I need to talk to him—'

'—and information he needs to hear—'

'Annie,' the chief commanded. 'Give Hiram the phone.'

Annie sputtered. 'Fine. But you need to know that all hell's breaking out. Moose says the explosions prove that they're fracking again, but they're doing it at night so no one can stop them. Ax says it's not fracking, not even the gas company – he says it's the government making a move to get us out of here so they can do what they want with the forest.'

Oh great. No facts, just rumors. 'Tell them both to sit on it, will you? Until we find out what's going on? Let me talk to Hiram.'

Hiram came on the line, his voice shaky. He said the explosion had happened a few minutes after twelve. Some of the membership – Ax, Mavis and a few of her women, Moose and Josh – had already gathered at the compound with him and Annie, convinced that whoever was setting off these blasts might blow up the whole forest by morning. The group of them wanted to form search parties and go hunting for the culprits.

The chief closed his eyes, made himself breathe slowly. 'Now hold on, Hiram. Put me on speaker, would you?'

The chief heard Hiram announce that he was on the speakerphone, and everyone began to talk at once.

'Everybody quiet down, I can't hear anyone if you're all jabbering.' He spoke quietly, so they'd have to settle down in order to listen. When they were silent, he began. 'I understand there's been another explosion. Do we know where?'

Voices said, 'No,' and 'Not yet,' and, 'I think out near the old campground.'

'Was anyone hurt?'

Nobody knew.

'How much damage did it do?'

Again, nobody was sure.

'Well, first thing is to keep our heads. I don't know who did this, but I can tell you that it's not fracking—'

'Yeah? How can you be so sure?'

'Think about it, Moose.' He'd recognized Moose's voice. 'They need permits for fracking. And big equipment – nobody's brought in any heavy stuff. Nobody's blocked off sections of the park. So nobody's fracking.'

'No? Then explain what's happening.'

'It's the government.' Ax's voice. 'I'm telling you they want to take the land—'

'Ax, we don't know that yet.' The chief remained patient. 'We can't go jumping to conclusions. What we need to do is cool down.'

'No, what *you* need to do is act like you're our sector chief and stand up to protect this place.'

The chief restrained himself. Ax had a temper; the chief would gain nothing by challenging him. 'I get how frustrated you are, Ax. We all are. But before we go on the warpath, we need to get the facts.' He didn't wait for the grumbles to subside. 'First of all, do you think this was a bigger blast than the one earlier?'

'Sounded about the same,' Hiram said.

Others agreed.

'So these are relatively small, isolated explosions. Timed far apart. Doesn't sound like what the government would do. So first thing we have to do is find out who we're up against. And if they're responsible for the killings or just the explosions—'

'What about that guy who's been testing the water?' Mavis asked. 'He might be part of some environmental terrorist group—'

'Yeah, trying to stir things up,' Annie said. 'You know, drawing attention to the pollution from fracking? Or the risks from the pipeline?'

'Maybe,' the chief said. 'But again, we're jumping to conclusions. We need facts. So let's split into groups and go find the second bomb site. See if anyone's hurt, what evidence there is, what damage has been done. Because count on it: Ranger Daniels is on top of this, and he's got the ATF on its way. We want the upper hand, so let's find out what the hell's going on before they even get into their cars to drive out here.'

The chief arranged for everyone to meet him at the compound. When he hung up, he chugged the rest of his drink, went for his vest and hat, headed for his car. Stopped, went back into his cabin, and got extra clips for his pistol.

Harper heard the boom, sat up, recognizing the sound. She'd heard enough IEDs and bombs, various sizes and types. This one wasn't big. Wasn't far away.

She nudged Hank, but he was sound asleep again. Nudged him again.

'Wha . . .?' He wasn't fully awake.

'Another explosion.'

He turned over, facing her. Listening. Hearing nothing.

'I heard it. Just now. We can't stay here, Hank. We can drive to a motel, but we have to leave. Now.' She shimmied out of the sleeping bag.

Hank grabbed her arm. 'You really want to pack up now, in the dark, and hike back to the campground? You're up for that?'

'As opposed to staying here and getting blown up?'

Hank sat, rubbed his eyes. 'I don't know what you heard, but I doubt anyone is going to blow us up.'

'Hank, I know what I heard—'

'Even so, I'm not up for trekking around the forest in the middle of the night. I think we're better off staying right here.'

She saw his point. Her head hurt where she'd bumped it, and her left leg throbbed. Her entire body ached from walking all day. As much as she wanted to leave and get home to Chloe, she couldn't imagine hiking anywhere right now. Fine, she'd stick it out until morning.

'But Hank, what about that explosion? Somebody's setting off bombs.'

Hank didn't answer.

'We're not safe here.'

'You're sure it was a bomb?'

'Yes.'

'You're positive?'

Really? He didn't believe her? 'You think I dreamed it, don't you? Or that I had another flashback.'

'I didn't say that.'

'But it's what you think.'

Hank took a breath, reached for her hand. 'Harper, I don't want to upset you. But tense situations tend to trigger your flashbacks. This day has been non-stop tense.'

'So what are you saying? That I imagined the explosion?' She pulled her hand away.

Hank reached for it again, grabbed it, held on. 'I'm saying that what you heard seemed real, but might not have been.'

Harper's body stiffened. She'd faced bombs and IEDs and sniper fire, had scars to prove it, and had the sounds, smells and sights of war burned into her brain. But when she said she'd heard an explosion, her own husband doubted her?

Outside the tent, an animal howled. Hank's grip on her hand relaxed. He rubbed his eyes again. 'Sorry. I shouldn't have said anything.'

She didn't answer. She simmered. Earlier, Hank had thought she'd imagined the creature; now he thought she'd imagined a bomb. If he didn't trust her perceptions, what did that say about their marriage? So much for a weekend of togetherness. She wanted to go home. She wanted to hug Chloe. She wanted this weekend to have never happened.

'Look,' Hank said. 'I sounded dismissive. I'm sorry.'

She reached for the flashlight, turned it on. Looked at him. Said nothing.

'I think we're safe until morning, that's all.' He waited for a response.

Harper said nothing.

'Come on, Harper.' He reached for her.

She resisted.

'What can I say? You're mad; I get that. But guess what? It's not easy living with someone with PTSD. How am I supposed to tell whether you're reacting to the moment or to something in your head? I do my best, Harper; I really do. Normally, I take you at your word. But tonight, admit it. You've been kind of bizarre, chasing a hairy monster in the dark, shooting at it. So I've got to wonder, when you say bombs are going off, if they're real or not.'

He reached for her, and she didn't resist. She settled back into the sleeping bag, her head on his chest, her eyes teary. Hank had never before complained about her condition, so she hadn't realized how profoundly it affected him. She lay quietly, hearing his heartbeat, pressing her cheek against his warm skin. And felt as if the war had separated her even from her own husband. As if she were completely alone.

When Harper opened her eyes, Hank was gone. She dragged her aching bones out of the sleeping bag and opened the tent, saw him salvaging what he could from the ravaged bear bag.

'Morning.' He nodded at the camp stove. It was still early – the sun hadn't risen over the trees yet. But he'd already managed to make coffee. 'The eggs got crushed, and the flour got spilled. So no pancakes or omelets today. Want some oatmeal? Or we've got granola bars.'

'Oatmeal sounds perfect.' Harper looked around. Saw the broken tree branch, their surviving supplies laid out on the tarp. Hank had been busy, sorting through the creature's mess.

'It took some weight to break that branch off,' he said. 'And whatever did it must have been pretty tall.'

It had been. Harper said nothing, didn't want to start another conversation about what she'd seen. She just wanted to brush her teeth. Getting a bottle of water, she glanced at the ground. And gasped.

The footprints were gigantic, ape-like, with toes and a thumb. No way had they been made by a bear.

'Hank, look—'

'I know. I saw them.' He faced her. 'I've never seen anything like them. I don't know what could have caused them.'

'I told you what caused them, but you didn't believe me. It was the Bog Man.' She went to him and held on, too alarmed to gloat. She stared at the prints, felt gooseflesh rippling on her neck, her arms. At least she'd been validated. The footprints backed her up. Maybe now, Hank wouldn't doubt her.

'The Bog Man.' Hank released her.

'Yes.' Harper looked into his eyes. 'The Bog Man.'

Hank looked away, went about making oatmeal. Harper said nothing. She got busy preparing to leave. She cleaned up in the creek, changed her clothes, organized her backpack, unzipped and rolled up the sleeping bag and put it beside Hank's soil and water samples. She was about to take the tent down when someone screamed her name.

'Harper! Thank God!' Angela hobbled in from the woods, covered with dirt, carrying a rifle, using a long stick as a cane.

'Angela?' Hank went to help her. 'What happened?'

'Please,' she panted. 'I need to sit.'

Harper unfolded one of their chairs, and Hank guided Angela into it. Her boots were unlaced; she raised the cuff of her khakis to reveal a swollen red and purple ankle.

'I'll get some ice,' Harper said, but Hank stopped her, shaking his head.

'I dumped it all.'

Right. They were leaving.

'Never mind. Ice won't help. I think it's broken. I hopped most of the way here.' Angela leaned back in the chair. 'I thought I'd die alone in our tent.'

Harper stared at the ankle. It looked bad.

'Here, drink this.' Hank gave Angela a bottle of water. 'I'm surprised to see you. I thought you'd left yesterday.'

'I was supposed to.' She winced, repositioning her leg. 'Captain Slader offered me transportation and got me a room in Philipsburg. It was generous of him, but, seriously, I couldn't leave. I just couldn't. Not without my Phil.' She took a long drink of water. 'No, I had to stay there in our tent. It might sound weird, but I felt like Phil was still there with me.'

Harper looked at Hank, recalling the weeks after his accident, when he'd been unconscious, barely alive. She'd spent nights clinging to his pillow, wearing his shirts, curling into his easy chair. His possessions had comforted her, made her feel less lonely, made him seem less gone. She understood why Angela had stayed in the tent.

'I couldn't sleep, though, without Phil. I was dozing,' Angela went on. 'And then, in the middle of the night – did you hear it? That explosion?'

'Yes, we heard it.' Hank glanced at Harper.

'You did? So why are you still here? Because I thought, sweet Jesus, they're bombing the place. I ran for it. Thing is, in my panic, I fell over my own two feet. I twisted my ankle – heard a pop, felt it snap. So I stayed up all night in my tent, swallowing aspirin, hearing strange noises. Waiting for the place to blow. I thought I'd die there.'

Harper made herself sound reassuring. 'That's over, Angela. You're here now. You'll be all right—'

'No, wait. I'm not done. That's not the half of it. So then this morning, I was in pain, but knew I had to get out of there even if I had to crawl. I made my way out of the tent and, guess what? I found out what those strange noises had been. Some animal had been in my campsite and torn it apart.'

'What?' Harper shot a look at Hank. He went back to preparing breakfast.

'I swear. Phil and I had great camping equipment. A stove. Lights. Collapsible furniture. Somebody smashed it all to pieces – so there I was, my poor Phil shot dead like a squirrel and all our things destroyed. And with my ankle, I couldn't even run away. I had to scuttle around on my backside until I got my hands on this big old stick. Then I had to make my way, hopping down the trail with my ankle swollen out of my boot. Thank God you two were here.' She rubbed her face with her muddy hands, smudging dirt across her freckles.

Harper didn't know what to say. She didn't want to tell Angela that their campsite had been destroyed, too. Didn't want to cause more panic. But Angela was looking at her, waiting for a response. 'Hank's making oatmeal,' she offered. 'Have some. You'll feel better.' Really? Angela's husband was dead and she'd broken her ankle. Oatmeal would fix it?

Angela looked over at Hank. 'I'd kill for some coffee.'

Harper went to the stove where a pot of water was boiling. Hank had already prepared mugs of instant coffee and bowls of instant oatmeal. He added dabs of brown sugar.

'I'll go to the ranger's station.' He gave Harper two plastic spoons. Kept one for himself. 'No way she can walk there. And we can't carry her, with all our—'

But Harper interrupted him. 'Didn't you hear what she said?' she whispered. 'The Bog Man tore up her campsite, too.'

'The Bog Man.'

'Yes. He must have gone from one campsite to another—'

'Harper, please don't—'

'It's no coincidence, Hank. He did the same thing to her campsite as he did to ours.'

Hank sighed. 'Let's eat, okay?' He carried coffee and oatmeal to Angela, who rambled on about Phil and Stan, insisting that Stan had killed him. Harper didn't listen. She ate silently, watching Hank wolf his food down, annoyed that even after he'd seen the gigantic footprints and heard about Angela's campsite, he still refused to believe that the Bog Man might be real.

Then again, just the day before, she'd agreed with him. She'd thought the creature was nonsense, too.

As soon as he finished eating, Hank stood. 'If you'll excuse me, ladies, I'll get ready to head out.'

Angela kept talking, but Harper said she had to get the first-aid kit and walked away, following Hank. She wasn't going to let him leave without telling him how upset she was that he didn't believe her. How she knew what she'd seen, how it had been real.

'Hank,' she began, but he leaned into the tent and pulled out the Winchester. He held it out for her. 'Keep this with you.'

Harper took it, relieved, and smiled. 'So you believe me about the creature.'

He hesitated. 'I believe you'll be safer if you have this with you.' He leaned over, kissed her cheek, and turned to put on his vest.

Her smile faded. Hank still didn't believe her. What was she supposed to do to gain credibility? Prove every statement she made? Gather evidence and document everything she wanted to tell him about? She thought back to the wad of fur she'd found. Damn – if Daniels hadn't taken it, she could have shown it to Hank. Maybe that would have convinced him. But no, he'd probably have insisted that the fur had come from a raccoon or bear.

She watched him pack. Two water bottles, snack bars, a knife, a pack of tissues. Damn. He was infuriating. She wanted to scream at him. Throttle him. Shake him until he believed her. Instead, she opened her backpack and took out the first-aid kit.

Hank finished loading his vest pockets, stepped over and kissed her forehead. 'I'll be back as soon as I can.'

She looked up at him, opened her mouth to tell him how she felt. But he was leaving. There wasn't time for a discussion.

'You all right?' he asked.

'Yes. Fine.'

He waved and walked off toward the trail.

Harper watched Hank limp away, his solid frame disappearing among the trees. Her chest tightened, and she had a fierce urge to call out and tell him to come back. Or to run and catch up with him, and go along. But that was ridiculous. He was just going a few miles to the ranger station. He'd be back soon. Then they'd have time to talk. And after the cops and Captain Slader were done with them, they'd leave, as planned. By early evening, they'd be back home with Chloe, and life would go on as if this weekend had never happened.

Harper squared her shoulders and took an ace bandage out of the first-aid kit. Sitting on the ground, she wound it around Angela's swollen, discolored ankle, trying to ignore the nagging tightness in her chest.

Hank hadn't been gone five minutes when Harper heard rustling in the woods. She froze, motioned for Angela to stop talking.

'Why, what's wrong?' Angela wouldn't quiet down. 'Did you hear something? Is someone out there?'

'Shh!' Harper put a hand over Angela's mouth, stifling her.

Angela pushed her hand away. 'What are you doing?' She pouted but didn't say anything else.

The rustling got louder. And more defined. It was definitely footsteps, running over dead leaves, coming closer. Harper picked up the Winchester.

'Who's there?' she yelled, aiming it at the sounds.

'Help – we need help.' It was a man's voice. Unfamiliar. Raw.

'What happened? What kind of help?' Harper didn't lower the gun.

Angela edged off the chair. Using her stick, she hobbled toward a fat tree trunk, taking cover behind it.

'Water?' a different guy called. He sounded breathless. 'Do you have water?'

'Water?' the first one said. 'We need a fucking machine gun.'

'I need water first.'

Harper listened to them, aiming at the sound of their voices, watching the woods. In a moment, two men burst out of the trees, their eyes wild, noses bloodied, gaits wobbly, clothes charred and tattered. They seemed to be unarmed. And they kept looking behind them, as if they were being chased.

'We made it.' One of them lifted a hand, maybe trying to wave. And sunk to the ground in a heap.

'Bob?' the other one yelled, kneeling to help him. 'Bob? Oh Christ.' He looked at the sky in despair, put his hands on his head.

Harper put the gun down and hurried to help, but stopped when she got close, recognizing the smells. Explosives. Fear. She gazed at the two men, the burns on their faces and hands. A skinless raw patch on one's nose, red blank spaces where the other's eyebrows had been.

Oh God. She needed to call for a medic, reached into her pocket for her radio.

'What happened, soldier?' she asked Pete. 'Are there other casualties?'

Bob opened his eyes, recovering, and the two men exchanged glances. 'Not that we know of.'

'What was it? IED? Ambush?'

'Say, what?'

The men whispered to each other, breathlessly watching the trees.

Where was her radio? She felt around inside her pockets. Found a pack of tissues, ibuprofen, a granola bar, a small flashlight, a lemon. A lemon? Harper stopped and looked around. Saw trees, a stack of supplies. Where was her unit?

One of the men was asking for water. Of course. Water. She spun around, went to the supplies, retrieved two water bottles. But she was still holding a lemon. Bite it, she told herself. Bite your lemon. She wasn't sure why, but she popped it into her mouth and chomped down.

The rind was bitter, the juice acidic, intense. Jarring. Harper puckered up, grimacing from the jolt to her senses. She blinked, swallowed. Looked at the two strangers. And, telling Angela to come out of hiding, she scrambled for her first-aid kit.

Angela emerged from behind the tree, wary of the two men. 'What happened to them?' She addressed Harper.

Harper didn't answer. She'd been unbalanced by her flashback, the speed and ease with which she'd been disoriented. The men gulped water. They were jumpy, jerking their heads around, looking over their shoulders. Whispering to each other.

'Was it that explosion?' Angela finally asked them directly. 'From last night?'

They gaped at her, eyes wide.

'Explosion?' one of them asked.

'What's she talking about?' The other one looked blank, blinked rapidly.

Harper crouched beside them. 'How about we start over. Who are you?'

'Okay, I'm Pete O'Neal, and this is Bob Dixon.' Pete held his hand out to shake, then, as if he remembered how burned it was, pulled it back. Bob glared at him, his eyes narrowed. 'What? I just told her—' Pete stopped mid-sentence. Then his mouth opened and he covered it with burned fingers. 'Oh. Right. Sorry, I must be in shock or something. My tongue got tied. Actually I'm Bob Pete. And he's Dixon O'Neal.'

'What? You don't remember your names?' Harper poured bottled water onto some bandages. 'So what happened to you?'

'You mean the burns?' They looked at each other.

'Our campfire,' Bob said. 'It got out of control.'

'We used lighter fluid,' Pete added.

'It got on my clothes, and Pete tried to help me, and we ended up on fire.'

'We had to put ourselves out. Thank God for middle-school fire drills: Stop drop and roll.' Pete tried to smile, but his face hurt. He couldn't stop shaking.

'You know what I think?' Angela eyed them. 'I think they got hurt in that explosion but they don't want to say so.'

Harper wondered. The men were certainly hiding something.

'We have hot oatmeal. You look like you should eat.'

'Thanks, ma'am.' Pete smiled, but Bob interrupted, 'We don't have time. No thanks.'

Bob and Pete leaned their heads together, talking in low, urgent voices. They appeared to be arguing. Harper approached them, reached out to place a damp bandage on Bob's seared nose.

Bob jumped back, slapping her hand away. 'Hey! What are you doing?'

'You should cover those burns—'

'No, we're okay. No time. We have to go back and get our stuff.' Bob tried to get up, teetered. Sat back down.

Pete shook his head. 'Let's just leave it and get the hell out of here.'

Bob set his jaw, enunciating each word. 'We need to get our stuff, Pete.' He tried to stand again. He grabbed onto Pete and pulled himself up, wincing. When he'd balanced, he looked at Harper. 'You should leave, too.'

They should? 'Why?'

'I can't leave,' Angela whined. 'My ankle—'

'Shh,' Harper cut her off. 'Why should we go?'

Bob looked around again, into the trees.

'Tell them,' Pete said.

'They won't believe us.'

'But if we don't tell them, it'll be on us . . .'

Bob nodded. He met Harper's eyes. 'There's something in the woods.'

'A monster,' Pete said. 'We're not lying. Just now, it was chasing us—'

'It was huge. And hairy. Like King Kong. A giant apeman.'

'An apeman?' Angela echoed.

Harper didn't move. 'You saw it?'

'I swear. On my mother's life.'

'Me, too.' Pete blinked rapidly. He was trembling.

So she wasn't crazy. They'd seen the creature, too. It was real.

'It's been tracking us.'

'I think it's hunting us.'

'When did you see it last?' Harper gazed behind them into the woods.

'Just now.' Bob pointed north. 'Like ten minutes before we ran into you.' He held onto Pete's arm, started back toward the trail.

'Bob, for Christ's sake. Why do we have to go back . . .?'

'We can't leave our stuff. Our backpacks. Think, for once. We need to take everything with us.'

Pete closed his mouth, nodded. Gave in.

'Be careful,' Harper said.

'You believe us?' Pete kept blinking. 'I didn't think anyone would.'

'I believe you,' Harper said.

Bob leaned on Pete's shoulder as they started off. 'You two should get the hell out of here,' he said over his shoulder. 'Before that thing finds you.'

They hurried off, half hopping, half tottering to retrieve whatever they'd left behind.

Hopping with her stick, Angela made her way over to Harper and stood, perched on one leg. 'You're not going to leave me here, are you?'

Harper turned to face her. 'No.' She went to get the Winchester, though, just in case.

'Because I don't believe those two for a second. A campfire? Really?' Angela plopped down into the folding chair, extending her injured leg. 'If they got burned by a campfire, I'm Angelina Jolie. No, those two were up to something. Did you see their faces when I asked them about the explosion? How they tried to look all innocent?'

Harper watched the woods for movement, didn't see anything. She couldn't wait to tell Hank about the men, though. Now that other people had seen the Bog Man, maybe he'd believe her. She took the Winchester and sat on a fallen log near Angela, who had resumed her non-stop talking.

'I lived with Stan long enough. I learned how to tell when a man's hiding something,' she said. 'And Bob and Dixon, or whatever their names were, they're hiding something. I wonder what they're really running from.'

'They told us.' Harper checked the rifle, made sure it was loaded. 'They're running from a—'

'Please stop, Harper. That's bull. There's no such thing as a Bog Man. Just like there was no campfire. No. I don't know why they're denying it, but I'd bet my ass those two got burned by that danged explosion.'

The sector chief's landline was ringing again. Another call from the compound. He'd been there most of the night, calming everyone down, organizing them into task groups. He'd finally come home around an hour ago, hadn't slept all night, and here it was, barely six a.m., and someone was calling to report more trouble. He swallowed the last of the whiskey in his glass, watched the phone ring. What if he didn't answer it? What if he just let the Hunt Club do whatever it wanted? Seemed like they were doing that, anyhow. How far would they take things? What would they achieve? He was beginning to doubt himself, his aptitude for leadership. Hell, he was beginning to doubt the whole effort. No way they'd really be able to overcome big corporations like the pipeline or gas company. The government was just a puppet of big money, and, if there was money to be made, they weren't going to let a little local militia stop them from confiscating and destroying God's natural forests.

He sat in his hand-carved chair, watching the still-ringing phone. Finally, with a sigh, he reached out and picked it up.

'I found the bastards.' It was Josh. 'The bombers for sure, maybe the shooter, too.'

'Yeah? Who are they?' The chief sat up, energized.

'Outsiders. They were having a meeting – that guy who's been taking water samples? They were all at his tent, having a meeting. A couple of them were hurt – looked like they got burned – must have bungled the detonation. But it's obvious. We're dealing with a conspiracy. Outsiders who are planning something. More explosions or more shootings. I don't know who they work for, but somebody must have sent them.'

'When was this?' The chief ran a hand through his hair, processing the news.

'Maybe twenty minutes ago. I came straight here to call you, but on the way I ran across the bomber's stash. Guess what was there? Backpacks with a couple of walkie-talkies wired as detonators. Blasting caps. Paraphernalia for setting off explosives.'

Shit. Hot seething rage churned in the chief's belly, rose up through his chest.

'So what do you want me to do?'

The chief needed to steady himself. But there was no time. What he wanted Josh to do was capture the perpetrators and rip their limbs off. But he was a leader, not a thug. He needed to remain calm. 'First, grab their belongings. Take everything.'

'Done. I couldn't carry all of it, so I told Ax and Moose to pick it up.'

'Any identification in it?'

'No.'

No, of course there wasn't. There wouldn't be.

'Okay. Gather up everybody. Let's meet again. The compound in half an hour.'

When he hung up, the chief went to the sink, splashed cold water on his face, ran a razor over his cheeks. Was Josh right about a conspiracy? And if so, who was behind it? He toweled off the extra shaving cream, figuring that whoever was behind the bombings wanted to terrorize the locals and convince them to scatter. Could be the government, the pipeline company, the gas company. They were all the same, really; all trying to take over the land and steal its minerals, and all of them would silence anyone who resisted them.

He peeled off yesterday's shirt, pulled on a fresh one. Replaced his socks. Grabbed his pistol and some ammunition. Headed for the door. The landline rang again. The chief picked it up, saw that caller ID identified the ranger's station.

But it wasn't the ranger who was calling. It was Hiram, using the ranger's phone, and he was whispering, his breath raspy.

'Has Daniels contacted you?' Hiram asked.

'No.'

The chief couldn't hear what Hiram said, had to ask him to repeat himself. When he did, the chief understood why Hiram was keeping his voice so low.

The ATF had arrived, along with state police and the media. They were at the ranger's station, and they were about to enter the woods.

The chief couldn't take a lot of time, needed to rein in the locals and get in touch with Daniels. He scanned the room, estimated forty or so had shown up. And every single one of them was steaming mad.

'Josh says they found the bombers' equipment.' Mavis barged up to him, right as he was about to call for order. 'What are you going to do? I say we find those sons of bitches and string them up, set an example.'

'That would be murder, Mavis.' He pushed her aside, stepped over to the gong. But she wouldn't be dismissed.

'Don't you dare push me. You may be sector chief and you think you're the law, but you're no better than anybody else.'

'Mavis, please. Sorry if I pushed you. I want to start the meeting, that's all.'

Ax was yelling at him, too. In fact, it seemed like everyone was. Angry shouts, bared teeth, fiery eyes all focused on him.

Be calm, he told himself. Set an example. He nodded at Hiram, who sounded the gong. People didn't quiet down, didn't give a damn about the gong.

Hiram hit it again.

The chief raised a hand, refusing to speak until the room quieted down. Gradually, it did, but even then the tension remained, electrifying the air.

He presented the information he had about Josh's findings and Hiram's call. People interrupted, calling out questions. Hiram asked them to wait until he was finished, but they couldn't contain themselves. He recognized their energy, knew that it was valuable, a resource to be channeled. He reminded them that they were stronger united together than alone and apart, that they shared the same goals. That they were fewer in numbers than their opponents, but that they were powerful in their resolve. He heard the timbre of his voice rise and the vibrato of his words; he marveled at the fluid unplanned phrases that flowed from his mouth like a battle flag in the breeze. When he finished his call to action, the members sat silent, moved. Then they stood, clapping and cheering, lining up in front of Hiram to volunteer for the tasks he'd outlined.

The chief's vision blurred. His people were responding. He had united them, motivated them. He was really their leader.

Angela kept going on, insisting that the woods were haunted. 'I can't wait to get out of here,' she said. 'I'll tell you why I couldn't sleep. It wasn't the explosion. Even before that, I could sense evil. Like restless spirits.' She lowered her voice. 'Every time I even started to doze off, I swear I saw Phil. I'm serious. He was there, floating out of the woods all bloody and dead, coming back to me.'

Harper tried not to listen. She packed up the supplies Hank had laid out, filled a bag with everything the creature hadn't destroyed. Hank had already bagged up the rest.

'And now those boys and you all say you saw a monster last night? Obviously, I don't believe that. But the fact that all three of you had the same dream or hallucination or whatever you want to call it—'

Harper stiffened. She was sick of having her perceptions challenged. But she didn't say anything, wasn't going to engage with Angela.

'—it tells you that this place is evil. You can feel it, can't you? It's in the air, all creepy and damp. Like the dark water and chill of the bog. You can actually see it if you look around you.'

Harper didn't want to, but she couldn't help it. She gazed into the woods. The sunbeams seemed exaggerated, off balance. The colors of the leaves were too bright, the shadows of the trees too harsh.

'I don't see anything,' she said. 'You're just tired. You've been through a lot.' Wow. She was doing to Angela what Hank had done to her – dismissing her impressions.

'Hah. You wish you didn't see it, but you do. It's not just me being tired and imagining things. You see it, too. I can tell you know what I'm talking about. This place is tainted, Harper. Or possessed. The air is filled with evil. It didn't used to be this way when Stan and I came up here. Then, it was fresh. Clean. It was our retreat from life. But something's happened. It feels like the forest is alive. Like it's watching us. I can feel it – like there are eyes in the trees.'

'Okay, enough,' Harper snapped. 'One minute you're saying there's no such thing as the Bog Man, then the next you're saying that trees are watching us? Please, Angela. Stop. You're only scaring yourself.' She'd been up all night, thinking about the creature, the explosions and the murders. She didn't need Angela telling her ghost stories. She went to the tent, took out the rods. Collapsed it.

'I'm not making this up, Harper. I swear Phil came back last night. I saw him. And I heard his voice, talking to me in the dark.'

Harper didn't say anything, didn't want to listen. Wasn't interested in what Phil had said. Was sure Angela would tell her anyway.

'He said he didn't understand what had happened, but he knew something was wrong with him. He didn't feel good. He asked me to help him.'

Harper began folding the fabric. She wanted Angela to shut the hell up. She didn't need to hear about a talking murder victim, had her own head full of restless ghosts to manage. Trying to ignore Angela, she focused on going home. On playing with Chloe. Or on riding her Ninja through the hills of Ithaca. But Angela's voice pierced its way into her thoughts.

'It was like he didn't get it that he was dead. I told him, I said, "You're dead, Phil." He couldn't comprehend it. I had to go through it all, explaining that Stan shot him.'

'You can't be sure it was Stan.'

'Oh, yes I am. It wasn't some local survivalist or a random hunter. It was Stan. I promise, Stan would do anything to mess me up. He saw Phil out there near the clearing and took his shot.' She was adamant. 'Hey, Harper. Can you get me more coffee?'

Harper got Angela's cup, refilled it with hot water, stirred in some instant.

Angela sipped, commented that it was bitter. 'No offense, but your husband makes it better. But I need something to warm me.' She looked over her shoulder. 'I can't stop shivering.'

Harper left the tent half folded, unfastened a sleeping bag and wrapped it around Angela's shoulders. The woman was annoying, but she'd just lost her husband and was injured, possibly in shock.

'Hank will be back soon with help,' she assured her. 'They'll get you to a hospital. You're going to be fine.'

'Will you sit with me?'

Of course she would. Harper went to the stove to fix herself a cup of instant, reached for the pot of hot water. When it exploded inches from her hand, she didn't think. She reacted in combat mode, hitting the ground and rolling away, seeking cover, looking around for the Winchester. Angela was screaming, but Harper couldn't help her yet, had to assess the situation. What had made the pot explode? Maybe it was nothing. Maybe the stove had malfunctioned, startling them. But damn, where was the rifle? She lay flat beside a log, peering out over the top. Saw nobody, but found the Winchester beside the tent, ten feet away. Crawling toward it, she glanced at the stove. Saw the pot on the ground, dented. Shimmied ahead, belly to the ground, listening to Angela moan that she'd been right, that the woods were possessed by evil spirits. Harper kept moving; the Winchester was almost within reach.

But she didn't get there. In the same moment, two things happened: Angela stopped shouting, and strong hands took hold of Harper's ankles, hoisting her into the air.

There were four of them. All men, all dressed in flannel shirts, down vests, caps and jeans. And three of them pointed rifles at Harper as she hung upside down.

'Put me down,' she commanded, trying to sound powerful.

The guy holding her was laughing. 'Look. She squirms like a trout,' he said.

Angela was wailing.

'Anybody else here?' One of the men walked toward the stream, searching, aiming his rifle into the trees.

'Don't see anyone.'

'Where are the others?' The question came from Harper's ankles.

'Put me down,' she demanded. Blood was rushing to her head.

She swung her arms, pounding her fists against his legs. He jiggled her.

'Tell me where your friends are.'

'What friends?'

He started twirling, letting Harper fly around him like a tetherball on a string. She sped, the ground racing under her – blurred fallen leaves, the edge of their tarp. The other men's shoes. The man holding her was laughing.

'Ax, enough. Put her down,' someone said.

'Hell, no. This is fun.' He whooped.

'I said, enough.'

When he set her down, the world kept spinning. Harper seethed, trying to get her balance back. Trying to locate the Winchester. Had they found it? Could she get to it? Who were these men? She needed to take them down.

'What do you want?' Angela's voice had risen an octave. 'We're just weekenders. We haven't done anything. Don't hurt us . . .' She was yammering.

'Shut up. You're worse than my old lady.' One of the men aimed a rifle at her face.

'I'll ask you again.' The one they'd called Ax stooped beside Harper. 'Where are your friends?'

'What friends?' Harper glowered.

'Her husband's gone to get help,' Angela blurted. 'I think I broke my ankle. Getting out of my tent.' She went on, telling them about hearing the explosion, running in the dark.

Harper's vision was stabilizing. One by one, she checked the men out. The oldest was maybe fifty. Kind of stout. She could take him, no problem. But Ax and the two others were built like lumberjacks. Fit, big, muscled. Ruddy. No way she could neutralize all of them.

Ax stood. 'When did your husband leave?'

Harper didn't answer, but Angela couldn't stop talking. 'About a half hour ago.'

'Where'd he go? The ranger's station?'

Angela nodded. 'Please. Don't hurt us. I just lost my husband.' She went on, explaining about Phil.

The men paid no attention. One of them waved his rifle at Hank's soil and water samples. 'What are those?'

'Nothing,' Harper said.

'Really. They look like scientific samples to me. What do you think, Moose?'

'That's what I think. What do you think, Ax?'

'They are samples,' Harper said. 'My husband's a geology professor. He takes samples wherever we go.'

'Did you hear that, Hiram? Her husband's a geology professor. He tests soil and water wherever they go.'

'Course he does,' the fourth guy said. 'And I just rode in on the hay wagon.'

'Oh God,' Angela whimpered.

The men huddled for a moment. Then the older man approached Harper. 'I'll ask you again: Where are the others?'

'She told you where my husband is. There are no others.'

'Look, we aren't messing around. We know you met here this morning with at least two men besides your husband—'

'Oh!' Angela cried out. 'He means those guys with the campfire.'

Harper winced at Angela, signaling her to be quiet. Not to give out information without knowing how it would be used.

'What campfire?' Ax crouched close to Harper, crowding her. He smelled like dogs and burning leaves.

'I don't know . . .' she began.

'They said their campfire got out of control. That's how they got burned,' Angela volunteered.

Harper turned, shot her a fierce look. Angela didn't seem to notice.

'They were burned?' One of the men turned to the older guy. 'Hiram, you roger that?'

'I do, Moose,' Ax said. 'Campfire's bogus. Those are the bomb guys.'

Hiram nodded. 'Unless they were just a couple of campers, unlucky enough to be too close to the site.'

'Bullshit.' The guy called Moose spat on the ground.

'So where are they?' Ax put his face up against Harper's. His breath was like stale tobacco.

'No idea,' Harper said. 'I don't even know their names.'

'Yes, you do,' Angela said. 'Remember? They got their names wrong the first time? But then they said their names were Bob and Dixon. They were going to get their stuff and leave.'

Ax smiled. Looked like a snake. He backed away from Harper, standing. 'So what do you want to do?' he asked the others.

'We're wasting time,' Moose said. 'We should move.'

'I agree,' Hiram said. 'We should get back.'

Harper turned her head slowly, looking for the Winchester. Edged toward it.

'Fine.' Ax stood. 'We can talk more later.'

Moose was the largest. He grunted as he picked Angela up and, ignoring her protests, flung her over his shoulder like a sack of barley. He was off balance. She slipped off; her head slammed onto a boulder with a thunk. Angela made no sound, though, not even a yelp.

'Angela?' Harper started to go to her, but Ax shook his head no.

'Don't even move,' he said.

'Bitch is fucking heavy,' Moose complained, hefting her up again.

'Angela, are you all right?' Harper called again.

Angela said nothing. Her arms dangled and her body swayed limply as Moose carried her into the woods. Harper watched, inching closer to her rifle, moving her hand slowly, holding her body perfectly still until her fingers made contact with metal. She pulled at it, dragging it closer.

A shot rang out, and Ax stood above her. 'What are you, crazy? You want to get killed? Look around you. There's four of us, and my breakfast was bigger than you are.' He kicked the Winchester away. 'Get up. Let's go.'

'What do you want? Money? I don't have any cash, but my—'

'We don't want your frickin' money. Move.'

Fear rippled along Harper's neck, down her back. If they didn't want money, what did they want? If they were just locals, members of the Hunt Club, why would they kidnap them? She kept her head down, looked from side to side, considered bolting into the woods, running a zigzag to avoid their shots.

Two rifles were aimed at her – Ax's and the fourth man's. Harper simmered, assessing her chances. Between the two of them, one would probably shoot her before she could make it to the trees. Maybe she could kick one of their rifles away, simultaneously diving for the other. But then what? They'd recover and outnumber her, outweighing her by a good three hundred pounds. Even if she darted away, they'd likely get the best of her. And before they did, Hiram might shoot her. So she didn't run, didn't kick or dive at anyone. Nostrils flaring, she met the eyes of each gunman before she stood. Then, at gunpoint, she let them lead her away.

* * *

Bob let go of Pete's arm and stared at their empty tarp. 'Fucking shit,' he said.

Pete rushed ahead, picking up their blanket, shaking it out. 'Where's our stuff?' He turned in a circle, examining the ground.

'Fucking shit,' Bob said again.

Pete blinked rapidly, stared into the trees. 'It's all gone.'

'Shit.' Bob limped over to Pete. His burns hurt, but he was getting used to the pain. 'Everything? They took everything?'

Pete shook the blanket again. 'This is it.'

'So wait. We have to think. What did they get? What was in the backpacks? Two detonators, blasting caps, wiring—'

'The weed,' Pete wailed. 'Fuckers took our weed.' He tossed the blanket on the ground.

'Forget your frickin' weed, asshole,' Bob snapped. 'Think. Is there any way they can figure out whose stuff it was?'

'Why? Wait – you think it was the cops? You think they'll look for like DNA and stuff? You think they're coming after us?'

Bob turned away, stared at his burned hands, then at air. This was bad. If the cops or the ATF had their stuff, then they were screwed. They'd left their fingerprints all over everything – the caps, the walkie-talkies. Everything. Hell, they'd planned to blow all of it up, so fingerprints wouldn't have mattered. And he'd had that DUI. It was supposed to have been expunged. So his fingerprints wouldn't still be in the police files, would they? But oh God, what about the walkie-talkies? Could they figure out where they'd bought them? Had they left anything else? Damn – the ham sandwiches from the snack bar. That waitress would remember them, would identify Pete as the guy who ordered them to go.

They were so fucked. Especially when the cops saw their burns.

Unless it wasn't the cops who'd taken their stuff. Maybe it was hunters. Or hikers. Or that creepy monster.

Somewhere close, a shot rang out. Bob wheeled around, looked at Pete, who was gaping at him, doing that blinking thing again.

'It's just hunters,' Bob said.

'Bullshit. That shot came from where we just were. Those women's camp.' Pete began walking in a circle, tramping on the tarp.

'You don't know that.'

'I do, and so do you.'

'No. It came from that direction, but you don't know where. For all you know, that little blonde chick just shot a pheasant.'

'Stuff it, Bob. This is bad.' Pete kept blinking, pacing. 'It might not be the cops who took our stuff. It could be the guy who shot those men. And he could be back there, shooting at those women.'

'Will you stop the fuck doing that eye thing?'

'Seriously?' Pete stomped over to Bob. He lowered his voice, held his head close. 'This place is fucking crazy. First, King Kong's chasing us. Now somebody steals our stuff – maybe the ATF, maybe some psycho lunatic. Either way—'

'We got to move.' Bob finished the sentence and grabbed Pete's arm. Together, Bob leaning on Pete for support, they backtracked through the woods, staying off the main trail.

As they approached the campsite where the women had been, Bob put a hand up, gesturing for Pete to stop. 'Shh,' he whispered, nodding to the left.

Pete hunkered down, followed Bob's gaze. A large man strode up the trail, carrying the woman with the broken ankle over his shoulder. The blonde trailed behind him, followed by three men with rifles.

'Shit,' Bob whispered. 'They've got our stuff.'

It was true. Their backpacks dangled from the shoulders of two of the men.

'Who are they?'

'Looks like locals.'

'Locals? But why? What are they gonna do to them?' Pete's eyelids fluttered at record speed.

'How should I know?'

They crouched low, watching the group pass. Then they looked at each other.

'Those women were decent to us,' Pete said. 'The little one tried to bandage us up. She offered us oatmeal.'

Bob nodded, wincing at the pain in his leg. 'Those guys stole our stuff.'

For a moment they were quiet, thinking.

'We got to make a choice here, Pete. We came here at our own risk to do something for the sake of the future and the environment. We decided to risk our lives to do what was right. Now, we have another decision to make.'

Pete closed his eyes to stop his blinking.

'Those bastards took our stuff. I say we go get it back.' Bob stood, squaring his jaw. 'You in?'

Pete sighed, accepting the inevitable. 'We don't have a plan.'

'Sometimes you got to wing it.'

Pete nodded. Bob was right. How could they turn their backs on a kidnapping? The little blonde woman had believed what they'd said about the ape monster. Had offered them breakfast. Pete held his arm out to help Bob, and the two of them turned around. Heading away from the Impala and their own safe escape, they followed Harper, Angela and the group of armed Hunt Club members into the depths of the woods.

Harper dawdled, limping, feigning leg pain. When Ax prodded her with his rifle, she explained that she had a war injury. Told him that she couldn't go any faster. She hung back while Moose, the big guy carrying Angela, moved ahead and out of sight. She lagged, pacing herself slowly, staying close to the campsite. Hiram and the fourth man passed her, leaving her behind with Ax. Harper limped, walking slowly, planning. Once the others were far enough ahead, she'd fake a stumble. She'd go down onto her knees, and when Ax came close to see if she was hurt, she'd come up fast, knocking his rifle away, butting his jaw with her skull, punching his gut, grabbing his gun. He'd be too stunned and winded to call his buddies, and before he could recover, she'd have the rifle aimed at his chest.

Of course, she couldn't be positive about her moves. She'd have to act and react, think in the moment. All she needed was enough distance between them and the two guys ahead of them. She slowed her pace, exaggerating her limp.

'Maybe I should carry you.' Ax nudged her. 'Hang you over my shoulder the way Moose's carrying your friend. You don't weigh but a hundred pounds.'

'Don't touch me.' As she spoke, she gave herself the go-ahead and stumbled, just as she'd planned. She landed on her knees, ready to pounce. But instead of coming to help her, Ax took a step back, watching her from a safe distance.

'You sure you don't want me to carry you? Because that sure was clumsy.'

She stood, brushed herself off. Kept walking. Hiram wandered back to join Ax. Harper tried to make another plan, but damn. Even if she could manage to take down one of them, she wouldn't be able to take them both. She needed a new approach. If she couldn't escape, then she'd need to make sure she was found. Which meant she needed to leave a trail.

Harper reached into her vest pockets, felt around. Found a wad of tissues, a Smokey the Bear pin. A bottle of ibuprofen. A lemon. A half-drunk water bottle. A half-eaten granola bar. A mini-flashlight. Band-Aids. Packets of wipes. A bottle opener, matches. A tube of bug repellent. She thought of the gear she'd carried in Iraq, how heavy it had been, weighing her down with ammo, weapons, helmet, water – no. Stop. She couldn't think about Iraq now. She needed to focus. She kept her hands in her pockets and worked her fingers, tearing the tissues into bits. Casually, she took a hand out, pretending to rub her back. And, while Ax was distracted, talking to Hiram, she dropped a small white swatch. She kept walking, bracing herself for a reaction. But there was none. Ax and Hiram were engrossed in their conversation.

Harper dropped another piece. And, a few steps later, another. Damn. They weren't heavy enough to drop straight down. They floated, drifting through the air to the side of the path. One landed out of sight, behind a cluster of undergrowth. Okay. No problem. She clumped a few pieces together, making them into a ball. And, when she was sure Ax and Hiram weren't paying attention, she dropped it.

She left the first several tissue balls only a few steps apart to make it clear that they weren't just litter, that they'd been left on purpose. Hank would find them, would show them to the ranger. And the police captain. And maybe the FBI or the ATF or whoever. But it would be Hank who would find them, who would know she'd left a trail. Who would follow it and find her. And take her home.

Oh God. Home. Chloe. Her bones ached, missing her.

No. She couldn't think of Chloe, couldn't be distracted by emotions. She had to leave another clue. She dropped another tiny ball. Eyed the rifle aimed at her. Wished she could throttle Ax and Hiram, the whole bunch of them.

'But it's not up to him,' Ax was saying. 'It's up to the group. Majority rules.'

'The chief has to have his say, too,' Hiram added.

'Fuck the chief. He's a passive wimp.'

'He's got a tough job, trying to keep the peace.'

'The peace? We're not about keeping peace. We're about striking fear. And expelling interlopers. And retaking our God-given land.'

He went on. Harper limped along, digging her heels into the

ground where she could, leaving as many signs as she could. When she ran out of tissues, she dropped the Smokey the Bear pin, then the matchbook. Then her whistle. Pieces of the granola wrapper. Band-Aids. When all of that was gone, she left ibuprofen pills, hoping that the birds wouldn't mistake them for seeds and scoop them up. And that squirrels wouldn't take the tissues to pad their nests. By the time they got to the barbed wire fence, she worried that, by the time Hank got back and realized she was gone, most of her trail would be gone, stolen by wildlife.

Moose waited at the chain-link fence, Angela hanging over his shoulder. Hiram unlocked a gate near the KEEP OUT sign, stopped at a ramshackle shed to drop off the backpacks, then proceeded to a nearby mound of dirt and rocks. A heap of firewood concealed a steel door built into one side of the mound. Hiram unlocked this, too, and they entered, descending a flight of stairs into an underground compound. The stairway opened to a rec room or lounge, lit with bare bulbs, furnished with worn sofas and chairs. About half a dozen people were gathered around a bar against one wall. One of them was talking on a telephone – a landline.

Harper looked around, tried to memorize details: A big bronze gong at the far end of the room. A big-screen television. Guns and rifles – dozens of them – mounted on a wall. Heads – several foxes, a bear, a buck hung over the bar.

Ax nudged her. 'Stop gawking. Move.'

A guy yelled from the bar. 'Who've you got now?'

'We'll be right there.' Hiram waved at him, telling him to wait.

'Heard from the chief yet?' some other guy asked.

'Just hang on, would you?' Ax barked. 'Let us dump them first.'

Dump them? Harper scowled. What kind of people were these, unalarmed, not even blinking when their friends came in with two kidnapped women? Who would sit at the bar, casually chatting with pals, watching captives being held at gunpoint? Her jaw tightened, but she had no choice. She followed Moose, watching Angela's limp arms, wondering how bad her head injury was. Finally, at the far end of the room, Moose stopped. Hiram knelt in front of him, lifted a chunk of linoleum from the floor, and opened a trap door hidden underneath. Ax grabbed a ladder from some hooks on the wall, and he and Hiram lowered it into the opening. Moose stepped forward, started to climb down with Angela.

'Hey, Moose,' somebody called. 'What are you carrying? You bag a sow?'

A sow?

People laughed. Started making pig calls. 'Suuweee!'

Really? Harper couldn't help it. She spun around, ready to dash across the room and knock out some teeth.

'Damn it.' Ax shoved her. 'Move!'

She heard him, but didn't move. Didn't go knock out teeth, either. Harper stood immobile, gaping. Trying to understand what she was seeing, why the people at the bar were laughing.

'What's so funny?' Moose climbed back up a step and looked around.

Ax chuckled. 'Nothing. Just Josh.'

Harper blinked to make the image go away. She dug her nails into her palms, causing pain to ground her in the moment and end what had to be a hallucination. But nothing helped. The Bog Man wouldn't disappear. He was there. In the room. Huge and hairy, and as real as the rifle poking her ribs.

Probably he'd come in behind them. But how? And why wasn't anyone frightened? At the bar, the guy was still on the phone. The others continued their conversations while the creature, too tall for the low ceiling, walked bent over to a sofa, took a seat.

Up ahead, on Moose's shoulder, Angela was regaining consciousness. She began arching her back, twisting her body, making breathless, hoarse panting sounds. She squirmed, pushing at Moose's butt, trying to get free. Finally, Hiram scolded him, 'Stop dawdling, would you? Hurry up and get down the ladder.'

Ax jabbed Harper with his rifle. She was aware of his voice, but not of what he said. She didn't move. Couldn't accept what she was seeing.

The Bog Man turned to one of the women at the bar. 'Hey, Mavis? Got any coffee?'

Harper's knees caved. Oh God. The thing could talk.

It wanted coffee.

Harper swayed unsteadily, watching one of the women fetch a mug and pour coffee. When she brought it to the Bog Man, he lifted his paws to his face and pulled off his head.

Harper closed her eyes and cursed. Damn. Of course. How stupid was she? She'd been fooled by some guy wearing a Yeti costume? She looked again. The guy's hair was mussed, but he was handsome.

Dark. Strong cheekbones. A mustache. Probably about thirty. She recalled her terror at seeing the creature in the woods. How had she been so easily bamboozled, so naive? She wanted to talk to the guy, to examine his disguise. The fur looked real. And the body had a not-quite-apelike, not-actually-human skeletal structure and skull. But how was he so tall? Was he wearing stilts? How could he run, or even bend his knees?

Ax pushed her again. 'Look here.' He was chuckling, using his rifle as a pointer. 'This one's white as a sheet. Looks like she's gonna faint.' He pushed her toward the trap door.

'Keep moving.' Hiram frowned.

She started down the ladder, but slowly, carefully. When she looked back at the Bog Man, not just his head, but both paws were off. She saw a long-legged guy in a fur suit, holding a mug of coffee in very human hands.

Bob and Pete kept their distance from the guys abducting the women. They walked a parallel path, off the main trail, far enough that they could turn and high-tail it away if they were seen. When they got to the chain-link fence, though, they had to stop and think.

'I don't know,' Pete said. 'We're outnumbered. Maybe we should go get the cops.'

'The cops.' Bob sat beside a tree, resting his leg. 'And what do you think will happen when the cops see our burns?'

'We can call them. On the phone. Nobody'd have to see us.'

'Great. Except we don't have phones. Besides, what happens when they come out here and find our stuff?'

'We don't know for sure that our stuff is here.'

'You're right. It probably just got up and walked back to the Impala.'

Pete's eyes blinked rapidly. 'So? Even if the cops find our stuff, they can't trace it back to us. I think we're okay—'

'Our fingerprints are all over everything.'

'So?'

'So I had a DUI, remember?'

'So wasn't that expunged?'

'My fingerprints might still be in the fucking system. It's not a risk I want to take.' Bob was fuming. 'Anyway, we have to go look for our stuff. Give me your sweatshirt.' Bob took his fleece off, grimacing as he aggravated his burned hands. He covered the barbed wire with the jacket, took Pete's sweatshirt and padded a few more sections. 'Okay.' He stretched his arms. 'Give me a boost.'

Pete stooped so Bob could stand on his shoulders, nearly screamed when Bob's boot scraped a singed patch on his neck. Nearly caved under Bob's weight. But he didn't, and with some effort, Bob made it over the fence, rolling onto the ground without a scratch.

Pete didn't have the benefit of a boost. He had to climb the fence, finding footholds in chain link, avoiding barbs. He slipped, tearing his jersey on the barbs, began climbing again. Slipped again, grimacing as his raw flesh hit the ground.

'Fuck, Bob. I can't do this.'

'Hold on.' Bob lay low on the ground, thinking. Saw the KEEP OUT sign. Maybe Pete could take that off the fence, prop it against the wire and step onto it, leveraging himself to get height.

Pete tried. He tugged at the sign until the boards came loose. It was a flat panel, but backed by two by fours. He leaned it against the fence, put his left toes on top of the sign and leaped upward, grabbing Bob's fleece, vaulting over the barbed wire. Almost making it. Tumbling back down.

On the fourth try, he cleared the top of the fence, but his left leg dragged, scraping the barbs. Sharp metal ripped through the fabric of his pants, tearing at his flesh. Pete yelped as he fell to the ground beside Bob. He lay moaning, his burns raging, his leg bleeding.

'Shh!' Bob lay on his stomach. 'Quiet.'

Pete managed to be silent, but his body screamed.

'You okay?' Bob leaned over, looking at his leg. 'Shit. It's just a scratch. Your pants are trashed, though.' He got up, retrieved the sweatshirt and fleece. 'Let's go.'

'Can't,' Pete breathed. He sat up, saw red trickling down his calf.

'Dammit.' Bob looked him over, sighed, gazed at the burns on his hands. 'Okay, sit. Pull up your shirt.' He tore strips off Pete's jersey, tied them around the cut on Pete's leg. 'It's nothing,' he said. 'Not deep. Just a scratch.' He looked at Pete. 'Ready?'

Pete's body reverberated from the shock of landing on hard earth. He was burned, cut, chilly and ragged. But he pulled himself to his feet and together, holding the fleece and the sweatshirt, they ambled ahead, noting a tall mound of dirt and rock ahead. And, to its right, a ramshackle shed.

* * *

When Angela regained consciousness, she was different. Out of touch. Disoriented. She talked to shadows. She often made no sense.

Harper helped Angela settle onto one of three cots that lined the walls of the bunker, examined the bloody bump on her head, realized she could do nothing for it, and tugged her boots off. Angela's ankle resembled a purple inflated balloon.

'Stretch out here,' Harper told her. 'Elevate your ankle.'

Angela didn't resist. But she didn't answer, either. Her eyes swam, watery and unfocused. Maybe she had a concussion. Maybe worse – a fractured skull? Internal bleeding? Harper had no idea. She touched Angela's forehead; it felt warm, inflamed. Angela rambled, talking about – or maybe to – Phil.

Harper sat on another of the cots under the cell's one dim light bulb, assuring herself that Angela would be all right. That they both would. That she'd find a way for them to escape. That help would arrive. But her mind was reeling. She needed to slow down, collect her thoughts, orient herself. Make a plan. She took a deep breath, closed her eyes. Saw the Bog Man pulling off his mask. Damn.

Angela moaned, uttered unintelligible syllables involving Phil. Probably she missed him, couldn't accept that her husband was gone. Harper couldn't imagine it. She thought of Hank, felt a pang. Bit her lip. No, she wouldn't think of Hank. Or of Chloe. She needed to focus.

Okay. Focus. She sat straight, surveying her surroundings. They were underground, locked in a dank concrete room that looked like a bomb shelter. It had three cots, one blanket and a portable toilet. There was a trapdoor in the ceiling, an air vent over one of the cots, a steel door in one of the walls. She got up, tried to open it, but it was locked.

Angela wailed. Her eyes were closed. 'Phil?' she asked.

Harper went to her, took her hand to reassure her. Did some addition, estimated that they were at least twenty feet underground. She studied the trapdoor, the vent, the walls. Felt buried. Her chest tightened. Oh God. She and Angela were stuck in a hidden tomb, a windowless, lightless chamber under a concealed trapdoor that no one might ever find.

Calm down, she told herself. Surely, Hiram and his friends would release them. Why wouldn't they? What could they achieve by keeping them prisoner? Nothing. Unless they were taking hostages. But why would they do that? She had to stop thinking the worst, had to remain positive. Hiram and the others wouldn't leave them there indefinitely.

Harper shivered. Watched the walls. If not indefinitely, how long would they leave them there? Why had they kidnapped them in the first place?

Angela sprawled on the cot, mumbling Phil's name. Saying something about his shooting.

'Angela.' Harper held onto her hand but Angela seemed not to notice her. She gave Angela's shoulder a gentle shake.

Angela looked at her vaguely. Stopped talking.

'Angela, listen. We're going to be all right. We'll get out of here. My husband will come for us. I left a trail—'

Angela's gaze drifted away, and she began mumbling again. Telling Phil something or other.

'Angela? Listen. Can you understand what I'm saying?' Harper tried again, but when Angela didn't respond, she gave up. She was talking mostly for her own sake, anyway. Giving herself a pep talk, reminding herself to stay hopeful. After all, it wouldn't be long until help arrived. Hank would find her trail. He'd follow it with Ranger Daniels and Captain Slader and the state cops. He'd rescue her and Angela, and take them home.

Unless the squirrels had grabbed the tissues for their nests and falling leaves had covered the ibuprofen capsules . . .

'Stan!' Angela yelled. Her eyes opened wide, and closed again.

Harper leaned back against the concrete, trying to remain calm. Think, she told herself.

Fine, so what was she supposed to think about? She chewed her lip and thought back, replaying events. Piecing them together. Tried to figure out why she and Angela had been kidnapped – and why that guy had been running through the woods dressed like the Bog Man. Wait – were these the people who'd shot Phil and that guy from the gas company? Had they set off the explosions? Harper stood, ran a hand through her hair. Nothing made sense. What could they hope to accomplish with all that violence?

Harper sat again, leaned back against the hard cold wall. She closed her eyes, saw Chloe's smile. Felt a welling of tears. Tightened her body, refusing them. Things were not dire. Hank would come for them, was probably on his way. Would appear any moment. Meantime, she had to stay strong.

She sat still, watching Angela.

'Angela?' she tried one more time. 'Angela, are you awake? Because we have to talk about what we're going to do.'

'Phil?' Angela asked. Then, breathlessly but clearly, she said, 'Go away. You're dead.'

Angela was delirious. Harper sat back, looked at the ceiling, the steel door, the blank concrete walls. Whatever was happening, she'd have to face it on her own. Her hand slipped into her vest pocket, felt around, and grabbed onto her lemon.

The sector chief had shut off his radio to quiet the endlessly blurting messages. He sat at the counter of the snack bar, drinking coffee and contemplating the torrent of events that were careening toward him, a tsunami rising up overhead, ready to strike havoc. His people had no idea how to deal with the forces amassing around them. They were out of control, delusional, believing they could win out against the gas company, let alone the government. He chewed a jelly donut, acting casual, taking in the scene.

And it was exactly that: a scene. The campground had become a circus of outsiders. ATF agents were there to look into the bombings. State cops to assist in the shooting investigations. Pipeline people and gas company representatives to assess damage and find the perpetrators. TV reporters to question everyone and record everything. And a small horde of campers and hunters to find out what in God's name was going on.

Same as he was.

Ranger Daniels was in the middle of it all. The cops pressed him to take them to the crime scenes and interview witnesses; the ATF and pipeline people wanted to go to the explosion sites. Reporters kept firing questions.

'One thing at a time,' Daniels bellowed. 'We'll get everything done, but only if you'll all quiet down and let me bring you up to speed. I've been up all night, so I don't have much patience. Bear with me.'

There were grumbles and mutterings, but everyone settled down. Penny, the waitress, was sweet on Daniels but flirted with everyone. She flashed a pink-lipped smile at the sector chief as she wandered around with a coffee pot, refilling cups.

'First, I'll address the explosions.' Daniels pointed to a map on an easel. 'Most importantly, no visible damage has been done to people, property or the pipeline. The first explosion occurred here, on the grounds of the old Hunting Lodge. It blew up septic tanks and a few trees. The second was here, right along the pipeline. It blew away the ground cover, exposing the pipeline, but it wasn't strong enough to do anything else. Mostly, it made a big old hole in the ground.'

A news reporter called out, 'So, no casualties?'

'None that we know of.'

Someone started to ask something else, but the ranger raised his hands, cutting him off. 'Hold your questions, please.'

More muttering.

The sector chief counted heads. Four ATF agents. Two state cops. Six media people. Five gas and pipeline officials. Including the police captain and the ranger, that made nineteen, not counting all the campers, hunters and hikers. Like it or not, Black Moshannon was in the spotlight. Unless he put the reins on hard and fast, his people wouldn't get rid of outsiders; they'd do the opposite, attracting even more attention.

'As to the two shooting victims.'

'Do you think Al Rogers was shot by the bombers?' A man from the pipeline company interrupted. 'Because it doesn't seem coincidental that a pipeline walker was shot the same day someone set a bomb off along his pipeline route.'

'If you don't mind,' Daniels began, 'Captain Slader and I will get to that.'

'And where's his partner? Jim Kinsella?' the man went on. 'We haven't been able to contact him. He doesn't answer his radio.'

'Maybe he got hurt in that second blast,' an agent said.

'Or maybe he's the one who set it off,' a reporter suggested.

The sector chief rubbed his eyes. He hadn't slept in over twenty-four hours. He needed to check in, update his people, find out what they were up to. Make sure they'd lie low until the ATF and cops left.

Daniels was calling for order. Telling everybody that there was no reason to believe that Kinsella was involved. That, in fact, Kinsella had been extremely upset by his partner's death and was eager to help Captain Slader with the investigation. He nodded to the captain.

Slader didn't want any part of this circus. Didn't want the state cops looking over his shoulder or the media misquoting him. But thanks to Daniels, everyone was looking at him, waiting for him to say something. He stood. 'Jim Kinsella hasn't been in touch since yesterday, but I'm sure we'll locate him after the meeting.'

'What about the second shooting?' a female news reporter asked. 'Was it related to the first?'

Damn. Now that he'd stood, everyone wanted to talk to him. 'It doesn't appear to be related. At this moment, it seems to be the result of a dispute between ex-spouses. We've taken a person of interest into Philipsburg for questioning.'

'Name?' the woman persisted.

'I'm not ready to release his name,' Slader said. 'He's not officially a suspect. But I can tell you that he had motive and opportunity.'

'Any chance either shooting was accidental?' a male reporter asked. 'A hunter mistaking someone for a deer?'

'Nothing has been ruled out.'

'Was the same type of ammunition used in both shootings?'

'Were the bodies found close together?'

'Did the victims know each other?'

Slader raised his hands, warding off the questions. 'We'll have statements for the press after we have a chance to investigate.' He turned toward Daniels, silently urging him to take over. Daniels watched him but didn't respond. 'Ranger Daniels.' The captain felt his face getting red. 'I think you can carry on now.'

'We'd like to get to the sites now,' an ATF agent said. The agents stood, ready for Daniels to escort them. The gas and pipeline officials stood as well. The media teams gathered their equipment, ready to follow.

'Fine. We'll head out. Meantime, Captain Slader will take the state police to the scene of the shootings.'

Damn. Slader was trapped. Had no choice. He finished his coffee and was about to start for the door when the door burst open and someone dashed in, calling for the ranger, asking for help. Too many people were standing in the way; the chief couldn't hear the guy clearly, couldn't see who it was.

But moments later, Daniels and the state cops came over to the counter, joining him. 'This is interesting,' he said. 'Angela Russo is the shooting victim's widow.'

'So?' Slader's shoulders tensed.

'She fell. Broke her ankle. So here again, I have another emergency and no staff to help me. All hell's breaking loose, and there's no one but me to deal with any of it. Now, on top of everything else, I've got a rescue operation. If I call an ambulance, it'll take hours.'

Slader sighed, had no choice. 'So what do you need?'

Daniels turned to the state cops. 'I figure you guys can help out, too. You're going to want to talk to her anyway, so how about you help us go transport her out of there, and then you can interview her while you drive her to the hospital?'

Slader bristled. Daniels had no business telling these guys they could interview his witness without him. But then it occurred to him that they were a godsend. If he let them take over the investigation, he'd be free to deal with other matters.

'Sounds good.' He stood tall and spoke with authority, reminding everyone who was in charge. 'And then we can meet in Philipsburg later. You can help me question the suspect.'

The sergeant crossed his arms, stuck his chin out. 'Fine.'

'So you've decided he's officially a suspect?' the corporal said.

'Sorry. I should have said "person of interest",' Slader corrected himself. He looked across the snack bar at the outsiders preparing to swarm the woods. The Hunt Club members weren't going to be happy. He reached into his pocket, left a dollar bill for Penny. Then he excused himself. 'Before we head out, I need to use the landline,' he explained.

He made his way through the outsiders and dashed to the ranger's office. As he made the call, his fingers were unsteady. And as he left a voice mail, he had the sickening sense that the locals had lost control, and that his message might be too late.

Without a window or a watch, Harper had no way to measure time. Had they been there an hour? Three? More? She wasn't sure. She alternated between staring at the trapdoor above and the steel door along the wall. Sometimes, she heard noises – voices filtering down from above. Or thumping from the other side of the door. She called out, asked if someone was there, but got no reply. She tried not to think of Chloe or Hank. Tried to focus on escape. Maybe she could take one of the cots apart, use the metal legs to . . . to what? Break through a steel door? Climb through underground concrete walls?

Harper closed her eyes, told herself there had to be a way out. She had survived much worse. Besides, Hank would come. In fact, he should be arriving any minute. Was it afternoon yet? How much daylight was left? Because, if he didn't find the trail before dark, he'd have to wait until morning. Damn, maybe it was already after dark. Maybe it was already morning. She had no idea.

No, she couldn't have been there that long. Probably it had just been a few hours. Her stomach was empty, though, so they must have been there a while. Oh God. She shivered. The room was damp and cold, and she'd covered Angela with the only blanket. Angela had quieted a while ago, seemed to be dozing. Harper leaned back, closed her eyes. Saw Chloe, her shining curls – no.

She stood up, started walking in a circle, swinging her arms. Getting her blood circulating. Keeping ready. On her twenty-third lap, the ceiling rattled and creaked.

The trapdoor opened, and slowly, the ladder came down. Hiram leaned over, peered down. 'You down there – keep away from the ladder,' he barked. Then he told someone it was okay to go down, but to yell if there was a problem.

A woman climbed down. She was middle-aged, wearing jeans and a sweater, her face weathered, her hair in a ponytail. Hiram lowered a shopping bag to her.

'Stay where you are.' She eyed Harper as she set the bag down, took a key from her pocket, and unlocked the steel door. 'Chow time.' She took a Styrofoam container from the bag, opened the door and took it into an adjoining chamber.

Harper stepped closer to the door, trying to see into the next room. Who was in there?

'Keep your stinkin' food,' a man grumbled.

'Suit yourself.' The woman backed up, started to close the door again.

Harper couldn't see the prisoner, but her adrenalin pumped and her muscles tensed.

'Wait – no. Please. Don't shut the door. Let me out of here.'

'Can't do that.' The woman stepped out, closed the door, ready to lock it. But before she could, Harper bolted at her, knocking her to the ground. Holding her down, telling her not to make a sound.

'Annie?' Hiram called. 'Everything okay?'

'Tell him, "Yes,"' Harper whispered, tightened her grip on the woman's hair.

'Yes,' she croaked. 'Fine.'

'Help us get out of here,' Harper breathed into her ear.

'There's no way. You'll never get past everyone upstairs.'

'Maybe we can. We have a hostage now.'

'Me?' The woman's eyebrows raised. 'You don't want to keep me down here. I'm the only one who gives a hoot about you. You hurt me, you'll be dead within a minute. Face it, you're outnumbered.'

'Annie?' Hiram called. 'Where the hell are you?'

Behind her, Harper heard the steel door open. 'Let her go,' the guy said. 'In a second, they'll be down here shooting.'

Harper looked up, recognized the pipeline walker. The dead guy's partner.

'Hurry up.' He pulled at her. 'Get off her.'

Harper glanced at the ladder, then back at the woman.

'He's right,' Annie said. 'Ax and some of the others will be happy for an excuse to kill you.'

Harper took a breath, released the woman's hair, then stood. The woman hopped to her feet, brushed herself off. Pocketed the key.

'Moose and I are coming down,' Hiram yelled.

Annie ran to the ladder, began climbing. 'I'm on my way. No need.'

'What took you so long?'

'That one woman.' Annie reached the top, and Hiram pulled the ladder up through the hatch. 'She's not doing so hot. I think she needs a doctor.'

'Fuck that,' Hiram said. He went on, but the door slammed shut, and Harper couldn't hear what else he said.

Jim Kinsella's eyes were bloodshot and his hands unsteady. Harper made him sit down.

'Did it take you, too?' he asked. 'The Bog Man?'

The Bog Man? 'No. It's not real . . .' Harper began.

Jim was on his feet. 'Oh yes it is. It brought me here. Dragged me.'

Harper shook her head. 'No, Jim. He's upstairs. I saw him myself. It's a guy in a monkey suit.'

Jim bent over, leaned into her face. 'I don't care what you say; I know what I know. It spotted me this morning and stalked me like a hunter. It must have hit me with something and knocked me out because when I came to, it was dragging me across a field to some locals, who brought me down here. So don't tell me the Bog Man isn't real. It's real. And the local people? They know all about him. In fact, they're working with him.'

Harper didn't disagree, didn't want to antagonize him by arguing. Jim was agitated, angry. He smelled of fear and sweat; his body was bruised and his clothing torn. She nodded, tried to calm him. 'I believe you. In fact, I saw him, too. Last night. In the woods.'

'You saw him?' Jim stood up, staring at her, breathing fast. 'So how can you say he isn't real?'

'Because I saw him upstairs before, taking off his costume. He's just a guy.'

'No. He's huge, too big to be a man. Too strong.'

'Look, I was fooled, too. I figure he's got artificial limbs or some kind of prosthetics to extend his legs.'

'No, that's crazy.' Jim ran a hand over his head, turned in a circle. 'Christ. What the hell is this? Why did they bring us here? What are they planning to do with us?'

Harper didn't know, didn't answer. She opened the bag that Annie had left them. Took out a bottle of water, handed it to Jim. 'Drink.'

He looked at the bottle, then at her. Finally, he took it. Drank. Eyed Angela. 'What's with her?'

'She's in and out. Head injury.' Harper tried to sound unconcerned. To create some sense of normal. She took out Styrofoam cartons, plastic spoons. 'Looks like chili.' She took a bite, mostly to help Jim focus on something besides their predicament. 'Not bad.'

'You're eating?'

'I'm hungry.' She wasn't, really. Her stomach was empty, but she had no appetite. Even so, she forced another bite. 'We need to keep up our strength.'

'So the Bog Man. You really think it's fake?'

'I didn't when I saw it in the woods. But now I know better.' She motioned for him to sit down. When he did, she offered him one of the chili cartons. 'He vandalized our campsite. Not only ours – and I'm not the only one who saw him. A couple of guys camping near us did, too.'

'So is that what happened to her?' He looked at Angela. 'The Bog Man?'

'No, no. She fell, running away from the explosion and broke her ankle. One of the locals dropped her on her head while they were taking us here. But the Bog Man? He's really just one of the locals. He was upstairs, drinking coffee. But it's no wonder we thought he was real. His fur and head – even in daylight, everything looks real.'

'You're saying the Bog Man is part of the Hunt Club.'

'Yes. He's just a guy.'

Jim didn't move.

Harper met his eyes. 'Look, he fooled me, too. When I saw him in the woods, I was so scared, I couldn't move.'

'Phil?' Angela stirred. 'Is that you? Are you here?'

'It's me, Angela,' Harper said. 'Harper Jennings. Try to rest.'

'I told you,' Angela muttered. 'A hundred times.' She lay back, mumbling something unintelligible. It sounded like 'fracking war.' Or possibly 'frickin' worm.'

Harper lowered her voice. 'She's delirious. Phil's her husband. He was killed yesterday morning, same as your friend. She keeps talking to him.'

'Shit.' Jim leaned back against the wall, pressed his hands against his temples. 'That other guy was her husband? Damn. So that explains it. These people holding us – they've got to be the ones who shot my partner Al and her husband – what's his name? Phil? And if that's the case then guess what – they're going to kill us, too.'

'Wait, slow down.' Harper put a hand up. 'You don't know that.'

'I get it about Al.' Jim stood, began pacing. 'They killed him because he worked for the pipeline – people around here hate us. They've torn up our campsites, messed up our equipment. They blame the pipeline for all their problems – if not the pipeline, then the gas company and the frackers. So I get why they'd mess with me and Al. But why would they kill this woman's husband? He had nothing to do with any of their issues. And why have some guy march around in a Bog Man suit, attacking and terrorizing campers? Why kidnap someone like you? What do they want? It's like the whole lot of them are declaring war on everyone who's set foot in these woods. And that's serious. Because these people have a militia. And the shootings make it clear they don't mind bloodshed.'

Harper thought of Ax, his cold eyes following her along the trail. She had no doubt that he'd been willing to shoot her.

'So we have a big problem.' Jim stopped pacing and faced her. 'I'm thinking there are two reasons they're keeping us. One, to hold us hostage as bargaining chips. Two, to use us as part of their scare tactics. Either way, the outcome's the same.'

'What do you mean?'

Jim's eye twitched. 'Don't you get it? It's obvious: We're dead.'

Harper put aside her carton of chili. She put her hand on Jim's arm, gently tugged on it, guiding him to sit down. 'No.' She met his eyes. 'We're not dead. Not even close.' She lowered her voice as if someone might hear. 'My husband is coming.'

He looked at her. 'What?'

'I left a trail. He'll find us. He'll bring the police.'

'You left a trail?' Jim repeated.

Harper nodded, smiled. 'Have some chili. You'll need your strength.'

'When's he coming?'

Harper started to say that she wasn't sure, but that it would be soon. But Angela sat up suddenly, looked into the air, and spoke clearly. 'Go to hell. All of you.' She lay back down, moaning. 'Stan,' she groaned. 'Stan.'

Harper opened a bottle of water, brought it to Angela, and lifted her head, trying to get her to drink. Angela slapped it away, refusing it. 'Phil? Stop – what are you doing?'

'It's not Phil. It's Harper.'

'No.' She squirmed, grimaced. 'No, go away.'

'Angela, take a drink,' Harper said. 'It's water.'

'Stop it, Phil.' Angela swung her arms, batting the bottle away. 'I said, go away. Don't touch me!'

Harper watched Angela, tried to make sense of what she was saying. She didn't sound very fond of Phil, telling him not to touch her. Was it possible that Angela had shot him? After all, she was an experienced hunter, could have easily picked him off. But why? What would be her motive? Besides, Angela's rifle hadn't held the kind of ammunition that had killed Phil; it hadn't even been recently fired. Stan's rifle had been fired, had the right ammo. More than likely, he'd been the shooter and Angela's ramblings meant nothing.

Harper retrieved the water bottle while Jim took napkins from the chili bag, began wiping up the spill. Above them, furniture scraped the floor. Harper looked at the ceiling, listening to the commotion. The Hunt Club must be holding a meeting. Jim stopped mopping and, eyes popping, pointed upstairs.

'Your husband better get here soon.' Jim stood up, holding the napkins. 'You hear them? They're up there gathering their forces. Getting ready.'

Footsteps pounded on the ceiling. Oh God. Maybe Jim was right. Maybe neither Stan nor Angela had shot Phil. And maybe Phil and

Al had been the first casualties of a violent uprising by the Hunt Club.

'Stan?' Angela shrieked. 'Is that you? Stan?' She looked directly at Jim. 'Who the hell are you? Did he send you? Go away. Go away!'

Jim introduced himself, said that he was also a prisoner. But Angela didn't seem to hear. She rambled, unsettled and restless, seemingly in a world of her own. It took Jim and Harper both to get her to drink a little water. She resisted, but with some effort, Jim got her to swallow some ibuprofen, too. He and Harper agreed that ibuprofen might not be the right medicine for whatever was ailing Angela, but it was all they had. And while it might not help her, it certainly wouldn't hurt.

Approaching the shed, Pete could see that it wasn't even locked. Its door was open a crack. All they had to do was look inside. If their stuff was in there, they could grab it and go.

Even so, Pete was uneasy. He and Bob were exposed. Between the fence and the shed was an open field. There were no trees to hide behind, no place to take cover. He half expected the guys with the guns to pop out of nowhere and start shooting at them.

But nowhere was exactly where they'd have to come from. Because those four guys and the women they'd abducted had simply disappeared. Where the hell had they gone? What had they done with the women? Pete had seen them pass through a gate at the fence. But after he and Bob made their way over it, they'd found no sign of anyone.

'Hurry up,' Bob whispered. 'We're trespassing.'

No kidding.

'They find us, we're dead.'

Pete didn't answer. He hadn't wanted to cross the fence in the first place. His body was wracked with burns and scrapes; he wasn't the one whose fingerprints were in the system. All he wanted to do was get back to the Impala and high-tail it home. But no. Bob had to have things his way. Always.

'Where'd they go, anyhow?' Bob looked back at the fence. 'They just dropped out of sight.'

'I know. I don't like it.'

Bob stopped. 'Hold on.' He looked at the shed. 'You think they're in there?'

Was he kidding? The shed wouldn't hold six people. Unless they were all standing up, pressed like sardines.

'Let's just get this done and go,' Pete suggested. 'They're not in there.'

'So where the fuck did they go? Are they watching us? We're like sitting ducks.'

Now? Bob was finally considering that they were completely exposed and utterly defenseless? Pete had the urge to dump Bob and run. He'd have trouble getting over the fence, but without Bob hanging onto him, he'd be able to move a lot faster. He pictured running back to the campground, getting into the Impala, flooring the gas – but damn. Bob had the keys.

'Fuck it,' Bob said. 'We're here. So let's do it. It's too late to turn back.'

They continued toward the shed, quickly, quietly. Pete didn't say anything, but he felt like telling Bob to go fuck himself. Bob was always bossing him around. Who'd put Bob in charge? When had he become a five-star general?

'You're doing it again.' Bob let go of Pete's arm. 'Will you stop your damned blinking?'

'Yes, Your Fucking Highness.' Pete faked a bow.

They were at the shed door. Pete looked around to make sure no one was watching as Bob pulled it open. Their backpacks were right inside, zipped up tight.

And behind the backpacks were other interesting items. Rifles. Boxes of ammunition. Shelves and shadowy forms.

'Check this out.' Bob stepped into the darkness. 'Jesus, I think it's a rocket launcher.'

Pete squinted, saw a mini refrigerator. Did they keep food here?

'Shhh.' Bob held up his hand.

There were voices outside. Distant, but coming closer.

'Shit.' Pete peeked out. Saw a half dozen people coming from the gate, heading toward them.

'Get away from the door.' Bob yanked him inside. He reached around for a rifle, handed it to Pete. Took one for himself.

'They're not loaded,' Pete whispered.

'They won't know that.'

They stood silently, waiting to be discovered. Listening as the people passed by. Hearing only snippets.

'. . . Josh had the right idea, taking that guy.'

'. . . make example . . . all out war . . .'

'. . . we're taking heat for those bombs anyhow.'

Bob and Pete held their breath, clutching unloaded rifles. But the people didn't stop at the hut. They walked past it, and then, abruptly, their voices disappeared.

'Take a peek,' Bob whispered. 'Where are they?'

Slowly, Pete put his eye to the crack at the door. No one was outside.

He opened the door another inch, saw open space between the shed and the mound of rocks and dirt. No people.

They'd simply disappeared. He stuck his head out a little further. No one was there. Just that mound. Which was a pretty odd formation. Wasn't natural. Someone had constructed it. Maybe to camouflage an entrance? But an entrance to what? Obviously something underground. Like a secret compound? Really? What the fuck was going on?

He turned to ask Bob what he thought, but stopped. More voices. Another gaggle of people coming toward them. Five of them, all women. He stood away from the door, clutching his rifle. The shed was tiny, the walls close. Pete closed his eyes, feeling trapped. Listening to Bob breathe.

When the women had passed, Pete picked up his backpack, opened the door a little for light. He was going to unzip it and look inside, make sure their stuff was all still there.

'What are you doing?' Bob pushed the door shut. 'They'll see you.'

'No one's out there. We need to grab our stuff and go.'

'Are you crazy? What should we say when we walk into the next bunch who comes in the gate? Obviously, they're having some kind of meeting out here.'

'But where? Are they going underground?' Pete pushed the door again, just a little, letting in some light. He noticed a light switch on the wall. The hut had electricity, a mini fridge. He was about to flip the switch on, see if the lights worked, when Bob shoved the door closed again.

Pete gritted his teeth, pushed it open.

'Dammit, Pete. Close it, the way it was.'

Okay. Enough. Pete was done. 'Fuck you, Bob. I'm out of here.' Pete opened the door and, ignoring Bob's frantic whispers, started out of the shed. Two guys walked toward him, deep in conversation.

Not looking his way. He darted back into the shed, not daring to close the door.

He stood in the shadows, waiting for them to pass, watching the ground outside the door. Not paying attention to indentations or markings, staring at them without seeing them.

Only after the men had passed and he was slumping on the floor to rest did the markings take on definition. Pete realized what he'd been looking at.

'I told you to stay in here. What the fuck's wrong with you?' Bob scolded. 'You'll get us killed.'

Wordlessly, Pete grabbed Bob's shoulder and pointed outside.

'What?' Bob resisted. Until he looked down and saw the ground.

The footprints were unmistakable. More than twice the size of a human's. How had they not noticed them when they'd approached the shed? But there they were, clearly defined, pressed into the dirt.

The monster they'd seen in the night had been here. Might still be nearby. Might even be kept here by the locals – that would explain the barbed wire fence. Bob and Pete might have walked right into its lair.

'Shit.' Bob sank to the floor, leaning against the wall. 'Shit shit shit.'

Pete sat beside him. His whole body hurt. He didn't give a damn about destroying the fossil fuel companies or blowing up the pipeline or becoming famous or changing the world. All he wanted to do was go home.

A parade left the snack bar, two by two. Ranger Daniels led ATF agents, state cops, gas company and pipeline people. Media. Hank and Captain Slader. Daniels carried a folded stretcher.

As they passed, Sylvie ran up to the news anchor. 'Did you read my report?'

The woman didn't stop, seemed not to recognize her.

'I gave it to you yesterday, remember? All about the Bog Man?'

The newswoman's photographer answered her. 'Of course. Thank you. It's great. We'll be in touch.'

Sylvie walked along with them, not giving up. 'Be careful out there. Don't underestimate him. He's unpredictable. They're saying another man's missing. Seems like the Bog Man's taken another one.'

Another reporter overheard. 'The Bog Man?' he asked. 'Who's that?'

The first newswoman winked at her photographer, nodded at Sylvie. 'This woman has all the details,' she told the reporter. 'We talked to her yesterday, got all the background. You might want to spend some time with her and catch up.'

Sylvie latched onto the new reporter, telling him about the Bog Man. She was still talking when the group reached the end of the campground parking lot where the trails into the woods began.

Daniels divided the group up, sending the ATF, pipeline and gas company people toward the blast sites. He was taking the state cops, the captain and Hank to the spots where the bodies had been found, right near Hank's campsite.

They set off, the captain following along, hearing Daniels complain about having to send the ATF and pipeline investigators off on their own. About how short-staffed he was. About the lack of control he had over what went on in the park. About his need to do four jobs because of budget cuts.

'Tell you what,' he said to anyone listening. 'Half the trouble we're having now wouldn't have happened if I'd had rangers out there patrolling the woods. We wouldn't be talking about bombers and explosions, that's for sure.'

Slader didn't comment. Daniels was a whiner, as far as he was concerned, grumbling about how impossible his job was. How he had two deaths and two explosions to deal with, plus an injured woman. How he had to deal with the local population, too, and assure them that they and their properties adjacent to the park were safe. How was he to do it all? Daniels didn't stop, just went on like a little girl. Slader wanted to deck him. He had his own problems, and nobody heard him bellyaching, did they?

At one point, Hank approached him. 'Captain, with everything that's happened, my wife and I want to get home. As soon as Ms Russo's ankle is attended to, we'd like to finish giving our statements and take off. This afternoon, if possible.'

The captain couldn't care less what Hank and his wife would like. But he didn't want to get into a discussion, so he simply said he'd do what he could. As Hank hurried ahead, Slader lagged behind, watching and listening. Assessing the state cops, wondering if they'd heard what Hank had said. What they'd thought about his request. Both walked in silence, not revealing anything. Not making small talk. They were strictly business, which might mean they'd be eager to push him aside and take over the investigation.

Slader hoped so. Maybe he could slip away right after he briefed them.

Up ahead, Hank picked up his pace. 'Harper?' He ran up the trail. 'We're back. Ready to go?'

Seconds later, Slader followed the others into the campsite. Saw Hank standing next to a half-folded tent, shouting Harper's name.

He got no answer.

The captain looked around. Saw the tent flattened on the ground. A half-empty pot of oatmeal congealing on the stove. An open first-aid kit on the ground near a log. A bunch of scientific stuff – looked like soil and water samples – along with water bottles, canned soup and other supplies spread out on a tarp beside the tent. And a Winchester lying in a clump of weeds.

What he didn't see seemed more significant. He didn't see Harper Jennings or Angela Russo with a broken ankle.

He didn't see anybody at all.

Dammit. Slader clenched his jaw. He had a pretty good idea what had happened. Fucking Josh had happened. Of all the locals, Josh was the biggest worry. He'd taken it upon himself to start trouble, and now he'd gone and collected more outsiders. It had been bad enough that he'd messed with the guys from the pipeline. But now he was taking weekenders? The captain could only imagine the women's reactions, screaming in terror as a Sasquatch came galumphing into the campsite, believing that he was real. Because, honestly, the first time he'd seen that get-up, even he'd been convinced. Real bear fur. Custom-made prosthetic limb extensions that allowed for balance and flexibility.

But forget Josh's ape suit – the man had become a liability. This time, state cops were involved – state cops who knew that two women were missing, who would call in reinforcements, who would instigate an all-out search and bring in the FBI. Christ, the situation was worse than he'd feared, and evolving too fast. Spiraling. He'd hoped to rein everyone in at the meeting, organize modest symbolic efforts, synchronize events, but, because of Josh, it could be too late. Slader crossed his arms, leaned against a tree. Josh was an idiot, overstepping his authority, unable to foresee the consequence of his actions. And he'd probably gotten the locals prematurely into an all-out war.

The state cops began to question Hank. 'When did you last see your wife?' the sergeant asked. 'Where exactly was she? How did she seem when you left?'

The corporal stooped beside a rock. 'Sergeant?' he called. 'You need to see this.'

Slader went over, too. Looked at the rock. Saw blood on it. A significant amount of blood. He watched the sergeant study the thing. Watched him look, narrow his eyes and squint at Hank. Slader knew the look. Knew what the sergeant would be thinking. Having seen blood, the sergeant would no longer trust Hank. In fact, might doubt Hank's whole story.

Hank didn't seem to notice what the cops were doing. No longer yelling for Harper, he was kneeling near the tent, examining the ground.

'Look here,' he called the others over. 'See? I found four or five distinct shoe prints.' He pointed them out, one by one, moving across the campsite, pointing out impressions on the ground. 'And look, a bunch of them – at least three – go off this way down the trail.'

The state cops exchanged glances. The captain watched, knowing that they didn't buy a word Hank was saying. They figured he'd planted the tracks, and they were going to let him keep going just to see where he'd lead them. Probably to his wife's body.

Slader didn't think the cops were right, but he also had doubts about his own theory. The campsite was orderly with the tent laid out, supplies neatly arranged. If Josh had been there, all that would have been trashed. Besides that, Josh's outfit was bulky. He'd have had trouble taking two people at once – especially when one of them had a Winchester around. Most confusing, though, were the footprints. Josh always acted alone, deliberately leaving one clear gigantic set of Bog Man prints. But, if this site had been trampled by several pairs of normal-sized feet, then – damn. What had happened? The captain's stomach wrenched, insisting that he might not want to know.

Daniels' radio squawked. Slader overheard Penny from the snack bar say that some hunters had come in, complaining that their campsites had been vandalized overnight. They'd found big footprints, and one guy swore he'd seen a huge Big Foot creature.

Daniels signed off and scratched his head. He stepped over to the captain. 'This weekend gets weirder and weirder.'

Slader nodded. Waited a beat. 'I'll take off in a few and deal with the hunters. You and the state guys can manage this.'

'Feeling all right?' Daniels asked him. 'You've been quiet.'

'I'm okay,' he said. 'Just don't like all the excitement. Cops, ATF. Media. I'm thinking the locals are going to get stirred up.'

'I hope not.'

'You never know with those Hunt Club people. They're at their limit with outsiders.'

'Well, they better get used to them.' Daniels looked back at the state cops. 'There's going to be a lot more outsiders around, at least for a while. Seems we got two women missing.'

Slader nodded toward Hank. 'Think he killed her?'

Daniels started to say no, but hesitated, eyeing Hank. 'Yesterday, I would have said no and sworn by it,' he said. 'But today? Christ, I have no idea. Nothing surprises me any more.'

According to the sun, it was mid-afternoon. Bob and Pete hid in the shed, beginning to understand that they'd be unable to get out of the place before nightfall. They'd stopped talking about the monster and its footprints. What was the point? Maybe it lived there, maybe it didn't. Maybe it had just been passing through. Maybe the reason the local people were gathering was to decide how to get rid of it, like the villagers in the Frankenstein movies. But the monster didn't matter; what mattered was how Pete and Bob were going to get out of there.

Pete had no ideas. The walls were too close, the space too dark. He couldn't get comfortable, couldn't sit, couldn't stand. Couldn't stay still. Fidgeting, he peered out the narrow slit between the door and the wall, aching for open space and sky. Watching slices of the two big lugs holding rifles, standing by the fence. Those guys had been there a while, unlocking the gate when people showed up. Standing there, never moving. Why couldn't they take a break just for a few minutes? Pete stood, shifted from leg to leg, felt like a prisoner.

Bob sat on the floor, sorting through the treasures stored inside the shed. 'Can you stop?'

'Stop what?'

'Singing opera. What do you think I mean? Stop jumping around.'

'I got to get out of here, Bob.'

Bob looked up at him. 'You'll be all right.'

'No, you don't get it. I've got to get—'

'What you've got to do is calm down. Because you'll fucking get us shot if you don't.'

Pete took a breath. Shook his arms, his hands. Ouch, mistake. Even moving through air hurt his fingers. They were tender, raw in spots. He closed his eyes. 'I'll be okay.'

Bob didn't seem convinced. If his burns bothered him, he didn't let on. 'I wish we could smoke. You need to mellow out.'

It was true. Some dope would really help. Pete was jittery. Claustrophobic. Armed guards were outside. And at least one hairy monster. 'What are those guys doing out there?' he asked. 'They've been there for at least an hour. Just standing there with their rifles.'

'They're guards. They're on watch.'

On watch for what? The monster? Or maybe they were like cops at a roadblock, watching for fugitives. 'Shit – you think they saw the sign? The one we took down and I used it to climb up on? Maybe they noticed it and they're looking for us.'

Bob made a tsking sound. 'Pete, think for a second. Why would they be looking for us at the gate?'

'They found our stuff and brought it here. Maybe they figured out we'd come looking for it.'

Bob didn't answer. He'd crawled to the corner of the shack, opened the mini fridge. A light came on inside it. 'Guess what – the electricity works.' He let out a gasp. 'Shit, what is all this stuff?'

Canisters were lined up inside. Who knew what was in them. Bob reached inside, took a gray wad off a rack. 'This looks . . . oh man. It looks serious.' He held it out to Pete.

Pete took it, held it in the slat of daylight. It was a gray clump, harmless looking, like molding clay. He swallowed, stared at it. Fought the urge to drop it and run.

'You thinking what I'm thinking?' Bob said.

'C fucking four?' Pete's voice cracked. 'Jesus.' C4 was powerful. The military used it. He handed it back to Bob. Gently. 'Who are these motherfuckers? What are they doing with explosives?'

Bob reached for his backpack. 'Maybe same as us. Putting an end to fucking fracking and gas pipelines.'

Pete leaned against the door frame while Bob took a quick inventory. A rocket launcher. Rifles. Military-style ammunition boxes. C4. And who were these people? Nobody. Hicks who lived out in the country. Thieves who'd stolen his and Bob's meager supplies when they didn't even need them. Damn. With their fancy arsenal, these guys would have no trouble taking out the gas pipeline. They'd be the ones to get all the fame and credit for standing up to the polluters and profit-mongers – even though he and Bob had planned it and tried it first – twice.

'Hungry?' Bob had emptied their backpacks onto the floor. The ham sandwiches sat beside their leftover blasting caps.

'Why'd you empty our bags? What are you doing?'

'Tit for tat.' Bob reached into the mini-fridge, grabbed a canister of something liquid. Stuck it into his backpack.

'Wait, what is that?'

'Not sure. But it's something these guys think is worth cold storage.' He reached for a wad of C4, stuffed it in beside the canister.

Cold dread wrapped around Pete's stomach. 'Bob, maybe we shouldn't mess with that stuff—'

'Bullshit. Serves them right.' He sounded cheerful, almost giddy.

'But what if the stuff in those containers is nitro?' Pete had done research. 'That stuff has to be kept cold. It explodes real easy if it gets above fifty degrees.'

'I'm being gentle.' He put in a second canister.

'Look. We came here to get our stuff back. Let's just take it—'

'Oh, we're taking it. With a penalty fine for stealing from us.' Bob grinned, his teeth shining in the dim light. 'Those fuckers are going to think twice before they rip anybody off again.' His bag was loaded. He zipped it up.

'Just be careful. Don't bump it.'

Pete didn't want to get blown up again. But maybe the stuff wasn't nitroglycerin. And once it got dark, maybe they could have another go at the pipeline, beat these guys to it. Maybe. But dark seemed a long time away, and he didn't know how he could stay cooped up until then. His body itched to move. His burns were raw. And the shed was suffocating. Craving air, he pressed his head to the narrow opening at the door and peered out.

The two guys had walked to the gate, rifles strapped to their shoulders. As Pete watched, they unlocked the fence for a wiry guy with bushy eyebrows. He dashed past them, a radio pressed to his ear, and sped past the shed over to the mound of dirt, barking into the mouthpiece, 'Wait. Not yet. I'm here. I'll be right there, tell them—'

Then, as soon as he disappeared behind the mound, there was silence. The guy was gone.

Pete turned back into the shed. The walls leaned in, moving closer. He looked outside again, down at the footprints of the monster.

'Think we're dead?' he asked.

'What?'

'I'm just saying. Maybe we got killed in the explosion.'

'Don't be a fucking asshole.' Bob dropped the blasting caps back into Pete's bag.

'I'm not kidding. Something's off. Like we're in some alternate reality.'

'What the fuck's wrong with you?'

'Think about it. A big tall hairy monster? Things like that don't exist in the real world. And people disappearing into a pile of dirt? It's not natural.'

'Stop doing that eye blink thing. Nobody's disappearing. There's got to be an opening back there. Get the fuck out of your psycho head. I mean it. Eat a sandwich.'

Pete leaned back, didn't point out that Bob hadn't explained the monster. He eyed the ceiling. It inched lower, teasing. He could almost hear it laughing.

Dead or not dead, something was seriously wrong about this place. He needed to get out of there, and soon.

'Soon as it's dark,' Bob answered his thoughts. 'We'll get the hell out of here. And this time, we're going to blow that sucker to fucking hell.' He reached for a sandwich, unwrapped it, and took a bite. With his mouth full, he grinned at Pete. 'Cheer up. When we're done, maybe we can go back to the snack bar. You can try your luck with that girl.'

Pete didn't answer. He was busy, caught up in a staring contest with a wall.

Captain Slader checked his watch. It was already after two; he needed to get to the Hunt Club compound. Everyone would be gathered there, simmering, ready to boil over. The locals weren't good at waiting. Didn't like to follow rules. Each one of them was a hothead, ready to pop, and collectively they were a rumbling volcano. He needed to get there, calm them down. Remind them that people were like sticks, much stronger bound together than acting on their own. Yes, he'd use that analogy again to contain them. And he'd put the kibosh on Josh. Whether or not he'd taken those women, what had he been thinking during the night, destroying campsites, stirring up hunters? Damned fool needed to lie low and leave his Yeti costume in mothballs for a while. When would the locals learn? That costume wouldn't scare people away; it would rouse curiosity and attract weirdos from all over the world who'd swarm the woods, searching for the creature. No, he had to get over there and talk sense.

But first, he had to get away from the state cops. The two of them stood on each side of Hank as if he were already their prisoner. Poor guy still didn't have a clue that they suspected him of anything. For the second time, he led them around the campsite, showing the oatmeal he'd fixed for breakfast, the dishes and spoons not cleaned up.

'Look.' His voice was urgent. 'It's obvious they left in a hurry. Their coffee mugs are right where they left them – and the camp stove was left on. Harper would never have gone anywhere with the stove still on.'

'So maybe someone took her by surprise?' the sergeant suggested. He was playing dumb. Playing with Hank.

'Exactly – that's what it looks like.' Hank went on, showing them that the tent was only half folded, as if she'd stopped in the middle. The cops stood with their arms folded across their chests, legs apart, unimpressed.

'So? Why are we standing here?' Hank's eyes were scalding. 'Someone's kidnapped my wife and Angela Russo.' He followed the footprints that led away from the camp. 'The tracks show that they went this way. I'm going to look for them.' He turned to the cops. 'You guys coming?'

The state cops didn't move. They stood like statues, arms folded, legs apart. 'Not quite yet, Mr Jennings,' the sergeant said. 'How about we talk a minute.'

'What?'

'Just for a minute.'

'Are you kidding?'

'No, sir. We need some background information.'

'Bullshit.' Hank turned back to Daniels. 'Ranger, can we please go look for my wife?'

Daniels opened his mouth, didn't have a chance to answer. The sergeant moved in, crowding Hank, raising his chin. 'Mr Jennings, tell us about your marriage.'

'Tell you about – seriously?' Hank sputtered. 'I'll tell you anything you want after we find Harper—'

'How have you and your wife been getting along?'

'Fine. Perfect.' Hank looked from one cop to the other. 'Look, I love my wife. My wife loves me. Okay? Now, let's go see where these footprints lead.'

The corporal blocked his way.

'What brought you to Black Moshannon this weekend?'

'Oh my God.'

'Mr Jennings?'

Hank turned to Slader. The captain felt sorry for him, but he wasn't getting involved. Was curious to hear the answers.

'We came for a weekend getaway. To spend time together.'

'What's all that stuff?' The cop pointed to Hank's soil and water samples, the geological testing materials that he'd laid out near the tent. 'What are those?'

'Nothing. Samples. I'm a geologist. I was testing—'

'I thought you said you came for a getaway.'

'We did.'

'But yet, you were working?'

'So?'

'So it seems like you're not being entirely honest with us, Mr Jennings.'

'What?'

Silence. The cops stared at Hank, and he glared back. A stand-off.

The captain checked his watch again. Two-thirty. Damn. He had to go. 'I'm off,' he said to Daniels.

But at that moment, Hank said, 'You guys can dick around all you want. I'm going to go look for my wife.' He turned around and started up the trail.

The corporal put his hand on his gun. 'Stop right there! Hold it!'

Daniels opened his mouth but made no sound, and Slader eyed the cops. They stood red-faced. Hank looked over his shoulder once, but continued on his way.

Slader's blood pressure surged. These cops were idiots.

Daniels urged the cops to go with Hank and see where the trail led. 'What's the harm?'

'Thank you for your opinion, Ranger Daniels.' The sergeant looked Daniels up and down, then faced the captain. 'What do you think?'

What Slader thought was that the sergeant was an asshole. But he shrugged. 'Your call.'

'Okay then.' The sergeant eyed Daniels. 'Why don't we all take a walk? What's the harm?'

'You guys go.' Slader backed away. 'I need to go deal with those hunters—'

'Hey, Sergeant?' Hank's shout cut him off. 'Come take a look – I found something!'

The cops glanced at each other, then the sergeant gestured to Daniels and Slader, indicating that they should lead the way.

The captain hesitated, but couldn't think of an excuse big enough to justify leaving so abruptly. He couldn't very well say that he had to get to the Hunt Club. But if he didn't get there soon, who knew what the locals would do? They had a mob mentality and an arsenal of weaponry. If one drew blood, the rest would, too, like a pack of maddened hounds. Slader had to get to them and provide a voice of authority. But the sergeant was waiting for him to walk up the trail. Okay. He'd spare ten minutes. No more. After that, no matter what, he was gone.

'Those guys are jerks,' Daniels whispered. 'Why'd you let them take charge?'

Slader didn't answer, just shook his head. Checking his watch again, he followed Daniels into the woods. Two-thirty-two. Shit. Ten minutes were too many. He hurried along the path with the others. Saw Hank up ahead.

'So? What'd you find?' Slader tried to move things along.

'Balled-up tissues.' Hank held out his hand, displaying a small white wad. 'Harper left a trail.'

They moved on, the five of them. Hank in front. The state cops at his heels, Daniels and Slader lagging behind. Hank didn't wait for them; he pressed ahead, studying the ground. A few yards ahead, he knelt, picked up another wadded tissue.

Wow. Slader was impressed at Harper's ingenuity and presence of mind. And he was also pretty damned sure where all her cleverly placed tissues would lead: to all his friends and neighbors at the Hunt Club compound. Damn. If the state cops followed it there, that would be the end. Everything would erupt in who knew what violence.

Luckily, the state cops didn't have any idea where they were heading. They had no idea about the locals and their group, let alone about their rabid hostility toward outsiders. No, the cops still seemed convinced that the husband was guilty of foul play – after all, wasn't the guilty party always the spouse? All those true-crime shows on television were full of men who'd murdered their wives. The state cops already assumed that Hank Jennings had followed the script, doing away with his wife, making the footprints at their campsite and laying the trail of tissues himself. Slader thought he'd buy himself some time and prevent a catastrophe if he encouraged their suspicions.

'Sergeant.' He gestured to him, indicating that he wanted to talk privately. And then he planted the lie. 'I think you should know. I overheard Mr and Mrs Jennings having an argument yesterday.'

The sergeant kept his head down, nodding slightly. 'You know what about?'

'I wasn't paying much attention at the time, had a couple of bodies to deal with. But now, looking back, and with that blood at the campsite, I gotta say it was pretty heated.'

The sergeant nodded again.

'And it occurred to me that a trail like this? Well, if I'd done away with somebody, I might very well plant it myself.'

A light flashed in the sergeant's eyes. 'So how do you want to play this?'

'Like I said, I've got to take off. You're running the show, so it's your call. But if it was me, I'd stop playing this game pretty soon and have a little conversation.'

'Thanks, Captain.' The sergeant puffed his chest out and ambled over to Hank, who'd moved up the path with the corporal. 'Wow.' He looked at the ground. 'I'm amazed you could see that little tiny tissue, the way it was hidden under the leaves. I'd never had seen it. Would you, Corporal?'

The corporal hesitated. 'Probably not, sir. I mean, no way.'

'It's almost like Mr Jennings knew exactly where to look.'

'Maybe he did,' the corporal suggested.

Slader kept quiet, letting the cops zero in on Hank so they wouldn't think of other possibilities. But those other possibilities plagued him. He kept seeing Phil Russo's body. Damn. Were the women dead, too? As soon as he was sure they'd stop following the trail, he'd go find out. Meantime, his blood pressure kept rising. He felt unsteady, and pain sliced his skull. Maybe he was having a stroke? Well, fine. If he died, he wouldn't have to worry any more. Not about missing women or shootings or explosions. Not about Mavis or Josh and their crazy Hunt Club. Or the city of Philipsburg and its outskirts, or fracking and polluting, or government encroachments, or the pipeline. None of it.

Slader rubbed his eyes, felt like a hatchet was buried in his forehead. He made himself draw a breath, smelled drying leaves, sweet air. Watched sunlight flicker through the trees. Felt his shoulders loosen. He loved these woods. Belonged there. Wouldn't mind dying there. In fact, he half hoped he would stroke out and die right then so he'd be relieved of his burdens.

When Daniels nudged him, he was startled, had lost track of the conversation.

'Tell them that's crazy,' Daniels insisted. 'They're saying he planted those tissues and they want to stop following the trail.'

Slader took a breath, kept walking, following the cops who were following Hank. Apparently, since he was still standing, he wasn't dying, wouldn't escape his troubles so easily. Daniels waited for a reply. He scrambled for an appropriate answer. 'Well, I guess they're exploring all possibilities.'

'Really?' Daniels tilted his head. 'But why would he plant the trail? That's a lot of trouble to go to—'

'People will go to a lot of effort if they have something to hide.' After all, he ought to know; he was going to a lot of effort himself right now.

'What?' Daniels' mouth hung open. 'No, we need to keep tracking. In case Harper left the trail, we've got to give this the benefit of the doubt. Follow it. See where it leads. We might be able to find the women.'

'Yes.' The captain spoke slowly, as if his point were obvious. 'But, if she didn't leave it, the trail might have been deliberately constructed to lead us in the wrong direction, wasting time so we can't save anybody.' There. That justified slowing Hank down, didn't it?

Up ahead, the sergeant puffed his chest out with authority. 'Mr Jennings,' he called. 'Wait up. We want a word.'

But Hank didn't stop. He seemed to have found a rhythm to the clues, and he moved along the path, stopping every five or six yards to look for another tissue. Collecting them as he went.

'Jennings, I said stop!' The sergeant didn't like being ignored. He quickened his pace, closing in on Hank.

'Sorry,' Hank called, not even slowing down. 'I can't stop now.'

'Jennings. Stop where you are. That's a police order.' The sergeant waited.

Hank stopped. 'Why are we stopping? We've got to find my wife.'

The sergeant and the corporal caught up to Hank, stood in front of him, putting a temporary halt to his tracking.

'This is nuts.' Daniels' hands were on his hips.

Slader lowered his voice, spoke confidentially. 'Okay. These two aren't the brightest cops in the force,' he said. 'Even so, we need to let them do their jobs. Which means questioning Hank and figuring out what he's up to.'

'Maybe he's not up to anything. Maybe he just wants to find his wife.'

'I agree, Daniels. But they can't just let him lead them all over the forest without being confident that he's legit. I'd be obliged if you'd stay with them and make sure they stick to procedure.'

'Procedure? I'm not sure I'm qualified—'

'Just don't let them shoot him. You'll be fine. But I've got to split. I've got a guy in custody, can't keep him there much longer.'

Daniels looked up the trail and saw the state cops badgering Hank. 'Captain, before you go – don't you want to intervene?'

'They're just blustering. If I call them on it, they'll pump it up even more just to prove they can. Better if I let them be,' he said. And before Daniels could reply, he waved goodbye, reversed direction and took off back toward the campsite.

When he was out of sight, he veered into the woods, moving parallel to the others, hustling to the Hunt Club compound. His face was flushed, his blood careening through his veins. He kept his gaze straight ahead, not daring to look into the trees, afraid of what he might see. Slader raced through the woods, praying that the locals had a trace of sense left. Or at least that he wasn't too late to pound some into them. He checked his watch again. Two-fifty-five. Damn.

Angela had quieted down, seemed to be asleep. Jim sat on the floor, leaning against a wall. He'd finished his chili and a roll, half a bottle of water.

'You should eat,' he told Harper.

'I tried. I can't.'

'You should eat anyhow.'

He was right. She knew that. In combat situations, it was

necessary to maintain your strength. Eating was essential, even when you had no appetite. She picked up her container of chili, a spoon. Looked at it, saw clots of red sauce, clumps of beans. Scooped some up, made herself chew. Fought the gag reflex. Swallowed. Repeated the process.

'So, your husband. You really think he's coming?'

'Yes.' She hoped so. 'Should be soon.'

'You left a trail?'

'Yes.' This guy kept asking the same questions, making her repeat the same information, over and over. She thought of Chloe looking at a picture book, heard her small voice repeating the same sounds, again and again. 'Cow moo. Doggy woof. Piggy oink. Kitty meeeow.'

Harper closed her eyes, pushing the memory away.

Jim leaned forward, whispering. 'What if he doesn't show up? How can you be sure he found the trail?'

She couldn't. 'He'll find it.'

'What if he doesn't? Or he does but they stop him? We need a back-up plan.'

A back-up plan? She'd love one. She'd been trying to find one ever since she'd landed there. 'I agree.' She looked around the chamber. 'Any ideas?'

His eyes darted left to right, right to left. 'Only thing I can come up with involves her.' He indicated Angela. 'We can tell them she's dying. When they come to look, we take one of them hostage. Or we can trap that woman next time she brings food.' He watched Harper, looking hopeful.

Harper nodded, but didn't comment right away. She didn't see the need to remind him that they were unarmed. That their captors had major weapons and could drop a tear gas bomb. Or shoot anyone not hiding behind the hostage. Or simply abandon the hostage. What would they do then?

She didn't want to rob him of hope, but was pretty certain that taking a hostage would be futile, probably self-destructive. Even so, she didn't have a better idea.

'Let's wait a while,' she said. 'Give Hank a chance to bring the cavalry.'

Jim nodded. He was jumpy, twitching. Probably feeling closed in, panicky.

'Where are you from?' Harper tried to distract him.

'Wilkes-Barre. You?'

'Ithaca.' She was about to ask if he was married, but a loud gong reverberated above them. Jim and Harper held still, listening. Upstairs, footsteps clattered, voices buzzed, furniture scraped.

'What's going on?' Jim stiffened.

Harper wasn't sure.

The gong sounded again. What did it signal? A meeting? A battle? Lunch? Something was going on, though. She looked up at the air vent in the ceiling. If she could get close enough, maybe she could hear through that.

She dragged a cot under the vent. Asked Jim to help her lift the one Angela didn't occupy. Together, they stacked the cots, one on top of the other. Harper looked up at the ceiling, down at the cots. The legs were spindly, not stable or secured. But she climbed up onto the top one, standing under the vent, hearing commotion and jumbled conversation.

'You okay?' Jim stood beside her, shifting his weight, worrying his hands.

The gong blared again, followed by an authoritative voice. 'Let's settle down,' a man said. 'This is an emergency meeting.'

'Where's the chief?' a woman asked. 'We can't start without him.'

'Hell if we can't,' someone shouted. 'He should be here. If he's not, it's our right to go on without him. We've got to move.'

'Let's have everybody's attention,' the voice said. 'Order. We have urgent business.'

'What are we going to do with the prisoners?' a woman asked.

'That's easy,' a man answered. 'I say we make examples of them. Stake 'em up like the first guy.'

Really? Harper's jaw clenched.

'Can you hear them?' Jim asked. 'What are they saying?'

Harper held a finger to her lips. 'Shh. Wait.'

'You're fucking nuts, Ax. We can't just kill them. Cops and ATF are crawling all over the place.'

'Besides, we didn't kill that first guy. Josh found him dead.'

'It had to be Josh, no matter what he says. Because if it wasn't, then who killed him?'

'Statistically, isn't it always the spouse?'

'Yeah, that's what they say. Had to be his wife.'

The talking went on, but Harper stopped listening. She stood on the top cot, staring at Angela, and considered what she'd just heard.

* * *

The gash on Angela's head had stopped bleeding quite a while ago. Her hair was matted and crusty around the wound, and she lay still, eyes closed. Harper thought back, replaying what Angela had said and done. Seeing her stumbling into their campsite in the morning, looking for her husband. Her pants had been covered with mud. Harper hadn't thought about it then. But where had that mud come from? It had to have been from the bog. But why would Angela have been near the bog? She hadn't left Phil near there; he'd been on higher ground in a clearing.

But Stan had been camped near the bog. Could Angela have gone there to see him? No, of course not. They hated each other. Harper recalled their ugly confrontation. Besides, Angela had been surprised to see Stan, angry that he'd take his new wife to their old camping site.

'What?' Jim asked. 'Why are you frowning? What are they saying?'

'Sorry. It's not them – just something I remembered.'

Jim fidgeted. 'Well, what's going on? Can you hear them?'

Harper tuned back in to the meeting upstairs. A man was talking.

'. . . must be working for the frackers. You saw the testing stuff, Moose and Ax. Spread out by their tent.'

'Yeah, I saw it. They took soil, water, who knows what all. I saw the two of them yesterday, collecting samples and testing stuff.'

Harper bit her lip. Damn. They were talking about her and Hank.

'So, obviously, those two aren't out here to camp. You're saying they're gas company people?'

'No doubt about it.' Harper recognized Ax's voice. 'And you know what else? I say we go for it. If we don't put an end to this now, more of them will keep coming. I say we make our prisoners into a message so loud and clear that all we'll see of the gas company frackers and pipeline freaks'll be their backsides on their way out.'

Cheers and applause drowned out his voice.

Harper glared up at the vent. A message? They were going to make her into a message?

'What's happening?' Jim stood by the cot, tugged at her arm.

Harper's nostrils flared. 'Shh. They're talking about what to do with me.'

'With you? Only with you?'

'So far.' She motioned for him to be quiet so she could listen.

'I don't get it,' a woman said. 'Are you saying that little blonde thing and her husband are the ones blowing everything up?'

'Maybe, maybe not,' Ax answered. 'But I'll tell you this: If they aren't doing it themselves, then they know who is.'

Voices jumbled in consternation. A voice called for order. 'One person at a time. Quiet. Mavis, you have the floor.'

'Thank you, Hiram. I'm confused. Ax, are you saying that that couple was sent by the gas company, and that the gas company is behind the explosions?'

'You bet I am. Either them or the pipeline company. Maybe both of them together. Look, fracking has lots of enemies, not just us. So does the pipeline. They've got tons of opposition. So what better way for them to gain public sympathy than to paint themselves as bombing victims? Who's going to remember how their fracking made water undrinkable and blew up a few houses? Or how the pipeline ruined acres of forest? Nobody. Not when the precious pipeline has been the victim of a terrorist bombing.'

Voices rose, commenting, agreeing. Calling for action.

'Damn,' Harper breathed.

'What? Tell me.' Jim's hands were on his hips. 'Or else get down and let me listen.'

Harper didn't move. 'They're talking about the explosions,' she said. 'It's not about us.'

Jim shook his head. 'Well, keep telling me. I have a right to know, too.'

'Shh. Quiet.' Harper strained to hear.

Ax was in the middle of a sentence. '. . . no explosion has actually damaged the pipeline. Anybody think that's an accident? I sure don't. I think it's because the bombers never actually intended to blow up the pipeline. All they wanted was to stir up sympathy.'

More consternation.

'Hold on,' Hiram said. 'Let's review what we know for sure. Two men were shot dead. Two explosions have gone off. But remember, we can't be sure that any of these things are connected or who's behind them.'

People shouted at him. 'Oh come on, Hiram.'

'Are you kidding?'

'Didn't you just hear what Ax said?'

'Okay,' Hiram insisted. 'Let's find out. If anybody knows why Al Rogers was killed or who killed him, speak up. Go ahead.'

There was a pause; nobody spoke.

'So, for all we know, Al Rogers was shot accidentally by some hotshot weekend hunter. How about this: Anybody know how – or even if – Al Rogers was connected to the other victim, Philip Russo?'

Another pause, and again no one answered.

'How about Philip Russo? He was just a weekender, up here with his wife. Anyone find out anything about why he got killed? Or who did it?'

There was a murmur, but no one replied.

Harper's gaze wandered to Angela.

'How about the explosions?' the guy continued. 'Anybody learn anything? Or know who's behind them?'

Someone coughed, but no one said anything.

'So we don't really know much about any of this.'

Jim nudged Harper's leg. 'Get down. Let me listen.'

Harper brushed his hand away. 'Hold on.'

'Come on.' Jim reached out to pull her off the cots.

'Don't even think about it.' Harper used her most ominous lieutenant's voice. 'Back off.' She'd deck him if she had to.

Jim met her eyes, looked away. Stepped back.

'I'll tell you what they're saying, just be patient.' Harper softened her tone, but made it clear she was in charge. Upstairs, a new man was talking.

'. . . we know more than Hiram thinks we do. We know that couple is doing testing and are probably involved with the frackers. But they – that big guy and the blonde – aren't the only ones involved. I'm pretty sure there's a bunch of them up here working together.'

People reacted, talking all at once. Hiram told them to give Josh a chance to explain.

'I saw them this morning while I was out.'

'You mean the Bog Man saw them,' someone heckled.

'Let him talk,' someone else scolded. 'What did you see, Josh?'

'They had a meeting. I was dressed as Bog Man, so I had to keep my distance. But I watched for a while. There were at least five of them. Those two downstairs, the blonde one's husband, and two more guys who looked like they'd been in a fire. They met at that campsite with the soil samples.'

For a moment, there was silence.

Then a woman asked, 'So what are you saying, Josh? That they're all working together? Those five and the energy companies? It's a conspiracy?'

'Imagine that,' another one said. 'A conspiracy. What a surprise.' She said something else, but Harper couldn't hear. The voices rose all at once, people clamored, furniture scraped. It took two beats of the gong to quiet them down.

When the reverberation faded, a new voice spoke.

'Friends and neighbors,' a man said, 'can I have your attention?'

'You finally decided to show up?' a woman called out.

'Enough speeches,' someone yelled. 'Time to get off our butts!'

'Where've you been, Chief?' someone else shouted.

'Order!' a third guy shouted.

People talked all at once, a jumble of tension and noise, ended by the chiming of the gong.

When it faded, the speaker began again. 'This is no time for squabbling.' His tone was quiet, unrattled. And familiar. 'Before we decide that the whole outside world is plotting against us, let's put things in perspective . . .'

Harper stopped listening. Stopped breathing. It was over. They were safe. She pointed to the vent in the ceiling. 'Jim.' Her eyes filled. 'It's okay. The police are here. The captain is talking to them now.'

'What?' Jim froze. 'The police? Do they know we're here?' He hopped up beside her, his weight collapsing the top cot.

'Damn it, Jim.' Harper slid off the mattress, shoving him off. She set the cot up again, climbed back up and began pounding on the vent, shouting for help.

'I'm not loud enough,' she said. 'Give me something – a shoe.'

Jim took off a boot, passed it up to her. Harper began thumping on the vent. Calling for Captain Slader. For the police. For Hank. For anybody. Jim yelled, too. They shouted SOS. Belted out their location. Made so much noise that Angela opened her eyes and gaped at them. But nothing happened. No one came running to answer their calls or to open the trap door and release them. No one even seemed to hear.

After a while, Harper's throat was raw from screaming. 'It's no use.' She stopped yelling, handed the boot back to Jim. 'The cops don't hear us.'

'What are they doing? Arresting everyone? Because someone will tell them we're here – that woman who brought food.'

'Harper? What's going on?' Angela looked at Jim. 'Who's he? Where the hell are we?'

'Shh, both of you.' Harper aimed her ear toward the vent again, listening. The captain was still talking? Why wasn't he arresting anybody? Unless there were too many people for his small force to take into custody. Maybe he was explaining that everyone would be questioned. That nobody could leave.

'. . . disagree with Josh,' his voice was reasoned, reassuring. 'The evidence doesn't support his conclusion that there's a conspiracy of any kind. In fact, I have a suspect in custody for the murder of Philip Russo, the man whose body Josh so creatively used to decorate a tree trunk.'

Wait. What? Harper was confused. The captain knew who'd tied Phil to the tree?

People were chuckling, whistling. Hooting.

Angela was complaining, asking why she had to be quiet.

'Hush,' Harper scolded. It was hard enough to make out what they were saying upstairs without Angela yammering.

'Who'd you arrest, Chief?' a woman asked.

Chief? Wait. Why was she calling the captain 'chief'?

'The ex-husband of the widow is in custody. There's lots of evidence – his rifle had been fired, his ammo matches that in the body. He had opportunity and plenty of motive, and so on.'

'Fine.' Josh's voice cut him off. 'Maybe the ex offed the new husband – which, by the way, I personally doubt because I think the wife and her husband are both involved with the frackers—'

'Like I said, there's no evidence to support—'

'Let me finish, Slader. You may be our sector chief, but we're all equals here, and I've got stuff to say.'

Sector chief? What? Captain Slader? Harper stepped backwards, turned to face Jim.

'What happened?' he asked. 'You look weird.'

She shook her head.

'Tell me. What?'

She had trouble making the words. 'The captain. He isn't here for us.'

'What captain?' Angela asked.

'But that's only because he doesn't know—'

'It's because he's one of them.'

Jim scowled, shook his head. 'That's crazy.'

'No. They call him "chief". He's in charge, Jim. He's their leader.'

Jim didn't say anything. For a long moment, his eyes darted back and forth. Then he sat on the floor against the wall, his head back, staring at the single light bulb hanging from the ceiling.

As Harper took her position at the vent, Angela pushed herself up onto an elbow. 'Why won't you answer me, Harper? Where are we? What's going on?'

The chief stood straight, with military dignity and posture. He didn't raise his voice, despite the fact that he'd had the floor and Josh had rudely stolen it. He'd give his people – even Josh – a chance to express their opinions. In return, they'd appreciate his patience and offer him the respect he was due. For the moment, he'd cede the floor to the rowdy, unwashed, unshaven moron who challenged him, knowing that Hiram was at his side, ready to sound the gong at his signal. Instinct told him to let the young fool have his say. Everyone knew that as a boy he'd tortured rabbits and that, more than once, he'd been reprimanded for his sadistic treatment of game animals. Josh was a sociopath. He would scare the crowd the same way his infernal Bog Man costume scared the tourists. After his extremist rhetoric, calling the locals to draw blood, they'd be hungry for a calm voice of reason.

'With all due respect, friends, let's pretend that our honorable sector chief is right. Let's assume that the outsider was killed by his wife's ex-husband. Is that the end of it? Should we all go home and have a beer?' Josh paused, holding his palms up. 'Let's consult an authority, a police captain. Let's ask Captain Slader if he thinks we're done here. Because, from my understanding, two men were shot. Does he say that the ex-husband killed them both? The husband and the pipeline guy, too? And was the ex responsible for the dead guy's partner's behavior? Did he make him go snooping around our compound fence? Because I saw him there myself.'

The crowd responded, a wave of mumbled comments. Hiram stood ready beside the gong. But the captain shook his head, held his tongue.

'And did the ex-husband arrange for that couple to sneak around taking more scientific samples?' The crowd got louder. 'Did he hire a couple of guys to blow up the old campgrounds? And to blast a hole near the pipeline?'

The crowd was a single unit, now. With one low, swelling voice.

'Here's what I say.' Josh's voice lowered in pitch. 'I say it's no accident that the pipeline guy downstairs was snooping here. And it's no coincidence that his snooping occurred on the same day that that couple was gathering scientific samples. And on the same weekend that not one, but two bombs went off.

'What I say is that they're working together, all of them. The fracking gas company's behind it, and we all know it. And the government's not going to do a fricking thing to stop them. They tried to scare us away. They poisoned our water – even today, we've got forty-four times more benzene, two thousand six hundred times more arsenic, and five times more naphthalene in our water than the government allows. Hell, do I need to remind you about Aden's house exploding? When was that, Aden, 2009?'

Josh looked around for Aden. Someone shouted, 'Yeah, 2009.'

The captain wanted to step forward, but Josh had the audience revved. He waited for the right moment to speak. He would acknowledge everything Josh had said, point out that it was either old news or unsubstantiated suspicion.

'And what about Gil?' Josh went on. 'Remember? Gil burned his mouth just by drinking his own water. His wife burned her lungs taking a shower – how long was she in the hospital? And how about the smell of gas everywhere? And the mud spill that leaked into the bog and the lake?'

The crowd's rumble swelled, louder, angrier. In a moment, Slader would remind them that all of these events had occurred four years ago. Things had been cleaned up. Aden's house had been rebuilt better than the old one. Most people could drink their water again. The point was that they needed to pick their battles, time them right, and plan a strategy for safe retreat. For now, they had to lie low.

But Josh was on a roll. And the crowd was rapt, following his cues. 'Face it,' Josh said, 'we've been passive too long. We've sat by while they've poisoned our water, polluted our air and land, blown up our homes, and made our families sick. What are we going to do now? Sit around and wait for their pipeline to burst like it does in hundreds of places across the country every single year?'

In a single voice, the crowd yelled, 'No!'

'Wait for them to get the government to run us off the land?'

'No!'

'Let them poison us one by one?'

'No!' The crowd's answer reverberated inside the captain's ears.

'Good. I agree – I'm right there with you. And the only way – I'm as sure of this as I am of my own name – the only way to stop them is to cut them off clean, sending a message so bloody shocking and final that they'll run their elbows and assholes all the way back to hell and never dare set foot in this woods, let alone try to mess with its people, ever again. I'm talking about war. Real honest to goodness, full-out war.'

The crowd erupted, cheering, clapping, standing up.

War? The captain's mind flashed back to the sounds. Sniper fire, the bam of an IED. Shouts and screams. And the smells. Burning rubber, burning flesh. He tightened his grip on his weapon and, when a gong sounded, he reflexively closed his eyes. Damn. He was losing control. Needed to step up. Be a leader.

But the people were all talking, not responding to the gong.

Hiram hit it again. And still, the din didn't fade.

'Order,' the captain blared. 'Order.' Stay cool, he reminded himself. Don't give that hot head subordinate any acknowledgement. Retain command. 'That's great enthusiasm, but let's not get carried away. We have business to accomplish, and not a lot of time.'

But nobody was listening. The sector chief stood at the head of the room, ignored by his people. He told himself to give them a minute, and he stood there waiting, blood pressure mounting, face burning red.

Hiram stepped over. 'What's your call, Chief? Want another clang?'

Slader turned to Hiram, his loyal old friend. But as he looked, Hiram seemed to have soft edges. His blurred, and the walls swayed. Legs caving, Slader leaned onto Hiram, who led him to a chair. Annie appeared, offering water.

'Chief.' She took hold of his hands. 'You all right? When did he eat?' she asked Hiram. 'Did you eat today? I bet you didn't. You need some sugar.'

Sugar? He tried to remember what he'd been doing. Had to get up and speak to the members.

'You stay right here a minute.' Annie ran off, shouting into the crowd for Mavis.

'What the hell?' Instantly, Mavis ran over, knelt beside him. Kissed his cheek, stroked his head. Hovered.

Annie came back with cookies and juice. Made him eat.

Damn. He hadn't eaten in a while. Couldn't remember when. He scarfed down the cookies, guzzled the juice. Felt his energy come back. He gave Mavis a quick hug, thanked Annie. And, as the Hunt Club members swarmed and buzzed like an angry hive, he stood up and walked back to his place by the gong.

It was the chief's turn to talk.

Bob pointed at Pete's sandwich. 'You gonna eat that?'

Eat? Really? Pete squinted out the crack beside the door, able to see only a sliver of open space. But in that sliver, he could see segments of the two armed guards still standing near the fence. How could Bob think about food? The walls of the shed squeezed him, taunting, suffocating. The burns on his face and hands had become inflamed and raw. They were trapped with a stash of explosives and ammunition. And according to the angle of the sun, it would be a couple more hours until it would be dark enough to try to escape. But Bob was thinking of food.

'Because if you don't want it, I'll take it.'

Fuck if he was going to let Bob have it. 'I want it.'

'Why aren't you eating it?'

Really? 'I'm saving it.'

'How about you give me half?'

'No.'

Bob didn't answer. Pete looked out at the guards, thinking. Maybe they didn't have to wait for sundown – maybe they could run for it now. If he and Bob carried rifles and took the guards by surprise, they might be able to get past them and climb over the fence. Except the guards had radios, would call for help. And the local people knew the woods better, would outnumber them. So, for it to work, the guards would have to be disabled.

'We'll need to tie them up.' He turned to Bob. Saw him swallow a mouthful of his sandwich. 'Fuck you, Bob. I said I wanted that.' He was on his feet, grabbing at the bread, snatching it out of Bob's hand so hard that he stumbled backwards. Bob grappled with him, tearing off a crust and a wad of ham.

'What the fuck's wrong with you?' Bob chewed.

'What's wrong with *me*? You're the one who took somebody else's sandwich.' Pete steadied himself, clutching what was left of it. Took a bite even though he doubted he could keep it down. He chewed slowly, his eyes on Bob. 'You had no right.'

'Jesus.' Bob met Pete's eyes. 'Stop being such a little girl.'

That was it. Pete had had enough. 'You know what, Bob? When this is over, I'm done with you.'

'Yeah? Good.' Bob grinned, got to his feet. 'I can't wait to be rid of your sorry ass.' He gave Pete's sternum a push.

'What, now you're pushing me?' Pete's eyelids twitched. Even with the sandwich in his hand, he pushed Bob back.

Bob's eyes hardened and he shoved Pete hard, knocking him against the wall. Pete bounced back, letting loose, kicking and punching, and the two of them fell over, rolling on the floor, bumping against boxes and crates, yelping in pain as their burnt flesh made impact with wood, fabric, stubble, or skin.

'Apologize.' Pete's voice was too loud, and they were making a ruckus. Pete didn't care. He was pissed. He locked his elbows around Bob's head and squeezed.

'Let go,' Bob hissed. 'They'll hear us.'

'Fine. Let them,' Pete said louder. He was ready to be caught. Anything would be better than staying closed up in this claustrophobic shack in a forest where hairy monsters roamed and your so-called friend stole your food. 'Apologize.'

'Shut the fuck up!' Bob growled, swinging his burn-covered fists onto Pete's back.

Pete tightened his vise-like grip on Bob's head. 'Only if you apologize.'

'Fine,' Bob winced. 'Sorry.'

'No. Like you mean it.'

'Fine.' Bob's voice quivered. 'I apologize. Sincerely. I shouldn't have taken your sandwich.'

'And you'll respect me and my property from now on.'

'Yes. I'll respect you and your property from now on.'

'Good.' Pete released him.

Bob whirled around and socked Pete in the jaw. Pete went down, landing hard on the stuffed backpacks.

Bob's froze. The blood drained from his face. 'Shit.'

'What?'

'Don't move.'

'What – why?' Pete held his jaw, looked around. Saw the backpacks under him. Glanced at Bob, remembering what was in them. Not just the C4 and their leftover pipe bomb, but those jars of unidentified liquid and gel. Possibly unstable stuff that might explode on impact. Pete took a breath and propelled himself forward, crossing the shed toward the door, running on his knees.

'Oh man.' Bob's hands covered his face. 'I thought we were goners.'

'Asshole. Knocking me onto that shit? You could have fucking killed us both.'

'Shh.' Bob looked out the open crack by the door. 'Keep your voice down. We're fine. They probably need a detonator.'

'You don't know that. We have no idea what that stuff is. The liquid could be nitro-fucking-glycerin. I told you. It blows up if you look at it wrong.'

'Jesus, Pete. I swear, if you don't stop whining—'

'What? You'll push me onto a bagful of nitro?'

'Cool it, would you? Nothing happened.'

Pete settled against the door, rubbed his jaw with one raw hand, held the crushed and filthy remains of his sandwich in the other.

Bob sat down beside him, crossed his legs. 'Fucking maniac,' he said. 'You weren't eating it anyway.'

'It's the principle. It was mine.'

'Yeah? Well, you're welcome to it. Bon appétit.'

Pete looked at it, dropped it on the ground. The sun hadn't moved. So they still had two more hours? His jaw throbbed where Bob's fist had landed. His burns killed. There was a ten-foot monster wandering around; women who'd disappeared. The walls of the shed were crushing him. And now, his best friend – the partner who shared responsibility for their whole plan – had turned on him. He'd known Bob had a dark side, but never suspected that he'd stoop so low as to take a guy's sandwich.

Pete looked out the crack near the door. Saw the monster's footprints in the dirt. The barbed wire fence across the field. Something was wrong, though. It took a while to figure out what it was: He didn't see the guards. Maybe it was nothing; after all, he could see only a narrow strip. Probably they'd moved out of his line of sight.

Still, he grabbed a rifle, motioned for Bob to do the same, opened the door another inch, widening his view. And saw the muzzle of a shotgun, pointed at his head.

Harper stood on tiptoes, stretching to reach the vent so she could hear what was going on upstairs, but Angela interfered.

'What are you doing, Harper? What's going on?' Angela sat up on the cot, repeating questions. 'What happened to me?' She touched her matted hair, felt her scalp. Winced.

'Angela, quiet. I can't hear what they're saying.'

'Oh God. My head got split open. I can feel it. Was I unconscious? The last thing I remember is eating oatmeal at your campsite – so what happened? How did I hurt my head? How did we get here? And who's this guy?' She tilted her head toward Jim. He was silent, sitting on the floor, still staring at the light bulb.

Harper turned to Angela, felt like knocking her out again. 'I'll explain later.'

'Why not now?'

Harper glared.

'Okay, just tell me – are we in jail?'

'Of course not—'

'Then what is this place? How come I can't remember coming here?'

'You said it yourself; you were unconscious for a while. You got dropped on your head.'

'Dropped on my head?'

'I'll tell you later.'

'But who dropped me? Was it him?' Angela tried to get up, moved her leg, grimaced. 'Oh God, my ankle.' She looked at it, saw the swelling, the garish purplish color. 'Wait – your husband. I remember, I hurt my ankle and he went to get help—'

'Angela. Enough!' Harper heard commotion from the meeting room.

'Why shouldn't I talk? Tell me what's going on – why are you standing up there?'

Oh God. Maybe the quickest way to quiet Angela would be to answer her questions. 'I'm trying to hear what they're saying.'

'What who's saying? Where are we? What are we doing here?' Angela scuttled to the edge of the cot, looked around. 'Where's my walking stick? I need to get out of here.' Her voice was shrill, rising in pitch.

Jim didn't move, just said, 'Good luck.'

'What?'

'We're locked up. Prisoners.'

'What?' Angela turned to Harper, squawking. 'What's he saying? You said we weren't in jail.'

'We were kidnapped,' Harper said. 'By some locals.'

'Locals? Why? I haven't done anything to them. I don't even know any of them. What could they want with me?'

With *her*? Harper rolled her eyes.

Angela turned to Jim. 'Who are you?'

Jim looked at her, said nothing.

The sound of a gong resounded through the vent.

'Angela,' Harper used her lieutenant's voice, 'that's Jim. He works for the pipeline, okay? Now, I need to listen, so quiet.'

Angela wasn't paying attention. Her eyes darted from left to right, up and down. 'No – no. This is crazy. I need to get out of here.'

The gong sounded again.

'Shh – they're starting again.'

'Starting? Starting what?' Angela shrieked. 'Oh God. I can't stay here. Let me out.' She pushed herself up, hopping on her uninjured foot, yelling. 'Help! Somebody! Help! Let me—'

She didn't finish because Jim got up, put his arms out and charged, growling, 'Just shut up!'

Angela landed on the cot, winded and stunned. She edged back against the wall, whimpering and huffing, and sat eyeing Jim. But, for the moment, she didn't say a word. Harper stood at the vent, listening to the crowd settle as the captain began to speak.

The captain stood on a crate, elevating himself above the others. It wasn't a tactic he preferred, but the members were riled up and rowdy. He needed to assert his authority, and visible stature was a symbol everyone would respond to. Gradually.

'Okay.' He raised his arms, motioning for them to settle down. Calling for attention, he noted that people had divided into groups. The biggest surrounded that lunatic Josh, who had just put everyone into a frenzy. But another bunch, mostly women, clustered around Mavis. He needed to unite them all, remind them that he was their leader.

'Let me get right to it,' he began. 'I've been briefed on what's gone on while I was out chasing bombers and fending off the Feds. I understand that some of us have taken it upon themselves to take hostages, and that we now have three people locked in the hole. That's abduction. It makes us a target for investigation by the Feds, as if we didn't have enough problems.'

Somebody shouted, 'They're prisoners of war!'

Somebody added, 'Stop being a pussy, Slader!'

Slader took a breath. 'As your sector chief, I need to talk to you about reasoned action. About planning. About control.'

'About bullshit.' That came from Josh's camp.

'You already know that the killings and bombings have made our little territory the focus of the state police, the ATF, the media, and the gas and pipeline companies. The woods are crawling with investigators.'

'What's your point?' a woman called out.

Slader didn't react, just kept talking. 'We have no reason to believe that any of the people you've taken prisoner have anything to do with the bombings. Nor do we have reason to believe any assertions of a conspiracy; there is simply no evidence to support that theory.'

Josh yelled, 'Except what I saw with my own eyes.'

'You calling Josh a liar?' Moose shouted.

Slader ignored the comments. 'You chose me as your leader, and I've been honored to act as sector chief. But if I'm to lead, you have to listen to me. I've told you that the best action right now is no action. That for now, our best plan is to lie low and wait for the investigators to do their jobs and leave. After seeing what's occurring today – the influx of media and cops – that is still my opinion.'

'Lie low and hide?' Josh stood up. 'Like that's gotten us anywhere before? We've laid low for years and lots of us still can't drink our water. I'm done being a chicken shit. It's time we make examples of people who mess with us. It's time to stand up and fight!'

People cheered.

Slader felt a vise on his chest, heat on his face. 'That's exactly what we need *not* to do. Remember our purpose here is unity. Each of us alone can break like a fragile stick. But when we stand and act together, just like a band of sticks, we become unbreakable. This is why we need to voice our concerns in unison to the authorities—'

'Listen to him. The chief wants us to line up politely and behave like good boys and girls. What do you want us to do, Slader, sign a fucking petition? Hold a sit-in? Or maybe just bend over and let them stick it to us?' People were shouting, applauding, but Josh put his hands up. 'Quiet down. I have a question, and I want everyone to hear the answer.' The Hunt Club became silent. 'Let me ask you this, Slader: Whose side are really you on?'

The air thickened. Everyone sat hushed, waiting for his answer.

'Go on. Tell us why you're so opposed to us taking action and fighting the people who've stolen our land and ruined our resources? I repeat the question: Whose side are you on?'

Slader stood at attention, raised an eyebrow. Sweat beaded on his forehead. 'What kind of question is that? I'm your sector chief.'

'Our sector chief?' Josh turned to the group. 'Slader's a gosh-darned police captain. Why didn't any of us realize it before? Slader isn't one of us. He's the fricking law – he's part of the establishment—'

'That's not true. This is my home—'

'—and he represents the government. Why else would he keep telling us to lie low and take it?'

'I've protected us and our interests—'

'And you've told us to do nothing but lie low and write letters to our congressman. Well, we're fed up, Slader. Finished. Done with you and your two-faced attempts to hold us back. I say, it's time to stop pussyfooting and go to war!'

Cheers interrupted him. He put his hands up again, calling for quiet. 'Outsiders have come to take our land. They've blown it up, raping it to satisfy their greed, stealing its treasures. They've been poisoning us, killing us slowly, one by one, and now they're picking things up, conspiring, setting off bombs, shooting folks. The only way to stop them is to show them we won't take it anymore. That we'll crush anyone who messes with us, starting with the conspirators we've got in the hole—'

A low murmur rumbled among the crowd.

'—and moving onto the rest of the invaders who come here to shatter the earth and poison our water and take our forest.'

The murmur built, gathering energy and density.

'We have no choice. They've pushed us to the brink. It's time we take a stand and spill some blood. Who's with me?'

Cheers erupted in a roar. People were on their feet, clamoring around Josh, declaring him their new leader, shouting that they were with him.

The sector chief stood on his crate, watching the fervor. 'This is wrong,' he shouted. 'We're out-manned. Out gunned. You're making a mistake.'

No one seemed to notice him.

He looked across the room, searching faces. For Mavis. She lusted for him, could never get enough of him. Surely now, when he needed her support, she would stand with him. There she was – he looked at her, met her eyes.

Mavis bit her lip and turned away, leading her pack of women toward Josh. The captain felt a stab. Took a breath. Raised his chin.

At least Hiram was still at his side. Hiram had clout. He would speak for him, sway everyone, bring them back to their senses. The captain turned to him.

Hiram shrugged, shook his head, and moved aside to make room for Moose and Ax. Unbelievably, they were coming for him, their jaws set and gazes cold.

'Moose,' he said. 'Ax? What can I do for you?'

But they didn't answer. Didn't say anything. Just took hold of his arms.

Stunned, the chief stepped off the crate, didn't resist as Ax and Moose took his gun and led him away. He stood tall, facing them with dignity and poise, but inside he crumbled to his knees, knowing how it felt to be Caesar, betrayed by his closest friends.

Harper climbed down from the pile of cots. 'They're coming.' She scanned the room. 'We've got to do something.'

'Like what?' Jim was jittery again, shifted his weight from foot to foot. 'What do you mean, "they're coming"? What did you hear?'

'What are we supposed to do?' Angela's mouth dropped. 'I can't even walk.'

'Harper?' Jim crossed his arms, uncrossed them.

Harper was distracted as she answered. Her mind was on defense. On coming up with a strategy. 'They're like a mob.' She examined the ceiling, the walls. 'And they want to use us in some war with the gas company or the government—'

'War?' Jim bit a nail. 'You mean like a stand-off? Like in Waco? Are these people in one of those crazy cults?'

'All I know is they're angry and violent. So when they come for us, we've got to be ready.'

'But I can't even stand,' Angela wailed. 'What will happen to me?'

Harper pulled the top cot down, turned it over.

'How can we be "ready"?' Jim fretted. 'What are you doing?'

She began twisting the screws that held the cot's metal frame together. 'We need weapons.'

'Weapons?' Jim stood over her, clucking and useless. 'You're thinking of the cots? The spokes? Are you kidding? They have guns.'

Damn. She couldn't loosen the screws. She looked around for a tool, saw empty chili cartons, water bottles. A blanket. Some blood-stained clips in Angela's matted hair. She didn't ask, just went over to Angela, took a couple of clips.

'Ouch,' Angela complained. 'What are you doing?'

'I'll give them back.' Harper slid a silver barrette into the slit on top of the screw, turned it like a screwdriver. The screw didn't move, but the barrette bent. Damn. She needed to slow down, finesse her movements. She took a breath and tried again with the barrette doubled over. Gently. Finally, even though the barrette was mangled, the screw gave way and came loose.

'Hold this.' She handed the screw to Jim, giving him a job.

'So when are they coming?' Angela sat up on her cot, hugging herself. 'Now? What will they do with us?'

Harper ignored her, concentrating. The hatch could open any moment.

Angela kept whimpering. 'You two can fend for yourselves, but what am I supposed to do? I have a broken ankle and I can't see straight. I probably have a concussion.'

Harper couldn't take the time to reply. She focused, working the screws.

Jim watched, perturbed. 'Seriously.' Jim eyed the trapdoor in the ceiling. 'Even if you take them off, how are we supposed to fight guns and rifles with a few metal rods?'

Harper didn't look up; kept working. 'You got a better idea?'

Jim was silent, shifted his weight to his other leg, watched the hatch.

'Point is . . .' Harper pulled a leg off the cot, handed it to Jim, who examined it, feeling its tip. 'They won't expect us to have any weapons at all. We'll be able to surprise them. If we can get close enough to knock out somebody or take a hostage or get one gun, we'll have leverage.'

'And then what?' Angela asked. 'In case you haven't noticed, I can barely move.'

Harper removed another leg from the cot. She held it, examined the end, its rough edges. If she had time, she could file those edges on the concrete walls, make them sharper. But even as it was, if she placed the rod right, aimed it at an eye or a throat, and if she was able to get enough momentum – well, she could make it work.

Angela fretted, Jim paced, and Harper worked on strategy. They would lay the legless cot on top of another one so no one coming into the room would notice it right away. She and Jim would each conceal metal legs behind them and wait for the right moment to strike. But that's as far as her strategy went because she didn't know how many would come for them, where they'd be positioned, or how many weapons they'd have. She needed to plan for a variety of possible scenarios.

She was still formulating the first scenario when the hatch opened. Even before the ladder descended, Angela started begging for mercy, crying that she was a widow who hadn't done anything to anyone. Harper braced herself. They weren't ready yet, hadn't discussed a plan. She shoved her metal rods under a mattress, nodded at Jim, signaling that he should do the same. But damn, it was too late.

The ladder dropped into place and someone yelled down, telling them to keep clear. Jim leaned against the wall, stuffed his metal rod behind his back. Boots descended. Harper focused, adrenalin pumping. Josh had promised to make examples of them, to spill blood. There was no choice but to fight, with or without a plan. She took a breath, thought of Hank and Chloe, and watched legs slowly lower themselves down, revealing hips, then a torso. As soon as the guy's feet neared the floor, before he could grip or aim his gun, she would pounce, grab his neck, and thrust her skinny metal rod into his throat. Someone might shoot from above, but if she positioned herself right, he'd cover her; the guy would take the bullet.

He was almost down. Harper got ready, picked up the metal bar, held it behind her back. Got to her feet.

'You've got a new room-mate,' someone called from above.

When the guy's head came through the hatch, Harper took a step back and dropped her stick onto a cot. Taking him down would do no good, and he would be worthless as a hostage. Wasn't even a danger to them. When he'd descended the final rungs, the ladder got pulled up, the hatch door slammed shut.

'You all right?' Harper asked.

When Captain Slader turned around, his eyes were wild and red, and even though he was looking right at Harper when she spoke, he didn't answer. He didn't even seem to hear.

* * *

Slader slumped on a cot, head in his hands.

'Captain Slader?' Angela shrieked. 'Oh God – did you come to rescue us? Have you called for backup?'

'Where've you been, Angela?' Jim's eyes bulged, staring at Slader. 'He didn't come to help us. He's with the Hunt Club. In fact, he's their leader.'

'No, he's not.' Angela scowled. 'He's the police captain – he's investigating Phil's murder. Captain? Tell him. You've come to help us, right?'

'I just told you,' Jim snapped. 'You were out of it before. Maybe you didn't hear. Slader's one of them—'

'Impossible.' Angela's voice went up an octave. 'I know him. He arrested my ex-husband. Captain, tell him how you took Stan into custody—'

'He's head of the locals.'

'He was, but not any more.' Harper flopped down, sat on the cot beside Angela. 'There's been a coup.'

'Why didn't you tell us?' Jim turned in circles, running his hands through his hair.

'I'm telling you now: Captain Slader's been ousted. Now he's just another prisoner.'

'Oh God,' Angela groaned.

The three of them gaped at Slader, who said nothing, just stared at his boots.

'Okay, enough. We're wasting time,' Harper said. 'They'll be back for us soon. So let's get ready.'

'Ready?' Angela scoffed. 'How? Fix our mascara? Pray? Plan our last words?'

'Shut the fuck up, would you?' Jim snapped. 'All you do is bitch and whine.'

'Yeah? Well, why shouldn't I? In case you haven't noticed, I have a broken ankle, my husband's been murdered, and I've been kidnapped by lunatics. I guess I have a right to bitch—'

'You know what? Your husband's lucky. At least he doesn't have to listen to you bitch and moan any more—'

A sharp, skull-rattling whistle interrupted them. As Harper took her fingers away from her mouth, everyone spun around and looked at her; even Slader watched her vaguely through glazed eyes.

'Okay?' She stood at attention. 'We don't have time for bickering or brooding. Captain Slader – or is it chief? Whatever you call yourself – we need your input. I heard what you said to your people before. The part about being stronger when they work together. Well, that's true for us, too. Each of us alone is powerless, but all of us together might succeed and get out of here.' She stepped over to the captain. 'You in?'

As she spoke, the glassiness in Slader's eyes cleared and his pupils contracted. Slowly, he got to his feet, stood tall, and faced her. Speaking in a soft, controlled tone, he said, 'Yes, ma'am. Jennings. I'm in.'

The whistle penetrated the cloud around the captain. The little blonde woman had sent the sound flying and, sharp as an arrow, it had cut into his brain. She belted out words and phrases with the authority of an army officer. Isn't that what she'd said she was? A lieutenant? Well, no matter what her rank was, it didn't matter; they were all goners. All dead. The locals had become an angry mob, led by Josh who was nothing but a twisted overgrown delinquent. He wondered what Josh would do to his body. Cut it up? Burn it? Put it on display? And how were they going to kill him? Probably hanging. Or they might shoot him. Might line up all four prisoners and do a firing squad.

The blonde woman was standing over him, firing off words. 'Each of us alone is powerless,' she said, 'but all of us together might succeed.'

Wait. Hold on. That was his rallying cry – the idea that even thin sticks, bound together, would be unbreakable. It was true, and this woman understood. She recognized his wisdom even when his own people had rejected and shunned him.

Well, it wasn't their fault, really. It was Josh. Josh had turned them against him. Josh. He should have locked him up years ago – animal cruelty. Vandalism. The list went on. Better yet, he should have eliminated Josh altogether, should have shoved him into the bog or the lake, held him under. Or shot him dead in his Bog Man costume, exposing his fakery to the outsiders.

But it was no good thinking about should-haves. It was too late. Josh had taken over. Slader kept seeing it happen, again and again. Mavis – hell. How many nights had he spent in her bed? Yet, when he'd needed her to stand with him, she'd walked away. And Hiram, his oldest friend, had turned his back. And Ax – how many times had he let Ax slide for driving under the influence? And Moose? He'd taught Moose to shoot a rifle – helped him bag his first buck. All of them had abandoned him. Annie, Wade – every single one of them. He couldn't stop listing the betrayals, seeing the backs turn. But now, this little blonde was talking about unity and power, staring at him. Why? What did she want from him? Couldn't she see that he was shattered? A broken, bleeding corpse of a man? A failure as a leader? What was the point of her repeating his words? His people would rather follow Josh on a suicide mission than follow him and survive. He was finished. His life over.

But the blonde woman was still watching him. Asking, 'You in?'

In what? He tried to recall what she'd said. Something to do with the stick thing, probably. Unity. Her eyes were bright, expectant. Strong. Yet they met his with a kind of shyness. No, not shyness. Deference? Yes. And respect. She looked at him the way enlisted men looked at officers, the way he deserved to be looked at. As if she wanted his leadership. He glanced around the room at the other faces. They were all three watching him, all waiting for his reply. These people – this ragtag little band of resistance – needed him.

Slader chewed his lip. Remembering his rules: A good leader responded to the needs of his people. A good leader put his personal needs aside for the sake of others. A true leader didn't dodge responsibility. Clearly, this little group was crying out for his help. For the sake of others, he would have to absorb the shock and pain of his own loss, muster his strength, rise to the challenge, and respond to the call.

'Yes, ma'am.' He got to his feet. 'I'm in.'

'So what are they planning?' Harper asked. 'What can you tell us?'

Slader pursed his lips, didn't respond.

'Just say it. They're going to kill us, aren't they?' Angela lay back on her cot, her voice flat. 'I know it. We're never getting out of here.'

'It's going to be tough.' Slader sounded grave. 'They intend to use us as an example.'

'An example of what?' Jim stopped pacing. 'I'm just a regular guy who works for a living. I haven't done anything—'

Harper cut him off, addressed Slader. 'Have you heard anything about my husband? He went to the ranger's station to get help for Angela—'

Slader looked away. 'He's been delayed.'

Delayed? How? Harper stopped breathing. Was Hank hurt? Oh God. 'What happened?'

Slader sighed, met her eyes. 'He found your trail and was following it with the cops and the ranger. I figured out that your trail was leading them here, to the compound, so I had to slow him down.'

'What did you do?' Harper stepped toward him, leaned up toward his face.

Slader backed away. 'Look, I was protecting my people – delaying the search party until I could get here and find out what the hell was happening.'

'Where's my husband?' Harper's voice trembled. Her fists tightened. Slader was a lot bigger than she was, but she didn't care. She'd taken down larger men.

Slader took another step back. 'Don't worry. He'll be fine.'

'Did you hurt him?'

'No – calm down. Nothing like that. I just made him take a detour. Look – if I'd known what Josh was planning, I wouldn't have done it. All I did was mention that you and your husband had been fighting—'

'But that's not true.'

'—and given that there was blood at your campsite, and that you were gone, I suggested that, statistically, maybe he'd done you in.'

Oh God. 'Where's Hank now?'

Slader paused. 'Last time I saw him, he was being questioned by state cops.'

Help wasn't coming.

'Asshole.' Harper couldn't help it. Her fist caught Slader on the jaw, sent him flying backwards onto a cot.

Harper rubbed her knuckles, turned away. Jim hopped from foot to foot, hugging himself. Staring.

'Great,' Angela said. 'They don't have to kill us. We can kill ourselves.'

Slader held his face, sat up. His lip was bleeding. 'Look, they won't keep him long. They have no evidence. I just made sure they'd question him. It's protocol.'

Protocol? To divert a search party? To interfere with – no, to prevent a rescue?

'Sorry,' he said. 'Like I said, I didn't know what was going on.'

Harper closed her eyes, saw Hank in custody.

'Point is,' Slader went on, 'it's getting dark soon. Even if they get back to it, the search party might not be able to track us here before that. So we're on our own. We'll have to take care of ourselves.'

'So what do we do?' Jim was quaking.

'My guess is they'll wait until it's late, when campers and hunters are asleep and no one's around. Then they'll come for us. So we have a few hours.'

A few hours?

Angela moaned that she didn't want to die. Jim crouched in a corner. Harper sat down beside Slader, put her hand in her pocket, and held her lemon.

'So? What are we going to do?' Jim asked. 'Just sit here?'

'Nothing we can do,' Angela said. 'We're all dead.'

Jim held up a metal rod. 'We've got these.' He turned to Harper. 'We can take apart the other cots, make more. When they come for us, we can rush them – like you said before, we'd have the element of surprise.'

Harper nodded. 'We can do that.'

Like she'd said before? When? Slader tried to follow. Where had that metal thing come from? He looked around, saw that he'd been sitting on a legless cot, placed on top of a normal one. This group had been enterprising, making weapons. Obviously, they didn't realize the arsenal they were up against.

'You might get one of them with a stick like that – even two. But the others'll shoot you.' He stood, smeared the blood off his lip. 'Our only hope is the ladder.' He pointed to the trapdoor. 'Once they lower it, we wait and let them send someone down. As soon as he comes through, we pull the ladder down so fast he can't help but fall. Before he can get up, we take his weapon. And we have a hostage, a gun, as well as the ladder—'

'They'll lock the hatch,' Jim said. 'What good's the ladder?'

'They only have one in the compound. They'll have to get another. So that buys us time. And in that time, who knows? The search party might find us.'

Harper didn't think much of Slader's plan. But she didn't say anything, didn't want to squelch the kernel of hope that Slader was planting. Didn't have a better idea.

'That plan sucks,' Angela said. 'Buying us time won't change anything. Nobody's coming for us, thanks to you. And even if they did manage to get here, they wouldn't find us. We're hidden under the floor. Stop pretending that there's hope. We're trapped here, and we're going to die here – all of us—'

'Shut up! Will you just shut up?' Jim turned to Harper. 'Make her stop. She's making things worse. I swear if she doesn't stop, I'll lose it.'

'Angela,' Harper began, but Angela let out a yowl, sobbing.

'No, Jim's right. This is all my fault. None of this would have happened if not for me.'

'That's ridiculous,' Harper said. 'No one's to blame but the locals.'

'No. I brought it on.' Angela kept crying, sniffing. 'Oh God. What was I thinking? If I hadn't brought Phil here, he'd still be alive – everything would be different. It's my fault. It's karma. What have I done?'

Nobody said anything. The others were absorbed in their own thoughts, preparing for the worst.

Karma? Slader leaned forward, elbows on his knees, watching Angela Russo. His cop antennae had begun buzzing. Experience had taught him to look for incongruities, things that didn't match up. And this Russo woman, well, her behavior was over the top. She'd lost her husband, but hadn't displayed much grief – in fact, her main emotion had been hatred for her ex-husband, Stan. That and self-pity. For sure, there was something off about her. It occurred to him that he'd been too preoccupied with the Hunt Club, hadn't really questioned Angela about her whereabouts when her husband had been shot. Hadn't asked if she'd fired a gun, or how their marriage had been going. Hadn't focused on the odd coincidence that she'd led investigators right to her ex-husband's campsite, right to his weapons and ammunition.

Fact was, Angela Russo had known about her ex's campsite near the bog; she'd camped with him in that very same spot for years. She must also have known what weapons he had, where he kept them. Slader looked her over, sizing her up. Figured that, if she'd wanted to, she could easily have snuck into Stan's camp early, while he was asleep, taken his rifle, shot Phil, and returned the gun without Stan knowing. Dagnabbit. The widow might have killed her husband and framed her ex.

Not that it mattered any more. With Josh in charge of the Hunt Club, they were all going to die.

Still, he was a cop. Couldn't let it alone.

'How come you say all this is your fault?' he asked. 'Care to explain?'

Angela froze like a hunted rabbit. 'Well, it's not really my fault. I just meant none of this would have happened if we'd stayed home. Phil would be home, raking the leaves. His body wouldn't have been carved and propped up like a scarecrow—'

'But I believe you said "none of it" would have happened if not for you. What about Al? Jim's partner? Wouldn't he still be dead?'

Angela looked away. 'I don't know about that.'

But she did know about her husband? Slader didn't back down. 'Tell us about your husband. How did you two get along?'

'Why are you asking me that? Phil was the love of my life.'

Really. 'I thought that would have been Stan.'

'What?' Her face blotched with red. 'No way. Stan's a snake—'

'You seem to have a lot of unfinished business with him.'

'Not at all.'

'Really? Because most times when a woman's done with a man, she doesn't care about him one way or another, as long as he steers clear of her. But you, well. the way you behaved, it was clear you still have feelings for Stan, even if those feelings show up as anger.'

Angela didn't answer. She glared at Slader, closed her mouth.

'How do you feel about his wife?'

'Wife?' Angela's eyes flamed. 'That title doesn't change anything. She's nothing but a slut.'

'She's wearing his ring.'

'That bitch pretended to be my best friend just so she could get close to Stan. They're both slime and I hope they rot in hell. What did they expect? That I'd just lie down and let them walk all over me?'

'They underestimated you, didn't they?'

'Damn right.' Angela's face was bright red, camouflaging her freckles.

For a few seconds, nobody said anything.

Slader studied Angela. She was still fuming mad, not the least bit repentant. 'Ma'am, did you know that Al Rogers and your husband were both shot with the same caliber bullets?'

'How would I know that?'

'I might have mentioned it. I know I told Daniels.'

'So? Lots of people use the same ammunition.'

Slader nodded. 'True enough.' He waited before going on. Looked around at his little group. Jim sat on the floor, no longer pacing, paying rapt attention to the exchange. Harper sat to his left on the cot, watching Angela with narrowed eyes. She'd outranked him in the military, but this was civilian life, and he was in charge. He was confident that he could count on both of them if he needed help with the suspect.

Not that it mattered, since they were all going to be killed.

Still, he was a leader. And a good leader served until his last breath.

'Thing is, both men were killed at about the same time, shot not far from each other. And they were both about the same size. Both wearing blue caps and blue plaid shirts.'

'So?' Angela's shoulders tightened. Her gaze wavered ever so slightly.

'So, it's possible that, from a distance, one of them could have been confused with the other.'

'What are you saying? That the killer got them mixed up? They were killed by the same person?' Jim's brows furrowed. 'Wait. So the locals killed her husband because they mistook him for Al, who was working for the pipeline?'

Slader kept his eyes on Angela. 'Maybe,' he said. 'Or maybe it was the other way around. Maybe the locals didn't kill either of them. Maybe someone killed Al, intending to kill Phil Russo.'

'Stan?' Angela's voice was flat. 'You're saying Stan killed them both?'

'Or someone wanted to make it look that way. Someone who knew where Stan was camped. Where he kept his guns and ammunition. Someone who could sneak into his campsite, take a rifle, use it, and return it without being seen.'

Angela didn't move. 'That's crazy.'

'Wait.' Harper stood. 'When you came into our camp, searching for your husband, you were all muddy.'

'No, I don't think so.'

'Yes. You were covered with mud, definitely. I thought you must have been to the bog looking for him.'

'Unless she was there, taking her ex's rifle.' Jim stood, faced Angela. 'Jesus – did you do it? Did you kill Al?'

Slader leaned back, crossed his arms, watched the cornered look in the woman's eyes. No question. Angela Russo was the shooter.

Not that it mattered.

'Why are you all staring at me?' Angela scooted backwards on her cot, pressed her back against the wall. 'I didn't shoot anyone. It was Stan—'

'Cut the crap.' Jim came at her, indignant. 'What's the point of lying? We're going to be killed in a few hours. Tell us the truth. What did you do?'

Angela cowered, her eyes filled with tears. 'You wouldn't understand,' she muttered. 'None of you.'

'Tell us anyway.' Harper's voice had authority, but it was soothing. Like a nurse's or a mom's. 'You'll feel better.'

Angela met her eyes. 'It was Stan,' she insisted. 'It's all Stan's fault.'

'Stan didn't shoot anybody.' Slader was tired of Angela playing victim. 'Why don't you just own it?'

Tears streamed down Angela's face. 'Own it? Why should I be blamed for ending a life? No one blamed them for ending mine.' She sniffed, smeared tears across her face. 'Because that's what they did. They took my house, my husband, my name – they ended the life I had. And nobody, not a single person, did anything about it.'

'So your ex-husband dumped you. How does that entitle you to kill your new husband? And my partner, who didn't even know you?' Jim's voice cracked.

Angela closed her eyes. 'Don't you judge me. You don't know what it was like. Having Phil as a husband was an insult. A mockery. A joke. But I don't admit anything, not a single blessed thing. I don't care what you think. Or what you do. I don't even care if these people kill me. Stan and Cindi finished me a long time ago. I'm already dead.'

Above them, the trapdoor opened.

'Angela Russo.' Slader nodded at her as he got to his feet, hitched up his pants. 'I'll read you your rights later, but consider yourself under arrest for the murders of Al Rogers and Philip Russo.'

While she protested, he motioned for Harper and Jim to join him. Armed with metal rods, they waited for the ladder to descend. There were only three of them, but together they'd be stronger than any one of them alone.

Harper didn't pay attention to the boots. She clutched her metal rod, ready to spring, watching the man climb down the ladder rungs. Captain Slader stood ready, eyes gleaming, but it was Jim who struck first, bashing the guy's legs even before his head came through the hatch.

When it did, Harper yanked Jim by the shoulders and threw him to the ground.

'What the hell?' Jim bounced back up, coming after Harper, but she'd whirled around, reaching for the newcomer. 'Hank?'

Hank was on the ground, favoring the leg Jim had hit, but he reached for Harper, embracing her. Holding her. 'Harper, thank God. Are you all right?'

Harper answered yes, but she didn't let him go. Didn't want him to see the worry in her eyes. How had he gotten there? What about the state police? He must have convinced them to let him go and followed her trail to the compound. But now what? Hank had been their last hope of rescue. Now that he'd been taken, he faced the same fate as the rest of them. Harper clung to him, picturing Chloe. She'd be okay. Trent and Vicki would take care of her. But she was so young – when she grew up, would she even remember her parents?

Never mind. There was no time for sentiment. Another man was descending the ladder.

'Don't hit him.' Hank put a hand in front of Jim. 'It's Daniels.'

Ranger Daniels stood at the bottom of the ladder, breathless. He looked around with wild eyes. 'Captain Slader? Damn. They've got you, too? These locals have gone crazy. The Hunt Club's starting a damned revolution.'

Someone shouted from above. 'Back away from the ladder. We're coming down.'

Harper finally let go of Hank, nodded at Slader, who motioned for them all to take a step back. Hunting boots stepped through the trapdoor and came down fast. A second man was on the ladder, just a few rungs up from the first.

'Now!' Slader said. Jim took hold of the second rung, Harper of the third and Slader the bottom one. 'Ready, and up,' Slader commanded.

The three picked up the ladder and yanked it backwards, pulling it down through the open hatch. The ladder fell flat, taking the men who were on it down with it.

They didn't fall far. As people shouted threats from the open hatch, Moose lay flat on his back, and Ax crawled onto his knees to get to his feet. Hank pounced, twisting Ax's arm behind his back while Daniels grabbed Ax's pistol from his waistband.

'You stupid fucks.' Ax bent over, glaring at Daniels, wincing when Hank tightened his grip on his arm. 'Are you nuts?' His eyes darted around. 'Moose! A little help, please?'

Moose bounded to his feet and struck Jim in the face, knocking him out. Pulling a hunting knife from his belt, he went after Slader. 'I'm going to gut you, Chief,' he growled.

Harper hung back, gauging her position, watching Slader edge back and around, armed with only a flimsy metal rod. They circled each other slowly until Moose swiped, knocked the rod from Slader's grip, and lunged. Blood spurted from Slader's shoulder, spattered the wall. Someone screamed – Angela? Harper couldn't wait any longer. She leapt at Moose, pouncing onto his back, wrapping her legs around his ribcage, grabbing his throat with one hand, clutching the wrist holding the knife with the other.

'Take the knife,' she barked at Slader. He was bleeding but still on his feet, holding his shoulder. But Slader didn't take it. He wobbled onto a cot, staring blankly.

Moose was too strong. Harper couldn't handle him alone. She tightened her thighs, moved her hand from Moose's neck to his eyes and dug her fingers in. Moose roared, shimmied, used his free hand to claw at Harper's fingers, peeling them away one by one.

'Huh!' Angela grunted.

Moose released Harper's fingers. Harper felt his body absorb a blow. She turned her head, saw Angela standing on one leg, swinging Slader's metal rod like a baseball, striking Moose's shins and knees. 'Huh. Huh.'

Moose spun around, bucking, trying to throw Harper off and deck Angela. But Harper held on and pressed her fingers deeper into his eye sockets. Angela slammed him again and again, hitting his shins, his knees. Moose grunted, careening blindly around the room, stumbling over Jim's legs, crashing into a cot, finally tripping over the ladder and falling to his knees. Still Harper hung on, not releasing him or his eyes even after he dropped the knife, even after Hank told her that it was okay, that they had him, that she could let go. No, Harper stayed on his back, clinging to it as if she could ride it to freedom. She didn't get off even when Daniels shouted, 'Look out,' and Hank called, 'Get down, damn it.' When the shooting started, she didn't move. Finally, Hank had to dive onto her, pull her to the floor and roll them both away.

* * *

Eyelids flapping, Pete stared at the shotgun.

'Put down your weapon and get up.' The guy had a long reddish beard, curly auburn hair. He motioned for Pete to come out of the shed.

Pete put his rifle down, stood up slowly. Didn't look around at Bob, but glimpsed him hunkering behind the rocket launcher as he stepped outside.

The guy's friend walked around from the back of the shed. He was chewing gum or maybe tobacco. He aimed his gun at Pete, smiling. 'Well, look at what you found. Who is this?'

'No idea. We haven't been introduced.'

'Who do you suppose sent him?'

Sent him? Pete looked from one of them to the other, didn't like their grins.

'Got to be the gas company. He doesn't look like a Fed – too young.'

'Not that it matters. He's trespassing, either way.' The darker guy chewed. 'He alone?'

The red-haired guy peeked into the shed, didn't see Bob hiding in the dark. 'Looks like it.'

'So what should we do, shoot him?'

'No – wait.' Pete took a step back, couldn't stop blinking. 'My name's Pete – I'm just up for the weekend with a friend.'

The men looked at each other. 'What friend?'

'No, he's not here. I got lost and wandered around for a real long time, and then I saw that fence, and I thought maybe I could find somebody here to help me . . .'

'Really?' The red-haired guy lifted his chin. 'Then what the fuck were you doing hiding in that shack?' The guy lunged forward, jabbing his muzzle into Pete's belly.

Pete bent forward, trying to protect his gut. 'Nothing. I swear—'

'I say we shoot him.'

'No! Wait . . .' Where the hell was Bob? Was he going to just sit there and let them kill him?

'What? You got some reason we shouldn't?' The red-haired one moved to Pete's side. 'Something to tell us? Like, for example, the truth?'

The truth? Pete's eyelids raced. 'Okay. Okay. I'll tell you.'

The darker one turned his head, spat out whatever was in his mouth. 'You got like thirty seconds.'

Pete tried not to turn and look for Bob. Tried to trust that his friend would rescue him. Tried to think of something to say, but all he could think of was the truth. 'Like I said, I came here with my friend—'

'Aw, he's just bullshitting. Let's just shoot him.'

'—to blow up the pipeline.'

'What?'

Pete repeated it.

The two men gaped at him. Glanced at each other. The darker one tilted his head. 'You're telling us that it was you set off those explosions?'

'Yes, sir.'

'You.'

'With my friend. Look.' Pete held up his hands. 'That's how I got these burns.'

The men eyed his hands, his face. They looked at each other. And burst out laughing.

'He came to . . .' The red-haired one guffawed. 'To . . .' He couldn't finish, he was laughing so hard.

The darker one was bent over, holding his belly. 'Can you believe that?'

'A couple of kids—'

'—blew up the old septic tanks.'

They roared with laughter, and while roaring, forgot about aiming their guns at Pete.

'That'll do.' Bob stood at the door to the shed, holding a backpack.

The two men kept laughing, couldn't stop right away. Took a moment to realize that someone else had joined them. When they did, they raised their rifles, aimed them at Bob.

'You don't want to shoot me.' Bob smiled, held up the backpack. 'You'd set off a terrible blast that would kill us all.'

'Bullshit,' the darker one said, but he didn't move.

'I was looking around in the shed, and guess what I found in the refrigerator?'

The men glanced at each other.

'I found lots of explosives. Plastic. Liquid. All kinds. And I packed it up in my backpack. Pete's, too. Thing is, I'm pretty sure some of that liquid stuff is sensitive. By "sensitive", I mean that unless it's kept cold, it will explode on contact. Like if somebody even bumps into it. So. Here's the thing. You two are going to escort us safely to the gate and send us on our way.'

The men looked at each other, grinning. 'Kid's got balls, right?'

'I've also got this backpack. Want to see what happens if I drop it? Or toss it at you?'

'All that's in this shed is ammo.' The red-haired guy turned to his friend. 'He's bullshitting, right?'

'Hell, Simon. You said that kid was alone. Didn't you even check?'

'Of course I checked. I didn't see anyone.'

'My ass you checked—'

'Gentlemen, please.' Bob's eyes gleamed. 'Stop bickering. Put your weapons on the ground.' He directed Pete to confiscate their rifles and radios, held the backpack like a bag of groceries.

The men hesitated, called his bluff. Pointed out that if his explosives would kill them, it would kill him and his friend, too.

Bob smiled. 'No doubt.' He held the pack over his head as if he'd smash it on the ground.

'For real.' Pete put his hands up. 'You don't want to fuck with him.' He and Bob had almost died twice in the last day, and it hadn't fazed Bob. Hadn't stopped him from coming back for a third attempt.

'I figure you guys want to kill us.' Bob lowered the backpack. 'If you really want to, that's fine. But if I'm going, you're coming with me.'

Pete couldn't stop his eyes from blinking crazy fast. Couldn't tell if Bob was bluffing, was pretty sure he wasn't. He took the two guys' radios, heard a woman asking for a check-in, or maybe a shift check. Some kind of check. He set the radios on the ground with the rifles. And, using some cord Bob had taken from a shelf, tied the men back-to-back, inside the shed.

When he was finished binding them, Bob was beside the shed, listening to a woman on the radios, asking about Ranger Daniels. A man answered that Daniels was in the compound. He and his friend were in the hole with the other conspirators.

'So this is real? We're going for blood?' the woman asked.

'Oh yeah,' the man answered. 'No prisoners. Full-out war.'

What was going on? Had she said *blood*? Pete looked around. The sun was dipping behind the trees. His burns throbbed and his stomach kept flipping. He was out of sync, disconnected, as if watching himself from far away. Forget about saving the environment and ending the use of fossil fuels; all he wanted was to run back to the Impala and fly back home.

'This has gotten weird, Bob,' he began.

'Sure has.' Bob grinned. 'I don't know what we can do for those women. Let's just gather up our stuff and do what we came here to do.'

The radio started again. A man's voice. 'Perimeter check-in.' Static. 'Again, perimeter? Simon? Dave?'

'I think they're calling those guys,' Pete said.

'Then we better get going before they come looking for them.'

Pete hesitated before lifting a backpack. 'That stuff in here – you were serious about how sensitive the explosives—'

'You bet your ass.' Bob cradled his pack, started across the field. 'Come on. Time to go make history.'

Someone pounced on Harper, throwing her off her prisoner. Just as she fell, a bullet whizzed past her head. Gunfire came fast, loud and she landed hard, face down. Someone was on top of her, holding her down. People were screaming, racing for cover. Bumping into each other. Falling. Harper had to get to her patrol – it was an ambush, and they were exposed. She needed to cover them. Needed a weapon. But the damned insurgent on her back was too heavy, holding her down. She fought, flailing, twisting, struggling to get free. Wait, where was her knife? Her prisoner, the man she'd taken down, had had a knife. She lay on her stomach, kicking and wriggling, looking across the floor for a metal blade. Seeing a pool of blood widening beside her head.

Shit. Had she been hit? She took a quick inventory of her body parts, searching for pain. But she remembered the suicide bombing, when her bones had been broken, her flesh seared and gouged, and she'd felt no pain. Nothing at all. So not feeling pain wouldn't tell her anything about a bullet wound. In fact, all she could feel was the weight of the attacker holding her to the ground. The blood pool was spreading, coming closer to her face. So, wait. It wasn't hers; couldn't be. If the blood were hers, the pool would start under her, not close to her. Why couldn't she think straight? What was wrong with her? Bullets kept coming, one after another, pop-pop-pop. A soprano voice stopped mid-scream.

'Come on,' her attacker shouted into her ear, hefted her up by her waistband, held her like a baby, except face down. He was strong, and she had no leverage, couldn't fight him off. Harper felt his unbalanced run, watched the floor rush under her. Saw her prisoner's face, half blown away. She turned her head, staring at him. Remembered riding on his back, poking his eyes. Oh God. Someone had pulled her away as a bullet had zipped past her head – the shot had been meant for her. Had hit him instead.

Someone had saved her life.

Someone from her unit?

'Go go go,' a man croaked. 'Come on!'

The floor flashed by. Harper passed over a casualty. A man – his back bloodied. She recognized him. One of hers. She turned her head, saw a woman crawling, one foot bare. Her ankle, swollen, purple. Splatted with blood. Harper's head passed through a door frame. The running stopped. The floor stopped moving. The man holding her didn't let go. She could feel his heart pounding.

'Okay, we're okay. Close it.'

'But that other guy . . .' The man holding her was out of breath.

'Jim's dead,' said another.

'How do we know?'

'If he isn't, he will be. We can't help him.'

Why were they speaking English? Shouldn't insurgents speak Arabic? Farsi? Were they spies? Harper scanned the room. No windows. A mattress on the floor. A portable toilet. Dim light spilling from above. Two men, plus the one holding her. Clearly she was in a prison cell. Someone closed the door.

Outside, the gunfire stopped. Nearby, someone was moaning.

'Put me down.' Harper tried to sound dangerous, authoritative.

Beefy arms lowered her gently to the floor.

'You okay?' The voice was familiar.

But it made no sense. Had to be a trick. A mind game, a form of psychological torture. She looked up. Hank knelt beside her, touching her forehead. Harper couldn't help it, let out a yelp.

'It's all right, Harper.' He leaned over and kissed her mouth.

Harper put her hand out, touching him. Making sure he was real. 'Hank?' She frowned, trying to understand. 'What are you doing here?'

'Daniels and I followed your trail—'

'Have you seen my patrol? Are they okay?' Harper tried to stand, needed to find them.

'Your patrol?'

'What's she asking?' one of the men asked.

'My patrol,' she repeated. 'They were at the checkpoint before the ambush—'

Hank put a hand on her arm. 'Harper? Where are you?'

What?

'I mean, are you with us?'

With them? She looked around. Everyone was watching her. 'I can't find my weapon. Or my ammo – everything's missing.'

Hank's hands moved across her body to her sides, into her vest pockets. Was he searching her?

He pulled out a lemon, held it out. 'Bite this.'

She looked at it, at him. Back to it. 'Why?' She knew she should, didn't know why. Something about lemons glimmered just beyond her memory.

'Go on.'

Harper looked across the tiny room. Saw a woman prone on the floor. Two men in the shadows, one leaning over the other, talking softly.

'Harper. Do it.'

Harper took the lemon, opened her mouth and chomped. Sour liquid assaulted her tongue, jolted her senses, short-circuited messages to her brain.

And propelled her out of wartime Iraq into a place where the danger was no less great, but the outcome far less certain.

The five of them huddled in the small dark closet where Jim had been imprisoned earlier. Angela had been hit in the back. Her wound wasn't bleeding too badly but her breath was labored. Slader had been shot in the side. His bleeding had slowed, and he lay on the mattress, weak and clinging to consciousness. While Harper recovered from her flashback, Daniels did what first aid he could.

Angela wailed steadily, a siren-like sound. Daniels, Hank and Harper sat against a wall beside the mattress.

'What now?' Daniels asked.

'I have the key.' Slader's breath rattled. 'Took it off Moose.'

The key?

'The locals . . .' He grimaced, paused. 'They can't get in here without it.'

Harper and Hank exchanged glances. Clearly, the locals could get in any time they wanted. They could, for example, take the door off its hinges. Or blast through it.

'Buys us time.'

Great.

'So, we have a key. Anything else to help us?' Harper raised her voice to be heard over Angela.

Daniels had managed to pick up Ax's gun. And Slader, even wounded, had confiscated Moose's knife.

Angela howled and cursed.

The four others sat silent. Nobody felt the need to state the obvious. They were outnumbered, out-armed, trapped in a concrete hole without food or water. They'd already lost Jim, and Angela and Slader needed medical attention.

'What do you think they'll do now?' Harper finally spoke.

'Depends,' Slader said. 'If it's up to Mavis or Hiram, they'll probably shoot us.'

Damn. Harper swallowed, pictured Chloe. Hank wrapped an arm around her, took her hand.

'But maybe it won't be up to them,' Daniels offered. 'Maybe someone else will take over.'

'I hope not. Hiram and Mavis shooting us – that'd be good news.' Slader stopped to catch his wind. 'Cuz if it's up to Josh and those guys, with Ax and Moose dead? They'll skin us alive. I mean that literally.'

Harper shuddered, gripped Hank's hand. Thought about how they could fight with one knife and one gun.

'Are we sure about Jim? He's dead?' she asked.

'Half his head's gone.' Daniels was sitting against the wall, his head back, eyes closed.

Silence.

Harper leaned into Hank, watching the door, waiting for it to break down. Listening for shouting or gunshots. Nothing.

Time passed.

She was thirsty, needed to think about something else. Again, Chloe popped to mind, grinning, eating string cheese. Asking for more. Oh God, she couldn't bear to think of Chloe. Needed to change channels in her head. Closed her eyes, saw Leslie, her shrink. Why was she thinking of Leslie? 'Because,' Leslie told her, 'you come to me when you have problems. You're hoping I can help.'

'So, can you?' Harper thought.

Leslie watched her with her patient green eyes. 'Mostly, I help you find a way to help yourself.'

What was that supposed to mean? Harper opened her eyes, saw dismal faces. Three men looking hopeless, awaiting imminent death. Angela lying behind them, ranting to her late husband. 'Phil,' she kept crying. 'Go away. You're dead. Leave me alone.'

Harper couldn't stand it. Had to breathe some energy back into them. Divert their attention.

'So, how'd you find us?' She squeezed Hank's hand.

'I wouldn't have if Daniels hadn't come with me.' He told her that the state cops hadn't released him until almost sundown; then they'd insisted it was too late to search, and they'd have to wait until morning to begin again.

'Your husband was pissed,' Daniels said. 'You should have seen him. I thought he was going to lose it and assault those two cops. But he didn't. He just grabbed a flashlight and stormed back out to follow your trail on his own.'

'Thank you, Hank.' Harper leaned up and kissed his cheek. 'You're so persistent.'

'Persistent? More like obsessed. He was pawing at leaves, looking for – what did you leave? Aspirin?'

'Ibuprofen.' Harper smiled. 'I was afraid the squirrels would take them.'

'It didn't take long for Daniels to figure out where we were heading,' Hank went on. 'And he says, your wife's got to be at the Hunt Club compound.'

'Trouble was the area's closed off with chain link and barbed wire,' Daniels said. 'The locals claim the whole parkland belongs to them, and they say the government stole their land.'

'Government fucking did.' Slader began coughing. 'Took the land right out from under us.'

'Anyhow, they've cordoned off a section where they hold their meetings and so on.'

'The government allowed that?' Hank asked.

'Course they did,' Slader said. 'They know the truth and don't want it to come to light, so . . .' He hacked again. 'So they let us be. It's a tacit agreement, or it was.'

'He's right,' Daniels said. 'The government hasn't given them formal title to the fenced-off land, but they also haven't done anything to take it back. My opinion? Angry confrontations cost money and cause bad PR. And the locals haven't been harming anyone. So the state just lets them block off a section of the woods and looks the other way.'

'So we got to the fence,' Hank went on. 'I used my hunting knife to rearrange some barbed wire. But once we climbed the fence, we found nothing. Not a single building, just a field and an old storage shed. And a mound of stones that looked like an entrance to an underground bunker. Nobody was around, so we went over to it and saw the door—'

'Your husband was fiddling with the lock when the door swung open and a couple of women greeted us with shotguns. I knew one of them—'

'Those had to be Mavis's women,' Slader wheezed. 'Tough as they come. They'd shoot you, then go home and bake a pie.'

'Well, they were kind enough to invite us in,' Hank said.

'And here we are.' Daniels sunk back into gloom.

Angela had been mumbling constantly, but no one had been paying attention. 'Phil, no. Go away. You're. Dead.'

Harper had been deliberately tuning her out. But now, she listened.

Angela thrashed. 'I swear I will. I'll shoot you again.' Kicking, she shouted something unintelligible, then was quiet.

Harper looked at Slader. 'Was that a confession?'

'Well, no one read her her rights.' Slader's breath rattled. 'But I told you she did it, didn't' I? She's batty, talking to her victim. Maybe her conscience is haunting her.'

Silence again. Harper put her head against Hank's shoulder, trying to come up with a plan.

The silence lingered. Finally, they heard movement on the other side of the wall. Hank grabbed the knife; Daniels took the gun. The three of them backed away from the door, braced for the unknown.

'What're you bothering about?' Slader breathed. 'They've got us. We're fish in a barrel.'

Not necessarily, Harper reasoned. Being underground as they were, they could only be approached from above. Which meant that the locals could be eliminated as they came, one at a time. Oddly, their position might actually give them an advantage.

Unless, of course, the locals dropped in a grenade.

As Josh slipped into his Bog Man suit, he felt his senses come alive. His breath quickened, and a fierce hunger rose in his belly. He could already smell their blood, see them twitching, hear their wails. He wasn't sure who was alive down there, but dead or alive, he would take his time with the chief, for old times' sake, and to show that even cops weren't safe around there. The blonde was spunky, had a nice rack, so Ax would want to spend some time with her. Fine. He didn't mind sharing as long as he could have her body in the end. He imagined the bunch of them, hanging from the trees like ornaments in the morning light. Who would find them first? Campers? The ATF? He hoped it would be the media, so the pictures would fly over the Internet and the news, announcing to the world that outsiders entered these woods in peril of their lives.

The Bog Man zipped up his chest, pulled on his head. Carried his paws up the steps and out of the bunker. He looked across the field, listening to the fury of his heartbeat and the threat of his breath, watching the shed. As soon as Simon and Dave brought in the last two prisoners, he would be ready. He was the new leader. The only one of his kind, and no one would stop him.

Pete and Bob hustled across the field toward the fence.

'This is going to be great,' Bob said. 'We've got enough power with us to send the pipeline to the moon.'

Pete glanced back at the shed. 'Think we tied them tight enough?'

'Shit. You tied them. You think you didn't?'

Pete had no idea. Had never tied anyone up before. 'I'm just saying. What if they get out—'

'We're gone, dude. They're not going to come after us. At least not until it's too late.'

Pete didn't answer. The radio kept squawking about the perimeter, about checking in. He worried that the men they'd captured were being missed. That someone would come looking for them. Meantime, the distance between the shed and the fence seemed longer than it had when they'd arrived. And the ground was bumpier, full of rocks and weeds and animal burrows. Hard to negotiate in the dark, and they couldn't risk exposing themselves by using flashlights.

Pete moved along, stepping cautiously.

The radio started again. A woman this time. 'Mavis? Are you going? Respond.'

There was a burst of static. 'Positive, Annie. We're heading out now.'

'Did you hear that?' Pete looked behind him, back toward the compound. 'I think they're going looking for those guys.'

'Then we better move. Hurry up, would you?' Bob scolded.

'I'm too sore to hurry. And you need to slow down. If we stumble and that liquid stuff gets shaken up, we're toast.'

'No, you know when we're toast? When they catch us, that's when.'

Again, Pete looked behind them. Saw somebody emerge from the mound of rocks across from the shed. Not just one somebody. Another, then another.

'Shit.' He jabbed Bob's arm, pointing.

Bob looked, cursed. Started running.

'Stop. Don't run.' Pete froze, unsure how sensitive the explosives were. Would the running motion set them off? Would it knock them against the other containers?

'Come on,' Bob growled. 'It's dark. They can't see us.'

Pete watched them, thought Bob was wrong: If he could see the group, they also could see him. And he saw them clearly, clumped together like a stampeding herd, coming fast.

The radio crackled. 'We've spotted two men heading to the gate.'

'Are they Simon and Dave?'

'Negative.'

'Bob.' Pete was short of breath. 'They've got us.'

'Hey, you two! Stop!' A shot whizzed past them.

The radio voice said, 'Try to keep one for questioning.'

Shit. Keep one? They were going to kill the other? Or a bullet might hit a backpack, killing all of them. Pete stopped, raised his arms. Surrendering.

Bob kept going, looked back. 'Fuckers,' he breathed.

Light beams flashed in Pete's face.

'Don't stop. Run!' Bob yelled.

Pete thought that was a mistake. 'No – don't run. Get down,' he called.

But too late. A beam of a light landed on Bob's back, and then the red dot of a laser.

'Stop!' a woman shouted. 'I'll shoot your friggin' ass.'

'Bob.' Pete carefully dropped to the ground. 'They've got us. Stop—'

Abruptly, Bob stopped, hands in the air. He turned, greeting the several men approaching with raised weapons.

'We got 'em,' one of them reported into the radio. 'We're coming in.'

'Great. See you in a minute.'

'On the way.'

With their rifles, the men indicated that Bob and Pete should turn around and head back where they'd come from. 'Move,' a man grunted.

Pete watched Bob, wondered why he didn't threaten to blow up these guys the way he'd threatened the ones in the shed. But Bob obeyed, silently marching toward the mound of stones.

'What's Josh going to do with them?' one guy asked.

The woman laughed. 'You mean where will he hang their skin?'

The others laughed too.

'In the morning, these woods are going to be draped with hides,' somebody else said.

'First, he's got to find out who sent them. How far the conspiracy's gone. Josh'll probably decide how to dispose of them depending on how they cooperate.'

Pete's mouth was dry. He felt dizzy, as if the ground were swaying. Were these people really talking about killing him and Bob? And, oh God – skinning them? Why had they come here? What did they care about the pipeline or the future of fossil fuels? And why had he let Bob steal those explosives? He thought of his mother. The girl in the snack bar. He didn't want to die.

The woman went ahead, led them around the mound of rocks to a steel door. Unlocked it. 'Go on.' She opened the door, gestured with her rifle.

Bob nodded, took a breath and started toward the door, but he faked left and full out raced away, heading toward the fence.

'Stop!' someone shouted.

Pete heard a gunshot.

'Don't – don't shoot at him!' Pete got down flat, hugged the ground, covered his head. Waited for a blast. But the blast didn't come. More shots went off.

The moonlight gleamed overly bright; the moment seemed unusually long as Pete looked up to see Bob clutching his backpack like a pigskin, running like a wide receiver, gliding through the air, sailing toward the ground. Diving head first to the earth. Whether Bob had been shot or simply tripped, Pete didn't know. And, as the earth shook and a blast of rolling hot orange swallowed him, Pete briefly realized that it didn't matter, either way.

A fish in a barrel, Slader thought. He tried to focus on the light bulb on the ceiling, but his vision kept fading. The light bled into the concrete, became a blurry glow. He squinted, forcing it back into the bulb. But the light resisted, spilling out of the glass, into the air. His pain was spilling, too. Maybe he'd lost too much blood. Maybe his blood had carried his pain with it, removing it from his body, spreading it onto the mattress, the floor. But that didn't matter. What mattered was staying alert. Being conscious when they came for him, exhibiting dignity right to the end. He was going to look straight into their pathetic eyes and shame them for their disloyalty. For following that clown Josh. The Bog Man. Really?

Wait. Where was the light? Slader opened his eyes. Had he been sleeping? He blinked at the halo on the ceiling. Where were the others? There had been others, hadn't there? People who'd been taken with him? He was sure of it. He closed his eyes, wondered when the traitors would come for him. The cowards. Hiram, Mavis, Annie, Ax. Felt a stab, worse than his gunshot. Maybe they'd be too late; maybe he'd deprive them of the opportunity to execute him. He could feel himself sinking. Was this how it felt to die? A gentle tug, an easing of pain? He watched the light, tried to hold onto the image of the bulb. But heaviness pulled at him, the sense of being swallowed. Well, he wasn't going to whine about it. Good leaders might lose sometimes, but they didn't whine, not ever. And as a leader, he needed to set an example, couldn't flinch, even when he'd been betrayed by his own people.

The light faded. Slader waited, listened to the rasp in his chest. Searched for the pain of his wounds. When the ceiling caved in on him, he wasn't thinking about his leadership any more, wasn't wondering what he could have done better. His final thoughts were of Mavis, how he should have married her. Maybe if he'd honored her that way, she wouldn't have abandoned him at the end.

Harper kept asking what time it was, and Hank kept saying it was five minutes or two minutes or four minutes after the last time she'd asked. Harper couldn't sit, couldn't stand, couldn't wait passively. She got up, turned in circles, examined the floor, the ceiling, the walls. She looked at Slader, who was unconscious. At Angela, who drifted, moaning occasionally, no longer talking.

Finally, Harper put her ear to the door, listening. Whatever had been going on in the outer room had stopped. She heard nothing. No one shuffling around or working on taking the door down. No one scuffling to remove bodies. And, if no one was coming down after them, she doubted that the shooters were still positioned at the trap door.

'I think they're gone.'

Daniels squinted at her.

'What do you mean "gone"?' Hank asked.

'I don't know. But it's been quiet. Maybe no one's watching the trap door—'

'But if they are,' Daniels said, 'whoever goes out there to look will get his head blown off.'

Harper crossed her arms. 'True. But if we wait here, we'll definitely get our heads blown off. At least there's a chance.'

Hank got to his feet. 'You're right. I'll go.'

'No you won't.' Harper stood between Hank and the door. 'Your limp makes you too slow—'

'You limp, too.'

'But I'm lighter. More agile.'

'Both of you are civilians.' Daniels stood. 'I should go.'

Harper shook her head. 'No. My idea. I go.' She went to Slader, took the key from his pocket. He didn't react.

'Harper, no.' Hank stood at the door, adamant. 'I won't let you.'

What? 'You won't *let* me?'

'Daniels or I will go—'

'Why? Because you're men? Hank. I was in combat—'

'You're not going.'

'Excuse me? Since when do you tell me what I can or cannot do? I'm going. Step aside.'

'Harper, I can't.'

Daniels stepped over to them. 'If we stand here arguing long enough, we'll miss the opportunity. One of us has to go. Now.'

'Hank, let me. I appreciate that you're worried, but I'll be quick. I'll just step out there and look. If no one's there, you'll come join me.'

Hank didn't move.

'Dude,' Daniels said. 'We might be able to get out of here. But we have to go now, while they're busy doing something else. We've got to move before they come back.'

Hank looked at Harper. 'Don't get shot. I love you.' He stepped aside.

Harper unlocked the door and slowly turned the knob. Opened the door a sliver. Then another. Finally, she pushed it open. The room was untouched. Jim, Ax and Moose lay where they'd fallen, cots upended. The ladder was flat on the concrete.

Harper stepped into the room, looked up at the trapdoor. It was shut tight.

They were locked in.

She motioned for the others to come out, pointed up at the door. Opened her mouth to ask someone to help her raise the ladder so they could investigate the lock, but never got a word out. A deafening bang interrupted, shaking the foundations of the compound. Harper pulled Hank down against the wall, eyed the ceiling. She recognized the sound, the reverberation.

Daniels held onto a wall. 'What the hell was—?' But the rest of his question was lost in another blast. Chunks of concrete dropped from the ceiling.

'Get down.' Harper motioned for Daniels to hunker with them by the wall and grabbed a mattress off a cot. Hank and Daniels helped her lift it, used it to cover their heads just before the next explosive crack loosened more chunks of concrete.

In the adjoining room, Angela was screaming.

'Don't panic,' Daniels shouted. 'Just keep your head down.'

But Angela's screams continued. Upstairs, people were also screaming, their panicked stampede pounding the ceiling, halted by another fierce blast. Then by a series of smaller pops in rapid succession, like a barrel of uncontrolled firecrackers. Or an onslaught by an entire army platoon, all firing at once. Bang bang bang bang. The vibrations rattled the room, cracked the walls, crumbled the ceiling. Soon, even the mattress wouldn't protect them. The light bulb flickered out. Left them in total darkness. Came back on again. Flickered out again. Chunks of concrete rained onto the mattress. A heavy slab fell beside them, thudded onto Ax's remains.

'Our Father, who art in Heaven,' Daniels began, but his prayer was drowned out by a resounding chorus of exploding ammunition. Harper knew the sound – hundreds of rounds, firing simultaneously. Sequentially.

Damn. There had to be a thousand men out there. This was no normal ambush. No typical sniper attack. This was a full-out surge by a huge military force. Harper stayed down, barked out orders, telling her patrol to keep down and hold their fire.

'What are you talking about?' someone asked. 'Hold our fire?'

'This isn't a discussion,' she snapped. 'Just follow orders.'

When the shooting finally stopped, the bunker was a shambles, the air clouded with dust.

'Everybody okay?' She kept her voice low, in case the enemy was close.

'Harper, are *you* okay?'

Harper? Really? 'Call me "Lieutenant".'

'Damn. Not again. Do you have your lemon?'

Her what?

The men lowered their mattress. Debris rolled off it.

'You're having a flashback,' the dark one said. He looked familiar. Like Hank.

Hank?

'Harper, you're not in Iraq. This isn't the war.'

She backed away from him. Why would he say that? Why did he look like Hank? Had she been injured? Was she imagining the resemblance? She grabbed a machine gun, held it up as she backed away, stepping over a corpse.

Somewhere a woman wailed.

'Come here, Harper. If you don't have the lemon, bite your lip. Hard.'

What?

There were two of them. She waved the gun. Stepped back.

On to something that moved. A woman screamed, 'My hand!'

Harper tripped, toppling backward, landing hard, not letting go of her gun. Pain radiated up her back, down her legs. Jolted her back into the moment.

Angela was next to her on her hands and knees, glaring at her, cradling her hand. 'You crushed my fingers!'

'Harper?' Hank came to her. 'You all right?'

She wasn't sure. She blinked, looked around. Got her bearings. Saw the metal cot leg she was clutching like a rifle. Dropped it. Felt her face heat up. Damn. She'd had another flashback? Two in the space of a few hours?

'Can you stand?'

Harper tried; Hank helped her up.

'Hey, can somebody stop fussing about Harper? What about me?' Angela was surprisingly alert, covered with dust. Blood trickled down her forehead. 'I'm the one with a broken ankle, a gunshot wound in my back, and a bashed skull. And now, I've got a crushed hand. You guys left me in there – I was almost killed. I had to crawl out here on my hands and knees like an animal.'

'The captain.' Daniels looked at the door.

Oh God. 'Slader?' Harper bellowed, turning, rushing into the next room.

The captain's boots protruded from a collapsed slab of concrete. Harper went to him. Found a hand in a heap of rubble. Felt for a pulse. Found none. Captain Slader was gone. Much of the ceiling, including the floor of the room above – had caved in on him.

But above them, where the ceiling had been, was a gaping hole. Which meant they had a way out.

Daniels insisted on going up first. It was, after all, his park. He pulled rank. Harper and Hank had held the ladder.

'Careful,' Harper whispered. 'Some of them might be up there. And they're armed. Be ready to duck.'

Daniels just began climbing the ladder, Ax's gun tucked into his belt.

'What about me?' Angela was losing energy. 'I can't climb a ladder in my condition – you guys aren't going to leave me alone down here.'

'Not for long,' Hank said. 'Only until we can get help—'

'No – you can't – don't leave me . . .' Her shouts were deflated.

Daniels' head was out. 'Mother of God,' he said.

'What?'

'What do you see?'

Daniels stood on the ladder, 'Lord Almighty have mercy.'

'What?' Harper snarled.

Daniels still didn't answer. He continued up the ladder and climbed onto the remains of the floor above.

Harper met Hank's eyes and started up the ladder. When her head poked through the opening, she saw why Daniels had been speechless.

'What is it?' Hank called from below.

Harper bit her lip, grounding herself with pain to fight off another flashback.

'Harper?' Hank asked again. 'What?'

Harper couldn't think of an answer, so all she said was, 'Damn.'

* * *

The foot was the first identifiable thing she saw. No shoe or boot. No sock. Just a seared bare foot, toes polished sky blue, ripped from the rest of its body. The past rose up, assaulting her with images: A boy whose face had been blown off. Detached limbs. The smell of burned rubber and flesh mixed with explosives. Cries of pain and horror. But Harper kept moving, climbing out of the hole. Staying in the present even as her memories clawed at her.

The compound roof had blown away, creating gaping holes above them. Exposing the night sky. Under the starlight, she saw devastation. Dust. Spots of fire where wooden beams glowed hot. An expanse of broken cement blocks, rocks, dirt, concrete chunks. And a terrible, deadly hush.

Hank climbed out behind her.

Angela's voice shattered the silence. 'Don't leave me down here! I'm coming up.'

The ladder wobbled. Angela cried out in pain. Daniels knelt at the opening. 'Be careful. Hold on – don't fall.' He turned to Harper and Hank. 'She's hopping. Even with that gunshot wound, she's pulling herself up. Can you believe her?'

Harper paid no attention. She waded cautiously through rubble, crawling over wreckage, looking for survivors. Her left leg throbbed, but she moved on, examining spaces between rocks and under concrete. Hank made his way to her.

'Anybody here?' he called. 'Anyone need help?'

Nobody answered.

A woman's hand protruded from under a heap of concrete. Harper took it, felt for a pulse. Moved on.

Hank stopped, wiped dust and soot from his eyes.

'You okay?' Harper asked.

He was standing near a burning beam. His eyes flickered, reflecting the flame. 'There's a bunch of them here,' he said. 'So far all gone.'

Harper wouldn't give up. Went in the other direction, into the far end of the space. Finding a boot. A rifle butt.

Daniels grunted, trying to pull Angela up the last few rungs as she cried out in pain. 'Ouch – be careful – you're hurting me. Oh God, my back. My ankle.'

Up ahead, the rubble lay in a convex pile, as if covering something. Maybe someone had taken shelter under a sofa or chair. Harper hurried, listening for movement, for a voice other than Angela's. Carefully, she lifted a chunk of concrete, pushed smaller pieces aside. Saw the shiny gleam of a gong. And under it, Hiram, his eyes wide, his hand clutching a mallet.

She was looking at him when the rest of the ceiling came down.

'Mrs Jennings?'

A light shone in her eyes. She blinked, turned away.

'Try to hold still.'

The light came back. Harper closed her eyes again. Turned away again. 'Stop it,' she said. Why was this kid blinding her with a light?

'Welcome back, ma'am.' The kid was in a white uniform. A sailor? Were they on a ship? 'I'm an EMT, ma'am. You've been out for a bit. I was trying to take a look at your pupils.'

'I'm fine.' She started to get up. Had to go look for survivors.

'Ma'am, please lie back.'

The ground was spinning. Harper couldn't step onto it. She settled back, closed her eyes. Waited for the spinning to stop. When she opened her eyes again, she saw the inside of a large tent. Cots. Medical supplies. Oh God. She bit her lip, but nothing changed. So this wasn't a flashback? Was this actually the war?

'Ma'am, please hold still. You've got a pretty impressive gash on your leg.'

She did?

'It's going to need some stitches. But honestly, even with the concussion, you were lucky.'

Lucky? What had happened? Where was Hank? 'Where's my husband?'

'Your husband?'

'Hank. He was with me . . .' Harper bolted up, looked around the tent. Saw a row of coroner's bags.

'Is that him?' the kid asked, pointing.

Harper looked. Hank was limping toward them.

'Yes.' She let out a breath. Sat back and allowed the kid to do his work. Hank was covered with dust and grime. His shirt was soiled and torn. He had a cut above his eye. Ragged scrapes speckled his arms. But as she took his hand, Harper's heart fluttered, and she had to slow her breath. In all their time together, Hank had never looked better.

Late the next morning, Harper sat talking to the ATF agents back at the ranger's station. Apparently, she had no memory of a chunk of time. She remembered searching for survivors, finding bodies and parts of bodies. And then, nothing until she was with the paramedic.

'We found the body of a man in what appeared to be an ape costume,' Agent Byrnes said. 'It was in the field just outside the compound. Do you know who that was? Or why he might be dressed that way?'

'It was Josh.'

'Josh.' An agent raised an eyebrow. His name was Meyer.

'I told you. The locals rebelled against Captain Slader. Josh was the new leader.'

'And he was dressed like that – why?'

Harper sighed. Didn't have the energy to go through it all. 'From what I can tell, Josh liked to dress up like a Yeti and roam the woods, scaring campers away. They called him the Bog Man. He and his followers were planning to kill us and decorate the woods with our remains. Maybe Josh put on his costume so no one would be able to identify him. If they saw him killing us or distributing our bodies, they'd blame the Bog Man.'

'The Bog Man.' Agent Meyer exchanged glances with his partner, Agent Byrnes. 'And this Bog Man. You said he's . . . what? A Yeti?'

'Like Big Foot. Or Sasquatch.' Harper explained that she didn't know much about it, except that he was an almost human creature in local lore. People said he lived in the bogs. She told them that Josh seemed to have been exploiting the legend to scare away outsiders and reclaim the woods for the locals.

'Reclaim the woods? But these woods are state property.'

'I know that, Agents. But I've been told that some local people believe that the government stole their land to create the park, and then handed that same land over to the energy companies, who fracked it, polluted it, and built a pipeline through it. In the process, homes were destroyed, water became undrinkable, and people became sick.'

The questioning went on. Harper felt no pain, only detached disbelief. God, what had happened? An explosion of fracking chemicals? A problem with the pipeline? Or had the locals planned a terrorist bombing but accidentally blown themselves up?

Agent Byrnes asked her again about Slader. 'So. You're saying that the police captain was the leader of this extremist group?'

'Yes.' They'd already been over all of that.

'And, in his role as police captain, Slader was in charge of investigating the deaths of Al Rogers and Philip Russo.'

Yes, as far as she knew.

'Do you think he was hiding evidence? Possibly covering for locals responsible for those deaths?'

She had no idea. She thought of Angela, wondered if she should tell them about what she'd heard in the bunker. Decided to wait. Didn't have the energy for yet another line of questions. Harper rubbed her eyes, slumped in her chair.

'Ma'am, I know you're tired. But there are a lot of unanswered questions here, so indulge us for another couple of minutes.'

Sure.

'We know that the explosion started just outside the compound, near the entrance. Two locals who are members of the Hunt Club were found tied up in a shed not far from there. You know anything about them?'

No.

'These two say the shed was used to stockpile the Hunt Club's ammunition. They say two young men ambushed them there and stole some powerful explosives not long before the blast.'

Harper said nothing.

'They said the men were outsiders, named Pete and Bob. Do you know anything about them?'

Pete and Bob? The same Pete and Bob who'd run into her campsite, freaked out by the Bog Man? Was that possible? She chewed her lip. Remembered their burns and Angela's suspicion that they'd set off the explosion the night before. But those guys were panicked, harmless. Running for their lives. Why would they have gone into the compound and stolen explosives?

'Do you know anything about those young men?

Harper hesitated. 'Not really.' She didn't really, other than that they'd been afraid of a guy in a Yeti costume. 'I might have run into them earlier, but they said they were taking off. Going home.'

Byrnes eyed her. 'You ran into them?'

'If it's the same two, they passed through my campsite on their way back to the campgrounds. They were leaving, so they shouldn't have been anywhere near the compound. Were they? Were they hurt?'

A pause.

'One survived. But he's not conscious.'

They watched her reaction, then made eye contact with each other. Harper couldn't read their expressions. Didn't try. She put her head back, shut her eyes for a moment.

'Okay, let's wrap this up. What do you know about the Hunt Club's arsenal?'

'Nothing. Except what you've told me.'

'What about the membership? Slader say anything about their plans?'

'Sorry. Nothing.' Except that they were going to either skin her and the others alive or shoot them.

Agent Meyer sighed, crossed his arms. Byrnes rubbed his eyes. 'Well, thanks for your time, Mrs Jennings. You know, there were over sixty people there. Only fifteen survived. You were lucky.'

Yes, she was.

'As we said, you're still in shock. Your memory might not be functioning clearly. So—'

'Definitely,' she answered before he could finish. 'I'll let you know if I think of anything else.'

The agents thanked her and escorted her out of Daniels' office. They invited Hank in next, which left Harper in the outer office, sitting next to Angela.

The media had gathered outside the ranger's office, waiting for updates. They'd been joined by campers, state cops, hunters. People who lived nearby. Gas company and pipeline officials had taken over the snack shop.

Hoping to doze off, Harper turned away from the window, closed her eyes. Saw broken bones poking through flesh, auburn hair – or maybe blonde colored by blood.

In the chair beside her, Angela fidgeted. Her ankle had been set in a boot, her head wounds stitched and bandaged. 'When will they let me go home? Haven't I been through enough?'

Harper didn't answer. Angela's whines scraped the inside of her skull.

'Isn't it enough that I've lost my husband? And broken my ankle? And gotten shot, dropped on my head, and kidnapped? No. Now, they're making me sit here for hours, waiting. Not that I have anything to go home to. How can I face all of Phil's things? His empty galoshes? His buttermilk? I don't know how he could stand that stuff, but he lapped it up.'

Harper didn't engage, didn't tell Angela that she could drop the act. That she had been busted. She watched the door to the inner office, wishing that Hank would reappear so they could leave. Thinking of Chloe, remembering the smell of her hair.

'You'd think they'd at least have interviewed me first. I should have had priority, being as I'm a widow. Don't they have any consideration? I can't even move with the bandages. The doctor said the gunshot was superficial. It sure doesn't feel that way. Lord, how long do I have to sit here? I have a funeral to arrange. Oh, and a notice to put in the newspaper. And I have to get the death certificate. Call the insurance agent. And Phil's boss, and his sister. Poor old Phil. Well, it's Stan's fault. I hope he fries for killing Phil. Him and Cindi both.'

'Oh, cut it out, Angela,' Harper finally snapped. 'Stop blithering.'

Angela looked slapped. 'What?'

'Because you did it.'

Angela's lower lip twitched. 'Did what? I don't – what are you talk—'

'Cut the crap. I'm tired. You know damned well what I'm talking about. You practically confessed when we were down in the bunker.'

'I did not. I have no idea what you're talking about.' Angela stiffened.

Harper turned and faced her. Realized she'd have to spell it out. 'Phil,' she said. 'It wasn't Stan. It was you.'

'What? No – it was Stan.'

'Stan didn't do it. He had no motive. You killed Phil.'

'But it was Stan's gun—'

'You snuck into Stan's campsite, took the gun, and returned it after you shot your husband. You knew where Stan was camping—'

'No – I had no idea he was even there.' Angela's voice went up an octave. She rearranged herself on the chair.

'Really? Because you knew he hunts here every weekend, every fall. And that he camps in the same spot. The two of you camped there for years.'

'So? That doesn't mean anything.' Angela shook her head. 'Besides,' she sputtered, 'why would I kill Phil?'

'How should I know? Was there an insurance policy?'

'How dare you!' Angela blanched. 'I'm not talking to you any more.'

'Fine.' Harper leaned back against the wall, slumped down. 'But you'll be talking to the agents. And then to the cops.'

'Oh God, what have you told them?'

'I told them nothing. Slader figured it out for himself and the others will too.'

Angela hesitated, eyed Harper. 'Well, you might think you know what happened. But you don't. And you can't prove it.' Angela's voice was low, like a growl.

Harper didn't comment, saw no reason to.

'And neither can Slader, being as he's dead.'

The crutch swung up in an arc and came down fast. Harper wasn't expecting it, wouldn't have thought Angela strong enough to assault her or foolish enough to try it with ATF agents in the next room. But there it was: the crutch speeding straight toward her skull. Harper's reflexes kicked in, and even before she'd comprehended what was happening, her arms went up, deflecting the blow, sending the crutch clattering onto the floor. And Angela along with it.

By the time they got back to campsite to pack up, it was late afternoon. Hank helped Harper finish folding the tent. They didn't talk much as they packed up the stove, the coffee pot. The folding cots and sleeping bags. Tarp. Chairs. Rifle. Hank's soil and water samples.

When everything was tied into bundles, they took a final walk down to the creek, sat on a fallen log. Hank put an arm around her. Harper leaned against his shoulder.

'You okay?' he asked.

She shrugged. 'You?'

'I'm glad we're alive.'

Harper took a breath, felt her lungs fill. She was glad, too.

'That was something.'

What was? Which thing?

'You broke Angela's friggin' arm.'

Harper looked up at him. 'It wasn't me – she fell on it.'

'You sent her flying.' Hank's eyes twinkled. He gave her a squeeze.

'I'm glad they finally let Stan go. But honestly, I pity Angela's cell mates. Having to listen to her for life? That's cruel and unusual punishment.'

Hank chuckled. They were quiet for a moment, watching the reflections of red and yellow leaves on the water. Harper watched the colors morph into bobbing blood and flesh, bits of exploded bodies. She thought of Ax and Moose. Annie. Captain Slader. Josh, the Bog Man. The other locals, so many of them dead. She clutched Hank's arm.

'I keep thinking that I should have sensed something in those guys, Pete and Bob. I should have stopped them—'

'What could you have sensed? You couldn't have stopped them.'

Obviously, Hank was just saying that. Trying to stop her from feeling responsible for what had happened.

'They didn't seem even a tiny bit threatening. They were running away from the Bog Man, practically wetting their pants they were so scared. It's hard to believe they were here setting off bombs.'

And yet, police had found maps of the pipeline and anti-fracking literature in their car. Along with blasting caps and walkie-talkie packaging. According to Daniels, who'd spoken to Pete, the survivor, the two had set off the first two explosions trying to blow up the pipeline, and then had broken into the Hunt Club's arsenal, tying up the guards and stealing substances far more powerful than they'd realized or known how to handle. In the end, they'd blown up not the pipeline, but the compound and dozens of people, including one of them.

Water rippled over rocks and mud, along tree stumps. A squirrel darted across a branch. A spiderweb glistened in the sunlight. The woods were busy and alive, as if nothing had changed.

'Ready?' Hank asked.

Very. Harper stood. Hank started up the path, but, hearing a rustle in the bushes across the creek, Harper glanced back. And froze.

It was at least seven feet tall, covered with fur that was dark as a shadow, camouflaged by the shade of the trees.

Maybe she was imagining it. She blinked, but it didn't disappear. It stood by the creek, watching her with shiny eyes. Neither of them moved.

Harper tried to call for Hank but couldn't open her mouth. Couldn't make a sound. Don't be an idiot, she told herself; it was just a costume. Maybe Josh's – but no. Josh had been killed in the blast, his costume burned and torn, the leg extensions destroyed. So, if not Josh, who was she looking at? Harper stared. Couldn't breathe, couldn't move. Couldn't trust her eyes.

'Harper? Coming?' Hank called.

The creature startled, let out a sound that was neither a bark nor a howl. And as swiftly and silently as it had appeared, it dashed away.

Harper kept blinking, peering into the woods.

Hank came back down the hill. 'What's up? We ought to—'

'I know. It's nothing.' She still didn't move. 'I'm coming.' The Bog Man. She'd seen it, hadn't she? Should she tell Hank? Would he believe her?

The woods across the creek didn't stir.

But the leaves rustled overhead. Trees surrounded her, obstructed her view. Closed her in.

Harper turned, hurrying, almost running up the path. 'It will be late when we get home.' Her voice was faint.

'What did you say?'

'Chloe. She'll be asleep.'

'Let's stop by Trent's and pick her up anyway. She probably won't wake up.'

No, she probably wouldn't. Harper thought of Chloe sleeping, her steady breathing. Her trust that her world was safe and loving.

'That way she'll wake up in her own room, and we'll all be together in the morning.'

Harper picked up her backpack, the folded chairs and the tent. Hank got the rest. She kept her mind on the morning. On Chloe. They would say goodbye to Ranger Daniels, dodge the press, and take off, leaving the woods and what happened there behind. All that mattered was that they were together. And alive.